WOLF'S HILL

BOOK THREE OF
THE BLACK ROAD

SIMON BESTWICK

Proudly Published by Snowbooks in 2018

Copyright © 2018 Simon Bestwick

Simon Bestwick asserts the moral right to
be identified as the author of this work.
All rights reserved.

Snowbooks Ltd.
email: info@snowbooks.com
www.snowbooks.com

British Library Cataloguing in Publication Data
A catalogue record for this book is available from the
British Library.

Hardback | 978-1-911390-49-7
Paperback | 978-1-911390-50-3
Ebook | 978-1-911390-51-0

For Laura Mauro,
With love from the King of the Bastards.

Previously

Twenty years after the nuclear attack, Helen Damnation came back from the dead.

For nearly four years she'd lived like an animal, after the defeat of the last rebellion against the tyrannical Reapers. But eventually her past caught up with her, and so did the vengeful ghosts of her husband Frank and daughter Belinda, demanding a soul in payment for their deaths – either hers or that of the traitor who betrayed their base, the Refuge, to the Reapers: Tereus Winterborn, now Reaper Commander of Regional Command Zone 7.

Helen spent the next year tracking down other surviving rebels and seeking new allies among the tribesfolk of the Wastelands. Then at last she returned to the city of Manchester, Winterborn's seat of power. Danny Morwyn, one of a rag-tag band of urban youths rescued from the streets by her old mentor, Darrow, helped her evade the Reapers.

Danny brought Helen to meet with Darrow – and with Alannah Vale, a one-time intelligence officer for the rebels. Alannah was still traumatised from her torture by Colonel Jarrett, an officer in the feared elite unit, the Jennywrens, but Helen badly needed her aid to discover the location of Project Tindalos, a new secret weapon being developed by Winterborn's chief scientist, Dr Mordake. Helen had been warned that Tindalos could potentially destroy all surviving life on earth.

Next, Helen and Danny entered the empty district known as Deadsbury, in search of its sole inhabitant, Gevaudan Shoal. Gevaudan, the last of the genetically-modified Grendelwolves, used as the Reapers' shock troops until they finally turned on their creators, wanted only to be left alone. He'd found a safe haven in Winterborn's territory, and a steady supply of the Goliath serum he needed to survive, by dangling the promise of future cooperation in front of the Reaper Commander, but had no intention of fighting again, for either side.

But something about Helen's determination impressed Gevaudan, and when she was captured by her old enemy Jarrett, the Grendelwolf ended his self-imposed isolation to rescue her. Meanwhile Danny, Alannah and Darrow had discovered Project Tindalos' location: a Reaper base in the Wastelands called Hobsdyke. With the city perimeter sealed, Darrow was forced to attempt an uprising to give Helen, Gevaudan, Danny and Alannah time to escape. He succeeded, but only he and a handful of his fighters survived.

At Hobsdyke, Helen and the others joined forces with Wakefield of the Fox Tribe and her warriors, but the base was empty except for the dead. They found, however, an entrance to a cavern system under Graspen Hill, where the base stood; there, they encountered near-indestructible, semi-human creatures that had once been the base's personnel – the Styr – and the grotesquely transfigured Dr Mordake.

Project Tindalos was an attempt to use the ancient ritual technology of a lost civilisation, the North Sea Culture, to awaken latent powers in the human mind, powers Mordake had hoped could undo the devastation of the War, and restore his dead wife, Liz, to him.

But the powers Mordake had sought to awaken had been implanted in humanity's ancestors by mysterious entities called the Night Wolves, venerated as gods by the North Sea Culture. Unable to survive in our world, the Night Wolves had influenced the development of the human race, implanting abilities that would enable their resurrection. The Styr, created by the partial success of Project Tindalos, existed to bring about the rebirth of the Night Wolves.

Helen and her allies managed to foil the materialisation of one of the Night Wolves. The resulting explosion caused the cavern system to collapse, destroying most of the Hobsdyke base and apparently killing Mordake.

In the following months, Helen's alliance against the Reapers grew, and in a hard-fought campaign over the bitter winter, they seized territory from the Reapers to create their own sphere of influence, controlled from a secret base at Ashwood Fort.

News of the uprising spread beyond RCZ7 to the Reapers' other Command Zones, creating rumblings of discontent across the British Isles. Determined to rule a reunified Britain, Winterborn set out to crush the rebellion before it could grow.

One of the tools chosen for this task was Dr Kellett, the creator of the Grendelwolves. Working with notes salvaged from REAP Hobsdyke, Kellett created the Catchman – a modified version of the Styr under electronic control. Almost indestructible, combining the relentlessness of a machine with the savagery of an animal, the Catchman could be programmed to home in on an individual's psychic signature. Since Helen never left the Fort, Winterborn ordered the Catchman targeted on her, seeking both to eliminate Helen and to pinpoint the rebel HQ.

Helen, meanwhile, had increasingly come to fear a possible repetition of the Refuge Massacre, should the Reapers locate

Ashwood, and called for the rebels' command structure and resources to be dispersed across a system of forts to make it impossible for the Reapers to deliver a single knock-out blow, but was voted down by the rebel Council. So was Darrow's proposal that he be posted back to Manchester to help organise a new network of in the city, which both Helen and Alannah feared would lead to his detection and death.

The Catchman worked its way across the Wastelands towards Ashwood, leaving a trail of corpses in its wake, When Helen went to investigate the scene of an attack, the creature altered its course to hunt her down. Helen fled, trying to draw it away from the Fort, and Gevaudan set off to aid her. But even the Grendelwolf proved unable to kill the Catchman – until Helen stabbed it with a steel weapon engraved with the North Sea Culture symbol known as the Hobsdyke Cross – the only weapon capable of destroying the Night Wolves.

Despite her efforts to lead the Catchmen away from Ashwood Fort, however, the Reapers had managed to locate the Fort. Now Winterborn deployed his second tool – Colonel Jarrett, together with the bulk of the Jennywrens, launched an all-out assault on Ashwood Fort, with Kellett and a detachment of Catchmen in tow. By now, Jarrett was obsessed with killing Helen to the point of mania and determined to accomplish her mission at any cost.

A ferocious battle for Ashwood Fort began, with both sides sustaining heavy casualties. Jarrett's forces breached the Fort's outer defences, but needed additional support in the form of heavy weapons to complete the task – so Danny's ex-lover Flaps found herself waging another, equally desperate fight out in the Wastelands to prevent the support convoys getting through. One of her men, Cov, discovered during the battle that his old friend Mackie had been turned by the Reapers and was now their spy, but Mackie killed him before he could be exposed.

Helen was critically wounded during the Reaper assault; while Darrow and Alannah took over the Fort's defence and Danny, Wakefield and Gevaudan led the fighting against Jarrett's forces, she hovered between life and death and confronted her murdered family for the last time. She relived the War, the murder of her mother by the Reapers, her joining the resistance – and becoming a surrogate sister to a young war orphan, Percy; the one emotional bond either of them formed.

When Helen married and had a child, her relationship with Percy was put under strain as Helen was no longer there to constantly support him through his recurrent panic attacks. By now, Percy had taken a new name: Tereus Winterborn.

When her marriage began to break down, they grew closer again, and eventually slept together. Appalled by what she saw as having committed virtual incest, Helen abandoned Tereus once more. Devastated by this rejection, Winterborn betrayed the rebels in exchange for an officer's commission in the Reapers. The Refuge was destroyed, Helen's family were killed and she was shot and left for dead before being flung into a mass grave. Ever since she crawled out of it, the angry ghosts had followed her, and now they demanded her death. But she said no, and recovered consciousness.

By now, Gevaudan and Wakefield had succeeded in launching an attack behind Reaper lines, while Danny had held back wave after wave of attacks. Gevaudan forced Kellett to destroy the Catchmen before shooting him. Kellett was left trapped in his burning control centre as the rebels broke out of the Fort and fell on the Reaper camp. As the Reapers fell back in ignominious retreat, Jarrett stayed behind, determined to kill Helen even at the cost of her own life.

Jarrett infiltrated the Fort and seriously wounded Danny before hunting Helen down. Weak and wounded, Helen had no chance against her – but Alannah arrived to confront Jarrett, and to finally kill her hated torturer.

Since the victory at Ashwood, the rebel command has, as per Helen's advice, been dispersed across RCZ7. Darrow finally gained approval to relinquish his position on the Council and return to Manchester to train a new generation of urban guerillas. A senior Reaper officer, Colonel Wearing, is now a rebel spy. The rebels have also produced 'the Book', a combination manifesto and training manual to help create new rebel cells and networks across the British Isles, and their agents have begun to distribute it.

Now resistance is growing across the Regional Command Zones, threatening not only Winterborn's ambitions, but the survival of the Reapers themselves. Fortunately he has acquired a new second-in-command: Dr Mordake, now back from the dead to offer aid in the form of his inhuman abilities and a new weapons system, based on Project Tindalos but deadlier still...

WOLF'S HILL

BOOK THREE OF
THE BLACK ROAD

Prologue

Piel Island, Barrow-In-Furness
Regional Command Zone 7 (North-West England),
British Isles
26th June, Attack Plus Twenty-One Years
0500 hours

The Black Road stretches through the waste of night, between twin cobble-tracks of white bone.

In the distance, broken towers, limned against the pale half-light of a dawn that never comes.

She walks the Road in a tattered coat, gun in hand. Alone: even her murdered family have left her now.

On the dim horizon, a vast clotted shape stirs. A wolf's head. Its ears prick up; great lamplike eyes gaze into her.

Tindalos, a voice whispers, a shadow on the wind.

Then the Wolf's gone, and only the Road remains. A lone figure stands on it – tall, black-clad, with long hair fine as silk. And a face she knows so well: long, pale and high-cheekboned, with full red lips. But it's changed: there's a jagged, Y-shaped scar on his left cheek, and hatred in his yellow wolf's eyes.

"Gevaudan?"

Claws slide from his fingertips, and the voice whispers again: *He will destroy you.*

His eyes glow, pale like the Wolf's; his lips peel back from yellow fangs.

She tries to raise her gun, but her hands are empty. *Run,* she thinks – but you can only go forward here, and there's no outrunning the Grendelwolf. And then he leaps.

*

Helen thrashed awake, tangled in the sweat-heavy bedsheets. She flung them back and lay in the cool dawn air.

Her heart thumped. She breathed deep, in and out: *only a dream.*

She got out of the narrow bed. Filled a plastic bowl from the jug of water on the table nearby and washed herself with a coarse woollen cloth, cleaning off the sweat. She wrapped cloth bindings around her chest and loins, pulled on boots and overalls and padded onto the landing.

Boards creaked underfoot, but no-one stirred. Downstairs, the Ship Inn's former bar had been converted into Fort Three's War Room. Two pool tables had been pushed together and a chart stretched over them; more maps covered the walls and at the far end, two techs hunched over their transmitters. The radios crackled faintly.

Outside, the air was dawn-fresh and brine-sharp. To the south, a look-out's light burned on Piel Castle's battlements. The low, gentle tide hushed and lapped on the beach; across the water, a tern called.

Helen crossed coarse grass, sandy soil, and a slope of till and rubble to the shingle beach. She stretched and limbered up, then ran north along the shore.

*

Walney Island and the Barrow Peninsula pointed, like an open pincer's jaws, to the Cumbrian coast; between them, in the Piel Channel, was the tiny speck of Piel Island.

Lights gleamed across the water on Walney as Helen jogged south along the western shore. The bigger island, with its barracks and armouries, was the obvious target for an attacking force, but the real prizes – the command staff and intelligence officers, with their lists of agents and broken codes – were all on Piel. If the Reapers came, they'd have a chance of escape.

While the people on Walney died.

You can always get them to die for you.

Alannah had said that; Flaps, too, and Frank's angry ghost. Helen ran harder, faster, emptied her mind of all but the land, the water and the run.

She cut across the island's southern tip, past the castle to the eastern shore, then back up towards the inn. This time, she was glad of her racing heart and the sweat.

At Ashwood Fort, she'd grown sluggish and soft, and it had nearly killed her. Now, Helen ran a full circuit of the island every morning, and felt sharper, clearer, than ever before.

She knelt on the shingle, splashed cold brine in her face and studied her reflection. A long white oval face; grey eyes and red hair with a single feather of white hair in it, just above the left ear.

Helen looked east towards the mainland, watched the sunrise spill its light across the bay. A few moments of peace. And then she recalled the dream.

He will destroy you.

She'd thought herself done with the Black Road, but it seemed not, and she didn't know why.

Helen stood and stretched again, then headed back to the Inn.

*

Ashwood Fort, RCZ 7
27th June, Attack Plus Twenty-One
1800 hours

Ashwood came in sight. On the hillside, the thin stream glittered in the twilight; at the top, the high crag of the Fort loomed behind the two defensive walls. *I nearly died here.* The scar above Helen's ear stung.

The landcruiser's radio crackled. "Who goes there?"

"Convoy 36a with Phoenix."

Phoenix: that was Helen.

They rolled up the hill, past trenches and barbed wire. Lush summer grass hid the battle craters. Closer to, there were other traces, like the wreckage of the little stone bridge that had forded the stream, and the bullet scars that pitted the Fort's outer walls.

The gates opened; they drove through the village. Where the old stone cottages had stood were tents, lean-tos and crude houses made from mortared rubble. Only the war memorial still stood, the cross on top shot away.

The inner walls approached, as scarred and pitted as the outer ones. The church tower's crenellated parapet was jagged and irregular, its stained-glass windows replaced with hide or scraped horn.

Helen's landcruiser drove through the inner gates and halted; she climbed out, stretching.

"Hoy!"

Four people approached. "Wakefield!" Helen called.

The small, sharp-faced tribeswoman grinned. "Welcome."

The second member of the group was, like Wakefield, of the Fox Tribe, and wore the head and skin of one as a headdress.

Helen knelt, her right hand out and open, her left on the ground. Weapon hand empty, shield hand down. "Chief Loncraine."

"Up, crazy ginger." Loncraine pronounced it, as always, with two hard 'g's. He was Helen's age, but grey-haired, his body scarred; the hard life the tribes led aged them fast.

A tall, grey-haired woman stepped forward. "Helen."

"Alannah."

They embraced. "You're looking well."

"So are you." Helen winked. "Being loved-up's done wonders."

"Bugger off. Come on, let's get in."

The fourth member of the party remained still, watching. "Gevaudan," Helen said.

He inclined his head. "You're well?"

She nodded. "You?"

"Fine."

"Good." Helen cleared her throat. "We should go in."

"Of course." They followed the others. "Might I interest you in dinner later?"

"Dinner?"

"I'm a reasonable cook."

He will destroy you.

Gevaudan kept his eyes on the ground. Helen touched his arm, drew back as he looked up. "I'd like that."

*

Bats flickered back and forth across the summer moon. Butter-warm lantern-light spread across the cottage's garden and over two wooden chairs and a table set with bowls and cups, fading as it reached the inner wall at the garden's edge.

Gevaudan opened a bottle.

"Wine?" said Helen. "Jesus. Can't remember the last time..." She trailed off, then held out her cup.

"Elderberry," Gevaudan said, ladling stew into the bowls. When they ate, he was relieved to find the meat and vegetables were tender, and that Helen seemed to find the taste acceptable. He hadn't cooked for anyone else in a long time.

"Thank you for coming," he said at last. "I've missed having company."

"You're in the middle of a small town."

"Most people here have a single room to live in, and many share even that. But no-one grudges me a house and garden to myself. They're glad I'm on their side – some even owe me their lives – but on the whole, they like me best at a distance."

"Even Alannah?"

"Especially Alannah. As for the rest – Flaps and Darrow are in Manchester raising a new cadre of urban guerillas, and you and Danny are... wherever you are. So," Gevaudan raised his cup, "as I said, it's good to see you."

Helen smiled. "And you."

"How are things with you?" he asked.

"Good," she said. "The Book's gone out by land and sea – it's all over the North, Wales, the Midlands – getting into Scotland now, and the Isle of M –"

"I meant you, personally."

"Sorry." Candlelight gleamed in Helen's eyes; she had no idea of her own beauty, and wouldn't have cared if she had. Even the thought felt wrong to Gevaudan; they might look of an age, but he could have been her grandfather.

A soft hand touched Gevaudan's wrist. "It's okay," said Jo. Gevaudan's breath caught; he hadn't ghostlighted in months. "Even you could die tomorrow, Gev. She's no child. She's a mind of her own. It's up to her, too."

"You okay?"

Gevaudan turned back to Helen. "I'm sorry. You were saying?"

Helen sighed. "You know what happened. When I was wounded, I had to face up to a few things. Not pleasant, but I feel... different."

"No more devils on your back?"

"Mm. Just hope that they weren't what made me good at what I do."

"What makes you good at what you do are years of experience, intelligence and good judgement."

"Don't know about that last one."

"You mean Winterborn?"

She'd told Gevaudan something of her history with Winterborn before leaving Ashwood; now, he suspected, she wondered if she should have.

"You didn't force him to become a Reaper."

Her eyes glistened; it wasn't just the candlelight. "He was family once."

Gevaudan reached out, but she drew back. "I'm sorry," he said, but it stung. Ridiculous – it wasn't as if she feared him too. She'd hardly be here otherwise.

Unless, perhaps, she was protecting her investment. *She's using you*, Jarrett had shouted after him once. But Jarrett was dead, and there'd been no truth in her words.

"What's wrong?" he asked.

"Nothing." But she wouldn't meet his eyes.

Best to change the subject. "When do you go back to Piel?" he asked.

"A week, ten days. They're swearing in the new Raider cadets. Want me to stand there and salute a lot."

"Not your thing at all."

She shook her head. "Too much like the Reapers."

"But necessary, on some level."

"Now that's a depressing thought."

Gevaudan smiled. "Yes, I'm not sorry to be missing it."

"Missing it?"

"A new cell's been formed on the Wirral. So they're sending a unit to link up with them, arrange some additional supplies.

Someone decided I'd be the perfect representative. I can only assume that drugs of some kind where involved."

"Great."

"Would some coffee help your mood?"

"Coffee always helps my mood. As long as it's the real thing."

Gevaudan stood, mock-bowed. "Then I'll fetch some."

*

Helen watched him go – that wolf's lope, too quick and fluid to be fully human.

What's wrong?

Nothing.

A lie, and far from her first to him. Like weeds in deep water, they caught and tangled her. And pulled her under to drown.

Part One:
The Breaking Strain

1.

Sick Bay, Ashwood Fort
Regional Command Zone 7 (British Isles)
3rd July, Attack Plus Twenty-One Years
0900 hours

Nestor Shelley rubbed his eyes, reached for his mug. The coffee was cold, but he drank it anyway: it was the genuine article, not roasted dandelion root. Gevaudan had given him two tins from his own limited supply, telling him it was the least he deserved. Nice to be appreciated.

"Okay," he called. "Next."

A chair, a table and a couch, screened off from the rest of the sick bay. Nestor had been here four hours already without a break; a couple more to go before he stopped for some food and to lie down for an hour or so. Not that there was the time to spare

– the demands on his time, his knowledge, his few resources was never-ending – but there came a point where sheer exhaustion made further work impossible.

The curtain rustled back. "Hi, Doc."

Nestor dredged up a smile from somewhere. "Colby."

Colby limped to the chair and sat, removing her shirt, and Nestor took out his stethoscope. Neither spoke as he worked, listening to her heart and lungs; they both knew what he'd find. She was in her forties, but looked to be in her fifties, and a hard fifties at that. Her brown hair was almost completely grey now, the blue-grey eyes bloodshot, though still alert. The yellow cast to her skin, at least, was no worse. But no better, either.

"So?" said Colby, when he was done.

Nestor shrugged. "Better than I thought you'd be, to be honest. That fresh air must be doing you some good."

"But?"

"But..." Nestor would be honest with her, as he always had. "Your condition's still deteriorating, Jane. I'm sorry."

Colby shrugged. "How long?"

"Six months. Maybe."

"Right, then." If she was afraid, she didn't show it. "That everything?"

"Do you need something for the pain?"

She shook her head. "Got to stay sharp. That everything? Got to get off."

"You're not staying for the ceremony?"

"Nah. Can't be doing with that crap."

Nestor chuckled. "No, me neither. Take care, Jane."

"You too, mate."

The curtain rustled back into place. Nestor breathed out. "Next."

The next one was Stock. Nestor inspected the scars where the Catchman's claws had all but gutted her. How many hours had he worked to save her? Enough, as it had turned out. "How's the pain?"

"Not too bad. Hardly anything now."

"Sticking to the diet?"

"Yup."

"Keep that up and you'll be fine. Need anything for the pain?"

"Nah. Fine."

None of them ever did. All out to prove how tough they were. Suffer in silence. "Okay, then. Come back in a couple of weeks."

"Will do." She grinned. "Starting in the Intelligence Centre tomorrow."

"I'm pleased for you." He was, too; he'd seen her in her bed in the months following her injury, usually with a tutor, determinedly learning to read and write. A new life, a new beginning; he'd helped that happen. It gave him some small measure of hope.

When Stock had gone, Nestor closed his eyes. A moment's rest. Just a couple of minutes, before the next one.

*

WINTERBORN'S OFFICE, THE TOWER
CITY OF MANCHESTER
0930 HOURS

A hot sun blazed in a blue sky. Winterborn felt a familiar urge – to go to the floor-length window and look over his domain, basking in the burning sun – but had to resist. An unfamiliar feeling, and not one he enjoyed.

His fingers itched for the music box in his desk drawer; even touching its scratched silver surface was often enough to restore his calm. But it was a private thing, not for other people's eyes.

Visitors to Winterborn's office were rare, and usually alone; today, though, a dozen TechSec Reapers were connecting old computer monitors and ancient TVs to consoles and transmitters. Two mounted a video camera on a tripod in front of Winterborn, doing their best not to look at him as they did, or at the silent, grey-robed figure in the corner.

"Nearly ready, sir." The chief tech wasn't meeting his eyes either. Reaper techs rarely found themselves in the Regional Commander's presence; besides, being noticed by Winterborn rarely turned out well.

"Lieutenant Cadigan?"

"Sir?"

"Look at me."

She obeyed unwillingly, eyes round and blinking.

"What, exactly, does 'nearly ready' mean?"

Cadigan licked her lips. "We have contact with nine of the other Commands. We're still establishing links with the island Commands, London and Cornwall."

"Then get on with it. I want to get started."

*

SICK BAY, ASHWOOD FORT
0945 HOURS

Nestor took a bottle of pills from his pocket: he hated using them, monitored their use rigorously. An addicted doctor was no use to anyone. Just one here, one there, now and again, to get him through. He tried swallowing it dry, but it stuck in his throat. He grimaced, drained the last of the coffee to dislodge it. There. He breathed out. "Next," he called.

The patient came in hesitantly, looking awkward, unsure as ever of her welcome. "Hello, Juliet," said Nestor. He nearly said *Miss Carson*, or just *Carson*, stopped himself in time. She was a patient like any other, whatever else she was or had been.

"Doc." Carson sat.

Nestor studied her: smallish, lean, pale, with cropped reddish-brown hair and hazel eyes. "How have you been? Any pain?"

"None."

He nodded, trying to think *patient* instead of *Reaper* or *Jennywren*. She wasn't one any more. Supposedly, at least. "You've pushed yourself pretty hard over the past couple of months."

"Had to."

"Hm." He put on the stethoscope. "Shirt off, please."

He listened to her heart and lungs. Strong. Healthy. *You should give them to Colby, and your innards to Stock*. He pushed that thought aside. *You're a doctor, a healer. The job's the same, whatever she's done.* "All good," he said at last. "You've healed incredibly well, you know."

"Yeah," said Carson. "Good job." She looked down at the floor. "Got a lot of making up to do."

Was there enough making up in the world for a Jennywren? Nestor's mother would have said so, if the repentance was sincere. *God sees all, knows all, forgives all, Nestor*, she used to say, *long as you ask for it*. Nestor missed her, and her faith. "Well," he said. "You're fully recovered, anyway."

Carson pulled her shirt back on. "That it?"

"That's it."

"Kay. See you, doc."

She went out. Nestor leant back in the chair and closed his eyes. Then the curtain swished back once more, and he opened them again.

*

WORSLEY CANAL JUNCTION
CITY OF SALFORD, RCZ7
0955 HOURS

From the woods above the Delph, Flaps watched the work team plod along the towpath, hauling the wide black barge down the canal. Their bare feet left red prints in the gravel and dust; flies swirled around them like smoke.

Through the binoculars Flaps saw slack, drained faces, cracked lips. Poor fuckers probably hadn't had water in hours. A woman stumbled and fell; the rest of the team trudged on. The woman moved weakly, then lay still.

The barge halted opposite Flaps' position. Traders rowed out from the deep, water-filled pit of the Delph to meet it, under the bridge and into the basin where the two big canals came together. Reapers paced on the canal quay.

Flaps eyed the road and the old village. There were small buildings with faded signs above the windows – shops, Darrow said they were called. One had landcruisers parked outside, and a newer sign above the door: black, with a picture of a wheatsheaf on it and the letters R.E.A.P. underneath.

There were houses, too – huge ones. Darrow said each one'd used to belong to one family, but Flaps recked he had to be taking the piss. Just one family, for all that space? Fuck off.

A Reaper handed food and water chits to the barge-team, while another bunch of thin, ragged scavengers shuffled forward to unload the barge. On the tow-path, the woman lay where she'd fallen.

The Reapers ignored the traders; they were concerned with the dock crew, making sure no-one was pilfering. The boat crew leant over to haggle with the traders; a few climbed down into the boats. So did several other people, who were quickly hidden under blankets.

Watching them climb down, Flaps glimpsed a couple of submachine guns. She noticed one especially, as it wasn't one of the usual Thompsons, Stens or Sterlings. It had a wooden stock, like an old rifle, a perforated barrel and a magazine that stuck out at the side. A Lanchester; Flaps only knew one rebel who carried one.

She glimpsed his face before they flicked the blanket over him: pale, dark-eyed, spiky black hair.

The boats rowed back under the bridge into the Delph. Flaps signalled, and five of her fighters slithered down through the undergrowth to the water.

*

St Martin de Porres Church, Ashwood Fort
1010 hours

Carson went in through the door, dipped her fingers in the font, crossed herself as she went up the aisle.

The church was pleasantly cool, after the baking heat outside. Empty, too, far as she could see; that was good as well. She walked up the aisle to the altar. Candles burned. There was silence, stillness, a sense of peace. She needed that.

She was used to the Reaper chaplains from SpiriCon division, and of course there were none of those at Ashwood. There were rebel Christians, too, but priests and pastors were in short supply, and she was still trying to decide which to go to. In the meantime, she had only a crude, basic belief that she was loved – yes, even her – and that redemption was possible. Somehow. Maybe those she fought with – would fight with, if they'd let her – wouldn't forgive her – you couldn't wipe the past from human memory so easily – but one day, God might.

Carson knelt at the altar, bowed her head, tried to shape a prayer. She reached into her pocket, took out a small, crudely-carved wooden cross, and clasped it in her hands.

Carson had been three when her parents gave her up to the Reapers; it was all she'd known. There'd always seemed a contradiction between what her faith professed and what she did, but the chaplain had always had an answer.

It had been Wakefield who'd found her after the battle, wounded and weak. With every reason to end Carson on sight and no reason to spare her, had let her live and called a medic. Carson lived because of her.

She gripped the cross, and closed her eyes. What should she ask God for? *Let today go well?* What did 'going well' mean? That she not be shunned or spat on? What right had she to ask for that? Repentance had to be more than words. The first Christians chose death, rather than to worship a false god: you had to know the truth, know what was right, and do it no matter the cost. Simple enough in principle, but a hard and narrow way in practice. As it should be: nothing good was easy.

Let them forgive me, Lord, let them see that I'm sincere? Ask God to soften the hearts of those she'd tried to kill, whose loved ones had been slaughtered by the likes of her? Again, by what right? By right of repentance? *Say you're sorry, and everything's okay again? It doesn't work like that, Juliet. You know it doesn't.*

She'd never be wholly one of the rebels, never be trusted by them, and the Reapers would kill her for a traitor if they laid hands on her again. A hard path, but Carson welcomed that; if that was forgiveness' price, she'd pay it.

Forgiveness: God's, not Man's. Was that would she should pray for? *Forgive me, Lord?* It might be closer, but it wasn't quite it.

A rustle of clothing; a man knelt beside her. He looked sideways at her, and his mouth thinned. "Move," he said.

Carson's praying hands tried to tighten into fists. The cross dug into her palm. *I've as much right here as you*, she could have said – but no. She nodded and rose, walked back to the pews. Most of them were newly built, rough planks laid on stacked bricks; the bulk of the original pews had been destroyed during the attack on the Fort. One or two were still intact, though; Carson found one and sat there, kneeling on a hassock.

At last, she found the words she needed: *Lord, make me worthy of forgiveness. Give me the courage to bear their anger and not be bitter, and to do what I must to atone.* Yes, that was it.

Juliet Carson closed her eyes, and prayed. And then, when it was time, she stood and went outside.

*

St Martin de Porres Church, Ashwood Fort
1015 hours

Helen leant on the parapet, watched the crowd gather below, milling and aimless. Orders were barked, and they formed up into ranks. She grimaced. *Parade-ground crap.* Below, someone came out of the church, marched to join the lines of recruits. The fighters around the woman shifted awkwardly; the gap between her and those on either side was wider than normal.

"There she is."

Beside her, Alannah took a swig of water. "Carson?"

"Yeah."

Alannah passed Helen the bottle. "She's put herself forward for Raider training."

"I heard."

Below, someone barked more orders, and the crowd fell silent. Helen could hear a fly buzzing; she took a last swig from the water bottle to clear her throat. "Here we go."

*

Worsley Canal Junction
1017 hours

Flaps watched the road and canal through the sights of her Sterling; beside her, others trained automatic rifles, two Bren guns and a GPMG on the Reapers, ready for the first sign of trouble. But none came, and a couple of minutes later the men and women who'd climbed off the barge joined her at the edge of the woods.

"Flaps?"

There he was – the spiky hair, the pale face, Lanchester slung across his back.

"Danny." She kept her face closed and hard. Give nothing. Show nothing.

"You're all right?"

She shrugged.

The rest of Danny's fighters were coming up behind him. A small wiry girl was the first of them: she was in ordinary scav's rags, but you could still tell she was a tribal, you looked close enough at the quick-eyed, weather-tanned, if birdlike face. She nodded and half-smiled. "Flaps."

"Wakefield." Flaps half-smiled back. She hadn't had much to do with the tribeswoman, but what she knew she liked.

Danny cleared his throat. "How's Darrow?"

Another shrug. "Getting on with it."

The rest of Danny's team filed up the slope. A couple she recognised: Harp, Lish. A couple dragging heavy bags after them. Supplies. One stumbled: a lean black lad. Reminded her a bit of Telo, the only boy in Scary Mary's crew. Long dead. "Brant?" Danny whispered. "You okay?" Brant nodded, heaved his bag the rest of the way up the slope.

The last one up was a bony Asian girl with a hard, pitted face. "All up," she said.

Danny nodded. "Thanks, Hack."

"Let's skate," said Flaps.

They went deeper into the woods, skirting clearings where the trees had been cut for shelters or fuel, filled with tents, bivouacs and lean-tos. The air turned foul with sewage and woodsmoke. Danny stayed close; Flaps felt his skin's heat on hers. Wanting him; hating him. *How're you? How's Alannah?* She wanted to know, and didn't; wanted him to be happy, wanted him to be miserable. No, she wouldn't ask. But there was someone else she *would* ask about.

"How's Gevaudan?" she said.

"Old Creeping Death?" Danny grinned. "Pining for Helen a bit, but he's okay."

"Thought they were getting together?"

"They're at different forts now," Danny said. "Bit awkward."

"But he's all right?"
"Yeah. She's sent him off to the coast somewhere."
"The sea?"
"Yeah."
"You ever seen it?"
"Nah."
"Me neither."

A bird clattered from a tree-top overhead. "So –" began Danny.

"This way," said Flaps. "Come on. Move."

*

COMMANDER'S OFFICE, THE TOWER
1025 HOURS

Cadigan wiped her forehead. "We're ready, sir."

Winterborn smiled at her, unblinking, till she looked down. "Good. Then let's get on with this."

Fourteen screens blinked and flickered into life. Fourteen men and women, old and young, appeared on them. Each, like him, behind a desk, and each, like him, wearing the gold rank badge of a Regional Commander on their black leather uniform.

Winterborn motioned to the door, and the techs made for it en masse. The figure in grey remained seated.

The door closed; Winterborn smiled. "Ladies; gentlemen. Let's begin."

*

St Martin de Porres Church, Ashwood Fort
1026 hours

Below, fires were lit; spitted pig carcases turned over them. Those cooked already were being carved on trestle tables. The new recruits, freshly sworn in, sat on the ground and ate. Helen could smell the pork roasting.

"Hungry?" said Alannah.

"Getting that way."

They climbed down the stairs to the inside of the church. Someone was sitting in a pew by the entrance; she got up as Helen approached, standing to attention. "Ma'am."

"Carson," Helen said.

The other woman's face was red. "Just wanted to thank you," she stuttered, "for giving me a chance. I know it was you, spoke up for me. I won't let you down."

A Reaper's gratitude; now *that* was uncomfortable. "You want to thank me, prove me right."

Carson flushed redder still. "I will. I will."

"Okay." Helen softened a little. "Go get yourself something to eat."

"Yes, ma'am." Carson spun on her heel and marched back outside.

Helen looked at Alannah. Alannah looked back at her. Neither spoke; a moment later, they followed Carson out.

*

Commander's Office, The Tower
1028 hours

"So, Winterborn." RCZ15's Commander Scrimgeour, a compact blonde woman with small, precise features and bright green eyes, folded her arms. "Let's talk about the balls-up you've made."

Winterborn felt a cold flood of fury, but smiled, remaining still. "I thought we might discuss the Unification Conference."

"Some damned hope. Word's out all over the country – you've an uprising in Seven and can't stop it. And now it's spread. I've even had trouble here in Fifteen."

Winterborn kept smiling. "I can see that coming as a shock to you, Naomi. But then the Orkneys and Shetlands are a soft billet. I doubt your liberal approach would last long here."

"Tobias is quite right," piped up Commander Fowler of RCZ1, a fiftyish woman with tangled grey hair, glazed eyes, and a tenuous grasp of reality at best.

"Tereus," corrected Winterborn, smiling, lips pressed together to hide his gritted teeth.

"That's what I said. Noreen here –" Scrimgeour opened her mouth to protest, then sighed and shook her head as Fowler carried on "– fails to recognise the necessity for a zero-tolerance approach. What we need to do is carry out air-strikes..."

No-one bothered reminding Fowler that the last aircraft in Britain had flown at the time of the Civil Emergency, and then only a handful of them, very briefly. There wouldn't have been any point. Thankfully, Commander Drozek of RCZ3 cut in on what threatened to become an interminable monologue.

"My worst enemies wouldn't call the Isle of Man a bastion of liberal values, Winterborn." Drozek lit a Monarch, leaning back in his chair. "And we've had fighting here, too – ever since your botch-up in March. They're smuggling that damned Book of theirs into every Command they can."

"Mine too," said Maguire of Northern Ireland. "Eight copies, in the middle of sodding Belfast. Christ knows how many more."

Commander Probert leant forward. "It took two years to mop up the rebel groups here in Wales after the Refuge fell," he said, "and even then we never got them all. Mountain ranges, valleys – they had a whole bloody country full of hiding places. Now they think their time's come, and it's all bloody kicking off again."

Johnstone, commanding the Scottish Highlands, scratched his red beard. "Major upheavals at my end, too."

"We've got 'em under control," said Treloar of Devon and Cornwall, black eyes dead as glass in her slack face. She licked her lips and smiled. "Anyone caught with a copy of the Book gets hanged – slow, so they strangle – and left to rot."

*

LIVERPOOL CITY CENTRE, RCZ7
1034 HOURS

Pin followed the Grendelwolf through the ruins, and gripped her rifle tight.

The ground was concrete, the tall buildings stone, cracked glass and rusting steel. Some had words on them. Pin could read now, so she spelt them out – FIVE GUYS, BURGER KING, NANDO'S – but they meant nothing. There were steel-backs on the roads, but different to the ones the Reapers had. They were huge, and built like two huge steel-backs stacked one atop the other, with rows of seats inside.

None of the buildings had fallen, but there'd been death: Pin saw skeletons inside the steel-backs, bones scattered on the road. Cones of purple buddleia on long green stalks sprouted everywhere; its sweet honey scent made her feel sick.

Pin felt dizzy. She'd been in ruined towns, once or twice – but there'd been edges to them. The Fox tribe's woods and hills'd been near, and she knew those like her own skin. But not here; this was a different place.

"All right," called Gevaudan. "Two minutes' rest."

He led them across a spread of paving and cobbles to a giant grey building with idols standing in front of it. Men on horses, huge cats with ruffs of shaggy fur. Gevaudan pointed to the stone steps in front. "Eat, and drink some water."

Pin climbed the steps till she was level with one of the huge cats. She touched it: stone.

"St George's Hall." Gevaudan put his Bren gun down and tied back his long black hair. "My daughter was married here."

"Married?" asked Neap, one of the younger ones. Like the others, he looked dazed by the city: except for the Grendelwolf, they were all tribals in this group.

"Handfasted," said Pin.

Neap looked round. "What happened?" he said. "None of it's smashed up."

"Radiological bomb," the Grendelwolf said. "Didn't smash things, just poisoned them."

"Poison?" Neap squeaked. "But safe now?"

"People can live here, if that's what you mean."

"Then why don't they?" Neap never stopped asking questions. Made Pin want to choke him sometimes.

"Too empty."

Pin nodded. "Too many ghosts," she said. Everything had a ghost — rivers, ruins, mountains, trees — but the city was full of people-ghosts, and angry ones, lost and wandering.

Gevaudan picked up the Bren. "Get your lanterns ready."

Up ahead, the road forked. Gevaudan raised a hand; Pin crouched behind a steel-back, shouldering her rifle. "Clear," said the Grendelwolf, and went left. Pin followed.

The road sloped down between two white stone arches; below was the tunnel entrance. An idol stood above it on either side — a bearded man and a woman, each with a crown. Cold air gusted up from below, foul with piss and turds and rotten things, but almost welcome after the buddleia's cloying honey-smell.

"Light your lanterns," Gevaudan said.

Tinder smoked and caught; a lighted taper went round.

"Now," he said, "with me."

Neap swallowed, eyes huge. Pin squeezed his shoulder, and they followed the Grendelwolf into the dark.

*

Commander's Office, The Tower
1045 hours

"We're straying from the main issue," said Drozek. "Our priority's to maintain order by stamping out the rebellion."

"I concur."

Silence fell; even Fowler, who'd been burbling softly on, ignored by all, stopped. The speaker was Percival Holland of RCZ12. A gaunt, craggy man in his sixties and one of the Reapers' founder members, he was the last of the original Regional Commanders. His word carried weight, and of all Winterborn's colleagues, Holland was the only one for whom he felt anything approaching respect.

"Reunifying the country is our ultimate goal," said Holland, "but only when the time's right to re-establish a central government. I don't think we're there yet. Acting prematurely will only screw things up."

Commander Grimwood of RCZ13 smirked. "Wouldn't expect Winterborn to understand that, Percival. Doubt he's ever done a thing that wasn't for himself."

"Glad you aren't allowing personal animosities to cloud your judgement," said Winterborn.

Grimwood's smile was as cold and empty as Winterborn's own. "We could talk about your recent record instead. You had Helen Damnation under your nose for years, alive and well."

"I'm with Holland," said Maguire. "First and foremost, we need to focus on restoring order in our own Commands. Unification's a sideshow. Irrelevant."

"I disagree," said McMahon from RCZ6. "We need a concerted effort. Tereus?"

"Graeme?"

"In the absence of other agreements, I propose a bilateral treaty between the North-Eastern and North-Western Commands. We can clear the rebels out of the North – cut the country in two as far as they're concerned."

"Hold the phone there, pal," said Carole McLeod of Lowland Scotland. "We're supposed to work towards union, not form power blocs. Especially on my fucking doorstop."

"I have to agree with McMahon about a joint effort," said Probert. "We haven't the resources we did during the Civil Emergency, and the rebels haven't a central command to destroy. We have to stop this *now*, whatever way we can."

"The questions is whether that way involves unification," said Holland. "I see no evidence of that."

*

Queensway Tunnel, Liverpool/Birkenhead
1055 hours

The smell was worse inside, and the dark was thick and cold from the river above. Gevaudan felt it press in around them as he led them on.

The stink of urine and excrement worsened. The tunnel curved first one way, then another, snake-like. It had ribbed white walls, now streaked with green and black, and four lanes, two going each way. In them were more vehicles: cars, trucks, buses.

The ground crunched under Gevuadan's boots. He glanced; it was littered with cockroach shells and animal bones – bats, rats, birds – lying in a soup of animal waste that had dropped from the ceiling. The mire clicked and scuttled as still-living insects scattered from his path.

Up ahead, something long and white hung down. A sheet of some kind, ragged and tattered. The lantern-light caught more of them, further down the tunnel. Then Gevaudan drew closer, and saw it wasn't cloth at all.

A gasp – he turned and saw Pin frozen, staring. She'd almost walked into another web, and the spider in it hung in no more than a foot from her face. The light gleamed in eight black shiny eyes; its legs seemed as thick as Pin's fingers, and three or four times longer, its body bigger than Gevaudan's fist. Pin shifted sideways, and it moved.

Neap screamed; the spider hunched, crouching. It was going to jump.

"Quiet," hissed Gevaudan, stepping forward; the spider scuttled upwards, haring up the strands of the web. "Keep quiet," he said, "and still. They won't be dangerous unless you panic them." He smiled. "They're probably more frightened of you than you are of them."

Pin didn't look convinced, especially as they carried on through the tunnel, skirting the webs, and encountered the shrivelled remains of birds, bats, rats and what looked like a small dog hanging in them. Nonetheless, she kept going – determined to set an example, Gevaudan guessed. She was doing well.

He kept low, staying close to the vehicles, the Bren gun at his hip. He passed a car, a truck – and then a double-decker bus, its windows unbroken, but streaked, like its two-tone green paint, with rust and moss and slime. Inside, the passengers were still in their seats. What he could see of them was little more than rag and bone, but they were barely visible, cocooned as they were in the ballooning clouds of spiderweb that filled the vehicle's interior.

One of the bodies raised a skeletal hand and pressed it to the window. Gevaudan froze, staring, then relaxed when he saw the hand had too many fingers. The spider stared at him through the dirty glass for a moment, then scuttled away into the depths of its lair. Gevaudan breathed out, and they all moved on.

A noise; movement. A snap and crunch. Gevaudan raised a hand, heard the movement of the others behind him stop, and dropped behind a car. He shouldered the Bren and inched forward, then stopped to listen again.

A soft drip of water; a faint rustle of things moving on webs and floor. Something larger moved on the ground nearby; Gevaudan aimed towards it. A rat glared beadily back at him, then scuttled away under the bus. Gevaudan rose, turned to the others and motioned them on.

And the darkness exploded into light.

Fiat lux, Gevaudan thought detachedly as his eyes tried to reattune themselves. The sheets of webbing glowed, the spiders black scrawls that zig-zagged up through them towards the ceiling.

Running footsteps thundered. "Remain where you are!" an amplified voice boomed. "Lay down your weapons!"

"Go!" shouted Gevaudan; he spun back and opened fire.

Webs jerked, flapped, tore. A clattering sound from above and blackness spilled from the ceiling to flood the tunnel; bats, frightened from their roosts.

Gunfire thundered in response. Webs jumped and tore again, some falling asunder. Dirt-covered windscreens exploded, and the bodywork of cars juddered and clanged as bullets slammed into them.

"Move!" shouted Gevaudan at Pin and the others. He could glimpse the Reapers through the webs – vague silhouettes, advancing and firing. He emptied the Bren's magazine in a long burst, saw two of them jerk back and fall. "Move!" he shouted again, then charged after his team, changing magazines as he ran.

One of the tribals blundered into a web that tore and flapped around him; the boy screamed, fell to his knees. There was a spider on his shoulder, biting at his neck. Gevaudan snatched it up, crushed it, but the boy fell forward and he saw three more of them clinging on.

"Keep going!" he yelled after Pin and the rest. "Stay low!" Cocking the Bren, he knelt to check the fallen boy, but the tribal's eyes were open and unblinking, and there was no pulse at his throat. Before he could turn to fire back at the Reapers, fresh light exploded in the tunnel, from the Liverpool end.

This time there was no warning. The Reapers' guns crashed again; Gevaudan's team got off a few bursts in reply, but one by one they dropped. Pin ran past him, shouting; then she spun, slammed against the side of the spider-filled bus and collapsed beside the door.

Gevaudan fired back, and then something smashed into him and he fell against a car. Pain in his stomach; he looked down and saw his black sweater was torn and wet. Another round hit him in the shoulder, but he kept hold of the machine gun, firing first one way down the tunnel, then the other.

Shadows ran towards him: he jerked the Bren their way, then pulled it up. It was Neap and two others; the last of his team.

The Bren gun emptied; Gevaudan threw it aside and straightened up. There was still the Fury. Injured as he was, he didn't know how long he could sustain it, but he could at least try, give the rest of his team a chance to –

A hissing screech echoed down the tunnel, and everything went still. The firing stopped; even the scuttling of rats and spiders was gone. The only other sound was the fading flap and squeaking of the bats as they fled away.

"What?" said Neap. "What's that?"

Gevaudan looked towards the Liverpool entrance, saw the hunched shapes advancing, silhouetted against the webs before they tore them down with their clawed hands. Steel-helmeted heads; round, palely-glowing lenses for eyes.

"Catchmen," he said.

"But they're dead," said Neap. "They all died."

"Not all, it seems." Gevaudan didn't reach for the pistols he carried; they'd be worse than useless here. Instead he crouched and drew the knives sheathed in his boots. They whispered free;

the light glinted on steel blades, and the symbol carved on either side of each one.

At first glance it resembled a crucifix, but a closer inspection would have shown the proportions weren't quite right, that parts of it weren't quite straight or at the right angle. Only one church he knew of depicted such a cross: the one that still stood in the village of Hobsdyke. Only it, carved on iron or steel, could kill the Night Wolves or one of their creatures.

"Get behind me," Gevaudan told Neap and the other two, and moved forward, still crouching, the knives in his hands.

How many of them were there? A dozen, twenty? Gevaudan was still trying to count them when they tore the last of the webs between them and him down. He heard Neap gasp as the Catchmen were revealed in full. A dull grey leathery hide covered their bodies and their mouths were lipless, bloodless slits, so their faces looked mouthless until they smiled, the grins stretching impossibly wide, up to where their ears should have been, huge red grins full of serrated teeth.

And then they rushed at him.

Gevaudan summoned the Fury.

He leapt and everything was fast. A Catchman came at him; he sprang aside, slashed it with a knife, spun to avoid another as it screamed. Drove the knife into the second attacker's back, spitted a third with the second blade as it lunged at him.

Another Catchman took its moment, clawed thumbs aimed at his eyes – Gevaudan kicked it in the chest, flipping it back. His knives slid free of the Catchmen he'd killed – they were just sacks of leathery hide now, the soft tissues frothing out of them in a bubbling pink slurry.

Gevaudan went for the Catchman he'd kicked but claws raked down his back. He cried out; more claws raked his stomach.

He kicked slashed stabbed, but they were as quick as him. Quicker. Then one had his arm, another his leg. He stabbed the one pinning his arm – it screamed but wouldn't let go. As it fell the one he'd kicked came to take its place. Gevaudan smashed his other blade through its right eye, deep into the skull – the blade stuck fast, wouldn't come free.

Behind him, screams – he twisted, trying to get loose, saw Neap and the other two vanish under the other Catchmen. Screams, then silence; the Catchmen rose from their kills, grinning mouths dripping red.

They ran at him, piled on. He stayed on his feet, didn't stop fighting – but then his legs buckled under the weight and he went down. The weight of them smashed into the tunnel floor's mire and filth; he couldn't breathe.

Before the black descended, he thought of Helen in the garden, the candlelight reflected in her eyes.

*

COMMANDER'S OFFICE, THE TOWER
1115 HOURS

"There's something I should like to say," Winterborn said. "I'd like to apologise for the lack of headway in putting an end to the rebellion. You're quite right that the movement here is the heart of the matter, and that they should have been stamped out at once. But measures are already being taken to break the rebel movement here in the North. And soon, a new weapons system designed specifically for this kind of insurgency will be in place – a final solution to the rebel problem."

Grimwood snorted. "Another of your pipe dreams?"

"You'll see results very soon," said Winterborn. "So perhaps we should postpone further discussion until the end of the month. Does everyone agree?"

"A show of hands?" said Holland. "Very well."

Winterborn counted. "Motion carried," he said. "Very well. Until then."

One by one, the screens blinked out. Winterborn gazed at them moodily, then turned to the grey shape in the corner. "Well?"

When the grey one finally spoke, two voices sounded as one: a male one, gravelly and deep, and a female, sweet and bitterly cold. "You'll have everything you want, Commander, before year's end. You have my word."

*

Queensway Tunnel, Liverpool/Birkenhead
1130 hours

It was a long time before the tunnel was quiet again. Pin pressed herself against the foot of the bus' stairwell, teeth gritted, lips pressed together, as cobwebs brushed her face and tangled in her hair. One of the corpses had slipped partly from its seat; its grinning face was an inch from hers.

The bus' door had been ajar, just enough for Pin to squirm inside.

She'd never seen a Catchman for herself, but she'd heard of them; heard how just one had almost killed Gevaudan. And how many were there here?

She'd heard Neap scream, as well; heard him scream and she'd done nothing. She screwed her eyes shut, she mustn't cry, mustn't sob. There must be no sound.

Blood trickled from her leg wound. Her rifle lay on the tunnel floor; she pulled her machine pistol out from under her jacket, eased the Stemp's bolt back very very slowly, so the click as it engaged was so soft, with luck no-one would hear.

The Catchmen's snarling subsided, leaving only muffled grunting noises, till at last an officer spoke. "All right. Get him out of here. Don't damage him any more than he already is. They want him alive."

Something tickled Pin's hair; a light, feathery touch. Then another, and another, and another, like little thin fingers.

Or legs.

She held her breath, kept still, as the spider crawled across her scalp, her forehead, down over her face. One of its legs wavered a fingertip's breadth from her eye, then settled on her cheek instead.

Down it crawled, down, then landed on the floor and scuttled across to another set of webbing.

Pin huffed out a relieved breath, crawled to the front of the bus and peered out through the main window. She couldn't see much through the grime, but she made out a half-dozen grey, steel-helmeted figures, clutching a tall, black-clad man between them. Gevaudan. She saw him move weakly; then they bore him off down the tunnel.

Footsteps; she ducked again, peering out through the crack of the door. Reapers filed past – the ones who'd been up the tunnel, waiting for them at the start, following the others, following Gevaudan back towards Liverpool.

Bastards. They'd been watching. They'd known the rebels were coming. Some had been waiting in the tunnel, others in the city, watching them go in and then following.

We never had a chance. Neap; it had been Neap's first time. So eager to show what he could do. Pin clenched her teeth and shook. Wait. She had to wait.

The last echoes of the footsteps died away. Pin stayed there, crouching, till at last the lights snapped off. She stood, putting her weight on her good leg, and wiped her face, then glanced back down the bus. Spiders hung in their webs, black blots amid the white and grey; she was sure they all watched her, but they didn't move. Pin turned away and squeezed out through the door, hissing to herself as pain shot through her wounded leg.

A couple of fallen candle-lanterns still burned. She picked one up and looked around, as much as she dared. Bodies were scattered across the tunnel, or pieces of them. Blood, still glistening and black, painted the cars.

Had to keep control. Had to stay calm. Had to find someone to tell. Pin peered under the bus and pulled her rifle out, then put on the safety catch and tucked the stock into her armpit, leaning on the barrel as a crutch. She looped the lantern's handle around her wrist and gripped the machine pistol in her other hand.

She wondered how far across they'd got before the ambush, how far she still had to go. Pin took a deep breath, and began limping down the tunnel.

2.

LISTENING POST 2, THE WASTELANDS
3RD JULY, ATTACK PLUS TWENTY-ONE YEARS
1140 HOURS

Colby parked the landcruiser in a nearby stand of trees and limped to the listening post, leaning on a stick. She stopped twice to catch her breath, coughing hard; at least she spat up blood. Nothing she hadn't seen before; least the air tasted clean.

Heather in bloom. Wind on her face. Green hills in the distance. Look in the right direction, and it was as though the War'd never been.

The bent, rusted pylon awaited her. Under it, she rapped her stick on the hidden trapdoor. It opened, and Swan grinned up at her. "Yer back."

"Well spotted." Grunting, Colby climbed down. The air was thick and muggy and close.

Home again.

*

Colonel Thorpe's Quarters, The Tower
1200 hours

Wearing circled her hips faster and faster; below her, Thorpe's hands slid up to cup her breasts, squeezing hard, rubbing the nipples between finger and thumb. His face was clenching; Wearing knew, from experience, his climax was fast approaching.

She moved faster still, feeling her own muscles tightening and the heat gathering between her thighs. Thorpe grunted, and she felt him swell inside her as he came, filling the sheath he was wearing. She gripped his hands, holding them tighter to her breasts, and kept riding him till her own orgasm hit her. Just for a few seconds, the world and its cares went away.

Then she slid off him and lay there panting and sweating in the narrow bed. Thorpe sat up to remove the sheath and knot it for disposal, then lay back down beside her and touched her shoulder lightly; she knew he'd prefer to snuggle, but that had never been her thing. Perhaps she should be a little kinder to him. Not only was Thorpe discreet, but, despite appearances, he wasn't actually a bad lover.

Wearing got up, climbed out of bed and reached for her uniform.

"Can't you stay?" Thorpe said. "Just for a bit."

"Sorry," she said. Her thigh muscles ached; that'd be hard to hide.

"When do you want to meet again?" She heard the hesitation in his voice as he said it; afraid she'd say this was the last time.

"I've got a lot on, next couple of weeks," said Wearing. "I'll let you know when I'm free."

"Okay."

She watched him struggle into his uniform. "I'll go in a minute," she said. "Give it a couple of minutes before you head off. Let's not make it –"

"Too obvious," he said, finishing the sentence as he so often did. "Okay."

Thorpe had just pulled his boots on when the first whoops and cheers sounded outside. He looked up at Wearing, frowning. "The hell?"

"Good news for someone, obviously," she said. And bad news for someone else. What if the Reapers had seized a rebel base, laid hands on information about the rebels' intelligence network? Almost unconsciously, she touched the padded, hidden pocket inside her uniform, felt the small pistol stashed there. Just in case she was ever found out.

Thorpe went to the door, opened it. She heard him speaking; heard another voice, wild with laughter. He shut the door, turned back to her. "The Grendelwolf," he said.

"What about him?"

"They've got him. Caught him in Liverpool." He grimaced. "Set the Catchmen on him. I hate those bloody things."

"Yeah. Me too."

"You mind if I go first?" Thorpe stopped briefly in front of his mirror, making sure everything looked right. "Winterborn'll want a full report five minutes ago and God help me if he doesn't get it."

"Sure."

"Thanks, Lee." Thorpe kissed her cheek. "Later."

He let himself out; Wearing stared after him, rubbing the spot where he'd kissed her. She hadn't expected the kiss; it had been oddly chaste, somehow. Sweet. She should have been irritated – their relationship was supposed to be strictly physical – but she wasn't.

Wearing sighed and shook her head. She'd better make her move: she had a report to make as well.

*

EASTERN STAIRWELL, FOURTEENTH FLOOR, THE TOWER
1230 HOURS

Reaper Axon plodded down the staircase till he reached the newel post. It was a square metal tube with a plastic cap. He prised the cap loose; inside, resting on a thick plug of cotton waste wedged inside the hollow post, was a small metal capsule.

Axon tucked the capsule into a pocket of his uniform, replaced the cap and started down the stairs. That was the last of the message drops checked; now to pass the message on. And quickly, before he could be caught with it.

*

LISTENING POST 2, THE WASTELANDS
1300 HOURS

Under the earth, Colby sweltered alone. She'd sent the rest of her unit up top; the dugout was baking hot without packing three people into it.

She wore only bindings over her loins and breasts; too hot for anything else. Sweat trickled down her back. She squinted at the old watch hanging on the wall. Another half hour and she could go up on the moors, let someone else take over.

The radio crackled. "Kingfisher to Sparrow. Come in, Sparrow. Sparrow Network, one of you please pick up."

Colby stared. Kingfisher was the callsign for the rebels' listening post in Manchester, within sight of the Tower itself. Of necessity, they were the calmest, most level-headed folk the rebellion could find, but there was an edge in the voice on the transmitter that wasn't far from panic. She swallowed and picked up the handset. "Kingfisher, this is Sparrow Two."

"Priority message for Osprey Actual."

Colby grabbed pencil and pad. "Standing by."

*

INTELLIGENCE CENTRE, ASHWOOD FORT
1315 HOURS

"He's definitely alive?" Alannah said.

"Kingfisher got confirmation from Honey Badger," Colby said,. "She notified them as soon as she heard."

"So where is he now?"

"The Pyramid in Stockport."

"Okay. Tell Honey Badger to monitor the situation, keep us updated hourly."

"Copy that."

"Osprey out." Alannah turned to Hei. "Monitor all Reaper chatter for references to: Gevaudan, Shoal, Grendelwolf, Pyramid, Stockport. And call all Council members to an emergency meeting."

*

OPS ROOM, THE TOWER
1318 HOURS

Winterborn felt the music box's contours through the material of his trouser pocket as he entered the Operations Room, squeezed it lightly, then took his hand away.

The music box gave Winterborn strength; it was therefore a potential weakness and normally never left his office, so that nobody saw it and guessed its value. But today he'd broken that rule. Events were in motion, much was at stake, and the outcome lay with Mordake. Winterborn hated relying on anyone to the extent he was depending on the good doctor, but in the end his power would be greater than ever before. Greater, perhaps, than he'd ever dared hope.

Reapers snapped to attention on seeing their Commander. Discipline. Good. Colonel Thorpe – stocky, plump and balding – saluted and stepped forward, licking his lips. He feared Winterborn, of course. That was good. Far better to be feared than loved; far more reliable.

*

Thorpe saw Winterborn smile as he approached, and swallowed hard. The Commander had always been hard to read, but even more so since Operation Harvest's failure and his new adjutant's arrival. Every contact Thorpe had with Winterborn now brought with it, at the very least, a jab of unease.

"Well?" said Winterborn. The blue eyes never blinked; framed by shoulder-length blonde hair, the pale face, smooth and inhumanly beautiful as a marble angel's, was calm.

"They have the Grendelwolf, sir."

"Alive, Thorpe?"

"Some injuries, but he'll heal."

"Yes. He tends to. Current status?"

"Sedated, sir, and en route to the Pyramid."

"Excellent. The Catchmen did the job, then?"

Thorpe swallowed. "Catchmen and Reapers, sir." He felt his mouth tighten as he spoke. Winterborn raised his eyebrows; Thorpe's stomach twisted. *You didn't let him see. You never let Winterborn see.*

"You disapprove, Colonel?" Winterborn's voice was soft, teasing. A faint smile touched the Cupid's bow mouth.

"Of course not, sir." Thorpe licked his lips again; his mouth was parched. "I just prefer to see Reaper victories won by Reapers."

"Speak freely, Colonel Thorpe." Winterborn moved closer. "You don't like the Catchmen, do you? They... make you uncomfortable? Repulse you?"

Thorpe managed to swallow. "Yes, sir."

Winterborn raised his eyebrows. "Which is it?"

"All of the above, sir."

Winterborn smiled for a moment. "All of the above." He leant close to Thorpe, till their faces almost touched. His breath was cold, rank; Thorpe fought not to flinch from it. "Do you know why we're going to win this war, Colonel Thorpe?"

Thorpe would have killed for a sip of water. "Because we're right, sir?"

"Right?" echoed Winterborn. "If I'd sent a platoon of Reapers to apprehend the Grendelwolf, do you know what would be en route from Liverpool now? A platoon's worth of cadavers and body parts. Instead I used the Catchmen. Distasteful as you may find them, they were the tools required to do the job."

Winterborn craned forward till his lips almost touched Thorpe's ear. Thorpe fought to remain still. "We'll win, Colonel, because we will not shirk the cost of victory, whatever it may be. They won't face reality, but we will. Sooner or later, one side will have to go further than the other is willing to. And that will be us, Thorpe. Us. Make an effort to understand that, before I replace you with someone who can."

Winterborn stepped back; the Ops Room's quiet daily hubbub washed back in again. Thorpe saw a few of the staff looking away. They'd been watching, listening. They'd all seen.

"I'm going to the roof," Winterborn announced. "Inform me of any important developments."

Winterborn strode away, hands clasped behind his back. Thorpe stared around the Ops Room. No-one met his eyes; a few hid smirks. A tremor shook his right leg; he forced it straight. His face was burning. He turned away and dabbed his forehead.

*

ROOF OF THE TOWER, CITY OF MANCHESTER
1330 HOURS

The wind buffeted Winterborn as he stepped out onto the roof. Since he rarely ventured outside the Tower, he'd almost forgotten the crosswinds that blew around it.

Below, the city spread out, the Pennines rising in the distance. If anything, the view was even more impressive than that from his window – an unbroken three-hundred-and-sixty-degree panorama, and in the open air. His domain felt almost close enough to touch.

Winterborn crossed the roof and stepped into the ring of domed cowlings in its centre where Mordake stood, his back to Winterborn, arms outspread. Mordake's hands clasped and unclasped; here one finger was extended, then three, then two. The arms gripped the air, rose and moved into new shapes. Then Mordake stopped and flicked his head. Winterborn determinedly remained expressionless when the hood fell back to expose the white female face on the back of Mordake's head. Its black void eyes fixed on him; the white lips bent into a smile. "Commander."

"Doctor Mordake." Winterborn cleared his throat. "The Grendelwolf has been captured."

"Good," said the white face. "The threads are being woven."

"Threads?"

"Of the web that will catch and destroy the rebels. That's what you want, isn't it?"

"A part of it."

"I know."

Mordake turned to face him. Winterborn breathed out; Mordake's own face, while no model of ideal beauty, was always preferable to the other. "You want to know about the other Commanders."

Winterborn stepped closer. "You said I'd have what I wanted."

"And you will. Dominion, that's what you want, isn't it, Commander? All this land, under your sole rule."

"Yes."

"It will come."

"How?"

Mordake placed a grimy hand on Winterborn's shoulder. Winterborn fought the impulse to recoil, even managed to smile. "Walk with me, Commander."

They paced anti-clockwise around the inside of the circle. What was the word Helen had taught him? *Widdershins*. Winterborn pushed Helen from his mind; she was the enemy now, nothing else. an obstacle to be removed.

"The other Commanders fall into three categories," said Mordake. "First, those who will support you: McMahon, Probert, Johnstone and Treloar."

"Four," said Winterborn, "of fourteen."

"Second, those who are neutral: Endabe of the Midlands, Wexford in East Anglia, Ishaque of the Hebrides and Commander Fowler of Greater London."

"Fowler is insane."

"And her Command's value symbolic at best. Nonetheless, she has a vote."

"Good luck getting her to inhabit the same reality as the rest of us even for five minutes. So – that leaves those who oppose me."

"Six of them. Less than half, you see? Some oppose Unification; others oppose you specifically. Six Commanders who must be persuaded or removed."

"I hope you're not suggesting assassination."

"There's a rule against it?"

"Unwritten, but no less unbreakable. Do you really think I'd tolerate some of those idiots otherwise? We may scheme and jockey against one another, but the one thing we do *not* do is that."

"Didn't you succeed by eliminating your predecessor?"

"Internal affairs are looked upon differently. He wasn't the first Commander to be deposed from within his own Command. A number of his subordinates were unhappy with his incompetence, and I emerged as the candidate of choice to succeed him. And some Commanders hold me in contempt for that. So even a suspicion of an attempted assassination –"

"Understood," said Mordake. "Don't worry about that. There are other ways. I guarantee you'll have what you need."

"I sincerely hope so, Doctor."

"Trust me, Commander." Mordake turned to face out over the city again, spreading his arms. "If there's nothing else –"

"Mordake?"

The white female face frowned. "Yes, Commander?"

"What, exactly, *are* you doing?"

"I told you, Commander. Weaving threads."

"How, exactly?"

"I'm ensuring," said Mordake, "that even if this fails, we've a way of neutralising the Grendelwolf."

"As long they lose him," said Winterborn. "One way or the other."

The second face smiled. "I think I can promise that."

Winterborn gestured to the cowlings. "You have everything you need?"

"So far," said Mordake. "If there's anything else, I'll let you know."

"Do so, and at once," said Winterborn. "Whatever you need. As long as it works."

"Oh, it will," said Mordake. "Project Sycorax will give you all Project Tindalos promised. And more."

NORTHERN MOOR, MANCHESTER
1345 HOURS

A house was still a house; most of the street was burned out, but nothing with walls stayed empty for long around here. The roofless ones had hide or tarp stretched over eaves and rafters; all were occupied, save one.

A road-shrine stood outside it, tallow candles flickering on its shelves beside withered flowers, crude pictures and cruder dolls. Darrow looked up from it to the front of the house.

The windows and doorway were ragged holes, the frontage pitted and pocked, chunks of it blasted away. Brick fragments still strewed the scrubby dead garden and drive. Heavy machine gun fire. They'd been wounded, dying. And then the Jennywrens had stormed in to end it.

Darrow wiped his forehead. It was a hot day, and hotter still in his heavy poncho. A deep breath; then he slipped up the drive and into the house.

Inside it was not only cool but cold, as if what had happened here last winter had frozen the house in time. Damp, rotten air: he could almost feel the mould taking root in his lungs.

Darrow picked his way along the hall to the former living room. Floorboards sagged underfoot, soft with decay. Living room, bedroom; those terms meant nothing now. They were just places to shelter, build a cook-fire, to huddle and sleep. And not even that, here, not any more. Was the house sacred ground now, or cursed?

He examined the walls closely, finding nothing, then went back into the hall, starting for the sagging splintered ruin of the kitchen door. The air stirred: movement. A floorboard creaked behind him, and Darrow turned. Four ragged figures – two men, two women – stood in the front doorway. As they crossed the threshold, a thin, sandy-haired woman drew a blade, the big man beside her a length of pipe. The others held lengths of rusty chain.

Darrow brought his Thompson gun out from under the poncho, braced it one-handed against his hip. He kept the barrel slightly lowered, not quite pointing at them yet. "Walk away," he said.

The four exchanged glances; the sandy-haired woman nodded and touched the big man's arm. The four of them backed out through the door; Darrow breathed out again.

He nudged the kitchen door open and went inside, but found nothing. Back in the hall, he gazed up the staircase, knowing that upstairs, where they'd died, would be the worst.

On the landing, in the front bedroom, cartridge brass crunched underfoot. The damp on the floorboards and bullet-shattered walls couldn't hide the blacker stains where blood had soaked in.

Which bloodstains had come from Mary? Darrow shook his head. Only Flaps had made it out of here, and even she couldn't have said where Mary had died; Mary had hidden Flaps before the end. She'd wanted one of her crew, at least, to get away, and Flaps had been the only one unwounded by then. Well, apart from Mary herself. But Mary Tolland would not have abandoned her crew.

Darrow shook his head. None of that, not now. He must be objective, look at the evidence.

He took out a clockwork torch and shone it over the walls. Nothing.

Darrow checked the remaining rooms up top – spare bedroom, bathroom – and climbed as far up into the loft as he dared, but found nothing in any of them either. He sighed and went down the stairs.

His bones ached. He had to smile; he'd always been in enviable condition, despite his years, even having long given up any hope of seeing an end to the Reapers' rule. Now that end might actually be near, but his age had seeped into him relentlessly since the winter, stiffening his joints as if with rust, as if determined to ensure he never saw the day.

Outside, the air was close and muggy, but welcome after the air in that house. A few scavengers, sitting outside on cracked pavement or broken garden walls, watched him sullenly. Darrow studied one particular pair for a moment, then approached them.

The sandy-haired woman reached for her knife; the big man made to rise. Darrow spread his arms, showing them empty hands. The woman kept hold of the blade, but the man settled.

Darrow crouched, wincing as his joints popped. "Have you lived here long?"

They exchanged glances; the woman shrugged. "Year."

"You were here last winter?"

She nodded. "Saw when the Reapers came there. Big fight."

"Yes, I know." Darrow didn't want to hear descriptions of Mary's last stand, or worse, what the Jennywrens might have left of her and hers. "But I'm interested in what came after."

He took out a can of meat from under his poncho, held it out. A mistake, he realised as soon as he did it: he could feel the gazes the sight of food attracted. He slipped his free hand beneath the poncho, got hold of the Thompson. "That house. People don't go in there any more?"

The woman shook her head.

"Not even strangers? Did you see anyone around that house that winter, after the fighting? A woman? Blonde-haired?" He hesitated. "Perhaps with children?"

Both scavengers shook their heads.

Darrow sighed. "Ah well."

He went back down the street, keeping hold of the gun, waiting for someone to come at him, but no-one did.

He turned onto the road that led into Northenden, started walking.

"Hey."

Darrow turned, raising the gun. A thin boy, one side of his narrow face striped with burn scars, raised his hands. "Easy."

"What do you want?"

"Heard what you said back there."

"And?"

"Got any more cans?"

"What do *you* have?"

"Uh?"

Darrow sighed. "Do you *know* something you want to tell me?"

"'Bout the cans?"

"Tell me what you know first."

The boy scowled, then nodded. "Back round winter. There was some bird in that house. Short black hair. Old, like you."

Mary. "I know."

"She had some young 'uns with her – black boy, girl with red hair. Reapers came. Shot shit out the place. Killed 'em all."

"I know that too."

The boy licked his lips. "Few days later – there was this blonde woman. Old. Bit big. Round face. Looked –" He hesitated.

"Yes?"

"Warm," said the boy.

"Warm," said Darrow.

"Warm. Yeah."

Darrow kept his face blank, but his stomach tightened. "Go on."

"She went in that house. Came out again. Fucked off." The boy shrugged. "That's it."

"Was she alone?" said Darrow.

"Thought she was to start off," said the boy. "But she wasn't. She'd made 'em hang back and wait for her. Bunch of sprogs." He held a hand about level with his waist.

"Kate," said Darrow.

"You what?"

"Nothing." He took the can from under his poncho. "Which way did she go?"

The boy pointed up the road – away from Northenden, towards Baguley.

Darrow nodded and threw the can; the boy scrabbled for it as it clattered on the ground, then bolted back to the ruined street, vanishing into an alley.

49

"Thank you," Darrow called after him. Then hid the Thompson under his poncho, and started walking.

*

THE WAR ROOM, ASHWOOD FORT
1405 HOURS

Sitting beside Alannah at the main table, Helen watched the other five Council members file in and take their places.

Loncraine nodded at her; Helen nodded back, her stomach hollow. Jazz half-raised a hand in greeting.

Jazz spoke for the rebels' field-base network, Loncraine for the Wasteland tribes. Next came Javeed Malik, representing the religious communities populating the Wastelands.

Justin Stewart and Nicola Thorn sat at opposite ends of the table, each trying to pretend the other didn't exist. Nothing new there, or remotely surprising. Thorn represented communities like the one Helen had grown up in before the Reapers came – scattered settlements of no particular denomination, mostly former farming communities, making as much of a living from the land as they could – while Stewart spoke for brigand and bandit groups who'd survived by preying on communities like Javeed's or Thorn's. The Reapers threatened both their constituencies, and the alliance against Winterborn had ended the brigands' depredations, but Thorn, like many others, had already lost friends and family to them. The brigands' involvement might be a necessary evil – a war on two fronts, against them and the Reapers, would have been impossible, and they needed every fighter they could find – but for Thorn, the emphasis would always be on *evil*.

"Thanks for coming at short notice, everybody," Alannah said. "I'll come straight to it. We're here to vote on one specific proposition, and we need a decision right away."

The others waited.

"The Reapers have captured Gevaudan Shoal. We don't know what they have in mind for him, but it won't be pleasant for him, or good for us."

Gevaudan's face in the cottage garden, the candlelight flickering in his eyes. Helen clenched her fists, focused on the faces around the table.

"Gevaudan's near the end of his cycle," said Alannah. "Without a fresh dose of Goliath serum within the next twenty-four hours, he's going to start coming apart."

"Coming apart?" said Thorn.

"Literally," said Alannah. Thorn grimaced. "From what I understand, it's slow and painful. But reversible – with a single dose of serum."

"Which, of course, he'll receive only if he betrays us," said Malik.

"Or just tells Winterborn whatever he wants to hear," said Jazz.

"I know Winterborn," said Helen. She kept her voice level. Mustn't think of what Gevaudan would soon be undergoing. "He'll have to do a sight more than that. Winterborn will hold out until he *believes* him. He'll break Gevaudan. Make him grovel. It's the kind of thing he enjoys."

"Gevaudan's been our ally since we started this," Alannah said.

An ally to me, and more. No, Helen mustn't say or think that. Remain focused on facts. Professional. If she let her emotions rule her, they'd kill either her, or others, as they had at the Refuge.

Alannah carried on: "The question is whether or not to attempt a rescue mission. While he's a valued asset, it would be a major effort, risk exposure for our crews in Manchester – risk a lot of lives, too, and with no guarantee of success."

Jazz leant back in her chair, arms folded, lips compressed. She'd been in a city crew until the December Rising, had seen first-hand the result of rebel crews and Reapers fighting in the streets.

"So you're putting this to a vote?" said Thorn.

"I think it's necessary," Alannah said. Thorn nodded, a frown creasing her smooth brow. "Thoughts?"

"What do we know?" said Stewart. "Where are they holding him, and what are they planning?"

"Alannah?"

Alannah squinted at her notes. Not that she needed them, with her memory; they were a prop to ease her discomfort at public speaking. "They've taken him to the Pyramid," she said. "It's their maximum security detention centre, and it's pretty much a fortress. IntelSec control it, using it for high-security prisoners. Reinforced concrete cladding, surrounded by guards and watchtowers, and slap in the middle of a cleared area so it's impossible to approach by stealth."

"Fantastic," said Stewart. "Any good news?"

"According to Kingfisher, they're keeping him in the building's maximum security section," Alannah said. "He's the only prisoner currently detained in that part of the complex."

"I said *good* news."

Alannah shrugged. "We don't know what they're after, but they went to a lot of trouble to get him alive. If they'd just wanted to remove him from the equation, it would have been easier to kill him."

"Does he know anything that could damage us?" Stewart asked.

"Gevaudan voluntarily recused himself from the Council after the attack here back in Spring. There shouldn't be anything he knows at this stage that they wouldn't have already."

"Do the Reapers know that?" said Stewart.

"Be surprised if they didn't," Alannah said. "They have a couple of agents with us – nothing high-level, but enough to know that he's been out of the loop a while now."

Malik cleared his throat. He was thin, quiet and softly-spoken, but the little he said was generally worth heeding. "A show trial, perhaps," he said, "or a public execution, to send a message."

"Perhaps," Alannah said.

"Or," said Malik, "they hope to turn him to their purpose."

Alannah nodded. "One of those."

"Gevaudan?" Loncraine snorted. He'd been briefed by Wakefield before taking her place on the Council, and she'd passed her admiration for the Grendelwolf on to him. "Betray us?"

"Even Grendelwolves feel pain," said Malik. "He's still only human."

Alannah raise an eyebrow at that, but didn't speak.

"Depends on what they want," said Stewart. "They want him to switch sides and fight for them – can't see that. But they could turn him to the extent of saying whatever they fancy – you know, a confession, or parroting whatever shit they wanna say about us. Jav's right." Stewart bared gapped yellow teeth in a grin. "You hurt 'em enough, you can break anyone."

"Well, you've had plentiful experience of *that*," said Thorn.

"Let's focus," said Helen. "We know what's at stake. What do we do about it?"

"Do?" snapped Loncraine. "You fight for those who fight with you. Else, why they fight for you?"

"So you're in favour of a rescue?" said Jazz.

"Course!"

"Well, I'm not," said Jazz. "I'm sorry. We've got to weigh cost and risk against the gain. And if this was anyone else, we'd have already written them off."

"Gevaudan Shoal isn't just anybody," said Thorn.

"Oh, I know *that*." Jazz was angry now. "Gevaudan's so much more *bloody* important than the rest of us, isn't he? Out of interest, how many of our lives would be an acceptable trade for his?"

"Jazz –" began Helen.

"No!" Jazz banged the desk. "What happened last time the city crews moved against the Reapers? A fucking massacre. We lost eight, nine tenths of everyone we had – friends, lovers. And yes, before you say it, there was a good reason – there always bloody is. But we weren't *ready*. And we were slaughtered. We're only just building our network in Manchester back to anything close to what it was, and they're surviving by keeping a low profile. You use them, and the Reapers come down on them like a fucking anvil."

"She's right," said Alannah. "They don't have anything like the level of strength or organisation we need." She was thinking about Darrow, Helen knew; she thought of how much older he'd seemed when she last saw him, almost frail. But he'd chosen to go back; he'd known what might be asked of him.

"We don't *have* to use the city crews," said Helen. "There's a Raider unit in Manchester right now to train with them. This kind of commando op's exactly what they're for."

"Danny's unit?" said Alannah.

"Yes." *For God's sake*, Helen wanted to snap, *he isn't a child any more, he's a man*. But of course, for Alannah, that would be the problem: Danny was *her* man now.

Alannah breathed out, looked down.

"I can't support the rescue mission," said Thorn. "I'm sorry. Many of the communities I represent had their doubts about this alliance. They were sceptical about our chances of victory, to say the least. Yes, what had been achieved already weighed in the balance, and the Grendelwolf joining our cause tipped the scales. If he's lost or turned, it would be damaging – but ultimately he's one individual and we'd find a way to deal with or respond to his loss. If we move prematurely in the cities, and suffer a repetition of what happened in the winter, the damage will be a damned sight worse."

"I'm against the rescue too," said Stewart.

"My God," said Thorn. "We agree."

"Jazz and Nicky –" Helen saw Thorn grimace at the nickname "– they're both right. Shoal's one man. You weren't ready in December, and it nearly finished you. I know – you came back from that, and now you might win. I wouldn't be here, I didn't think that. But when the time comes, we'll need the city crews, in Manchester most of all. We don't have much there now. The Reapers pull another crackdown, there'll be nothing left. Might be no way of building 'em up again. I get what Nicola's saying, 'bout him being a symbol an' all, but that's to communities that haven't done much fighting. No offence."

Thorn pursed her lips.

"You want to convince folk we can still win? That's simple. You show you can make the Reapers pay. They hurt us, we hurt 'em back. Retaliatory raids. If they *do* turn Shoal, we plan a hit. Take him out. But to be going on with we leave the city crews out of it – let 'em rebuild, so when we *really* need 'em, they're there." Stewart shrugged. "Sorry, but that's it."

From a rescue to an assassination – but the cold logic of it was hard to refute. If it had been anyone but Gevaudan – or if she'd known him as little as Stewart did – how would Helen have voted herself?

Helen looked round the table. Alannah wouldn't meet her eyes; no telling which way she'd jump, not with Gevaudan's life weighed against Darrow's and Danny's. "Javeed?"

Malik put a finger to his lips. "I think we must," he said. "Not because he's the Grendelwolf, but because we can."

"But we *can't*," said Jazz. "That's the point. No one person's worth the kind of blowbacck we'll get."

"I know that in many cases we wouldn't think twice," Malik said. "But we *are* thinking twice. The Grendelwolf is a creature of God. Compassion dictates that if a rescue is possible, we should attempt it."

"So that's you and Loncraine in favour," said Helen. "And Jazz, Justin and Nicola opposed."

"What about you?" said Loncraine.

What had Gevaudan said? *I don't fight for a cause. I fight for you.* And there was – whatever she felt for him, even if she didn't dare name it yet. How could she not vote to save him?

Not vote to send Darrow, Danny, Flaps, to likely die in the aftermath if not in the fight itself? Throw away the city crews, all to save him? *You can always get them to die for you.* But refuse to risk them, and she abandoned Gevaudan to the Reapers.

The same choice, either way; only the order of magnitude differed. Helen felt Alannah's eyes on her: Jazz's, too. All their eyes.

Helen took a deep breath, nodded. "I vote yes," she said. Of course she did. It wasn't even a choice. She tried not to look at Alannah – hers was the deciding vote now – but in the end she did.

Alannah met Helen's gaze. "I'm sorry, Helen. Jazz is right. The last time we did this, we lost so many. It was necessary so we could take out Hobsdyke, but this? I'm sorry, but no. If it's Gevaudan or the city crews, then the crews are more valuable right now. That's my judgement. I vote no. Four votes to three. The motion is denied."

"What?" said Loncraine. He looked appalled.

"This is a mistake," Helen said.

"We've voted, Helen," said Alannah quietly, no longer looking at her.

Helen stood, swaying.

"Wrong," said Loncraine. His voice rose. "This is *wrong!*"

"Democracy, Chief." Stewart gave a snaggle-toothed grin. "Get over it."

Helen heard Loncraine's voice behind her as she made for the door, raised in shock or anger. She wasn't sure which as she wove down the corridor, legs unsteady; too dazed from the death sentence Alannah had just passed.

And how many death sentences would you have passed, otherwise, to get him out?

She saw Gevaudan's face in the garden, the calm trust in his eyes. Then his changed, scarred face from her nightmares.

He will destroy you.

If he died, at least, that could never happen. But if he survived, and learned he'd been abandoned to the Reapers, what then?

Helen straightened her back and walked on, fists clenched at her sides.

*

INTERROGATION CELL, THE PYRAMID, STOCKPORT
1500 HOURS

The first things Gevaudan registered were nausea and joint pain. He hung in a grey haze, feeling as though he were tumbling end over end. Free fall. He hadn't felt like that since his twenties, last time he got thundering drunk. But even then he hadn't felt this sick, and his arms hadn't felt as though they were being slowly wrenched from their moorings.

He opened thick, heavy eyelids with an effort. Pale, stinging light; the grey haze became a greyish solidity: bare concrete walls and floor, blotched with red-brown stains. There were two armed Reaper guards, and an officer – a gaunt, high-cheekboned man with dark, grey-threaded hair. His arms were folded, and he studied Gevaudan with small black shark-eyes, like a butcher viewing a carcass. "Welcome back," he said.

A fluorescent strip-light glowed above. Gevaudan hadn't seen one of those in years. A Reaper facility, then: no-one else had such resources. He remembered the tunnel, the Catchmen swarming over him. He'd been certain this was the end – but instead they'd pinned him, held him still. The Catchmen were almost as strong as him: in those numbers, he'd stood no chance. Then a needle had pricked his neck, and after that – dizziness, sickness, everything blurred. Then nothing.

His mouth was dry and tasted foul. Strangely, he was standing, and the pain in his shoulders was worse.

Gevaudan tried to move his arms, and couldn't; his wrists were immobile, above his head. When he tried to straighten his legs, he found his ankles pinned as well.

He looked up; hanging from the ceiling, bolted to the concrete in their turn, were lengths of thick chain, wound tightly around his wrists before connecting to a heavy manacle. When Gevaudan looked down, he saw the same had been done to his ankles. He hung from the first set of chains, and the second only just allowed him to straighten his legs.

It was only then that he realised his clothes were gone. Of course. Immobile, struggling for breath and naked: his captors clearly wanted him vulnerable and exposed.

Gevaudan frowned, despite the circumstances. Tereus Winterborn was many things, none pleasant, and enjoyed making his subordinates squirm, but this brand of petty sadism somehow wasn't him.

A dull, heavy clank, and Gevaudan looked round to see an iron door swing open. Outside, something clicked and scraped on the floor.

The Reaper guards took up positions on either side of the door. The click and scrape sounded again; now accompanied by a dragging sound, and stertorous breath.

Someone came through the door, hunched over and leaning on a black, silver-pommelled cane. He wore a black leather coat and a fedora, brim tilted over his face, and dragged his left leg. The skin of the left hand was buckled and shiny, like wax half-melted and re-set, the last two fingers fused together in a foreshortened clump: keloidal scarring, caused by burns.

"Major Lewis," he said. "I'm sure your services are needed elsewhere."

The gaunt man shrugged. "Just wanted to get a look at him."

"Well, now you'd had your little treat," said the man in the coat. "So go away."

Lewis's face tightened. He drew himself up, glaring. "Now," said the man in the coat.

Lewis stalked out. When he was gone the man turned and approached Gevaudan, breath rasping. Finally he looked up and removed the hat.

More burn scars covered his scalp, leaving only a few clumps of pale, straggly hair. Another sheet of keloidal scarring had obliterated the left side of his face: the eye was gone, as though it had never existed. But Gevaudan recognised the right side instantly: a muddy brown eye, simian features, a prim, puckered mouth – the half of it that wasn't an immobile slit, at least. You didn't forget such a face, not after you'd seen it gloat over you time and again, as the treatments it had devised warped your body into that of a Grendelwolf.

"Kellett," said Gevaudan.

"Shoal." Kellett's half-mouth pulled upwards in a smile. He took a syringe from his coat pocket, pulled the cap off with his teeth and brought it towards Gevaudan's neck; Gevaudan bared his teeth. Kellett's smile faltered for a moment; then he shrugged and plunged the syringe into Gevaudan's right arm. Gevaudan grunted, glaring at him. Kellett spat out the cap and smirked. When the syringe had filled with blood, he stepped back.

"You and I," he said, "are going to have great deal of fun together, Shoal. But first, someone wants to see you."

Kellett limped out of the cell, the Reaper guards following. The door swung shut, the lock clanked, and Gevaudan hung there, waiting.

And the hours began to pass.

*

INTELLIGENCE CENTRE, ASHWOOD FORT
4TH JULY, ATTACK PLUS TWENTY-ONE YEARS
0245 HOURS

"Alannah!"

She blinked as she entered the centre; Hei ran towards her. "I was just coming to find you," he said.

"What? What is it?" Cold fear, a knot of it in her belly. A Reaper attack, or something closer to home; something about Darrow, or Danny?

"Here." Hei held out a signal flimsy. "You need to see this, now."

3.

Canteen, Ashwood Fort
4th July
0302 hours

Helen sat alone at a table, studying the water that had splashed on it from a beaker. She dipped her finger with it, tracing symbols on the table-top: the clenched-fist symbol of the rebellion, the wheatsheaf of the Reapers, the Hobsdyke Cross.

The canteen was empty; the only other occupant was a young lad with a mop and bucket. Helen knew him by sight: Mackie, that was his name.

"Crazy ginger," said a voice. She looked up: Loncraine stood over her. "Sit with you?"

She nodded. Loncraine pulled back a chair and sat.

"You couldn't sleep either?" she said.

Loncraine shook his head. For a time after that, neither of them spoke. Loncraine shifted, his mouth working. Helen waited.

"Wrong," he said at last, and looked up at her.

"Wrong?" she said. But she knew what he meant; of course she did.

"The Council," said Loncraine. "Wrong."

Helen nodded. "Yes," she said. "I think so too."

"Leave him to the Reapers like this. It's a..." Loncraine raised his hands. He was struggling to find the words he needed. If this had happened with one of his warriors, there wouldn't have even been a debate on whether or not to attempt a rescue: *how* would have been the only question. "A wrong thing," he said at last.

"I agree."

"Darrow," said Loncraine. "Would he think this?"

"I don't know," said Helen. "Probably not." There was a reason Darrow and his crews had survived so long – *until you came back, Helen* – while the tribes had been driven to the edge of extinction by the Reapers.

*

Mackie kept his eyes on the floor, mopping closer to Helen's table. The word was out, course it was, 'bout the Grendelwolf, and these two'd have come straight from the Council meeting. That's what they were talking about.

"But if he got an order," Loncraine was saying. "From you, from here. What then?"

"Having a good snoop, are you, mate?"

Mackie gasped, half-turned, then looked down again – they were looking at him, staring, they'd heard him. But only him. Not Cov, even though Cov was standing next to their table, arms folded, smirking at Mackie. Only he saw Cov, 'cos Cov was dead.

"Who you gonna stab in the back this time, mate? Them? Well. Makes a change from shooting me in the face, dunnit?"

The mop clattered to the floor. He couldn't stay; couldn't hide things enough, not here, not like this. Mackie turned, stumbling away.

*

Helen watched him go, shook her head. "Sad."

Loncraine frowned. "What wrong?"

"He's always been a bit – simple." That was the best word she had. "He was at one of the field-bases when the Reapers hit back in the Spring. His best mate was killed. He's never been right since."

Loncraine shook his head; Helen couldn't tell if it was out of sympathy or lack of comprehension for the weird ways of non-tribals. Then he looked up at her again. "So?" he said.

She remembered what he'd been asking. "If he thought it was genuine? Yes. He would."

"So?" Loncraine said again.

And condemn how many of his crewboys and crewgirls to death? And what would Darrow say, when he found out? Or Alannah? It could shatter the whole alliance from within. But if Loncraine would do this for Gevaudan, how could she not?

Running footsteps sounded; Helen turned, saw Hei burst into the canteen and run towards their table. Relief: she'd been spared, at least for now, from making that choice. "Helen," Hei puffed. "Chief Loncraine. You're wanted in the War Room, now."

*

MAJOR LEWIS' OFFICE, THE PYRAMID
0313 HOURS

Lewis breathed in and out. Hours later, his fury at Kellett kept coming back. *You've had your little treat, so go away. Now.* No-one, *no-one* had spoken to him like that in years. Decades. He could have taken Kellett by the throat, snapped his neck with a twist. But Kellett was Winterborn's pet, at least for now.

So he sat at his desk and read the latest field reports, tried to make it go away. Sifting the crap, looking for the gold.

And then there was one report. Short, but detailed, from an observation post in Northern Moor.

Lewis stopped. Re-read it. Could be something, could be nothing. But if it was something – it would be a coup, all right. Something to be proud of. A small *fuck you* to Kellett. He put it to one side. He'd look at it again later. Once he'd cleared some more of the crap away.

*

INTERROGATION CELL, THE PYRAMID, STOCKPORT
0330 HOURS

Winterborn's personal guard surrounded him; three in front, one to each side, three behind. Excessive, perhaps, especially on what should have been home ground, but Winterborn would rather be excessively cautious, and live, than the alternative.

Besides, no caution was excessive where Shoal was concerned. Fear twitched in Winterborn's belly at the thought of the Grendelwolf, but he dismissed it. Fear was a useful servant, but a poor master; besides, he wouldn't deny himself the pleasure of this encounter at any price.

Two CorSec Reapers stood guard outside the cell; at a nod from Winterborn, they unlocked the door and stepped aside.

Inside, chains rattled and clanked. Winterborn's guards marched in ahead of him; four took up positions with one in each corner of the cell, rifles aimed at the Grendelwolf. Two others, marching abreast, entered the cell. The last two followed Winterborn in.

Shoal looked up, veins and muscles bulging in his neck and arms. The chains on the left arm were stretched tight; he was exerting his full strength in an effort to break free. When he saw Winterborn, the yellow eyes narrowed; fear flickered in the Commander's belly again, but he forced a smile.

"I suggest you save your strength," he said. "You'll need it."

"Are you here to gloat, Winterborn, or just to ogle my manly physique?" Shoal settled back into the X-shape the chains naturally held him in, displaying himself unselfconsciously. A CorSec guard came in with a chair and placed it behind Winterborn.

"You disappoint me." said Winterborn. "I thought you understood that my interests are nothing so petty. My mind, as they say, is set on higher things."

"I'm sure."

"You do realise," said Winterborn, "that this is our first real meeting? We've communicated via messengers, radio, telephone, but after all these years, this is the first time we've met face to face."

"I can assure you, Winterborn, the pleasure's all yours."

Winterborn sighed. "I'd hoped we could be civilised about this, Shoal. Oh, and by the way, you can pull on those chains to your heart's content. Dr Kellett's been very thorough in calculating both their strength and yours, and it would take at least three of you to break free of that little set-up. So we won't have any annoying little distractions like your trying to disembowel me." Winterborn sat. "So, let's begin."

"Winterborn," said Gevaudan, "I'm tired, cold, uncomfortable and more importantly, bored. Let's stop playing games, shall we? What do you want?"

A smile touched the pale, marble-angel's face. "What do you *think* I want, Shoal? What I've always wanted, where you're concerned. I want you to fight for me."

Gevaudan laughed; he couldn't help it. "You know, Winterborn, my mother had a saying."

"Oh?" Winterborn raised an eyebrow. "I never knew mine, so others' experiences in these matters fascinate me. Do tell."

"The saying," said Gevaudan, "was 'I wants don't get'."

For a moment Winterborn's face was still, a mask; the blue eyes didn't blink. Then he laughed. "A novel way of putting things. But no more than I expected."

"Then why ask me?" But Gevaudan realised there was something he'd actually forgotten, with all that happened. Winterborn knew it, though, and before Gevaudan had even finished the sentence, he already knew the answer.

And Winterborn saw he did and leant forward, still smiling; Gevaudan managed not to wrinkle his nose at the sourness of his breath. "It's very simple, Shoal," Winterborn murmured. "Because now we're going to change your mind."

*

THE WAR ROOM, ASHWOOD FORT

0345 HOURS

"Thank you all for coming." Alannah sat and took a deep breath. "I've decided to change my vote in favour of a rescue mission."

"Too late," said Stewart. "We voted. Decision's made. Get over it."

"I'm sure you'd say that if *your* side had lost," said Helen.

"This isn't about sides," said Malik. "It's about the right course of action."

"Sod this," said Jazz. "We've got to make decisions and stick to them."

"We've received new information," said Alannah. Helen looked at her; the other woman's eyes met hers. "As a result of which, I move for a second vote."

"What information?" said Jazz.

"It changes nothing," Stewart said. "We agreed: the rebellion's bigger than the Grendelwolf."

Jazz bit her lip.

"There's something else." Alannah gave a tight smile. "You could say it sweetens the deal."

"You're not going to shift me on this," said Stewart.

"Not even if I told you we had a chance to take out Tereus Winterborn himself?"

"What?" said Helen.

"We had a message from Honey Badger," said Alannah. "Winterborn's gone to the Pyramid to personally oversee the interrogation."

"Winterborn *never* leaves the Tower," said Jazz.

"Except he has," said Alannah.

"If he's there, security'll be even tighter," said Stewart. "Getting in'd be impossible."

"Difficult, yes," said Alannah. "Impossible, no."

"The crew network —" began Jazz.

"The Raiders are in the city too." Alannah swallowed hard. "Danny's team." When no-one said anything, she continued. "Winterborn's either removed any potential rivals, or put them in roles where they're pitted them against one another. We're still not clear on who his new Adjutant is, but we do know it's someone from outside the Command, and whoever they are, they're not popular. So if anything happens to Winterborn, there's no clear line of succession."

Jazz whistled. "And if they start fighting among themselves..."

"Not to put too fine a point on it," said Helen, "we can knock seven balls of shit out of them."

"Wish I could vote yes twice," said Loncraine. Even Stewart smiled at that.

Warmth spread through Helen's belly, and a cold tingle of excitement. *We're going to do this.* "At the very least, we deprive the Reapers of a propaganda victory and get one of our own. And at best —"

"We might even have won the war," said Malik.

"Second vote, then," said Alannah. "All in favour?"

Her hand, Helen's, Loncraine's, Thorn's and Malik's all rose. Jazz nodded, raised hers too. Stewart looked at them all, then scowled. "Fuck it," he said. "Let's do this."

*

INTERROGATION CELL, THE PYRAMID

0350 HOURS

"Until lately, Dr Kellett's had a rather quiet few years," said Winterborn. "After the Sheffield debacle, as you can imagine, he was somewhat out of favour."

"I thought I'd killed him during said debacle," said Gevaudan. "My aim must have been off."

"And again at Ashwood," said Winterborn, "and yet, here he is. What was it Colonel Dowson used to say? Ah yes – a bad penny. Always turning up like one."

"An annoying habit."

"He was initially listed as missing, presumed dead, after Ashwood," said Winterborn, "but he managed to crawl out of the fire you left him to burn in —"

"Believe it or not," said Gevaudan, "I'd intended to give him a bullet in the head. Quick and painless. Things didn't go as planned."

"Oh, I believe you. You're boringly moralistic about that sort of thing. But I digress. Kellett's fall from favour ended very suddenly back in the winter, when it became clear he was the only scientist with the knowledge to make the CATCH Program work. Since then, we've had a few very illuminating chats. He's been very informative about Grendelwolf biology. Quite fascinating to discover how you work."

"You didn't know that previously?"

"Oh, the essentials. The speed, the augmented strength and senses, the healing ability – the immunity to old age was a particularly fascinating feature. I must put him to work developing certain aspects of *that*. But the specifics were very interesting. You're a triumph of human technology, Shoal."

Gevaudan waited, jaw clenched.

"Which, to continue running," Winterborn went on, "requires two things. Food, of course – and this."

Winterborn took a phial of greenish fluid from his pocket and swung it back and forth. The liquid sloshed about inside; nausea rolled through Gevaudan.

"The Goliath serum," said Winterborn. "Kick-starts the entire process. Keeps that remarkable biology of yours running like a well-oiled machine." He held up the phial, swung it to and fro. "As long as a fresh dose is administered every thirty days. The price of all the advantages you have, and a very, very useful means of control."

"Always assuming," said Gevaudan, "you know when it'll wear off. After all, give the rebels enough time to mount a rescue mission..."

"Not going to happen, Shoal."

"Surely you've been cured of overconfidence by now, Winterborn? Don't tell me you've come to believe your own propaganda about the invincible Reapers. Or rather, please do. I could do with some amusement."

Winterborn dropped the phial; it shattered on the floor. Gevaudan pulled against the chain, straining at them reflexively. The serum glowed faintly, then faded, soaking into the stained concrete.

"You're quite right, of course." Winterborn chuckled. Eyes like a starved rat who'd seen its prey was helpless. "I've no doubt that Helen will work very hard to get you back. But she hasn't much time, has she?"

Gevaudan said nothing. Nothing to say.

"There was always the danger you'd take your dosage early, of course," said Winterborn, "being out in the field. But I've little appetite for gambling, Shoal; I prefer certainties. You like your habits, your little routines. Dr Kellett's blood test proved me right: your body will start crying out for its monthly fix any time now. And I don't need to tell you that the withdrawal symptoms will be a *bitch*."

Fear. Gevaudan hadn't known it in a while, not like this. "Your sadism's positively adolescent, Winterborn."

"I'm just stating facts, Shoal, although it *is* pleasant to have the upper hand with you at last. I leave the sadism to Dr Kellett, and he took great enjoyment telling me all about what will happen to your body. He was quite vivid, in fact." Winterborn smiled. "It would please me greatly to have you on my side, Shoal, but your dying a hideous, agonising death would hurt the rebels almost as much. So I'll settle for that, if needs be."

He leaned back in his chair, smiling, and for now said nothing more.

*

DEADSBURY, MANCHESTER
0430 HOURS

Grey pre-dawn twilight; the twitter of birds. Darrow trudged up Barlow Moor Road through drifts of rotten leaves, then turned left up Wilmslow Road, passed faded but undamaged shopfronts. Well, undamaged except for one, which was bullet-riddled and glassless. *Helen was here.*

A little further along, he glanced back and went still, staring at one building's faded signage. He walked back, looking in through cracked, dusty windows. Chairs and tables, tarnished silver, upturned glasses; draped with cobwebs, filmed with dust.

Empty chairs at empty tables... Darrow hummed a snatch of the song, then stopped. Too close to the bone.

And besides, one table was occupied. Almost hidden in one corner of the restaurant, a woman in a black evening dress sat alone at a table for two, drinking from a wineglass.

Darrow watched her in silence for a full minute, perhaps even two. Then he went to the door and pushed it open.

No-one had entered in a long time; it squealed and grated. A smell of damp and dust and old, old rot swept out to meet Darrow; dust swirled up in the sudden draught, pale and faint as smoke.

Darrow approached the table, pointing the Thompson down at the floor. The woman looked up at him and set down her glass; it was half-full of spiders and rain.

"Hello, Niamh," he said, and indicated the chair opposite her. "May I?"

She motioned to it and nodded. Darrow sat, the Thompson across his lap. "I was surprised to see you," he said. Niamh raised her eyebrows. "No, not unpleasantly. But I'd forgotten we came here."

Niamh smiled back at him.

"We only taught about half a mile away, didn't we? What was this place Italian? No – Spanish, that was it. You were mad about tapas."

Niamh inclined her head and raised her glass.

"How long did it take me to find the nerve to ask you to dinner?" Niamh shrugged, sipping rain. Darrow sighed. "All for nothing, as it turned out."

He drummed his fingers on the Thompson, looking at the dusty crockery and cutlery. "I wonder, sometimes – even now. Was it just that there was some sort of spark missing, so it never would have worked – or was there something I said or didn't say, or did, or didn't do, that would have changed everything? Do you understand what I mean?"

Much as Darrow had expected, Niamh's smile answered nothing.

Darrow sighed. "I never did have any idea how to talk to women. Not in that way." He shrugged. "Funny, though, the things that haunt us. We don't choose them."

Darrow toyed with a wineglass. The other paths, the roads not taken, would always be unknown; there was only ever the choice you made, and how you lived with its consequences. "How did you die?" he said at last. "In the War, or afterward? From a bullet, or disease? Or did you last as long as the Civil Emergency?"

Niamh didn't speak; her smile faded, and she studied her glass, swirling its contents around.

"Could have been later, couldn't it?" Darrow said. "Could even have been the December Rising. And who killed you? A Reaper or a rebel? Or are you actually still alive somewhere? Is that it?"

Niamh smiled again, and drew her pinched-together fingers across her lips, miming the closing of a zip.

"That would be funny, wouldn't it?" Darrow said. "We might have passed each other in a shanty town, or a camp in the Wastelands. And then there was that boy of yours."

He toyed with the wineglass again. "I'll never know, will I? Any more than I will where we'd be now if that evening had gone differently."

Weariness blew over Darrow in a wave; he sagged, tired and aching. "Ah well," he said. "I enjoyed the conversation."

At the door, he looked back; the restaurant was empty.

Empty chairs at empty tables.

"It's good to talk," Darrow murmured, and went out.

*

Past the Fletcher Moss Gardens, Darrow stopped at the church. There was movement in the bell tower. Darrow held up four fingers, then lowered the little finger so only three remained.

Two short whistles sounded from the tower. If anything had been wrong, there'd have been three, because Darrow would have stuck out his thumb instead of tucking the little finger away.

Darrow pushed the church door open, started down the aisle. Heads nodded at him from the pews. He nodded back, heading towards the altar, where Danny and his group sat in a huddle with the small, flame-haired figure of Flaps. She leapt to her feet. "The hell have you been?"

Darrow raised an eyebrow. "For a walk," he said.

"Long walk."

"Danny," Darrow said.

"Darrow." The boy had changed a lot: both since Helen had first come to Manchester, and since the battle for Ashwood Fort. He still seemed quick and nimble, but not quite as much as he had. And Darrow thought, although he hoped he was wrong, there were flecks of silver and grey in the spiky black hair. But wounds, of body or mind, did that; they aged you, made you ache.

"You're well?"

Danny nodded. "You?"

"Still alive," said Darrow. "Wakefield," he nodded; the little tribeswoman grinned back.

He didn't look directly at Flaps, but saw out of the corner of his eye that her arms were folded, eyes narrowed. "Ashwood want you," she said.

"Did they say what for?"

Flaps shook her head. "Not hard to work out, though."

"What?"

"Kingfisher just told us," she said. "The Reapers. They've taken the Grendelwolf."

A cold fist, metal-gloved, closed tight in Darrow's belly, crushing his innards in its grip. Sudden weakness in his legs; he steadied himself against a pew. Helen, ordering him and his into battle again. They hadn't been ready in December, and they'd been slaughtered. And they weren't ready now. Darrow straightened up, breathed out. "All right," he said. "Contact Osprey."

*

INTERROGATION CELL, THE PYRAMID
0502 HOURS

At length, Winterborn grew bored with the silence. "You've gone rather quiet," he told Shoal. "Which is a shame. I'm usually rather stuck for intelligent conversation. Most of my subordinates are terrified of me."

"You surprise me," the Grendelwolf said through gritted teeth. His colour had shifted, from alabaster white to a sickly grey, and his eyes were reddened. "And you so full of native charm."

"Don't get me wrong, Shoal – their fear's as useful as it is gratifying. I'm just saying there's a downside, in that it tends to cut conversations short. They can't get out of my presence fast enough. Except for my adjutants, and I don't pick them for their sparkling social skills. Those are thin on the ground in REAP Command at the best of times, and they're not exactly essential to the role." Winterborn sighed. "Dowson had the imagination of an engine block – and about the same level of aesthetic charm – and as for Jarrett… did you ever have the doubtful pleasure of a conversation with her?"

"Once or twice." Shoal's teeth chattered, and his forehead glistened; a film of greasy sweat covered the Grendelwolf's limbs and torso. "But there wasn't much opportunity for small talk."

"There wouldn't have been," said Winterborn. "She didn't really have any interests outside work. Other than killing Helen, of course."

"I thought that was her job." Shoal's fists clenched; he was starting to shake.

"Her job, her hobby, her religion and her main goal in life. It did get rather tedious after a while. I wanted – want – Helen back in her grave as badly as Jarrett did, but I do occasionally find other things to occupy my mind."

"I hadn't noticed."

Winterborn sat back, stroking his chin. "Kellett tells me that the early stages aren't unlike radiation sickness. It's the fast-dividing cells that are affected first, you see – mucous membranes, hair and so on. After that, the necrosis sets in – extremities, skin cells, progressing inwards as your body tries to conserve vital organs and core functions, restricting supplies of serum-rich blood to essential areas. You literally decompose, while alive. Alive, and fully conscious, to the very end."

"I refer you to my earlier comments about adolescent sadism."

"Sticks and stones," said Winterborn. "The process only takes a few hours, but I imagine it feels decidedly longer. Time can be a very subjective thing, after all. But, where there's life there's hope. As long as you're still respiring, Kellett says a single dose of Goliath serum will restart your regenerative capacities at full strength and repair all damage in little more than an hour. All you need do is convince me you've sincerely chosen to switch sides."

"Winterborn?"

"Shoal?"

"Go to Hell."

"After you, Shoal. After you."

4.

Intelligence Centre, Ashwood Fort
4th July, Attack Plus Twenty-One Years
0530 hours

"So," said Helen. "Can it be done?"

The silence at the other end of the line was so long that she thought they'd lost contact. Then there was a long, crackling hiss; a sigh, she realised. "In theory, yes," Darrow said finally. "But my crews haven't seen much action – most of them are still in training."

"Not all of them, though."

"No, not all of them."

"Plus Danny and his Raiders. With their help –"

"With their help, yes," said Darrow. "Given enough information about the target –"

"Alannah'll brief you on everything we've managed to glean."

"Glean?" A faint chuckle. "Haven't heard that in a while."

"Roger?"

"Just my past as an English teacher coming out." Darrow sounded bone-weary; Helen heard him release a long, heavy sigh. "All right," he said. "Put Alannah on and we'll get to work."

*

Interrogation Cell, The Pyramid
0601 hours

Sickness swept through Gevaudan in waves. The queasiness he'd felt on waking had returned, worse than ever. At first he'd told himself it was the after-effects of whatever drug they'd dosed him with, but now he was struggling not to vomit and stabs of pain shot through his abdomen; no denying what this was.

Gevaudan's stomach contracted; bile flooded his mouth. He tried to choke it back down, but couldn't; vomit splashed down his chest and onto the floor, inches from Winterborn's feet. Gevaudan saw the fluid was thick, laced with red. The Commander made a little moue of distaste.

"The lining of your stomach's starting to break down." Gevaudan looked up: Kellett stood by the cell door. Hadn't heard him come in. "Very painful, that'll be. You'll start to dehydrate, too."

Gevaudan blinked sweat from his eyes. Cold. Shivering. Feverish. "The biggest regret of my life will be not killing you."

"Oh, I'm sure you'll have bigger ones before we're through." Kellett limped closer. "Of course, all you have to do is –"

Gevaudan spat blood and bile at him; Kellett recoiled, spluttering in disgust as he wiped it off. He glared; the unscarred half of his face was bright red. "Enjoy yourself while you can, Shoal. You'll be begging me before the end."

A fresh wave of sickness hit as Gevaudan opened his mouth to speak; his guts twisted. For a moment his only thought was that his bowels were about to fail, another humiliation for both Kellett and Winterborn to revel in. He clenched his fists, shut his eyes; in the distance, Kellett was laughing.

*

ST JAMES' CHURCH, DEADSBURY
0614 HOURS

Darrow spread the sketch-map out on the floor in front of the altar. "The area around the Pyramid's been cleared, and the perimeter secured with a fence. There are watchtowers, with searchlights and machine guns. The Pyramid's original outer surface was bullet proof glass; that's now clad in reinforced concrete. Two gates, front and back, both heavily guarded, are the only ways in or out. Main entrance can only be accessed via the Hollywood Way Bridge – over a river which is, incidentally, heavily mined. Thoughts, Danny?"

Flaps' fists clenched. She'd been Darrow's right hand ever since he'd fucked off back to the city, but now Danny-boy was back she wasn't even asked what she thought. Danny rubbed his chin, studied the map. "Frontal assault's out, then."

Darrow nodded. "It'll have to be our approach for the exfiltration, though. Distract them, hit them hard, create an opening to get you and the Grendelwolf out."

"My job," said Flaps. "Right?"

"Yes. You've done that before, so you should be fine."

Should? Fucking well *would*. "Still gotta get in, though." She looked at Danny. "Any ideas?"

*

Interrogation Cell, The Pyramid
0702 hours

Shoal hung limp in his restraints; bloody vomit streaked his chest, and urine pooled on the floor beneath him. He was shivering, teeth chattering, face grey.

Winterborn leant in close. "All those years," he said. "Keeping me hoping you'd fight for me, all the while never having any intention of doing so. And look at you now. If I'd only called your bluff."

"Then one of us would be dead," Shoal glared yellowly at him. "Or both, perhaps. I might have taken you with me before I ended up like this."

"Or not," said Winterborn. "Most ideals and loyalties tend to prove quite fragile if you apply enough suffering. As we shall see." He stood. "I'm told things are about to get rather messy, so I think I'll watch the rest from a distance. I'll leave you in Dr Kellett's capable hands."

The cell door clanged shut behind him.

*

Deadsbury
0734 hours

"What 'bout tunnels?" Danny said. He looked knackered already. The air in the church felt stale. There was a reek of old smoke where some of the rebels had been chaining Monarchs. Made Flaps feel sick.

Darrow shook his head. "They learned their lesson after Station Five. They found and blocked all tunnels under the site and blocked them fully. Multiple heaps of rubble, booby-traps in places. No sewerage system – everything goes to an on-site septic tank."

"Maintenance? Repairs?" said Flaps. She wasn't having Danny plan it all himself.

"All done by TechSec," Darrow said.

"So to get in or out," said Danny, "you're either a Reaper, or they're bringing you in."

"Obvs," said Flaps.

"We got any Reaper uniforms?"

"Two or three." Darrow looked grey and tired and lined. Something was preying on him, sucking the insides out. What? Where'd he gone, before? "What we *don't* have are the security passes without which, Reaper or not, we won't even get past the front gate."

"Can't sneak in, can't smash in." Danny folded his arms, bit his lip. *Not so easy, is it?* Flaps thought, but then he smiled. "Got it."

*

INTERROGATION CELL, THE PYRAMID
0806 HOURS

Gevaudan's arms and shoulders ached; the nausea was a heavy, rolling ball in his stomach that the rest of him seemed to be spinning drunkenly around, and his bowels were getting closer and closer to giving way. He clenched his muscles against the growing pressure to stave off that final humiliation; Kellett was there.

In a way, his presence was beneficial; the world around Gevaudan was melting away into a grey haze in which he floated, alone with the pain and sickness, but Kellett was an anchor of sorts, a reference point; he was like a cold black light whose intensity seared the skin. That beady, ratlike eye was on Gevaudan, waiting, watching; gloating, feeding off the pain like a leech on blood. Gevaudan's fists clenched; he'd starve the bastard for as long as he could.

"You can't win this, you know." Gevaudan didn't answer; Kellett came closer, wheezing, leaning on the cane. "I said –" Louder now, close to his ear. Cold, rank breath. "I said, you can't win this."

The hectoring voice was high, thin and irritating; a wasp in a jar. Ignoring him wouldn't work; he wouldn't let up until he had a response. Probably not even then. Gevaudan coughed up bloody-tasting phlegm; he tried to spit at Kellett, but it spilled down his chest. "You think not?"

"We've been here before." The cane clicked and tapped at the floor. Kellett was circling him; Gevaudan closed his eyes. "Remember your training, Gevaudan? I know I do. All your prissy ideas about pacifism and disobedience, like some snotty teenager rebelling – but no, it wasn't adolescent rebellion. It was a *lifetime's* worth of convictions."

That smug, gloating voice; Gevuadan's fingers twitched. If he could only get free, lay hold of Kellett – even kitten-weak as he felt, he knew he'd find the strength to finish him.

In the grey haze, he half-saw, half-felt Jo standing there, shaking her head to see him yield to hatred and cruelty. But it wasn't about that any more; Kellett was something that shouldn't be in the world. He was worse even than Winterborn; to die knowing you'd at least put an end to him would be something, at least. But Gevaudan was pinned fast, and couldn't move.

"And yet," said Kellett, "you broke. You threw all those things away, and became what I wanted."

Something dug under Gevaudan's chin, forcing his head up. Kellett's breath rasped against his face. "Look at me, Shoal. Look."

The object under his chin dug in harder, threatening to tear the weakened skin. Gevaudan opened his eyes; Kellett's half-molten face was inches from his. He supported himself against the wall with the fused paw of his hand; the other gripped the cane, forcing the pommel under Gevaudan's chin.

"Your looks haven't improved," Gevaudan managed.

Kellett's half-mouth twisted in a sneer. "You broke," he repeated. "*I* broke you. I broke you then, and I will again now. And I'll be here to see the moment you do. After what you did to me, I've earned that right."

*

DEADSBURY

0832 HOURS

"So what d'you reck?" said Danny. He stood, stretched. Bright morning sunlight glowed through the stained glass windows, made coloured patterns.

"Extremely dangerous," said Darrow.

"We'll lose people," Flaps said. "You know that, right?"

Danny nodded. "Obvs." He knew Darrow was seeing what'd happened before, back in the winter. All the ones he'd lost then. He didn't look at Darrow, not straight on; couldn't.

"But it's the only way you're gonna get in," Flaps said. "Nowt else we can do. Yeah." She nodded. "It's a good plan."

She didn't meet his eyes either. Not easy, saying owt good to him, not after what he'd done. Couldn't blame her for that. Still hurt, though.

"Even if it works, we'll take heavy casualties." Darrow sighed: a long wind, blowing through dust. Danny saw the lines on his face, the grey hair, like he'd never seen them before. *He's gonna die. Sooner, later, he's gonna die.* Daft really; everyone was. But Darrow'd always been there: a rock, part of the world, permanent. But he wasn't; even if he didn't get shot, age or sickness'd get him one day. Funny thing to realise, specially now; Danny could have done without it.

"But you're right, Flaps," Darrow said. "It's the only way."

"It's a good plan," Flaps said again, almost whispering; didn't look up.

"Yes," said Darrow. "It is. Excuse me."

He got up, wincing as his joints cracked, then headed off towards the vestry. Head bowed. Looking so fucking old.

Danny glanced at Flaps; she was watching Darrow go as well. When the vestry door clicked shut, she turned back to him. "Right, then," she said. "Let's get started."

5.

INTELLIGENCE CENTRE, ASHWOOD FORT
4TH JULY, ATTACK PLUS TWENTY-ONE YEARS
0858 HOURS

"Your desk."

"Thanks." Stock breathed out as she sat. Her guts still twinged with pain, even with the scars healed. Her hands shook; she balled them into fists and pressed them into her lap.

"And your radio set." Hei passed the headphones to her. Awkwardly, Stock took them. "Already tuned to a specific frequency, covering a specific area, so don't touch controls for now." He handed her a pad and grease pencil. "Anything you hear, write down. They use a lot of codewords – know we're listening and we've broken some of their scramble codes. So just write down what you hear, best you can. Okay?"

"Right."

Hei studied her. "Let me know if you're ill or tired. Know you got to take things easy."

"Thanks. I'll be right."

Stock took a deep breath, put on the headphones and picked up her pencil.

*

St James' Church, Deadsbury
1058 hours

"So that's the first part," said Flaps. "Gonna have to get in close, but you can do that. It's the landcruiser crews, gonna have the toughest go of it."

"Not fucking kidding," muttered Jukk.

"Well, that's how it goes," said Flaps. "Gotta be done. But yeah, not gonna shit you. The Reapers'll hit back fucking hard. So make it look right, but get out fast. Don't wanna lose anyone."

They would, though – every fucker stood or sat round the chart did. They just weren't saying it, and hoping – praying too, the ones that did – that it wouldn't be them.

"After that," she said, "we get well clear, and out of sight. We've got hideouts sorted, close by as we can get away with, so we can keep watch."

"What for?" said Jukk.

"What do you think for, you mushroom? Signal from the Raiders. And when we get it, we go back in."

*

Intelligence Centre, Ashwood Fort
1149 hours

"Alannah?"

She looked up from her reports. "Yes, Hei?"

"Darrow for you."

A deep breath, then she nodded. "Put him through." Alannah picked up her headset. "Osprey Actual."

"Osprey, this is Falcon."

So tired; he sounded so fucking tired. "Go ahead, Falcon."

"All set," he said. "This evening."

"This *evening*?" Alannah winced as she heard the edge in her own voice. "The target's going to be deteriorating rapidly, Falcon. Estimate eight, nine hours max, before he's at the point of no return."

"We'll only get one go at this, Osprey. If it goes wrong we're all dead."

Alannah breathed out. "I know, Falcon."

"That's the earliest we'll be ready. And if we can get him out alive, we will."

*

Deadsbury

"Once we're there," said Flaps, "two teams. One gives covering fire, other one gets the Raiders and the Grendelwolf out. Questions?"

"Just one." Jukk again. Should have fucking known.

"Yeah?"

"Why are the Raiders doing this? It's our job."

Mutters and grunts: agreement. "Screw it down!" It came out louder than Flaps'd meant; sharper, too. Part of her agreed with them. Fucking Danny, waltzing in. She kept seeing his face, whether she wanted to or not. "This shit's what they train for," she said. "And it's why they're here – we learn from them, they learn from us. We'll have fun too, mate, don't worry."

And a better chance of getting out.

*

INTELLIGENCE CENTRE, ASHWOOD FORT
1330 HOURS

Stock pushed the headset's earpiece tight against her head, shut her eyes and wrote. She'd only learned how in the last couple months, in hospital. Had to, if she wanted to work here.

And she had. If Alannah knew who Stock was, it didn't show, but Stock'd be dead without her. The Catchman had ripped half her guts out; Danny had reckoned she was done for, but Alannah had told him to put Stock on a landcruiser and get her to the Fort. Nestor had spent three hours working on her to keep her alive. She owed him too, obvs, as much or more, but she never wanted to see the inside of sick bay again.

She wouldn't be much of a fighter either, though; not now. So – flat on her back in sick bay, fuck-all to do, why not learn to read and write? Specially as she'd need to, to work in Intelligence.

And here she was at last. Just starting out – listening in on standard, boring transmissions – that was all, for now. But she'd show she could do more. Head down, hard work, get the job done till they trusted her with more. So she could make Alannah proud, thank her properly.

Something new came through the static. A voice, muttering. Stock reached for the control dials, pulled her hand back. Wasn't sure what to touch and what not to, not yet. But the voice was getting clearer now, enough that Stock could make out the words.

They didn't mean anything she could understand, but Hei'd said the Reapers used code. Stock picked up her pencil. *Write it down. All of it. Get it right.* Listening properly, she could tell it was the same few sentences, repeated over and over. She started writing.

*

ST JAMES' CHURCH, DEADSBURY
1346 HOURS

"Right," said Flaps. "Take a break now. Rest up till it's time."

She needed the bog; she went to the one set up in the vestry. When she came out, she almost walked straight into Danny. "Yo," he muttered.

After a moment, she nodded back. "You all right?"

He nodded. "You?"

"Yeah. See you."

"Flaps?"

She turned back. "What?"

He wanted to say something, make things right, but he didn't have the words and nor did she. In the end he said: "Ask you summat?"

"What?"

"There's this woman."

"Another one?" Flaps felt a mean little throb of pleasure at the thought of Alannah getting cheated on too.

"Not like that."

"How then?"

"Fighter. Wants to be a Raider."

"She good enough?"

"Oh yeah."

"So?"

"She's a Jennywren."

The warm thick air went stiller. "You what?"

"Used to be. Got shot at Ashwood, taken prisoner. Anyway – reckons she's seen the light and everything."

"Bollocks."

"Might be true. Anyway, she wants to join the Raiders. She could do it, and having an ex-Reaper on board – be fucking handy for this job, wouldn't it?"

"If she *is* ex."

"Yeah."

Flaps tapped her fist against her flat belly. "What's this saying?"

"I dunno, Flaps. I'm in a right knot."

"Thinking 'bout it too much." Flaps tapped her belly again. "Go with this."

"Right."

Flaps sniffed. "You got everything you need?"

"Yeah. Reminds me – summat to show you." He motioned her to the altar, opened one of the bags. "New toys."

Pistols, Flaps realised. She took one from him: a thick, stubby cylinder with a pistol grip and trigger, and a bolt you pulled back to cock it. "Fuck's this?"

"Blap-guns, Zaq calls them."

"Blap-guns?" Flaps snorted. "Shit name."

"'Cos of the sound they make." Danny tapped the barrel. "Silencer."

"Okay." Flaps studied it. "They work?"

"Yeah. 'S just a .32, so you gotta be up close, but..."

"You'd wanna be anyway." Something like this wasn't exactly a marksman's weapon. "You taking these with you?"

"For the Pyramid?" He nodded. "Some. Rest are all yours."

"Ta," she said. "Owt else?" Flaps didn't wait for a reply, just turned away. "Laters then."

She left the church, padded to the gardens nearby. They were overgrown in summer, a mad blur of tangled colours. She sat there, breathed in the flower scents, looked at the blooms. So many different colours and shapes. Gevaudan'd kept his memory stones here. She'd found the old cairn under a willow, by the brook that wound through the gardens. He'd offered her an old book on flowers and plants, to help her name and learn about the flowers, but Flaps had said no. Never been a big reader. She wished she'd said yes, now.

Flaps crossed the brook to the willow tree, crouched by the scattered stones. She chose one grey pebble, smooth and round, and pocketed it. For the Grendelwolf, if they got him out. *When* they did.

Then she walked back through the gardens, not looking back, to the house, just up the road; she lived in with two others. One room was hers; in it, she sat on her straw pallet with her Sterling SMG and her Browning Hi-Power, and set to work: stripped them, cleaned them, put them back together, loaded them.

Then she got up, stood. Deep breaths. A tense knot in her guts. Cold. Hands shivering.

Deep breaths. *Calm. Be solid. Hard. They'll all look to you. Show them you're not scared, even if you are.*

But she was. She hadn't fought, not properly, since the Devil's Highway. And not in the city since the December Rising. Not since Mary and the rest of her crew'd died. *You're my best, Flaps*: pretty much the last thing Mary'd said to her before –

Flaps huddled in a corner of the room, rocking. Let herself shiver; let herself cry, too, biting her hand so no-one heard.

"It's true, Flaps."

Flaps looked up. Mary stood over her.

Ghostlighting again.

Mary crouched and touched her face, fingers cold and cobweb-light. "You're my best," she said. "Always were. You can do this, Flaps. Show them all. And bring them back alive."

Another touch on Flaps' cheek, and Mary was gone. Flaps shivered, but she was calm again.

*

ST JAMES CHURCH
1600 HOURS

In the graveyard, the Raiders sat, letting the sun warm their faces. Danny fiddled around with some twigs and strips of plastic sacking, Harp dozed with his head in Lish's lap, Wakefield and Filly snuggled beneath a willow tree and Hack leant back against a gravestone, whetting the blade of her knife.

She liked knife-work best; you got close to what you killed, could feel the blow hit home. See the blood run out, see it in their eyes too – the knowing that it was over, that they were done. Then the light fading in them, till it was gone. And then there was one less Reaper, just a blank-eyed doll left cooling on the ground.

Guns were easy. For cowards. Pull the trigger, watch someone fall. The Reapers'd done that to her brother. Raj hadn't even done anything wrong; hadn't even been one of the ones throwing stones. He'd had his hands up and everything. And that Reaper cunt had just flicked his submachine gun towards him and fired. Short burst. Raj had screamed. Nine years old and shot in the guts. Of course it'd hurt. He hadn't died right then. Took a couple of days. Hack'd held him the whole time.

Hack had never found that Reaper. Or maybe she had. A helmet had hidden the man's face, and she'd cut enough Reaper throats in her time. Shot plenty, too. All she knew, she might have got the cunt after all. If she had, she hoped it'd been with the blade. Maybe the Reaper had looked in Hack's eyes and known who she was, even if Hack hadn't. Remembered her from that day. Understood why. That would've been good.

In the meantime, any Reaper would do.

Hack tested the blade with her thumb. Blood welled up. She sucked it from the wound, spat it into the long grass and cleaned the knife. Then sheathed it, and lay back in the grass to rest. Eyes closed, till it was time to go and kill more Reapers.

*

Danny sat, tongue-tip poking from the corner of his mouth as he bound the twigs with the plastic strips. One twig was forked, so there were legs: a crude man-shape. He wrapped the last strip around the 'neck', till it made a lump that looked sort of like a head.

It was rough, but it'd have to do. *Keep me safe. Get us all out alive.* But even as he mouthed the prayer, he knew the second part wasn't happening. Just have to hope most of them got out. And that what they got out of this'd be worth the ones who didn't.

He stood up. The other Raiders sat or knelt or lay in the graveyard grass: some'd been making talismans like his, or praying. Others'd just been closing their eyes to rest: Brant was one of those, curled up against a gravestone. Hack was another, lying on her back with her hands folded on her chest, like they were about to bury her. Fucking creepy. "Everyone ready?" Danny said.

Almost as one, the Raiders jumped to their feet. Danny had to smile. He'd trained them well. Well enough? They'd see soon. Brant uncurled, yawned and stood, rubbing his face. Hack still lay there, eyes moving to and fro beneath the lids. "Hack?" called Danny; he was tempted to poke her in the ribs to wake her, but knowing Hack, he'd get stabbed if he did. There were times when he wondered if he'd been right to pick her.

Hack's eyes opened, and she sat up. "Ready," she said, and stood.

"Right, then," Danny said. "Let's go find some Reapers."

*

Northern Moor, Manchester
1631 hours

Lewis picked his way up the creaking stairs, reached the derelict house's landing, pushed the bedroom door wide. A Sterling swept round to cover him, then lowered. "Sorry, sir."

"Forget it." Lewis crouched down and crawled to her side, grimacing. The room stank: sweat, spoiled food, the bucket in the corner. "Harris, isn't it?"

"Yes, sir." A small, lean woman; a tough, plain face, short brown hair.

"Take me through it."

Harris peeked over the windowsill, pointed. "Older guy, grey hair, but seemed pretty spry. Matched the description. Wearing a poncho. Not sure, but there may have been a long weapon under it. Anyway, he went into there, was inside a few minutes."

"That house?"

"Yes, sir."

"Alone?"

"Few scavs went in after them, then cleared out. Looked pretty scared. But he came out later and talked to them for a couple of minutes. Waved a food can in front of them. Didn't look like he got anything from them, but he let them have it anyway."

"Any sign of them?"

"Not since. But there's another one. See there? Thin boy, scarred face."

"I see him."

"He went after the old guy. Came back holding a can. Stashed it quick, but I saw."

"That boy there, for certain?"

"Yes, sir."

"Good work." Lewis put his communicator to his lips. "Korth? Stand by to make a pick up. Alive, Korth."

Intelligence Centre, Ashwood Fort
1638 hours

"Stock?" A hand touched her shoulder; Hei was looking down at her. "With me, please."

Stock's fucked-up innards clenched: cold, hard, painful. What'd she gone and fucked up? Were they gonna kick her out now? Already? First day?

Hei walked her towards Alannah's desk. Stock's ruined guts knotted tighter. Fuck. What'd she gone and done?

Alannah looked up. "Stay with us for a minute, Hei."

Hei nodded. Stock's belly hurt; her skin felt greasy with sweat. She made herself stand straight.

"Sit down before you fall down," Alannah said.

"Th-thanks." Stock's guts unknotted; now she felt giddy and faint.

Alannah held out a sheet of coarse paper. Stock saw her own spidery letters printed on it. "Remember this?"

"Yeah."

"It said this? Exactly this?"

"Deffo."

Alannah nodded. "You're monitoring Sector 11, right?"

"Yeah."

"Okay. Anything else like this, you bring directly to me. Right away. Wherever I am. Clear?"

Stock nodded. *Directly to me.* And on Stock's first day. "Got it."

Alannah half-smiled. "Okay. Now get back to it. Remember – anything else like this –"

"Straight to you."

"Straight to me. That's right. Carry on."

Dismissed, but gently. "Yes'm." Stock got up and limped back to her desk, trying not to grin.

*

Alannah watched her go. "Hei?"

"Yes?"

"Contact the Sparrow network. I want bearings on that signal. Then triangulate so we can get a fix."

Hei made a note on his pad. "Understood."

"That's all. You can carry on."

Hei nodded. Alannah watched him go, too, and then a long breath escaped her. She looked again at Stock's note, and felt cold.

6.

Listening Post 2, The Wastelands
4th July, Attack Plus Twenty-One Years
1702 hours

In her earth burrow, Colby adjusted the dial on her radio. Voices rose out of the fog of static and vanished back into it.

A voice emerged. She turned the dial another fraction of a notch, and the voice became clear. The message was the same few phrases, spoken over and over again. She nodded to herself and reached for her map. Now to get a bearing.

*

CANTEEN, THE PYRAMID
1705 HOURS

Axon could hear them as he worked: the canteen was empty, 'cept for two Reapers at a nearby table. An older one, Asian, and a young one with sandy hair.

"You gonna ask him?" the young one said.

"Am I fuck," said the older man. "It's a load of old bollocks."

"You reck?"

"I reck."

Axon pulled the spent fluorescent tube from its housing and climbed down off the table. "Wanna bet?" he heard the younger one say.

"How much?"

"Pack of Monarchs."

"You don't even smoke."

"Got some, though. Well?"

Axon picked up the new tube, laid it on the table top and clambered up again. "All right, then," the older Reaper said. "Always up for some free cigs."

The younger Reaper stood up, walked over. "Yo," he said. "Axon, right? I'm Twemlow."

"Can I do you for?"

"Wanted to ask you something."

"'Bout the Grendelwolf?"

Twemlow blinked, then smiled. "You get that a lot?"

"What do you think?"

"You really met him?"

"For about a minute. He killed my mate."

He'd told Benny to just let the big bastard go, but the older man'd had to take a shot at the Grendelwolf. A second later Benny had been dead and Axon had been on the ground, his gun slapped out of his hands. And that white, yellow-eyed face, close to his. *Helen Damnation. Is she alive? Where did they take her?*

"But not you?"

"Nah. I told him what he wanted to know." *And fainted.* He wasn't going to mention that. Or how he'd got to thinking about how no Reaper would've shown that much mercy, and, as the fighting began, about which side he wanted to be on. And now the Grendelwolf was in a cell here. "And so would you."

"I bet."

Twemlow opened his mouth to ask something else, but then a voice barked out. "Having fun, are we, Water?"

Twemlow's face reddened and he snapped to attention. "Sarge."

The NCO strode in. Stone: Axon'd run across him a couple of times. Squat, bald-headed; a broken nose, no neck. He moved in close to Twemlow, almost nose to nose. "Nice to see you two taking it easy." He eyed Axon. "Carry on," he said, then turned back to Twemlow. "Don't shit your pants, Water. I'm just here for a brew."

The Asian Reaper let out a loud breath that sounded remarkably like 'prick.' Stone wheeled. "Something to say, Ahmad?"

"No, Sarge."

"Good." Stone looked up at Axon. "Know why he's called Water?"

"No, Sarge."

"Because he's wet," said Stone, leaning in close to Twemlow and grinning with yellow teeth. "And he runs away. Right, Twemlow?"

Twemlow's face was redder than ever.

"Isn't that right, Reaper Twemlow?"

"Yes, Sarge," Twemlow said at last.

"Certainly is," said Stone, then nodded to them all. "Carry on," he said, and strode on to the counter. Twemlow turned away, face still red and went back to his table. Not looking at him, Ahmad slid a pack of cigarettes over to him. Axon picked up the new tube, started fitting it into place.

*

INTERROGATION CELL, THE PYRAMID
1728 HOURS

A thick grey haze filled the burnt and burning streets, scorching Gevaudan's lungs when he tried to breathe. He coughed and retched; his fingers ached from gripping the coarse fabric of the sack he dragged behind him and the weight of it made his arms and shoulders ache, but he didn't let go – couldn't, mustn't.

"I have promises to keep," he mumbled through thick, heavy lips. *"And miles to go before I sleep."*

A dozen people shambled past; they were scarlet and black, towing flags of dead, ragged skin behind them. Further along, men and women in tattered clothing groped unseeingly towards him. They had no faces, only blackened masks of seared skin, resembling alligator hide. No eyes, no features, only mouths like red holes. The only sound they made was a faint murmury whisper; Gevaudan thought of crickets on a summer night. He stepped aside and made himself utterly still to let them pass, and to avoid their touch.

Roofless, doorless, windowless houses. Bodies on the pavement, emaciated and near-bald from the creeping doses that had killed them.

Gevaudan ached, bone-tired. But he was nearly home.

He rounded a corner, and there it was. A Victorian townhouse with shattered windows and one wall almost completely gone, baring the rooms to the elements. Carrion crows gazed beadily down from the bare rafters.

The front door swung open as Gevaudan reached it. "Hello?" He stepped over the threshold into the hall, dragging the sack behind him.

"In here," his father called from the front room.

His father, his mother, Jo, Michaela, Keith, David, Gloria: they all watched him, cold-eyed, unsmiling. Ashes blew into the house on a cold wind, clinging to their hair.

"Well?" his father said. "Where's your brother?"

Gevaudan's muscles moaned their relief as he released the sack, but there was no cause for joy. Because now he had to tell them. He upended the sack; out slid soot, charred friable pieces of bone, part of a skull. "I'm sorry," he said. "I was too late."

But there was no answer. Gevaudan didn't want to look up; he knew what he'd see. But he had to look. It was the price of his failure.

They were all dead, in their chairs or on the floor, bloody vomit crusted round their mouths. Flies crawled on them. Their hair had fallen out or faded; David and Gloria, in their mother's arms, looked like tiny ancients.

"I'm sorry," he said again, but there was no-one to hear.

The nausea hit him abruptly, with the force of a punch to the stomach; he doubled over, fell to his knees in the black, greasy ashes and threw up. Strings of blood and tissue fell from his mouth. When he reached up and touched his hair, it came out by the handful.

Creeping dose. Same as them – as Mum, Dad, Jo, Michaela, Keith, David, Gloria. Every Shoal claimed by it, in the end: only Gideon had escaped, reduced in seconds to ash and bone instead of this.

But Gevaudan hadn't died then; he couldn't have. He hadn't been a Grendelwolf when the bombs fell – that had come later. And if he'd died then, he'd never have met Helen. Helen. This was a dream, he realised. A dream. A dr –

*

The hank of hair came out with almost no resistance, leaving the scalp raw and bleeding. Shoal's head jerked up; pain and delirium blurred the yellow eyes, but hatred gave them focus when they found Kellett.

Kellett smiled back at the Grendelwolf; his stomach twitched and rolled with mingled fear and excitement. "You're coming apart, Shoal." He held up the hair, then tossed it aside. Bruise-like patches of black and green spotted Shoal's skin, taking on a greasy sheen, and already the toes and fingers had started to blacken in earnest. "Your skin will start coming off soon. That, I can promise you, will *really* hurt."

"Fuck off." Shoal's voice was little more than a phlegmy wheeze.

"Not up to your usual standard, Gevaudan."

Shoal tried to spit at Kellett, but the gobbet of bloody phlegm only fell onto his chest. Kellett chuckled and leant forward to watch more closely, humming an old pop song from before the War as he did. Its title, if he recalled correctly, was 'I Don't Want To Miss A Thing.'

*

FALLOWFIELD, MANCHESTER
1735 HOURS

The last Reaper tried to run, but Harp's throw-stick hit the nape of her neck with a dull crunch. The Reaper pitched forward, arms and legs shivering. Harp ran over, gripped her head and twisted; the spine cracked, and she was still.

"Get a skate on," called Danny.

Three landcruisers sat idling on the pavement beside the row of gutted terraces, their crews scattered dead around them. Hack wiped the blood off her knife on a Reaper's hair, spat once on the body and stood; Harp and the others dragged the corpses inside one house, stripped them and squeezed into the uniforms.

The tight leather pinched and scratched at collar and cuff, and in the summer heat Harp was soon sweating like fuck, but he squinnied at himself in the 'cruiser's windscreen and hardly knew it was him. *Reaper.*

"Stop poncing." Lish poked him in the side. "Get aboard."

The black leather brought out the white of her skin, the red of her hair. Clung to her arse, too, as she climbed aboard ahead of him. Harp pulled his helmet on, lowered the visor.

Their legs brushed together as he sat beside her; he touched her thigh. She smiled at him as the landcruisers pulled out, took his hand in hers.

*

St Martin de Porres Church, Ashwood Fort
1750 hours

In a pew near the back, Carson knelt on a threadbare hassock, hands clasped before, head against the wooden shelf in front.

She blinked. She'd been drowsing – nearly dozed right off. *Sorry, God.* She focused. Pray. Pray for the Grendelwolf; pray for the Raiders. Pray for Wakefield; pray for Filly.

Wakefield standing over her, rifle aimed down, Filly beside her. Carson lying there, blood in her mouth, knowing it was all over. And then Wakefield had lowered the rifle, let her live.

The Raiders were the Jennywrens, but with mercy – with all the things Carson had told could have no place in a Jennywren's life. And Filly, Wakefield's Filly – she was so beautiful. She'd never touch Carson, of course, but that didn't matter. Being a Raider would be being close to her, and that would be a joy and a penance in one. Just to have Filly smile at her once, to look at Carson and not see a Reaper but a woman, a friend – yeah, that'd be enough.

She didn't know the Grendelwolf, had only ever seen him at a distance, but she wished she was with the Raiders now – with Filly – to get him out or die trying. Because then they'd know. They'd see, then, she was on their side.

*

INTERROGATION CELL, THE PYRAMID
1800 HOURS

Kellett poked the wet black glisten of Shoal's fingers with his crippled hand; a chunk of rotten flesh fell off the bone, hit the floor with a wet plop. Shoal grunted weakly.

"Falling apart," Kellett said again. "Your hands and feet are already necrotic. Rest of your skin's well on the way too." He shifted his bad hand to the pommel of his cane, drew a vial of serum from a pocket with the other and tapped Shoal's forehead with it. The Grendelwolf's eyelids twitched and opened; the eyes themselves were rheumy and bloodshot.

"See this?" said Kellett. "All yours. You just have to accept the price."

Shoal closed his eyes; Kellett tapped his forehead with the vial again, harder. He grunted and his head jerked up, yellow eyes narrowed in hate. The cracked lips peeled back from his remaining teeth; several had already fallen out, and lay in the mire of piss and blood on the floor.

"All this can stop," said Kellett. "And in fact, it *will*. We both know it's not if, but when. Why not give in sooner rather than later? You've done your part – shown your defiance, suffered for your rebel friends. You think any of them would have lasted this long? Seen their bodies disintegrating like this, and not given in? You know they wouldn't."

Shoal fought for breath; each one must hurt like hell, Kellett knew, but finally he spoke. "You really do love the sound of your own voice, don't you?"

"And you clearly enjoy suffering," said Kellett. "I'm not the one hurting you, Gevaudan. You're doing it to yourself. I made you, and I own you, yes. Doesn't mean you can't be happy. You just have to make your peace with the facts. And in the end, you will."

"Dear God, you're boring."

"And your insults are getting weaker, Shoal. Just like you."

*

Hollywood Way, Stockport

1900 hours

The Pyramid reared up ahead, like a giant spear-tip poking the sky. Beside Danny, behind the lead landcruiser's wheel, Wakefield was breathing faster; he glanced over at her, then dug out a piece of rag and handed it over. "Here."

Wakefield wiped the sweat from her face. "Sorry."

"S'okay. I'm shitting it and all." He grinned at her and winked. Wakefield half-smiled back.

Had to be worse for her – this was a different kind of fighting, pretending to be one of the people who killed tribals on sight. Danny got that. He was half-sure everything about him screamed *rebel;* Wakers probably thought everything about her screamed *tribe*. But, any luck, their uniforms were all most Reapers'd see. Most people didn't look far, Helen'd told him that. Saw what they expected to.

Danny hoped she was right.

They were approaching the bridge. At the checkpoint, a Reaper sentry held up a hand, stepped forward; Danny pushed the transmit button on the handset beside him. "Ready?" he said, not moving his lips.

"*Say the word,*" said Flaps.

*

OBSERVATION SUITE, THE PYRAMID
1902 HOURS

Winterborn leant towards the monitor. Shoal, naked in his chains, arms and legs black with rot, rags of skin hanging from shoulders and chest; Kellett, taunting him with that vial of serum; Shoal's head straining towards it, the rotten remnants of his fingers twitching.

He wanted it, needed it, was ready to beg. Yes. What Winterborn had sought so long was almost here; the Grendelwolf was ready to break.

He'd sat, watching the process of Shoal's decay for the past few hours, almost entranced by it. But this moment had to be seen, not over a video-link but face-to-face. Winterborn stood, and motioned to his guards.

*

NEAR THE PYRAMID, STOCKPORT
1904 HOURS

The Reapers had destroyed every building around the Pyramid, scorched every blade of grass, to leave a bare, almost completely flat plain.

On the outer edges of the plain, though, there were still heaps of rubble and earth, pushed back by landcruisers with 'dozer blades during the clearance – closely watched, obvs, but nothing experienced crew-members couldn't get to without being spotted, given time and patience.

Flaps and a half-dozen of her crew now huddled behind one such heap under a camouflage net. They might get clocked if Reapers drove straight past – which wasn't impossible since there were 'cruisers circling round the Pyramid twenty-four-seven –

but for now they were out of sight. A half-mile away, in a narrow terraced street in Edgeley, four landcruisers were parked, ready to move.

Under the net, her crew unpacked. They had two Carl Gustaf 84mm anti-tank launchers which Flaps'd used against Reaper convoys on the Devil's Highway. The rebels had a handful of them, much to the frustration of the Reapers, who'd sought the few surviving caches in vain. The old Second World War PIATs still used by both sides were useless outside a hundred metres – the 'Charlie G' had a longer range and harder punch, so they had to be risked here.

"Get a bead on your targets," Flaps said, "but wait for the order to fire. Got it?" She put the communicator to her lips. "'Cruisers, move out on my mark."

Beside her, Jukk put his eye to his launcher's sight.

*

Through the rangefinder, the checkpoint on the bridge sprang into focus, and the three landcruisers halting before it.

"Wait for it," Jukk heard Flaps say. Wait for what the fucking Raiders wanted. Twats.

Jukk sighted on the lead 'cruiser. Morwyn's cruiser. One pull of the trigger, that'd be all it took. But he pursed his lips and shifted his aim, till the third and last 'cruiser was in his sights.

Flaps' radio crackled. "Now," said Morwyn's voice.

"Hit it," said Flaps.

Jukk squeezed the trigger.

7.

Interrogation Cell, The Pyramid
1905 hours

Gevaudan had only known worse pain than this during his conversion into a Grendelwolf, and perhaps not even then. Every inch of skin on his body felt raw and weeping; it burned at the air's lightest touch, and when the weeping dried out, the raw, swollen flesh split at the slightest movement.

His throat felt like drought-cracked mud, even though every cough brought up more tissue and blood; he was drying out – losing moisture through the damaged skin. He was burning hot, but when the air brushed against him it was like being stroked with ice.

Despite the pain, he was aware enough to feel humiliation too. Despite his best efforts, his bowels had given way; hot liquid faeces ran down his legs, fell into the foetid mire on the floor – the blood and vomit, the urine and the putrefying tissue that had been his skin and musculature. He might have slipped his chains if he'd had strength to move – he didn't dare look at his lower limbs, but they were probably little more than bone by now.

"Straighten up, soldier," his father said. "Back straight. Feet together. Come on, boy. You can do it."

"Shoal. *Shoal.*"

A thin cold voice, sharp in his ears, like a blade or drill. Gevaudan groaned; it just added to the pain.

"Look at me."

Obey the voice and it might stop; he forced his eyes open.

Winterborn's face came into focus. "You can stop this," he said. "Even now, you can *live*. In fact, I can offer you something that Helen and the others certainly can't. More than a simple supply of serum. Much more."

Gevaudan closed his eyes.

*

Winterborn opened his mouth to speak again, but then stopped, turning. Very, very faintly, the Pyramid had shivered, and a sound rumbled through it.

The dull thud of an explosion.

*

MAIN GATE, THE PYRAMID

"Prisoners for interrogation," Wakefield heard Danny tell the checkpoint-Reaper, and then the rocket shrieked.

Even though she'd been waiting for it, she jumped. Her fists clenched on the wheel – what if they missed, hit Danny and her?

Then, a flash; the earth jerked and the bang slammed her ears between its hands.

Their steelback lurched forward. The second one slewed round; the third jumped in the air, back end on fire, and crashed down.

"Shit!" screamed the checkpoint-Reaper.

A machine gun chattered on a watchtower, till another rocket shrieked; the tower-top vanished, and instead there was an orange flower, turning black, the clap of the explosion. Wakefield looked back at the third steelback; Harp scrambled out, Lish beside him.

Another rocket shrieked past Wakefield; a section of wall near the gates blew apart. "In!" the Reaper shouted, haring across the bridge. The gates swung wide; Wakefield drove the steelback across the bridge towards them. The running Reaper leapt up into the flatbed.

The second steelback stuttered forward then died, boiler hissing steam; its crew piled out, swept up Harp and Lish, rushed them through as well.

Wakefield was through the gates. The rest of the team poured through them, and then they swung shut. The rest of the steelback's occupants jumped out. Most were in Reaper uniform, but Hack and Brant were dressed as scavs, hands roped behind their backs. The gate-Reapers shepherded them all towards the Pyramid.

Wakefield looked back, saw bodies scattered round the third steel-back. The Reapers they'd killed to take it – dead even before the carefully-aimed rocket had hit, but they'd made it look real. Outside the gates, more steel-backs drove straight at the Pyramid, .50 cals chattering.

Wakefield ducked as the Reapers fired back, didn't look back again till they were at the Pyramid's main entrance. Flaps' steelbacks had already turned, heading back where they'd come come – all but one which stood still, boiler steaming, bodies scattered around.

Carry their souls, Wakefield said to the Fox Spirit – but then they were in through the door and it was shut behind them, and all that remained was the fear she had to keep locked down, no matter what, in order to live.

*

LOBBY, THE PYRAMID

The lieutenant behind the main desk stood, wide-eyed and gawping, as they ran in. *In through the front door, open arms.* No Reapers around him; they'd all legged it outside to shoot at Flaps' lot. "Fuck," Danny heard him mutter. "Fuck. Fuck."

Probably barely out of training. Good. "Interrogation block," shouted Danny. The lieutenant blinked at him. "Where?" Danny said, and motioned to Brant and Hack. "They know about this shit. There might be a follow-up."

The lieutenant pointed. "That way. Just follow the signs."

Take control, move quick, act like you belong. "Will do." Danny motioned the others, and they herded Hack and Brant down the corridor.

*

INTERROGATION CELL, THE PYRAMID

The Grendelwolf hung limp in his chains. Winterborn stepped away, disgusted, snapped his fingers at one of the CenCom guards. "What's going on out there?"

"Not sure, sir."

Winterborn sighed. "I know *you're* not sure. So find me someone who is. I want a full report immediately."

"Sir."

The guard dashed off, and Winterborn turned back to study Gevaudan. "Dr Kellett?" he said. "Wake him up, will you? We've things to discuss, and very little time to do so, by the sound of it."

*

OUTSIDE INTELSEC UNIT, THE PYRAMID
1921 HOURS

Marching through the Pyramid's corridors, Wakefield felt giddy, scared, dreaming, all at once. They were far from the tribe-lands, the Wastelands, the places she knew – they were in Reaper-land, the heart of it, pretending to be Reapers themselves.

The rifle weighed heavy. The leather uniform pinched and chafed. Under it, more weapons: a blap-gun, and her knives. Might or might not be of use, but they were hers; were *her*. That mattered.

They marched together, in step, arranged to form a box around Harp and Brant. Hard to do – not the tribal way – but they had to look like Reapers. Wakefield gripped the rifle tightly, looked sideways at Filly. "Eyes front," Filly mouthed.

Wakefield faced ahead again. Danny marched in front; he wiped first one palm, then the other, on his uniform. Sweat: he was scared too. That made Wakefield feel a bit better. A bit.

They reached a checkpoint. A barred gate; Reaper in a cage, holding out a hand to Danny. Danny took out a pass, handed it over. "What's this about?" the Reaper in the cage said.

"Picked these up in Heaton Moor." Danny jerked a thumb at Hack and Brant. "Under orders to get them to interrogation rapid."

The Reaper squinnied at the pass, yawned, nodded. There was a buzz, and the gate swung open.

*

INTERROGATION CELL, THE PYRAMID
1928 HOURS

Gevaudan's teeth felt loose and weak in his mouth. His raw flesh wept; the dried flesh split at the slightest movement; his shoulders ached as he sagged against the chains. Every inch of him seemed to sing its pain, and his hand and wrist bones must be nearly fleshless – any moment, they'd snap like stale bread and when he fell he'd burst open on impact with the floor, his head exploding like rotten fruit. But that might not be so bad. The pain would end.

"Mum," he whispered.

A hand stroked his few remaining strands of matted hair. "Hush," Jo whispered, and kissed his cheek; Gevaudan flinched, but it didn't hurt. It actually dulled the pain for a few seconds. "Not long now," she said. "Soon be done."

*

INTELSEC UNIT, THE PYRAMID
1940 HOURS

Offices, cells and interrogation rooms: that was IntelSec, that and the sounds of muffled screams.

Danny'd sneaked a glance in through one of the interrogation rooms. Stained floor and walls, a floor drain clogged with hair. He touched the pistol on his hip. If it all went tits-up and they took him, there'd be no rescue; never pull this stunt off twice. Better off finishing it quick.

Not far now, though. Soon be at the block. Just a bit further.

"Lieutenant?"

Shit. "Keep walking," Danny muttered out of the side of his mouth.

"You! Lieutenant, I'm talking to you."

Shit shit shit. "Ma'am," said Danny, halting.

A Reaper captain marched up, four men with her. Her shoulder-flash was a black eye, etched on white. IntelSec. "What are you doing here?" she said.

"Prisoners for interrogation, ma'am."

"I can see that. Why are you here? Processing is back that way."

"Under orders, ma'am. High-Sec Block."

"Oh, really?" The officer folded her arms. "That's interesting, Lieutenant, considering that only the Regional Commander can authorise that. Your papers. Now."

"Yes, ma'am." Danny took his fake ID out, held it out to her. As she took it, he said: "Kiwi."

The officer looked up, and there was a dull, muffled sound: *blap*. A small black mark appeared above her eyebrow. She blinked. Blood trickled out of it into her eye. As she fell, there was another *blap*, and then another. A second Reaper pitched backwards, mouth open.

Danny drew his own blap-gun as one of the remaining guards reached for a weapon. *Blap blap blap. Blap.* Two more Reapers fell. One writhed, coughing blood. The last one ran: Danny aimed after him and fired three shots, then went in close to finish him. One more *blap* sounded behind him; he looked back to see Brant standing over the writhing Reaper, who wasn't writhing any more. Brant looked up, raised his eyebrows. "They work," he said.

Harp got a cell door open. "This one's empty."

"Get 'em out of sight," said Danny. "Then let's move."

*

INTERROGATION CELL, THE PYRAMID
1946 HOURS

Jo was gone; neither Mum nor Helen were anywhere to be found. Unless he counted Kellett – and he'd rather not – Gevaudan was dying alone. The doctor's seared face was a blur, but he remained unpleasantly audible.

"Still time," Kellett said. "There's still time, Shoal."

Gevaudan tried to shut out that thin, droning voice. There *was* time, but not much more, not now. He need only hold out a little longer, endure the pain till it was done. And then he wouldn't have become a slave again, or betrayed Helen and the others. *Death is part of the process.* Where had he heard that? Didn't matter. It would soon be done, and if his loved ones were anywhere, he'd be with them. Gideon; would Gideon still be angry, or did death heal all? Gevaudan hoped so; an eternity in this state was too horrible to contemplate.

"Do you hear me?" Kellett's voice wouldn't be shut out; it burrowed deep under the skin, gnawing away at his resolve. "I know you can hear me, Shoal. there's still time."

Still time. Still time. No, there wasn't. To hell with Kellett. *Everyone breaks, everyone gives in, everyone becomes the thing I want them to be*: that was Kellett. Gevaudan had to deny him him that victory.

So you'll die, and he'll think you mad or a fool. But that was Kellett's problem; he couldn't understand anything else.

Why die for the rebels? They all fear you; none of them trust you. Helen will never love you – and even if she could, what then? She'll grow old and die; you'll go on and on. Unless you stop taking the serum, in which case you're back here again. You could find a less painful way to kill yourself, I suppose. Or, of course...

Or you could say yes.

Gevaudan grunted weakly, shook his head.

No, don't dismiss it. Think. You could have what you had before. Your own place. Music and books. Instruments to play. A little haven amidst the ruin. You'd just have to swallow your pride.

No. He wouldn't give Kellett what he wanted. Or Winterborn. Winterborn was there, too, waiting for him to break. He wouldn't. He wouldn't.

But now that vow felt hollow. The pain was so terrible, the temptation so strong. Once he'd have said he was indifferent to whether he lived or died, but life, even in this ruined world, was suddenly sweet – even a friendless life, led alone.

Gevaudan groaned and shook his head. Death had to come now, *right* now. Because unless it did, he wasn't going to hold out.

*

1950 HOURS

"Report," Winterborn said, turning away from the decaying Grendelwolf at last.

The Reaper lieutenant swallowed – he looked as though he'd rather face whoever had attacked than break news of it to Winterborn. Gratifying, but there were more pressing concerns just now. "Well?" Winterborn said.

"Rebels, sir. Rocketed the front gates and watchtowers, then rushed the gates with landcruisers."

"Christ," said Kellett.

"Control yourself, Doctor. What's our status?"

"They fell back under heavy fire, sir. Units are in pursuit."

"Good." So, they'd tried and failed. Darrow must be slipping. Winterborn turned back towards Shoal, then stopped.

"Darrow doesn't slip," he said.

*

OUTSIDE HIGH-SECURITY BLOCK, THE PYRAMID
1952 HOURS

They rounded the corner: up ahead, metal bars across the corridor. There was a door in them, and a steel cage holding two Reapers on gate duty – a hard-faced female sergeant and a scrawny private. Two more Reapers flanked the door. A layer of sweat thickened between Danny's palms and the Lanchester; he wanted to wipe it off, but if they saw, they'd wonder why he was afraid. Maybe they'd put it down to the summer heat, but he wasn't chancing it.

"Prisoners for interrogation," he said. Nearly ready to kick off. Till then, stay calm. Get close. Let them think you're on their side till –

"ID, please," said the sergeant.

Danny fumbled in his pockets for it. Might still bluff their way through here. But his pockets were empty.

*

INTERROGATION CELL, THE PYRAMID
1953 HOURS

"Sir?" Fear in the Reaper lieutenant's voice. Winterborn sighed. Weakness everywhere, when he needed it least.

"Roger Darrow," he said. "You've heard of him, yes? Controls rebel operations in this city? An old man who'll soon be dead one way or the other, but no fool. And he doesn't slip up."

Shoal let out a weak moan; Winterborn spared a brief glance for what had been the Grendelwolf, then turned back to the lieutenant. "Using rockets to disable the gates and watchtowers was a bold, effective move, using weapons that are valuable and in short supply. And yet given that advantage, the rebels failed to press it home. How many landcruisers attacked the gates?"

The lieutenant fidgeted – desperately wishing he could back away, no doubt. "Three, sir, maybe four."

"They have more landcruisers than that. Three or four of them against the Pyramid is suicidal lunacy, and they fell back almost immediately. Darrow wouldn't squander resources like this on a half-baked plan."

*

OUTSIDE HIGH-SECURITY BLOCK, THE PYRAMID
1954 HOURS

"Bollocks," Danny said. "Must've lost it when they hit us."

"What happened?" said the boy, then fell silent as the sergeant gave him a look.

"You wouldn't have got this far without ID," said the sergeant, eyeing Danny. "What name is it?"

"Lieutenant Robb."

The sergeant squinnied at a clipboard. "Nothing about you here, sir. Sorry. Can't let you in without –"

"Look, we nabbed three rebel suspects in Heaton Moor. One of them started blabbing and this one," he nodded at Hack, "knifed him. Neither of them are talking so my CO said get them here ASAFP."

"What's the fuss?" said the sergeant.

"They're gonna try and spring the Grendelwolf."

"Just did. They got fucked."

Danny shook his head. "Just a diversion. We got *that* much out of them. They're gonna try again, summat big. So these two need getting to the interrogators now."

The sergeant bit her lip, then nodded. Her hand inched towards the switch that unlocked the gate.

*

INTERROGATION CELL, THE PYRAMID
1956 HOURS

"Did anyone come through during the attack?" said Winterborn.

"Come through, sir?"

Winterborn controlled his anger with an effort. "Did anyone enter the Pyramid?"

"No, sir – well –"

"Well, what?"

"Just a Reaper unit, escorting some prisoners. They came under fire –"

"And were rushed inside?"

"Of course, sir."

"Without stopping to carry out the normal security checks."

"They would have been –"

"Sound the alarm, Lieutenant."

"Sir?"

"Sound the alarm. *Now*."

*

OUTSIDE HIGH-SECURITY BLOCK, THE PYRAMID

Wakefield's eyes didn't leave the sergeant's hand. It slid across the desk with intolerable slowness, the slowness things moved with in battle. But at least in battle there was something you could do; here, Wakefield could only watch.

But the sergeant's hand was going where they wanted it to go; towards the switch that controlled the gate. One click, and they'd be through.

The sergeant extended a finger to push the switch.

It was almost touching it when the bells began to ring.

8.

Outside High-Security Block, The Pyramid
4th July, Attack Plus Twenty-One Years
1957 hours

When the bells rang, Danny saw it in the sergeant's eyes: she knew. Her mouth opened; he pulled the Lanchester's bolt back and swung it up. "Don't fucking move!"

They didn't, but the Reapers at the gate did. Wakefield swung her rifle towards them as they raised their submachine guns, but Brant was quicker. The rope wrapped loosely round his wrists fell away; his blap-gun came out from under his rags and thudded half a dozen times, very fast. The two guards flew back against the gate-bars, then dropped. Hack had drawn a Stemp from under her gear, but already too late to do anything.

Danny shouldered the Lanchester, aiming at the sergeant. "Keys. Slowly."

The sergeant obeyed. "You can't get in through the gate with them."

"I know. You're gonna buzz us through in a sec." Danny tossed the keys to Brant. "Crack open the armoury."

"No," he heard Harp shout, but then a burst of gunfire sounded, deafening in the narrow space. A bullet whipped past him. Danny yelped and ducked.

When he looked up, the sergeant's right eye was a red hole; the boy slammed into the wall and slithered down it, a dazed look on his face, one hand still inside his jacket. The sergeant fell across her desk, then to the floor. Hack blinked, still aiming her Stemp at them. Smoke and sparks spat from inside the cage. The gate control – a stray bullet had fucked it.

Stupid fucking – Danny grabbed her, slammed her against the wall. "Fuck are you doing, you thick c –"

"He was going for a gun," Hack spat back at him. "The boy."

Danny looked. The boy's hand slipped out from under his jacket and opened. Inside was a crushed, broken effigy of mud and twig – to watch over him, keep him safe.

"Danny," said Wakefield.

Shouts and running footsteps sounded from inside the Interrogation Block, and the gate was still locked.

*

INTERROGATION CELL, THE PYRAMID

2001 HOURS

The CenCom Reapers closed in tight around Winterborn, guns raised. "Move out," shouted their CO.

Winterborn glanced at Kellett. "Coming, Doctor?"

Kellett turned back to Shoal, moving closer and breathing deep to savour the stink of the Grendelwolf's rot. "They won't get through," he said. "And I'm not missing this."

Winterborn sighed. "Sometimes, I wish just one person around me was normal."

He nodded to his guards. The cell door slammed, and Kellett was alone with Shoal.

*

OUTSIDE HIGH-SECURITY BLOCK, THE PYRAMID
2006 HOURS

"Brant, Harp, Lish," Danny said, pointing back the way they'd come. "Get a Gimpy, rifles, crate of grenades. Cover our arse. Filly?"

"I know," she said, "the gate." Brant shouldered past with the GPMG, Lish with the rifles; Harp dragged a box of grenades. Filly darted past him and started rummaging.

A knot of Reapers squeezed out of a cell halfway down the block. Danny only glimpsed the man they were clustered round, but only one bloke'd get that much fuss made of him, and 'sides, the Reapers had blue shoulder-flashes: *CenCom*.

"Winterborn!" he shouted: the blond head turned. A white face; blue eyes, narrowed in a frown. *Who are you?* Well, 'course – Winterborn wouldn't know Danny. *But I know you, you cunt.*

And this was all he was? Skinny, pale – but most of all, in killing range. Danny fired through the bars, then dived as the blue-flashed Reapers fired back. Bullets kicked and whined from the walls; Ren fell, clutching his throat. Hack swore and blasted the full clip from her Stemp through the bars at the Reapers.

"Filly!" Wakefield scrabbled across the floor: her girl lay face-down beside the gate. Danny's breath caught; when Filly looked up, grinned and squeezed Wakefield's hand, he breathed out. "Get Winterborn," he yelled.

Still prone, Wakefield poked her rifle through the bars and fired, but the Reapers fired as they fell back, raking everything from floor-level up. Wakefield and Filly rolled clear of the gates, huddled against the walls. Danny fired a couple of bursts after them: one Reaper fell, but that was all.

Fucking hell, if they'd just had Scopes here – she'd have dropped Winterborn without even blinking. But she was gone, like Trex and Thursday, Scary Mary, Mike Ashton, like Nadgers and –

He stopped himself; he'd nearly seen them, all the dead, and now was no time for ghostlighting. "Filly," he shouted, "get to work."

Filly nodded and crawled to the gate. She'd grabbed a block of plastique from the armoury; she wrenched off a chunk and started moulding it into place around the lock.

Danny squinnied through the armoury door; it was a fair-sized room, and a fair chunk of it was taken up with stacked sandbags. "Grab some of those," he said.

"Company!" Brant shouted.

*

CORRIDOR LEADING TO HIGH-SECURITY BLOCK, THE PYRAMID
2010 HOURS

"Move it!" Stone barked. "I've got my eye on you, Water. I even think you're falling back and I'll shoot you myself."

Cunt. Twemlow gripped his Sten as the squad jogged up along the corridor. "Stick close," he heard Ahmad say from the side of his mouth.

"Will do," he muttered back.

They rounded the bend in the corridor, and the guns started firing. Three Reapers went down ahead of them; Ahmad grabbed Twemlow and threw him to the floor. Hit the ground beside him, fired a burst back with the Thompson, scrambled back around the corner. Twemlow scuttled after him.

"Stop fucking hiding," roared Stone, firing a burst round the corner. "Get out there and take them – *fuck*." He ducked back as bullets smashed dust and chipped concrete from the wall inches from his face. "You," he barked, pointing at another Reaper. "Get reinforcements, and an MG. We need more bodies here."

*

INTERROGATION CELL, THE PYRAMID
2012 HOURS

A faint, reedy noise came from Shoal. Was the Grendelwolf crying? Oh, that was sweet; the sound of a breaking soul if ever he'd heard it. Kellett's cock twitched and stirred.

"Dry your eyes, Shoal," he cooed. "Help is at hand. You only need ask."

Shoal looked up, a grin stretched across what was left of his face, and Kellett realised he hadn't been crying at all.

"Oh, Dr Kellett," the Grendelwolf wheezed. "That's the last mistake you'll ever make."

*

OUTSIDE HIGH-SECURITY BLOCK, THE PYRAMID

Danny emptied the Lanchester, and a Reaper fell; he pulled out the spent magazine to reload. Harp's rifle fired five rounds rapid, and then it, too, clicked. "Reloading," Harp shouted. Brant snapped off another burst from his Stemp; Lish pushed past Danny, rifle shouldered, and opened fire. Hack ran to Harp's side, tossing the last of her scav rags aside, and fired a burst from her machine-pistol.

"Sorry," said Filly. "Think I cut the fuse a bit short."

"No fucking shit?"

"Move it, you two," yelled Danny.

Wakefield fired a burst back at the Reapers; Filly grabbed her arm and they both ran through the gate.

*

HIGH-SECURITY BLOCK, THE PYRAMID

Four Reapers remained outside the cells, and as Danny barrelled past the others he saw three of them fall, one after the other. A rifle clattered to the floor, and the last Reaper fell to his knees, hands raised. Fucking hell. What was Danny supposed to do with a prisoner, now? He opened his mouth to speak, but Hack'd already raised her Stemp, aiming. "No," Danny shouted, but it was lost as the Reaper screamed the same thing. And then Hack fired a burst and the Reaper's face exploded. He pitched forward, was still.

"The fuck?" Danny grabbed Hack's arm. "He'd surrendered."

"My brother surrendered too," Hack said. "Didn't save him."

"We're not them," said Danny, then bit down. *Not now; later.* Would Helen have minded what'd just happened? No idea, but he thought Gevaudan would've. Funny, that. "Which fucking cell's he in?"

"Here," called Lish, opening one cell door's hatch. She ducked down as a gunshot sounded, slammed the hatch shut. "Fuck." She tried the door, standing to the side of it. "Locked," she said.

"Filly," said Danny. The girl nodded and knelt in front of the cell door, moulding plastique around the lock.

A bullet punched into the corridor wall – Reapers, coming round the corner, moving in towards the gate. "Harp, Wakers – you keep 'em back. Rest of you with me. Lish, stick close. Gonna need you."

The cell doorways were recessed into the walls – the Raiders huddled into them as the Reapers fired into the interrogation block. A dead Reaper lay beside Danny's position, still holding a Sten gun; Danny knelt and pulled the spare clips from the dead man's belt.

Something flew from the gate, clattered along the floor towards him. Round and black, smoke trailing from it –

"Grenade!" he shouted. It was two feet away; Danny grabbed it, cocked his arm back. How many seconds on the fuse? Three? Five? Then he snapped his arm forward, ducked back into the doorway as it sailed back up the corridor.

A dull thump; the walls shook, and there was a gale of concrete dust. Muzzles flashed through the dust haze; Danny fired back at them. His ears hummed, from the grenade and the guns. He'd be bastard deaf by the time this was –

"Fire in the hole," shouted Filly. Danny heard *that*, thank fuck, and ducked down, hands over his ears. A moment later came the bastard fucking mother of all THUDS: the floor jerked under him, dust rained down and something cracked above. For a sec he thought the ceiling'd come down. And the cell door toppled out into the corridor with a clang, the lock and hinges blown,

Little popping noises – a pistol going off. Filly pointed to the doorway; Danny ran to it as two more shots rang out, followed by a dull clicking.

Empty.

"Let's go," Danny shouted, and swung in through the door.

9.

INTERROGATION CELL, THE PYRAMID
2024 HOURS

Seeing what was inside the cell froze Danny up for a second; if the fucked-up thing with the walking stick's gun had been loaded he'd have been dead. But it was empty, so the stick-man – it *was* a man, just about – cobbed it at his head. Danny ducked, and the spell was broken.

"In!" he shouted. "Wakers, keep those fuckers back."

"On it." Wakefield motioned to Hack and Brant.

Danny advanced, gun aimed at stick-man.

"No!" Stick-man stumbled back into the wall, shrank down. The unfucked side of his face twisted; the one eye looked fit to start skriking. "Don't shoot."

"Cover him," Danny said. "Lish?"

"Here."

Stick-man was a nasty sight, but that wasn't what had frozen Danny. He pointed at what had; naked, red and black nearly all over, hanging in chains with blood, piss and shit pooled under it. A few bits of long black hair hung from its head.

*

Kellett huddled against the wall. Guns aimed at him. *Him.* This couldn't be happening. How had these animals got in? They were feral. Near-beasts. He was sure some of them were tribals. Subhuman. How could they have got in? Even dressed as Reapers, how could the guards here not have seen what they were? Kellett wanted to weep. To die because of these shits, because of the guards' incompetence. It couldn't be happening. Not to him.

The boy in charge came at Kellett, gun aimed. Its black, perforated barrel smoked; the muzzle jabbed towards Kellett's face.

"No!" Kellett hated himself for cringing and screaming, hated *them* even more for seeing it.

The boy jammed the gun's muzzle to Kellett's forehead. It was hot from firing, and Kellett hissed in pain. "Keys," said the boy, jerking his head towards Shoal. "Fucking now."

"Yes. Yes." Kellett fumbled in his pockets. Something dug into his forearm. It was the sheath he'd strapped to it. After Ashwood, he went nowhere without weapons. His pistol was already gone, but he still had the knife. Not much, but something.

He pulled out the keys; the boy snatched them. "Watch him, Filly," he told a black girl, who aimed a machine pistol at Kellett. The boy ran to Shoal. A red-headed girl held a vial to the Grendelwolf's lips, a vial of luminous green liquid.

"No," shouted Kellett. The black girl raised her machine pistol. *Fuck you, you nigger bitch.*

"Shut the fuck up." The boy raised his gun, lowered it again, then set about unlocking Shoal's restraints. He took hold of a forearm to steady it; Shoal moaned and the boy recoiled with a disgusted cry; blood and strands of tissue hung from his hand. He wiped it on his uniform, glared at Kellett. "He dies," he said, "I'll gut you myself."

No you won't. Kellett pressed back against the wall; his fingers probed his shirt-cuff, seeking the catch that released the knife. *I have a weapon you don't know about, and when I use it, you'll see. You'll see.*

*

HIGH-SECURITY BLOCK CORRIDOR, THE PYRAMID

2026 HOURS

Wakefield ducked as a bullet hit concrete above her head, fired back. Thought she heard someone scream.

Half a clip left. After that she'd only have her pistols and her tribe-weapons.

Tight. But Ashwood had been worse. Wakefield grinned, aimed through the dust and smoke and fired again.

*

INTERROGATION CELL, THE PYRAMID

2029 HOURS

Gevaudan was dying, or so he assumed. It no longer burned when he breathed, and the he could no longer his skin splitting. That only made sense if he was losing all feeling as the last of him rotted away.

At least he hadn't betrayed Helen. He'd come close; if the pain had persisted, the pain and Kellett's endless taunting voice, he wouldn't have endured.

A taste in his mouth; he coughed and spat, but it wasn't blood. This taste was different. Familiar. Then he realised parts of his skin were pain-free, but not numb: in fact, he could feel the air brush against it, and it didn't hurt.

"Hey."

A voice he knew, but didn't hate. Not Kellett then, nor Winterborn. His shoulders weren't hurting either: no strain on their joints. He wasn't held upright any longer, but sitting on stone or concrete, propped against a wall. There was still pain, but it was fading.

"Oi. Creeping Death."

Danny?

Gevaudan opened his eyes. Faces. He recognised some. Red-headed Lish, and Harp, too. And Danny. Danny was there. Trying to smile, but his face...

Gevaudan looked down at himself. Big patches of white skin had regrown, but other parts were still raw and wet, and in some places he saw exposed bone. His hands and feet were lumpen, misshaped: pink swellings marked where missing toes and fingers had begun growing back.

Danny was trying to hide the disgust on his face. Gevaudan licked his lips: the familiar taste was the Goliath serum, he realised. They'd come for him. Of course they had.

They hadn't let him down, but would have let *them* down. He'd so nearly betrayed them.

Was he going to weep? Gevaudan didn't know, but he couldn't bear the horror and pity on Danny's face any longer. He covered his face with his hands.

*

Kellett watched the nigger bitch. A fucking half-ape savage with a machine pistol – well, even *they* could learn to use a gun. Monkey see, monkey do. But the others were busy either with the Reapers or the Grendelwolf. What was left of him. Kellett would smile about that no matter what came next, because he'd stripped everything from the bastard once again; another minute and the cunt would have been grovelling, begging for his serum. Kellett would hold onto that. *He was going to break. He knows it, I know it, and he knows I know. It's a cancer in him, a slow wound: bleeding out, turning septic. It'll kill him in the end, whatever happens to me.*

But Kellett knew what would happen to him: he was going to live, and to get out of this cell. One man with a knife, crippled or not, mightn't have a chance against a bunch of thugs with guns, but those weren't the odds now. The only one watching him now, the one he had to deal with, was the nigger bitch. He could out-think her kind any day of the week.

His fingers found the release catch, and the knife slid from its sheath. Kellett's fingers were moist with sweat, and for a horrible moment he thought it would slip and clatter on the floor. But no: he had hold of it. In an instant he could have the knife in hand and ready to use. But not yet: the nigger bitch was still watching.

Guns crashed outside; the sharp-faced little tribal ducked back inside the cell, fired her machine pistol around the door. In the cell's corner, Shoal moaned. The red-headed girl tugged at the blanket on the cot-bed, trying to pull it free.

Sweat stung the corner of Kellett's eye. The nigger bitch still had her gun on him. *Look away just for a second. That's all I'll need.* But it had to be soon, while the others were still occupied, or he'd have no chance. And before they could move out, because they'd kill him before they left.

Shoal groaned again, and the nigger bitch looked round. *There.* Kellett flexed his fingers; the knife slid from his sleeve. When he shifted his grip, there was a moment of fright where he thought he'd drop it, but then he was gripping the hilt.

Kellett lunged forward, punting himself at the nigger bitch with his cane. She turned back, lifting the machine pistol, and he struck at her as if throwing a punch. *Aim for the heart.* The impact went up his arm; the nigger bitch's face slackened. Kellett left the knife in her as she started falling, grabbing the machine pistol and throwing himself at the redhead.

He cannoned into her and they almost fell across the bed. *No! Keep your balance!* He clamped his stick-wielding arm across her throat and pulled her back against him, shoving the machine pistol to her head. "Still," he said.

"Fuck!" The boy swung round, gun shouldered.

"Filly!" The tribal bitch started towards the nigger bitch.

"None of you move," said Kellett. "I'll blow her fucking brains out. Lower your guns." He dug the gun into the redhead's temple; she gasped. *Pathetic little bitch. You don't know pain, not like mine.* "Do it."

The boy lowered his weapon. "Do it." The tribal bitch didn't lower hers; her hands shook and her eyes were wet. She kept looking from him to the nigger bitch in her pool of blood. Kellett knew that look. *A dyke, too?* He hadn't thought the tribals that evolved, but this one must be, at least. An added bonus, that; a little bit of unlooked-for pleasure.

His bad leg hurt. "Don't try anything," he told the redhead. He dragged her backwards, till he was up against the wall. That eased the discomfort, a bit.

"Now," he said, "you're going to put out a white flag. Don't worry, you aren't surrendering. You can have your heroes' deaths if you want. But first, you and those Reapers are going to have a little ceasefire. Just long enough for me to get out."

*

Gevaudan was ravenously hungry, but the pain was nearly gone. He took his hands from his face; the rest of the cell swam into focus:

Danny and the others were still; Kellett had an arm across Lish's throat, a Stemp to her head, while Filly lay unmoving on the floor in a pool of red; from the doorway, Wakefield stared down at her, nearly crying.

"The white flag," Kellett said, inching across the cell with Lish. "Now. And get that tribal bitch out of my way."

Filly, Wakefield; two more lives Kellett had stained and marked. Kellett was a blight, corrupting all he touched. And next it would be Lish – he'd kill her as soon as he got away.

Gevaudan looked down at himself; most of his skin was healed. One finger hadn't quite fully regrown, but otherwise his hands were nearly back to normal.

The serum had worked quickly. But the damage done had been vast; he still felt weak. But he was still a Grendelwolf. Gevaudan only needed a little strength; a few seconds worth, a minute's at the most.

He drew his knees towards his chest, braced his feet on the floor and pressed his palms against the wall behind him.

He could leap at Kellett, but for this to work he'd have to be fast. Dare he try to use the Fury yet? He had to; he owed them the attempt at the very least.

Kellett edged towards the door. "Move," he told Wakefield. In a moment, he'd be away. It had to be now.

Gevaudan pushed down with his feet and hands; it threw him upright, drove him forward, but even as he summoned the Fury he knew it was too much, too soon.

Kellett, Lish held in front of him, the gun at her head, the hand on the gun.

Gevaudan's heart hammered, shaking his body, and he couldn't breathe, but it didn't matter. He needed only seconds.

The claws slid from Gevaudan's fingers. Kellett half-turned; his half-mouth opened, finger whitening on the trigger. *Lish –*

Gevaudan's arm swung up and over, a blur of motion.

Kellett's trigger finger tightened, whitened; the trigger was about to give, the gun about to fire.

Gevaudan's claws hit Kellett's forearm and sheared through flesh. For the briefest split-second he felt them snag on bone, then shatter it.

Kellett's good hand separated from the forearm, just behind the wrist joint. It spun through the air; the Stemp fired into the ceiling. Dust; a ricochet whined.

Gevaudan grabbed Lish, flung her aside. Out of his way; just Kellett and him.

His heart thumped so hard his whole body shook. Weak; short of breath; sick. Vision narrowing: red haze, dark spots.

Soon he'd be unconscious, or even dead. One thought: *finish this*.

Kellett's half-mouth stretched open in a scream. *No more*, thought Gevaudan. *No more of you.*

Gevaudan's claws seized Kellett; gripped, tore.

Screaming.

Blood on Gevaudan's hands, his face.

Rip the bastard apart.

And then, beyond Kellett, he saw Jo. Only for a moment, only a flicker of her. Ghostlighting, maybe for the last time. Watching him, with sorrow in her eyes

Was this how his life was to end: revelling in another's death and pain, even Kellett's?

Kellett: everything about Kellett was a taint. Gevaudan flung Kellett away from him; the ruined body hit into the wall and then the floor, tangled and bloody. Twitched once; was still.

Gevaudan's heart hammered and skipped; he couldn't breathe. *Helen. Jo. Danny.*

His legs gave way; he fell to his knees.

Too much, he thought again. *Too much, too soon.*

A shout; people ran towards him.

And then he pitched forward, and there was only darkness.

*

Wakefield jumped over the Grendelwolf; he didn't matter now. Only Filly mattered – Filly, lying still in her own blood.

She mustn't cry – not here, not now, in front of the others. But to love and then to lose it, have it torn away, the pain of it was like nothing she'd known before. At Ashwood, she'd thought Filly dead in the fighting at one point – but that had been before the first kiss, the first night together, before all the rest. And now Filly lay stabbed and still in her own blood, dead –

Filly groaned as Wakefield knelt by her. She twisted, rolled over and clutched her wound. Wakefield's first cry had no shape, meant nothing but shock, relief and joy. The second was a name: "Lish!"

Lish ran to them – wide-eyed and shaking, but ready. "Sit her up," she said.

Behind them, Danny knelt beside Gevaudan.

*

For a sec Danny thought the big fucker had carked it; be fucking brilliant, that, after all this. But the Grendelwolf was still breathing. "Lish!"

"One sec." The medic secured a dressing to Filly's chest. "Should be okay," she said. "Blade turned on your rib. He was going for your heart, by the look, but he missed that, and your lung. Didn't hit anything vital." She grinned. "You were lucky."

"Twat wouldn't have stabbed me if I had been," Filly grunted. Wakefield helped her up.

"We going or what?" Brant shouted from the doorway, firing a rifle he'd pirated from a dead Reaper up the corridor.

"In a sec," yelled Danny. "Lish!"

Lish crabbed over to Gevaudan, touched the Grendelwolf's throat. "He's breathing," she said. "and his pulse is regular. He'll make it. Just needs rest and food."

"He won't get either here," Filly said. "So, we going or what?"

"Yeah." Danny pulled the blanket from the cot-bed. "Harp, giz a hand."

Danny and Harp helped Gevaudan stand, the blanket round his shoulders. "We head out the back way," Danny said. "Lish, Wakers, you cover us. Filly – think you can leave the cunts a prezzie or two?"

She gave a taut, painful grin. "I'll need a bit of help, but yeah."

Danny and Harp dragged Gevaudan out into the corridor, keeping low as bullets chipped the walls. Danny unzipped his jacket, reaching for the flare pistol.

*

OUTSIDE HIGH-SECURITY BLOCK
2042 HOURS

"They're falling back!" Stone shouted. "After them!"

Twemlow ran after the others, head down and wanting to be somewhere else. He'd been under fire precisely once, on a convoy on the Devil's Highway, and that'd been enough – he was in no rush to be at the front of the charge. Stone knew that, of course; that was why he liked to make Twemlow's life hell. Even though Twemlow was pretty sure that for all his preening, the only action Stone had seen was against hungry, stone-throwing scavs, probably from a couple hundred feet away, holding a rifle.

Two Reapers went down in the rebels' covering fire as they retreated, but then the corridor was clear. "Check the cell," Stone shouted. Tremlow dropped to one knee, aimed down the corridor to where the rebels had gone, in case they came back. That's what he'd tell Stone, anyway.

"Clear," shouted Stone, and kicked Twemlow in the thigh. "On your feet, Water. Move your arse."

Ahmad clapped Twemlow on the shoulder he drew level. Stone smirked and blew them both a kiss. "Get after them," he said, then motioned to a couple of Reapers. "Check the cell."

The Reapers went into the cell, through the shattered doorway. Stone followed.

"Wait," Ahmad shouted, then "Fuck!" He body-slammed Twemlow, sending them both to the ground for the second time that day. There was a bang and thud, and the floor jerked under Twemlow like a pulled rug; smoke and dust blew out the doorway and something hit the far wall with wet slaps before dropping to the floor in a black and red heap. It was still moving, for a few seconds at least: after a moment, Twemlow realised it was Stone. Or at least his top half.

In the cell, the bomb'd left scorch-marks and wreckage. There was blood on the floor, and a reeking stain beneath the chains hanging from the ceiling. And in one corner, in a red pool under a wet red mark on the wall, was a smashed-up thing that'd been a man.

"Let's get after them," Ahmad said. "Come on."

Twemlow turned to follow, teeth gritted, then stopped. He could barely hear it for the humming in his ears and the shooting still going on nearby, but it was there: a faint, agonised whimpering, from inside the cell. He turned and looked around, and realised that the mangled thing in the corner was still – just about – alive.

*

STOCKPORT COUNTY FC GROUNDS
2102 HOURS

The old football pitch was wild with brambles and fruit trees, planted over the years since the War, but the grounds were deserted. People came from time to time to scavenge, but no-one stayed. A match had been in progress here on the day of the War; most of the players and spectators had died here too. The place felt haunted.

But the club building was large and spacious on the inside: perfect place to stow their landcruisers and heavy gear. Rats in the walls, pigeons in the rafters, but the roof was still in one piece, and from it Flaps and her team had a pretty good view of the town: easy to spot Reapers coming, and most of all to watch the Pyramid.

Peepo lay prone on the rooftop with a pair of binocs. She was stocky – bit porky, even, which took some doing – round-faced, toothy, smiled a lot. Cos of that, Flaps never really trusted her – who the fuck smiled that much? – but she had the best eyes in the crew.

The others cleaned their guns, smoked, chilled out however they could. That'd been the first fight for of them, and soon they'd be in their second. Half-wanting it, half shitting it at the thought. Flaps knew how it was.

She paced, stopping when she reached Jukk huddled against a cowling. He was puffing on a Monarch; half a dozen others lay stubbed out beside him.

"You right?"

Jukk nodded, but he was shaking, pale. Flaps knuckled his shoulder. "First one's worst," she said. "Gets easier as you –"

"Flare!" shouted Peepo. Above the Pyramid, a point of red light fell earthward. Another shot up a couple of seconds later; from behind the building. "They're round the back," said Peepo.

"Fucking great." Flaps turned. "Tool up," she said. "Let's skate."

*

LOADING BAY, REAR OF THE PYRAMID
2113 HOURS

Danny sighted down the Lanchester, nailed a Reaper running towards their position with a grenade. The Reapers coming up behind the one he'd dropped scattered, and Danny ducked as the grenade blew. Two more Reapers ran in from the other side and he fired three short bursts at them, winging one. He'd have got the other Reaper, but the gun emptied.

"Fucking shite." He pulled out the clip, slapped a new one into place. One left, stuck through his belt.

Harp threw the GPMG aside. "Empty," he said. Lish, kneeling beside Gevaudan, threw him a Sten; he cocked it and aimed it back inside the building.

"Last mag," shouted Brant. He'd lost his rifle, and was pulling back the bolt on a Sterling.

They'd fought their way through to the Pyramid's rear exit, but the soldiers in their watchtowers and on either side of the yard had them pinned down in the recessed entryway. Between that and holding off the ones inside the building trying to follow them out, they were already running low again.

One good thing: the gates were still open. The Reapers hadn't had the chance to close them after Winterborn had got clear. Danny and his crew couldn't get to them and escape, but the Reapers couldn't get near enough to shut them either. Pity they hadn't got here a minute earlier – if nowt else they might have had a crack at Winterborn – but all they'd seen was the landcruisers skidding off. If Scopes'd been there, that'd probably have been enough; she could have slotted the twat, no trouble. But Scopes was gone.

Anyway, Winterborn'd never been the main job; the main job was huddled behind Danny, shivering under a blanket. Though fuck knew what chance they had of getting him out now.

A Reaper edged towards the gates; Danny fired a burst. Stone chips exploded from the edge of the recess as the machine gun in the nearest watchtower fired in response. Danny ducked back; Wakefield – the only one left who still had bullets in her rifle – tried to aim at the tower, but recoiled with a yell, clutching her eyes. Hack poked her SMG round the corner and fired a burst up at it, then ducked back from another hail of fire.

"Lish –" Danny shouted.

Wakefield waved him back. Her eyes were red and streaming, and tiny beads of blood flecked her cheeks and forehead, but otherwise she wasn't hurt. "Just dust."

Gold light and long shadows; a blood-coloured sky. Air that stank of smoke and dust and frightened sweat. The gunfire a muffled thunder beneath the whining in their ears from firing in the narrow concrete space. Throats raw from screaming at one another because they were all half-deaf.

Come on Flaps, get your arse in gear.

Wakefield's lips were moving; even without being able to hear, Danny could tell what she was saying. *Fox's Spirit, run with us. If we die, carry our souls.*

He could hear something else, just about: sirens, wailing. Through the spraying dust and stone chips, Danny saw the Reapers at the gates, pushing them shut. But beyond them, there was movement: landcruisers, arrowing in towards the gate.

"Thank fuck," said Harp, but then the 'cruisers' guns fired and the top of the entrance exploded into fragments.

"Jesus fucking Christ," yelled Lish, "you are shitting me. You are fucking shitting me."

But the guards were pulling the gates open again, and the landcruisers rolled towards them, Danny saw a small figure in a Reaper uniform behind the .50 cal in the lead 'cruiser, spraying the rebels' position.

Something wasn't right, though, Danny realised as the first landcruiser came through the gate. One thing'd kept them alive: the Reapers couldn't aim directly into the recess. But the 'cruisers were coming straight at them – she'd wanted to, the gunner could've blown them all to chunks. She was aiming high on purpose.

Hack's rifle came up, aiming at the small machine-gunner, but Danny knocked the barrel down. "Wait," he shouted.

The landcruisers' .50 cals swung away from the recess, towards the Reapers. Something shrieked through the air: a flash, a thunderclap, and the top of the watchtower was gone.

The lead landcruiser swerved to a halt, broadside-on to the loading bay. The gunner pulled her cap off, and Flaps' red hair caught the light. "Get your fucking arse in, you lazy cunt."

"Love you too," muttered Danny. "Move it!" He jumped into the flatbed; Brant helped Lish bundle Gevaudan into the back with him. Another rocket shrieked in and exploded; the other landcruisers were raking the yard in both directions.

Another landcruiser pulled in; Wakefield helped Filly aboard. Hack dived in after them. Only Harp remained, firing his Sten down the corridor.

Flaps swung the .50 cal back towards the loading bay. "All aboard," she shouted; Harp took one look at the machine gun's smoking barrel and bolted into the second 'cruiser.

A second later, three Reapers came through the door; Flaps fired, and they vanished in a red and grey haze. Pieces of them flew out. Flaps aimed down the corridor and fired a long burst. "Let's go," she shouted.

The landcruiser pulled out and turned, surging for the gate; the second 'cruiser followed. More rockets shrieked in – two, three of them. The landcruisers juddered as the rockets hit the Pyramid; then they were through out the gates, sirens wailing behind them.

*

HEATON LANE, STOCKPORT
2122 HOURS

The 'cruiser swung side to side, zigzagging on the potholed road.

Wakefield cradled Filly, stroking her forehead. Peepo worked the .50 cal, firing back down the road; there were Reaper 'cruisers after them already.

"I'm okay," said Filly. "Don't fuss, love."

Love; Wakefield's eyes prickled. To fight, hunt, run and hide, kill Reapers – she knew those things, but to be called that? Much less to *be* loved? She felt like a newborn in this, falling on her arse whenever she tried walking. But long as Filly was there, she'd learn.

The Reaper 'cruisers wove back and forth across the road. Guns flashed; Peepo cried out and fell back into the flatbed, clutching her arm. The .50 cal's barrel swung about, unmoored; Wakefield got up and grabbed the handles as more shots whipped past. She aimed at the nearest Reaper 'cruiser's cab, squeezed off a burst. Glass shattered; the 'cruiser slewed sideways across the street and into a wall.

Wakefield fell on her rear as the landcruiser hit a roundabout and tore around it. She scrambled back to her feet, looked at Peepo; the other woman was pulling a dressing tight around her arm with her teeth. "I'm okay," said Peepo. "You deal with them."

Wakefield hunched low behind the gun, and aimed again.

*

Heaton Lane/Stockport Viaduct
2127 hours

The landcruiser jerked and bounced on the road; the surface had gone even rougher than usual. Huddled under his blanket, Gevaudan groaned; Danny ducked as bullets spanged off the bodywork. "How far now?"

Flaps pointed. "We're there."

Danny looked ahead; a long, high bridge of brickwork spanned across the road, and beyond that, the river. "Stockport Viaduct," Flaps said.

Water gleamed. Danny looked back; behind them, half a dozen Reaper landcruisers were gaining. "They're right on top of us."

"Course they are." Flaps put her radio handset to her lips. "Ready."

Ragged shapes moved up on the viaduct. Rifles and submachine guns glinted.

"Set," said Flaps, as the first Reaper cruiser came down the road; Danny saw flames bloom in the dark, dozens of tiny points. "Wait for it," Flaps said. "*Wait.*"

Danny looked at her; she was gripped the handset so tight the casing creaked.

The last of the Reaper 'cruisers rolled onto the viaduct; Flaps pushed the transmit button down and said "Go."

The points of flame leapt up and over, towards the Reaper 'cruisers. Burning rags stuffed into clay jars; sheets of fire flew up, fell on the Reapers and clung on. There were screams and gunfire, muzzle flashes.

"Stop here!" Flaps yelled. Their 'cruiser slewed to a halt in the middle of the viaduct; the others braked behind them. "Everybody out!"

Brant and Lish dragged Gevaudan from the flatbed as the others bailed out. Hands caught the Grendelwolf, helped lift him clear. More crew-folk came out of the viaduct's shadows and jumped into the landcruiser. Flaps pointed to rope ladders hanging down the side of the viaduct. "Up here."

They tied a rope around Gevaudan's waist; the crewfolk on the viaduct winched him up.

"This way." Flaps ran along the viaduct, till they were out over the river, then snatched a rope-coil up from the clinkered ground and tossed the bundle over the parapet; it unravelled down the viaduct's side, stopped and swung just above the river. Danny saw it was lashed to a heavy spike driven into the brickwork. Crew-folk threw two other ropes over, and lashed a fourth around Gevaudan's waist.

Flaps and Danny stood over the Grendelwolf. He looked gaunt and shrunken, and when he blinked up at them, Danny saw he looked fucking wretched, too. Reaper bastards.

The Grendelwolf looked away, staring down at the ground. Flaps knelt, took a long white hand in hers and squeezed, then breathed out. "Get him lowered."

"More Reapers coming!" someone shouted.

"Move it, then." Flaps climbed over the parapet.

Danny looked over the side. "Oh, fuck me."

"Bit busy right now," Flaps said.

Lish climbed over the side, looking even paler than usual. Hack practically jumped over, like it was nothing. Danny had to look to make sure she hadn't gone and banzai'd herself, but no, there she was, clinging to the rope and shuttling down it, fast as fuck. Brant took a deep breath and followed.

Down on the road, the Reaper landcruisers were burning; a second group had come up as the last screams and shots faded. The rebel landcruisers rolled on up Heaton Lane with their new crews. The second Reaper group was trying to get around the remains of the first to go after them. Out across the city, sirens wailed. Danny spat on his hands and climbed after Lish, doing his best not to look down.

He climbed most of the way with his eyes shut. The rope swung and knocked against the brickwork, and Danny muffled more than one yelp as his knuckles got banged and skinned. But he held on, and finally his feet were on solid ground.

"Move it," said Flaps; her crew were pulling coracles out from under one of the arches. "Everybody in." She nodded to the water.

The river rushed and rattled, streaked white with foam. "Fucking seriously?" Danny said.

"Got a better plan?"

They dragged the last coracle to the water together; Danny got in beside Flaps. She looked at him for a second as she pushed the coracle clear of the bank with a paddle. "Hang on," she said. "Gonna get bumpy."

Flaps warded their boat clear of the rocks; as they went on, the going got easier. Her knees pressed against Danny's, and they both did their best to pretend nothing was happening. In a coracle ahead of them, Gevaudan shivered under his stained blanket. Danny realised he was shaking too. So was Flaps; he could hear her teeth chatter as they went.

Behind them, the viaduct shrank away; the flames from burning landcruisers reached up into the black sky. Someone had set light to the ropes, which blazed and fell apart as he watched; they must've been treated with something that'd burn fast. Flaps glanced at Danny. "Good job," she said at last.

"Thanks."

"Glad you're okay."

She looked away from him, keeping her eyes on the river. Danny couldn't be sure in that light, but thought she might have gone red. He didn't say owt about it; on a fast river in a small boat, Flaps might might do to him what the Reapers hadn't.

10.

THE BAILEY, MANCHESTER
4TH JULY, ATTACK PLUS TWENTY-ONE YEARS
2203 HOURS

A grey concrete room, blood and shit soaked into the floor. A chair: tied to it, the scarred boy from Northern Moor, stripped naked. Bloody and bruised; burned and cut. Weeping. Broken.

Sergeant Korth released the boy's head, let him slump forward. Lewis wiped the knife and returned it to the table. Its job was done: he didn't need it any more. He lit a Monarch, listening to the sobs subside. "Cigarette, Korth?"

"Thank you, sir." Korth took one. She was a short, lean black woman, with a shaved head. When Lewis gave her a light, the flame glinted on her smooth scalp.

"Anything else you want to share?"

In the chair, the scarred boy shook his head. Tears and blood; a smell of piss. "Told you everything. Swear. Please."

Behind him, Korth raised her eyebrows, reaching for the garrotte at her belt. Lewis gave a small, fast head-shake. Not yet, not quite yet. "One more thing." He moved in close. "This grey-haired man," he said. *Roger Darrow.* "Which way was he going?"

*

Winterborn's Office, The Tower
2212 hours

Winterborn felt dizzy; the room spun around him and it took all his self-control not to fling the intercom, the music box or both across the office. "Find them," he said at last. "Whatever it takes." But Shoal was gone; barring a miracle, there'd be no retrieving him. He shut the intercom off and gripped the edge of his desk.

Sweat prickled on Winterborn's forehead. Breathing fast. Losing control. Of his breathing, his Command, even of his life. He scrabbled for the leather bag in his desk drawer, put it to his lips and breathed. In, then out, slow and steady. After a few breaths, he fumbled across the desk for the music box, listening to it play. That helped. Better; not much, but a little.

A knock on his office door; Winterborn jerked upright in his chair. "Who is it?"

"Just me, Commander."

"Mordake." Winterborn tucked the bag away, shut the music box lid. "Come in."

Mordake entered, sat slowly down. "I came as soon as I heard."

"My most secure prison." Winterborn's teeth chattered; he clenched them tight. "And they got in. Just like at the Bailey. And they took my prisoner." He kept his voice level; he wouldn't whine like a spoilt child. He was more than that. Stronger. "No matter my defences, they always find a way through."

"They've won one round, Commander," Mordake said, "nothing more. We play a longer game, you and I. *There are many events in the womb of time, which will be delivered*' – if you remember your Shakespeare."

"Very apt, Doctor," said Winterborn, "but I prefer to make the classical allusions around here."

"Apologies. Should we reschedule your video-call?"

"Absolutely not." Winterborn returned the music box to his drawer, but kept his hand on it. "See to it."

Mordake opened the office door; Cadigan slipped in. Winterborn tried to decide which of them she seemed more afraid of, and decided that it was still him. He turned in his chair, studying the city below. The distant Pennines were faint low humps in the summer haze.

Cadigan coughed. "Ready, Commander."

"Good." Winterborn swivelled back into place. The screen came on, and Commander Probert blinked out at him. "Testing," he said.

"You're coming through loud and clear, Stephen." Probert looked nervous; Winterborn gave what he hoped was a reassuring smile. "Are you receiving me?"

"Yes."

"Good." Winterborn waved Cadigan away; Mordake sat in his chair in the corner, out of shot. "So, to business. Thoughts on my proposal?"

"Certainly tempting," Probert admitted.

"Commander McMahon's already made bilateral arrangements with RCZ7. He knows I want to extend the same terms – on behalf of both our Commands – to you, and he's wholly in favour. My Jennywrens have extensive counter-insurgency experience."

"You've any left, after Ashwood?"

Winterborn's mouth twitched. *Careful*. For now he had to keep a friendly face; after Unification, things would be different. "I have enough," he said. "We had a recruitment drive ongoing since the December Rising. Many of our new recruits received direct combat experience at Ashwood."

"Of defeat."

"Lessons have been learned. The rebel virus has mutated and evolved. To defeat them, we have to do the same. As a single entity, we can isolate them, cut them off... finish them."

Probert sighed. "I'm sorry, Tereus." Winterborn gripped the music box. *Is he to refuse me?*

"I didn't mean to cast aspersions on your men," said Probert. "God knows I need all the help I can get, and your proposal's very attractive. And I agree, Unification's the way forward. It's the other Commands I'm concerned about."

"Indeed?" Probert was sharper than Winterborn had thought.

"Some of them are more worried about other Commanders than the rebels. You in particular. Fucking retarded, obviously. They look at you and they don't see the future, or a final end to the rebellion. They see a threat."

"Yes," said Winterborn. "I'm afraid so." *Rightly, of course.*

"Me, I don't give a shit – I've enough on my plate with Wales. But we need someone in overall command, and you've shown you've the brains and skills. But it's too much too fast for others – McLeod, for instance."

"I know," sighed Winterborn. "She believes in checks and balances. A balance of power and resources between the Commands. To her, agreements like this create factions within the Command, and threaten that stability."

"Exactly." Probert's forehead glistened with sweat; Winterborn felt a twinge of distaste. "She's resisted Johnstone's Caledonian Alliance plan for the same reason."

"I should tell you I'm approaching Johnstone, too. I know he's eager for such an alliance, so I've already drafted a treaty between our putative accord and his." Winterborn smiled. "Effectively, another bilateral agreement."

Probert smiled back. "Leaving McLeod out in the cold, unless she ditches her blessed scruples."

"Precisely."

"Right." Probert nodded. "So get the treaty to me for signing and sort the deal with the Jocks. Soon as I hear they've agreed, I'm with you."

"I've set things in motion." Winterborn stroked the music box. "I should have news for you very soon."

"I'll look forward to it, Tereus. And to crushing those rebels once and for all."

"Now that I'll drink to."

"I'll be sure to lay on a bottle of something good, next time we meet."

"I'll look forward to that." Beyond a token sip for form's sake, Winterborn wouldn't touch the stuff; alcohol and its loss of control disgusted him. But like Mordake's odd rituals, one had to say the right things, make the right gestures, to get the desired result.

*

The War Room, Ashwood Fort
2322 hours

A cigarette-smoke haze filled the room and made Helen's head ache; she wafted a signal flimsy in front of her face, but it didn't help.

Alannah sat, arms folded, staring down at the charts. If she actually saw anything, Helen couldn't tell. Nothing to do but wait. The others sat and stared as well – Jazz and Loncraine, Stewart and Thorn, Malik. Still no-one spoke; nothing left to say or do.

Footsteps; the War Room door opened. "Signal from Falcon," said Hei. "Mission accomplished."

Helen was fairly certain that everyone around the table breathed out in unison. "Casualties?" said Alannah at last.

"Some," said Hei. "But Colonel Morwyn's uninjured."

Colonel. Helen still couldn't square that with the puppy-eyed boy she'd met by the Irk last winter. But seven months could be a long time.

"Thank you." Alannah's voice was small and choked.

"Thanks, Hei," Helen said. "Oh, and could you leave the door open?"

As soon as Hei had gone the silence broke. Stewart whooped; Jazz laughed. "Thank God," said Malik, while Loncraine only smiled. Thorn touched Alannah's arm, and quietly said "Glad to hear it."

Gevaudan, *and* Danny, out alive. Helen looked at Alannah; the other woman smiled, but it quivered at the edges and her eyes brimmed. Helen went and hugged her; Alannah hugged back briefly, then the moment broke and they stepped apart.

*

INTELLIGENCE CENTRE, ASHWOOD FORT

"Ma'am?"

Alannah looked up; the thin, white-faced girl with the limp blonde hair – what the hell was she called? – held out some rumpled notes, grimy with nervous sweat. "Got those bearings, ma'am." *Ma'am?* Where the hell had she picked that up? "One from Sparrow Station Two, one from Eight."

"Okay." Alannah took the notes from her. The girl's wide eyes were half-hopeful, half-afraid; wanting to hear she'd done okay. Alannah remembered her name, just in time. "Thanks, Stock." Despite the sweat-stains, the notes were neat and easy to read; thorough, too, and precise. "Good work," Alannah said. "That'll be all, Stock. You can call it a day now." The girl had been on since nine o'clock; she'd earned some bloody rest.

Stock nodded. "Yes, ma'am." She limped away with as much of a spring in her step as her condition and exhaustion allowed. Alannah smiled, too; it faded, though, as she remembered Danny:

still in the city, far from home. *Work; make it go away with work.* She studied the notes again.

*

THORNLEA COURT
BAGULEY, MANCHESTER

6TH JULY, ATTACK PLUS TWENTY-ONE YEARS
0400 HOURS

The low-rise blocks seemed deserted, but Darrow kept low and to the shadows, free hand on the Thompson's cocking handle. Wings clapped, then huffed softly at the air; a pigeon rose from an empty window and across a courtyard strewn with cinders and ashes, remnants of bone.

Desolate; empty. There was no-one here; what Darrow was looking for certainly wasn't. The question was whether it ever *had* been.

Darrow crossed the courtyard and pushed aside the rusted tin covering a doorway. He flicked on his clockwork torch, steadying the submachine gun's barrel with it as he climbed the stairs.

The floors were empty and silent. When he reached the third floor, Darrow crept along the rotten carpet and sagging floorboards till he reached the door marked 14 and crouched there, listening.

From inside came a faint scuttle. He prodded the door ajar with the gun barrel, and heard tiny paws scurry away. Darrow half-smiled, then pushed the door wide, before stepping sideways, out of any potential line of fire. But there was only silence.

He stepped through the door, sweeping the room with the Thompson. Bare boards; bullet-flecked, soot-marked walls. Empty cans and dried faeces in one corner; window-frames with jagged broken glass and cobwebs of rotten tattered curtain.

Slowly, Darrow paced the room, going from one corner to the next. As he went he studied the walls from top to bottom, searching for marks, but the only ones he saw were those left by bullet and fire, animals and decay.

Until:

Darrow's breath caught. His arms and legs shook; he almost dropped the Thompson. Wincing as his joints creaked, he crouched, then reached out and touched the wall.

The marks looked to have been scorched into the wood: a heated blade, perhaps. A smiling face; below it, a dozen dots in rows of three. He leant closer, studied the face; the eyes were circles, each with a tiny mark at the centre. In the left eye, a 1. In the right, an 8.

Eighteen.

Darrow stood, wincing; a sound rang across the courtyard, through the shattered window. He turned, crouching, and inched to the window, but saw nothing other than dead, sodden ashes and the flats' lifeless emptiness.

Darrow breathed out and retreated to the door. She was alive, or had been. And so had the others, all twelve of them. And now he had a place to look for: *Eighteen.*

*

Flaps moved further back through the doorway, burrowing further into the shadows. She glanced down this time, though, to check she wasn't about to tread on any more more pigeon bones. Something in her pocket dug into her hip; she winced and gritted her teeth.

Darrow came out of the building, walked straight past her hiding place. Head down, tired-faced – weighed down, but by what? He was old, but he was still good; he should have been ready for something when he passed her doorway at least, but she could've dropped him in two seconds if she'd wanted.

Flaps peered out, watched him go. *What's he hiding? Who?*

She fumbled in her pocket for the object that'd dug into her, took it out: the pebble from Gevaudan's cairn. Bollocks. She'd forgotten to give it him before he left. Flaps shrugged to herself. There'd be another time.

She put the stone back in her pocket; then, when she was sure Darrow had gone, she padded towards the building. She'd seen his face at the window; she knew where he'd been.

*

After Flaps had gone, a silhouette broke the line of the apartments' flat roofs.

Reaper Harris stood, stretched aching muscles. Then she knelt and packed her camera away. Her jaw was clenched; the old man had kept moving at the wrong moment. Most of the pictures would only show the back of his head, or a blur. But she'd keep watching, keep following. Sooner or later, he'd slip, and she'd have what she needed. She lay back down, reached under the rags she wore as a disguise, and took out her radio.

*

INTELLIGENCE CENTRE, ASHWOOD FORT
0902 HOURS

Alannah laid the ruler on the map, drew a grease-pencil line from Ashwood across the paper. Then she moved her protractor to Sparrow Station Eight, marked off the bearing and drew another line, then leant forward to study its intersection with the first.

"Jesus." Alannah breathed out. "Jesus Christ."

*

WINTERBORN'S OFFICE, THE TOWER
1003 HOURS

"So," said Winterborn. "Let's lay our cards on the table, Carole."

McLeod scowled, arms folded. "I think you know where I stand, *Tereus*."

A calculated insult; one day, she'd pay for it, but for now Winterborn smiled. "I understand your concerns, but what if I could reassure you?"

"I doubt that."

"I've signed a treaty with Probert and McMahon. You know what that means. Wales and the North will become an alliance, a unified bloc. On your doorstep."

McLeod's mouth twitched. *Johnstone wants his Scottish power-bloc, remember?* Mordake had said. *Ishaque will support that if it'll get her off the Hebrides. They make a bilateral agreement with you and your allies – with McMahon on your side you control the entire North of England, and Mcleod's Command will be caught between you and Johnstone.*

"At the same time," Winterborn continued, "I've also been negotiating a bilateral treaty between my little... union and Jim Johnstone – along with any other Commands that join his Scot-Bloc. Fair terms. Favourable, too. Jim and his allies will get the same levels of access and support that Stephen and Graeme will. Needless to say, Commander Ishaque is hot to trot."

Despite herself, McLeod smiled. "That's Nadia. Anything to get back to the mainland."

"Jim's also very eager. Which leaves only you."

"Forgetting Scrimgeour, aren't you?"

"She's easy to forget, I admit, but no. Scrimgeour can't afford to antagonise Jim or Nadia. She's occupying a very lonely, isolated position out there in the North Sea. Her Command's only been tenable with support from the three of you."

"And of course, on my own, I wouldn't be much help to her."

"I suppose you could send aid by sea. A long, hazardous trip – and in return for what?"

McLeod bashed out the Monarch she'd been smoking and lit another from the embers. "And anyway, in that scenario I'd have problems of my own. I'd be caught between you and Johnstone, trying to beat the pair of you off."

"Now there's an image."

"Fuck off, Winterborn."

"As I said, Carole, cards on the table." Winterborn's smile was gone. "You don't *have* to see this situation as a threat. Believe it or not, I've no desire to fight you. My enemies are yours – the rebels and their allies. To deal with that threat –"

"I've heard the sales pitch."

"Alternatively," said Winterborn, "consider this. You see yourself as caught in a pincer movement – Johnstone to the North, me to the South. But that's only true if you consider us enemies rather than allies. Looked at another way, you're part of something greater. The heart of it, in fact – a reunified Britain, from the Humber to the Hebrides. Anyone wanting to attack you will have to come through the rest of us, and you can count on our aid if your rebel problem worsens."

"And in return?"

"*You* aid us when *we* need it, and help us extend the scope of unification."

McLeod smiled grimly. "And of course, support your bid to become Supreme Commander?."

Winterborn smiled back without blinking. "That's a matter for your own conscience, Carole."

"Course it is." McLeod sighed. "Okay. I know when I'm beaten."

"Look on it as an opportunity, Carole, rather than a defeat."

"Whatever. Get the treaty to me."

The screen went black. Winterborn swivelled towards Mordake's corner and clapped, slow and silent. "Bravo, Doctor. Bravo."

Mordake shrugged. "I merely pointed the way, Commander. The achievement itself is yours."

"I know it is." Winterborn looked into the open drawer, stroking the music box. If Mordake would just leave the room – but then, what need was there? All was well; everything was, at long long last, coming together. And yet part of him still craved the melody from the box. Almost as if there were some pleasant association –

And there was none. None. Helen was nothing to him now. An enemy to be destroyed: a final barrier to the order he required. Nothing more.

The intercom buzzed. "Yes?"

"Colonel Thorpe, sir."

"Show him in."

There was sweat on Thorpe's forehead and bald pate; he was frightened enough of Winterborn in the Ops Room, but in the Commander's office itself he looked ready to liquefy, like so much jelly. Boneless, spineless. Repulsive. But – for now, at least – useful. "Colonel. Your report, please."

"Yes, sir." Thorpe's eyes had strayed from Winterborn to Mordake. The good doctor's hood was down; Mordake turned his head so the second face looked directly at Thorpe; it smiled, then blew him a kiss.

"Doctor Mordake," said Winterborn. "It's impolite to play with your food."

"Didn't mean to break your flow, Colonel. Please carry on."

Thorpe licked his lips, managed to look away from Mordake. "We've intercepted communications from the rebels. They've got Shoal out of the Stockport area – he's now en route to a rebel fortress."

"Is he now? And how did they pull that little trick off, given that you allegedly sealed off the entire town?" Winterborn went on, before Thorpe could answer: "I suppose it would be too much to hope that we have anything so useful as the name of the fort he's en route to, or how they're trying to get him there? You know, so that we might stand a chance of intercepting them?"

"No, sir." Thorpe licked his lips again; the man was dripping sweat. "Not yet, I mean. But –"

"Find out, Colonel," Winterborn said. "And do it now, instead of wasting my time with news I don't wish to hear."

"Sir." Thorpe backed away to the door; if Winterborn hadn't been watching him every step of the way, he suspected Thorpe would have turned and run. The door clicked; Winterborn chuckled.

"You should watch him," Mordake said.

"He's spineless."

"A coward, yes," Mordake agreed. "Which is precisely why he's dangerous. If he fears you more than the rebels, he may decide you're the greater threat. And if he turns on you, he'll do so treacherously, in secret."

"You're saying Thorpe will betray me?"

Mordake pursed his lips. "Not for sure."

"You do surprise me, Doctor. It's not often I hear you admit to uncertainty."

"Even I can't see all that lies ahead, Commander. Only possibilities."

"So Thorpe *might* betray me?"

"Yes."

"I'm not concerned with who *might* betray me, but who *will* – and more importantly, *how*. Anyone *might* betray me, Doctor." Winterborn smiled. "Even you."

*

Ashwood Fort

2140 hours

The summer sun sank in the west; dusk crawled across the broken horizon, purple, red and gold. The bats wove back and forth above the outer wall's battlements, skimming past Helen's head.

She looked down, waiting.

They got him out; they're bringing him back. But with so many dangers between the city and here, she'd believe nothing until he was home.

A pair of lights gleamed on the road; then another, and another.

"Landcruisers approaching," a sentry said into his radio. Along the battlements, rifles and light machine guns were shouldered; .50 cals swivelled on their mounts. Helen clasped her hands behind her back.

"Approaching convoy, identify yourselves," the sentry said.

"Convoy 36a. We have Harrier. And Cormorant."

Cormorant was Gevaudan. Helen breathed out and leant against the parapet. "Ask them how he is."

"What's Cormorant's status?"

Danny's voice crackled out of the speaker. "How do you think? Nearly rotted his bones off today. He's alive, if that's what you mean. And he'll be okay. I think."

Helen climbed down the steps, to be there as the gates opened. Danny was driving the lead 'cruiser; Helen circled behind the vehicle, leaping up into the flatbed. A big, pale shape scrambled away from her, pulling its blanket tighter round itself.

"Gevaudan?" He hunched in a corner of the flatbed, looking shrunken and afraid. "It's me." She reached out to touch his shoulder, but he flinched away. "It's Helen."

He looked away, and didn't speak.

They drove past the church; the inner gates opened, and the landcruisers halted before the Fort. The engines fell silent; doors slammed. "Medic!" Wakefield shouted as she helped Filly down from a neighbouring 'cruiser's flatbed, holding her lover close; Nestor and one of his nurses ran to meet them.

"Gevaudan? We're home."

But still he didn't look at her, much less answer, just shuffled past and climbed out of the flatbed, letting the blanket fall away. He wore tattered, ill-fitting clothes that threatened to split when stretched over his big frame, but even so Helen saw how gaunt he was, how the muscles at his throat stood taut through the skin. "Gevaudan –"

He half-raised a hand. "I know," he said, "and I'm grateful. But for now, at least, I need to be alone."

He still didn't look at any of them, just shuffled away – a broken, old-man's walk – across the courtyard towards the cottage. Helen started after him, but Danny put a hand on her arm and shook his head, unshed tears in his eyes. Harp and Lish stood pale and hollow-eyed, his arm about her shoulders, passing a cigarette back and forth.

Gevaudan's cottage door clicked shut; no light came on inside. Where was he now? Huddled on a bed, or in the corner of a room? "Bastards," Helen said at last.

"Never thought I'd see him like that," said Danny.

Helen took a deep breath. "They'll pay for it," she said.

"'Bout him?"

"Give him time. When he needs us, we'll be there." She looked back to Danny again and the other Raiders. "You did a bloody good job," she said. "I'm proud of you all."

But it sounded hollow, empty, seeing how little of Gevaudan they'd brought back, and how many of theirs they'd left behind.

*

CANTEEN, ASHWOOD FORT
2200 HOURS

Helen sat at a table in the corner and watched the Raiders eat. She had no appetite of her own; only weariness, and Gevaudan's gaunt, broken face in her mind's eye. *You bastard, Winterborn.*

Alannah came in; Danny looked up from his food, then stood. His hands clasped hers; she rested her forehead against his. More intimate, somehow, than a kiss. Helen smiled. Sweet. It was good to see. She was glad Alannah had finally stopped caring about how they looked together, or about the years between them. Love was like that, or could be: absurd, but glorious.

How would you know? That voice again, so like Frank's.

She knew. She'd loved. Once upon a time.

Do you still?

She thought of Gevaudan, and refused to answer.

Alannah murmured something to Danny and kissed him, then came over to Helen. "Hey."

"You okay?"

"Yeah." Alannah glanced over at Danny, then looked back, her smile faidng. "And no." She pushed a folded sheet of paper across the table to Helen. "We picked this up yesterday, and again today."

"A transmission?"

Alannah nodded, said nothing else. Helen unfolded the paper. As she studied the spidery capitals on the page; a cold, long-fingered hand reached inside her and squeezed. "It can't be," she said at last.

"It is," said Alannah. "It's starting again."

Part Two:
Deus Ibi Est

1.

ASHWOOD FORT
17TH JULY, ATTACK PLUS TWENTY-ONE YEARS

A lid of dull cloud pressed down overhead, thickening the hot damp air till it was like trying to breathe wool. *Rain soon*, Helen thought, as she crossed the inner courtyard.

She'd strayed close to Gevaudan's cottage several times, but never gone in. He'd wanted to be by himself until further notice, and she'd respected that. Should she have defied the ban and gone to him? Love was a foreign language to her – assuming that was what she felt. When had she last loved? She wasn't sure if she'd ever loved Frank, and whatever she'd felt for Belinda had only ever been a fitful shadow of the all-consuming mother-love she'd heard of; she'd only felt anything like it after Belinda was dead. Hard to admit, but true.

The only time she'd really loved – unconditionally, without reservation – had been her mother. And that had been something very different. This was *terra incognita* to her.

Nonetheless, she walked to the cottage now straight-backed and unhesitating. *It helps when you've got an ulterior motive.* She grimaced and knocked; the front door swung open.

"Gevaudan?"

No answer; she stepped inside.

The cottage smelled rank and stale, the air thick with sweat and decaying food. She went from room to room; books and empty food-tins were strewn about. On the kitchen table, three empty wine-bottles.

The cottage garden had been left untended; thick grass reached almost to Helen's knees, and weeds had choked the flowers Gevaudan had tended.

Gevaudan leaving made little sense: where would he go, and more importantly, why?

Perhaps he just wanted solitude, and to be away from the people who'd seen him broken and weak. The memory cairn at the foot of the garden was undisturbed; if he was leaving for good, he'd have taken the stones with him.

Unless, perhaps, he no longer cared. He'd lived a long time, outlasted so much and so many; perhaps this had been the final straw.

She refused to believe that, but whatever the truth, Gevaudan was gone, and she didn't know where.

*

Gevaudan huddled in the chill damp dark, the jagged rock against his back. Water dripped; the only other sound was the breath of the dead.

For anyone else, the dark would have been a refuge, but having a Grendelwolf's eyes meant he was spared nothing. He saw them all, surrounding him, watching. None spoke; all were silent. Mum and Dad; Jo, Michaela and Keith; Gloria and David. And Gideon, of course, his stare the worst of all.

*

DANNY'S OFFICE, ASHWOOD FORT

Danny poured water from the jug into the bowl and splashed it on his face, then filled a cup and drank it off in one. It was fucking boiling. He slumped down behind the desk.

A tap on the door. "Yeah," he said.

Carson came in, snapped to attention. "Reporting, sir."

Straight, disciplined: like a Reaper. "At ease," Danny said. Still wasn't used to this, rapping out orders like some strutting twat.

Carson at-eased, still staring straight ahead. "Stand easy," said Danny. And she did.

"You still wanna be a Raider, Carson?" he said at last.

Her face, flushed red and bright with sweat, twitched. Scared. Wanting to hope, but afraid to. "Yes, sir, I do."

"Then you are." He saw her face brighten, and pointed at her. "Just don't let us down. Make me look like a cunt and I'll fucking do you."

"I won't, sir. I won't. Thank you."

She'd go on like that for half an hour if he let her. "Right, then. Dismiss."

"Yessir!" She snapped to attention and saluted so hard he thought she'd brain herself, then wheeled and marched out.

Danny sighed, then reached for the water-jug again.

*

HELEN'S OFFICE, ASHWOOD FORT

A tap on the office door. Helen looked up. "Yes?"

"They're here, ma'am."

"Show them in."

A dozen men and women traipsed into the office. "Thanks for coming," Helen said. "As you know, we've a potential situation. The Grendelwolf's missing. All indications are that he's left the Fort, and we need to find him. Last anyone saw of him was last night. You were all stationed as lookouts on the outer wall, so if any of you saw or heard anything, I need to know about it. Doesn't matter if it wasn't in your reports, or why. What matters now is finding him."

No-one spoke.

"Nothing? Seriously?"

None of them met her eyes.

"None of you saw a thing? He can't have just vanished into thin air."

Perhaps he hadn't left the Fort; below, after all, were the miles of caves, honeycombed and winding, most still uncharted; you could search a small eternity for someone in there without finding them. Most likely you'd be lost yourself, die alone in the dark. Helen's fists clenched at the thought. Was Gevaudan hiding there? Or – she wondered again – had he gone there to die, the shadow on him having grown too thick to bear? No; she wouldn't believe that.

"Nothing? Any of you?"

Heads shook. Helen sighed. "All right," she said. "That's all."

She closed her eyes and pinched the bridge of her nose. What next? Down into the caves to try and find him, or his body? She didn't think she could handle either the trip, or what she might find at the end of it.

Another tap on the door. "Yes?"

"Ma'am?" One of the lookouts crept back in; a tall thin bony girl, angular and awkward like a metal ladder folded too many times. An awkward tangle of brown hair grew out from her head instead of down, making her look like an elongated mushroom. "Can I have a word? Private, like?"

Helen was tempted to tell her to go away, but resisted. "Come on in," she said.

The pulled the door shut behind her. "It's about the Grendelwolf, ma'am."

Helen sat up straight. "What about him?"

"Do you – do you think he's okay, ma'am?"

"What's your name?"

"Blob, ma'am."

"Blob?" Helen decided not to ask. "Well, I doubt it. I don't think he's been okay since the Pyramid. Do you?"

"Didn't really know him before. I'm new." Blob scratched her neck. "From what folk were saying, he's not exactly the sociable type."

Helen snorted, then chuckled. "He has his moments," she said, remembering Gevaudan in the canteen with his guitar.

"You worried 'bout him?"

"Of course I bloody am." Helen reined her irritation in. "Yes, Blob, I'm worried about him. As a friend. So if you know something, or think you might – I need to know. Please."

Blob bit her lip. "He went east," she said. "The hills."

"The hills?" The hills to the east of Ashwood were rough and craggy, with little strategic value; the rebels had largely left them alone.

"He's been out there a few times, last couple weeks. I've seen him come and go – don't think any of the others have. He saw me one time." Blob coughed, reddening. "Asked me not to tell anyone."

"It's okay." Helen motioned to the chair before her desk. "Think you can show me where he went?"

INTELLIGENCE CENTRE

"Boss?"

Hei approached Alannah's desk. She smiled at him tiredly "What have you got?"

He held out a flimsy. "From Honey Badger."

"About time. What's she got?"

"Nothing yet, unfortunately. Whatever Project Sycorax is, the files on it are high security. Very hard to access, especially without being spotted."

Alannah snorted. "That's her problem, not ours. Get back to her. I want that information, and I want it now."

*

THE EASTERN HILLS

Helen took a water-bottle from her knapsack and swigged; a greasy skin of sweat covered her, the air had grown thicker still, and the sky above was nearly black. Not the best idea she'd ever had, on reflection: the storm would break any second, and she was the tallest thing around.

As if in answer, a fork of lightning appeared further along the hills, a glowing white crack in the sky; a clap of thunder sounded a second later. Warm fat drops of rain splashed her face; a few at first, then a torrent, pummelling her like hail. Lightning flashed again, just over the brow of the hill in front of Helen. The thunder shook her bones.

She needed to find cover. Helen pressed on towards the crag Blob had pointed out, head down. Up ahead, sunk into a recess in the rocks, was a cave entrance. Of course. Where better to hide?

The rain was hammering Helen so hard she felt breathless. She went to the cave entrance, peering into the dark. "Gevaudan?"

No answer. Helen looked up at the black sky. Thunder rolled again. *Fuck this*. Helen stepped into the cave.

The sound of the rain faded as she groped further into the dark, replaced by a quiet, steady dripping. And then another sound, like a gust of wind: a long, weary sigh.

"Hello, Helen." A match struck, and a candle-lantern began to glow; the spreading light glistened on the cave floor, on damp stone walls and Gevaudan's gaunt pale face. "What part of 'I want to be alone' didn't you understand?"

Helen sighed, picked her way over to him and sat down, ignoring the chill damp soaking through her coverall. "I was worried about you."

The white face was blank and cold. "I take it you found a way to loosen Blob's tongue."

"She's worried about you too," said Helen.

"How touching."

"Don't be an arsehole, Gevaudan."

"An *arsehole*?" He snorted. "I haven't been called that in a while."

"Then it was about time," said Helen.

Gevaudan chuckled; it went on and on, shaking him. He breathed out. "You know, that didn't feel bad at all."

"Blob hasn't told anyone else," said Helen. "And neither will I. If this is what you need, fine. Whatever gets you through this."

"This?"

"Whatever you're going through." Helen looked around. "Can't say I see the appeal, personally."

"The solitude."

"It obviously wasn't the scenery."

"Aren't you supposed to be back at Fort Three by now?"

"Yes." Helen shrugged. "But I'm not."

"Rank hath its privileges."

Helen looked around. "So, what have you been doing here?"

"Remembering."

The water dripped. "Anything in specific?"

"Certain things have a habit of coming to the fore."

"Kellett?"

"And all that goes with him. My conversion, my training – not pleasant memories, as you can guess. A substantial helping of survivor's guilt, too. But you can relate to that."

"Shall we talk about something else?"

"Why not? I'm open to suggestions. I'm rather knowledgeable about the music of Claudio Monteverdi, if that's of any interest. I particular admire the *Vespers*."

"You're full of surprises, aren't you? Or full of something." Helen pursed her lips as the water dripped; the scant light, reflecting from puddles on the cave floor, rippled and wavered on the Grendelwolf's face. "Actually, there is something I've wondered for a while."

"Oh?"

"How you ended up with a name like Gevaudan."

"Ah, that. Surprised you took this long to ask. I could tell you, but then I'd have to kill you."

"What?"

Gevaudan sighed. "That was a joke."

"And you said *my* sense of humour would be the death of me?"

"The name was my mother's idea. She wasn't a typical army wife – fancied herself as something of a Bohemian. Artistic." He smiled. "I really have no idea how she and my father worked, but they did. I was born prematurely on a holiday in Languedoc, in France. A part of it formerly known as Gevaudan."

"Okay..."

"There's a French – well, not legend, exactly. The Beast of Gevaudan. An animal of some kind, killed around a hundred people in the region back in the eighteenth century. No-one's quite sure what it was, or where it came from. It's an enduring mystery, and something of a source of weird and wonderful theories. Or was. I have no idea what's left of France these days. Or even most of Britain."

"And?"

"And, the legend fascinated my mother, so she and my father, with me *in utero* – were visiting the Gevaudan, when she went into labour. Middle of nowhere, and in the days before mobile phones. While these are the days after them."

"Stick to the point."

"As you wish. A local farmer drove them to his house and delivered my mother of two twin sons. I was named for the location; the farmer's name was Gideon Chastel, so my brother was named after him."

"You've mentioned him before. I didn't realise you were twins."

"It didn't seem relevant. He died in the War."

"You told me. You must have been close."

Gevaudan sighed. "Once."

He looked at the cave wall, but Helen knew he wasn't seeing it, probably wasn't even seeing her. She waited; sometimes it was better to say nothing. "I think I've told you some of it," he said finally. "He was a soldier, like my father. As nearly all the men in the Shoal family had been, going back nearly two hundred years. I broke with that tradition – I was a pacifist, if you recall."

"Yeah, I remember." He'd told her after the battle of Ashwood, sitting on the hillside with her in the spring sunshine. She'd been recovering from the bullet that had nearly killed her then; now he was the wounded one. "We became different people."

"You said your dad wasn't too happy."

Gevaudan snorted. "Something of an understatement. But Gideon was even angrier. The word 'traitor' was used." He pushed his fingers back through his hair. "When we were about eleven, twelve years old, we visited some relative or other – a great-uncle, I think – in a military convalescent home. He'd been wounded in the First World War and horribly disfigured. There were others there, too, from this war or that. I remember seeing them as we went along the corridor to his room."

Gevaudan sighed. "Up until then, Gideon and I had been like one person – liked the same things, disliked the same things..."

"But not this?"

"No. Not this. Gideon decided, I suppose, that what had happened to those men was terrible, but that was the whole point – a soldier knew something like that could happen, but fought anyway, to keep others safe. That took real courage, made it a noble calling. But I couldn't see any nobility – just stupid, pointless violence. The kind of thing you never heard about in the stories you read about war, or the films you watched." Gevaudan hunched forward, clasping his hands.

"Are you okay?"

"Of course I'm bloody not. I'm not sure I'll ever be again." Gevaudan breathed out. "But that was where things began going wrong. The start of the fracture. I went one way, he another. It made him angry."

"And you?"

"Sad. Another difference between us. I became a pot-smoking hippy..."

"A what?"

Gevaudan chuckled. "I grew my hair, took drugs – lived in a commune for a while. I didn't wash, I played the guitar very badly and sang truly terrible songs about peace and love that I thought would change the world." He looked at Helen and sighed. "I think you had to be there. I was too late anyway. The 'sixties were very much over by then."

"You've pretty much lost me."

"It was a different time. The gist of it was that I had no time for the Army, or for words like tradition or duty. My father was furious, but Gideon was angrier still. I'd betrayed everything our family stood for. And as the other half of me, he had to make up for that." The last of the smile left Gevaudan's face. "Gideon joined the Army on our seventeenth birthday, and for a few more years, I smoked my drugs and sang my terrible songs."

The rain slashed at the hillside, hissing. A lightning flash lit the cave's damp walls; thunder echoed off the stone. "And then?"

"I realised I actually wanted to do something, achieve something, So I took fewer drugs and played a few of my songs in pubs – where I realised just how terrible they were, not to mention my guitar playing. I took some evening classes to learn how to play the damned thing and then before I knew it, instead of learning about music, I was teaching the subject at a local college. Is any of this making sense?"

"A bit," said Helen. "I can remember… enough of that world." Bits and pieces of the time before rushed back to her. Some of them she hadn't recalled in years – not until she'd been shot at Ashwood, anyway. And some of them not even then. "So what happened next?"

"There was another teacher there," said Gevaudan. "A couple of years younger than I was." He smiled. "Jo."

Helen felt a flicker of jealousy. "Your wife?"

"We went out, became lovers, and yes, eventually we married. And we had a daughter, a beautiful little girl called Michaela. By then I was on speaking terms with my father again – giving him his first grandchild didn't hurt, I suppose. My mother had never stopped caring anyway – family trumped politics every time as far as she was concerned. My father and I agreed to disagree. But Gideon…" He trailed off and shook his head.

"When brothers fall out, it can get pretty bitter," said Helen, thinking of Percy.

"Yes, it can," said Gevaudan. "By then he was a highly decorated officer, with some sort of special forces unit. I don't know the details, but I think it's safe to say he did some questionable – even terrible – things in the name of serving his country."

"He sounds like a Reaper."

"I know."

"So what happened?"

"Something went wrong on an operation he commanded. There was a death – a civilian– and the screw-up was public enough that somebody had to be seen to be punished for it."

"And that somebody turned out to be him?"

"He was stripped of his rank and dishonourably discharged. So just as things improved between my father and I…"

"Now he was the embarrassment."

"It wasn't easy for him."

Gevaudan sounded sorrier for Gideon than Helen thought the sod deserved, but said nothing. Families were strange things.

"He struggled to adjust to civilian life," Gevaudan sighed. "Ex-soldiers often did. He ended up in debt and homeless, took drugs. I helped out where I could – financially, or getting him into this or that rehab programme – but it always went wrong. And first of all Michaela was growing up, and then she met Keith and got married. There were other priorities. I couldn't help as much as I'd have liked to."

Gevaudan leant back against the wall; outside the rain beat down. "He hated me by then, anyway. He was the one who'd worked hard to make our father proud and I was the traitor – but now *he* was the black sheep, and *I* was the favoured child. I suppose I did feel responsible, to a degree."

"Remember what you told me about Winterborn, Gevaudan?"

He looked down. "Yes."

"This is no different."

"Easy to say."

"Tell me about it. Anyway, sorry – go on."

"Not much more to tell, really. He'd become involved in illegal activities of one kind or another over the years since his discharge – and of course the way things had gone for him, he had fewer and fewer legal options open to him. He got in trouble again – serious trouble – and ended up in prison, about a month or so before the War. And two or three weeks before I did, too."

"How come?"

"I'd become a peace activist by then, remember? I was detained as a subversive a week, two weeks before the War. I was one of the lucky ones; I managed to escape after the attack, and went looking for my family. Other than Gideon, they'd all been at my parents' house. Michaela had a family of her own by then. Her husband, Keith. Two children – David and Gloria. My grandchildren. They survived the attack, but the radiation had got them."

He'd told her before, but that didn't matter. Helen nodded.

"After that, Gideon was the only family I had left, even if he hated me. I found the prison he'd been in, but..." He shook his head. "It was burned to a shell. All I found was ashes, some pieces of bone."

Thunder rumbled, but further off. The rain's roar was fading.

"Things are a little blurred after that. I wasn't quite sane. Some other survivors found me and took me in, looked after me until I came back from wherever I'd gone. By then we'd left the city. I lived in the Wastelands for over a decade after that. I wouldn't say I was happy, but I was better off than most, and I had something like a family again. And then the Reapers came. I don't need to tell you what happened then."

"I can guess."

"After that, they put me to work on a clearance crew, where the late, unlamented Dr Kellett found me. The rest you know."

Helen couldn't think of anything to say. "I didn't think I'd have a family again," said Gevaudan, "but it seems I do after all." His face tightened. "You came back for me," he said. "And I – I –"

"Gevaudan?"

He held his thumb and forefinger a quarter-inch apart. "I was *this* close to giving Winterborn what he wanted. I was about to betray you."

Helen hesitated, then reached out and laid her hand on his. He flinched, but didn't withdraw. "You torture someone enough, everyone breaks. Ask Alannah. It was the same for her. If we hadn't got her out in time –"

"It doesn't help," said Gevaudan. "Because you always know how close you came."

"The point is, you didn't betray us. That's the important part. Hold onto it."

Gevaudan sighed. "What is that you want?"

"Eh?"

"You're here because you want something."

"I'm here because I'm your friend." Had she hesitated over the word? If so, it wasn't because she had any doubts about it; only whether another, more intimate word should be used.

He smiled grimly. "You need me for something."

She sighed. "Can't it be both?"

"With you, I suppose, it'll have to be. Go on, then."

"There's something I need to look into. And I could use some help. If you're up for it."

"And if I'm not?"

"I'll have to go without you."

He shook his head. "You always find a way to get the horse out of the stable."

"It's for your own good."

He laughed; it echoed in the cave, and Helen realised the rain had stopped. "All right," said Gevaudan, and stood.

2.

WINTERBORN'S OFFICE, THE TOWER

"Our agent at Ashwood," said Winterborn, "indicates that Shoal's a virtual shut-in. Long may it continue, eh?"

"What happened to him at the Pyramid will be with him for a long time to come," said Mordake, "but it won't keep him out of action forever."

"Ah."

"But I wouldn't worry, Commander. He's loyal to Helen. They all are."

"Yes, Doctor, she tends to have that effect. I fail to see any cause for optimism there."

"It's her weakness, Commander. The entire rebellion's weakness."

Winterborn raised his eyebrows. "I'm not sure I follow your reasoning here, Doctor."

"You soon will, Commander. You can trust me on this."

"I sincerely hope so, Doctor." Winterborn maintained eye contact with Mordake, willing the other man to look away. Mordake smiled, then stood.

"I believe you have more video calls to make, Commander. If you don't mind, I'd like to meditate in my quarters for a few hours."

Winterborn shrugged. "I have no objection. I believe I can deal with this myself."

"Of course." Mordake smiled. "You only needed to be shown the way."

I need nothing and no-one, thought Winterborn, but restrained himself. "Until later, Doctor."

Mordake pulled his hood up and went out. When the door clicked shut, Winterborn reached for the intercom.

*

MORDAKE'S QUARTERS, THE TOWER

Mordake's quarters were Spartan: a narrow bed, a desk and chair, a bowl, cup and a jug. He lay on the bed and closed his eyes.

"None of that." The thin, cold voice was muffled by the cowl. Mordake's hands crept towards the hood, fingers hooked and poised: *stuff the cloth into her mouth and nose, suffocate her.* Then he lowered them; he knew it would be useless. "Up and about," said the voice. "You have work to do."

Just let me sleep, for Christ's sake. "You aren't trying to rebel, are you, Doctor?" said the voice. "You know that's pointless. We two are one. We're happiest when we accept it. Now we need a word from our sponsors, so be about it."

God damn you. But if God existed and damned anyone, Mordake knew – what little of him that wasn't simply an extension of his devil twin's will – then it was him, and deservedly so. He dragged himself from the bed, knelt and took a small, battered suitcase out from under it. He took two items from the white hessian bag inside, then set them on his desk before pulling the chair aside and placing it neatly in a corner of the room.

The first object was a small stone idol of a wolf sitting upright. It had no muzzle, only a hole beneath its glaring, slitted eyes. Mordake opened the second object, a small stone jar. The jar was three quarters full of wet clay; he dug a thick, slippery gobbet out, wedged it into the hole, then pinched and shaped it into a crude muzzle. Mordake nodded to himself, recapped the jar and washed his hands in the bowl; when they were clean he dried them on his robe, knelt before the wolf idol and began to whisper softly, in an old, dead tongue.

*

WINTERBORN'S OFFICE, THE TOWER

"Thank you for your time, Padraig," said Winterborn. "We're both busy, so I'll keep this brief."

"Appreciated," said Maguire, taking a sip from the cup on his desk. "So, fire away."

"I have a deal to offer you, Padraig," Winterborn said, "and it's one I think you'll like."

"I'm guessing this is about Unification?"

"Correct. But please do hear me out."

Maguire shrugged. "I'm listening."

"There are two key components to it," Winterborn went on. "The first is that you'd be guaranteed effective Home Rule over Ireland. Your own little kingdom, to rule as you will. However – the second point – you would also be guaranteed logistical support from mine and any allied Commands, as required, in annexing the Irish Republic and incorporating it into Regional Command Zone Two. 'Allied Commands', in this context, would

– so far – mean mine, McMahon's, Probert's and the Scottish Command Zones."

Maguire pursed his lips. "Not bad. I'll give you that."

Winterborn inclined his head. Mordake really had an unerring instinct for what the other Commanders wanted most. Maguire wanted not only to rule his little dominion in Northern Ireland without interference, but also to expand it. Foolish as far as Winterborn was concerned: any force trying to take Ireland would be up to its neck in its own blood. But life was cheap, and Eire largely uncontaminated – potentially, a rich prize, even cleansed of its population.

"In return for?"

"Supporting me for the position of Supreme Commander, of course."

"Of course."

"Padraig, I have no interest in trying micromanage Northern Ireland from Manchester, far less any campaigns you have planned in the rest of the Emerald Isle. As long as I have your loyalty when it counts, you have mine. I doubt you'll get the same latitude from any other prospective Supreme Commander."

Maguire breathed out. "Probably not. You've these others on board?"

"The treaties have already been signed."

He nodded. "All right. I'm in."

"Good," said Winterborn. "I'll have a copy of the treaty dispatched at once." In fact, he'd done so earlier that day. "Thank you, Padraig. The future looks bright."

*

MORDAKE'S QUARTERS, THE TOWER

Mordake stopped chanting and looked up. The wolf's clay muzzle rippled and twitched; it split open and yawned wide; its jagged edges shaped themselves into teeth. The jaws closed, then opened again. A thin growling sound escaped them, and then a voice.

"Mordake."

"Masters," said Mordake, and bowed his head.

"Project Sycorax. Report."

"It progresses," Mordake said. "Ahead of schedule."

"This is satisfactory."

"And Helen Damnation?"

"She comes to us. We see this."

"The plan remains the same?"

"You are unconvinced?"

"I don't believe the rebels will accept."

"The path we offer shortens their pain and brings them a swifter victory. Why would they refuse?"

"It's their way."

"Unlikely. The probability of their ultimate victory is high; such outcomes rarely arise from an excess of scruples."

"I think you underestimate them."

"The decision has been made and events set in motion. We shall see what we shall see."

*

COLONEL WEARING'S QUARTERS, THE TOWER

Wearing lay on the bed fully clothed, eyes shut. She had an hour; just long enough to nap, to rest a little. But sleep wouldn't come. She heard every tiny sound and it stopped her slipping away. A voice in the corridor outside; a mouse or a rat scuttling somewhere in the walls. And, a moment later, the rustle of paper pushed under the door.

Wearing's eyes opened; she sat up, rubbed them, then focused on the square of folded notepaper lying on the worn carpet. She got up, ran to it, snatched it up. The sooner she read it, the sooner it was disposed of and could no longer be a threat.

She unfolded the note; it was in code, but short, and soon translated. When it was done, she shredded the notes, put it in her mouth, chewed and swallowed. It stuck in her throat; she poured a beaker of water and took several gulps.

No excuses. All info re Project Sycorax required immediately. Priority.

No excuses, was it? Fuck you, Alannah Vale. But there was no fighting it; she was caught.

The sooner it was done, the sooner it was over. Wearing went to the door and let herself out. Go find the files, and now.

"Lee?"

Shit. She turned. "Richard."

Thorpe came up, smiled shyly. "You okay?"

"Fine. What you want?"

He blinked, hurt by her abruptness. "Just wondered – well, when you might be free."

"Christ knows. Can't you think about anything but your dick?"

Hurt flickered on his face again, but he forced a smile. "Occasionally. Look, don't worry – if you're sleeping with Soper now, I get it. He's better-looking than me."

Soper was Wearing's assistant, and all of sixteen years old. Wearing snorted with laughter. "You're disgusting, Thorpe. He's a boy."

"Bloody worships you, though," said Thorpe. "I've seen the sheep's eyes he makes."

Wearing snorted again. "Things are complicated enough without me shagging around *that* close to home."

"You look stressed."

"What else is new?"

"Just so that you know –" Thorpe was flushed, she saw, and stumbling over his words "– I'm here for you as a friend as well."

Like the kiss he'd given her before, it surprised her, and not wholly unpleasantly. Doubtless Alannah would expect her to view it as something to exploit, but Alannah could sod off. "All right," she said.

"Okay." Thorpe harrumphed and turned to go. "Later."

"Richard?" she called when he was halfway down the corridor; he turned back. "You free tonight? About twenty-one hundred?"

"Yes. Yes, I think so."

"Okay, then. Your quarters?"

"Fine by me."

Wearing grinned. "I know it is."

Thorpe grinned back. She watched him go.

*

WINTERBORN'S OFFICE, THE TOWER

"Leave us," Winterborn told Cadigan. When she and her team had left, he sipped his coffee – that beautiful rarity, the real thing – and smiled. "Stefan. Are you well?"

On the screen, Drozek scowled. "Let's skip the pleasantries, shall we? I have a Command to run."

"Very well."

"We both know what you want, and I won't give it you. But say your piece."

No more than Winterborn had anticipated. Unlike Maguire, Drozek was happy as he was; a pragmatist, with no ambitions beyond keeping his little kingdom ship-shape and Bristol fashion, like the good Navy officer he had been.

I'll enjoy this. "Simple enough," said Winterborn. "If you support Unification – under my overall command –"

"Naturally –"

"You'll retain complete autonomy within your own Command, but with full logistical support available at any time from myself and any allied Commands."

Drozek snorted. "I'm disappointed in you, Tereus."

"Really?"

"Yes. You're a conniving little sod, but I expected something better than that."

"How so?"

"This is the same shit you'll have offered Maguire. Might have worked with him, might not, but I expect you thought *they're both islands, give them the same deal.*"

Winterborn opened his mouth to speak.

"But I'm not Maguire, am I?" said Drozek. "I'm not interested in invading the next-door neighbours and building some tinpot little empire. I've no interest in fighting a war – apart from the one I'm already fighting because you couldn't stamp out your rebellion before it spread. But I can fight my part of that without your help."

"Have you quite finished?" said Winterborn. "Then let me bring you up to date, Stefan. Yes, I made a similar offer to Padraig, which he accepted."

"More fool him, then."

"I've also negotiated bilateral agreements with McMahon –"

"No surprises there."

"And with Commanders Probert and Johnstone, who has in turn brokered treaties with the other Scottish Commands, including Commander McLeod."

Drozek's smile stiffened. Winterborn felt a smile forming, and stifled it; it wouldn't do to appear too smug. "So," he went on, "you'll have a unified alliance every inch of the Welsh, English and Irish coasts close to you. An excellent position, I'm sure you'll agree, if you were to need any logistical aid."

Drozek took a Monarch from his packet and lit it. "Or a potential invasion from either side," he said at last.

"I'm hurt by the suggestion," Winterborn said. "Come now, Stefan. Yours is one of the best-organised and most stable Commands. We both know that. Which is the very reason it would make such a tempting target for the rebels. Destabilise you, and they can destabilise any of us. You have, of course, a proven track record in dealing with such unrest yourself, which I'd be foolish to interfere with. Your Command would still be your Command, to run as you see fit. But with an alliance such as this alongside– any attempt at destabilisation, no matter how well-organised, would be doomed from the start."

Drozek clapped slowly. "Well played, Winterborn. Well played."

"So?"

Drozek stubbed out his cigarette. "Send me the damned treaty."

*

MORDAKE'S QUARTERS, THE TOWER

"What about Helen Damnation?" said Mordake.

The wolf's clay muzzle writhed and yawned again. "The probability of her presence when the rebels come to us is high."

"She'll never agree to your offer."

"Of course not. But we already have the means to neutralise her. The only question was how and when to use it. We will increase the probability of the rebel accepting our offer, while simultaneously disrupting their unity. Either works in our favour. Whoever wins, all lose. Except us."

The idol's jaws closed, then shrivelled and crumpled; the ball of clay clattered on the table top; smoking and charred. Mordake returned the idol and clay-jar to the hessian bag and stowed it under the bed in the suitcase once more. Then he rose, and drew up his hood again.

3.

THE WAR ROOM, ASHWOOD FORT

"Sure he's ready for this?" said Alannah.

Helen shook her head. "No way to be sure. I don't think even he knows. He needs something. I just don't know *what*. I'm hoping it's something like this."

"If it isn't," said Alannah, "it might damage him even worse than he is already." And God alone knew how bad *that* was; it wasn't as though Gevaudan wore his heart on his sleeve. No telling how deep the damage lay, how close he was to coming apart, or what form that unravelling would take if it did. Only that it was likely to be far deadlier in a Grendelwolf than in a normal man.

"I know. But we've got to try something. Not just for his sake, either."

"I know."

Alannah shuffled her papers one last time, then pressed her hands flat against the table. Nothing more to say; they waited, silent, for Gevaudan.

*

WINTERBORN'S OFFICE

"I can see you've been busy," Endabe said.

"I'll take that as a compliment."

"You shouldn't," she replied. "It's a simple statement of fact." The picture and sound on the video-link were the clearest yet: cold, mechanical efficiency characterised Endabe's Command. She was known, behind her back, as the Droid, and had never been seen to smile or to display any other emotion. "You've achieved a great deal in a short period, certainly. Seven Commands, including your own – eight assuming Commander Scrimgeour bows to the inevitable."

The inevitable. Winterborn smiled. "I suspect she will. She's many things, but not a fool."

"Nor am I," said Endabe. "I'm a realist. There's a clear trend here, and it's gathering momentum. To oppose it would be counter-productive, even dangerous. And there are clear advantages to the agreements you outline. So I'll agree in principle, subject to a detailed review of the terms and conditions and your acceptance of any amendments."

"Of course."

"I assume the necessary documents are en route to me already?"

"You know me too well, Kowsar."

"My Command works efficiently because I know the people I work with, both inside it and out, Tereus. You contacted me when a substantial alliance was already in place, because you knew that I would almost certainly accept the offer under those circumstances. Therefore it made logical sense to dispatch the documents beforehand. Hardly complicated." Endabe raised her eyebrows. "Is that everything?"

"I believe so," said Winterborn. "Although it feels almost like an anti-climax. This is certainly the simplest and easiest conversation of its kind I've had."

"Life isn't a drama, Winterborn. I'll be in touch. Over and out."

The screen went blank. Winterborn stared at it silently, then chuckled. "Brr," he murmured, then he took out the music box and leant back in his chair. The chimes began to play; tinny music filled the room, and Winterborn closed his eyes.

I dreamt I dwelt in marble halls, with vassals and serfs at my side...

*

THE WAR ROOM, ASHWOOD FORT

Footsteps sounded in the corridor outside; Helen stood as the door opened.

Physically, he was restored, the man – the Grendelwolf – she knew. Despite the heat, his long black coat flapped around him, although he'd changed his black sweater for a shirt; his hair hung glossy and fine below his shoulders, and he was no more gaunt than was normal for him. The lips were full and red, the yellow eyes clear; it was only on close inspection that they showed anything less than their former strength and confidence.

"Helen," he said. "Alannah."

Alannah coughed and stood too. "Gevaudan."

"So," he said. "What's the problem?"

"Alannah?" Helen said.

Alannah coughed. "Couple of weeks ago – when you were taken –"

Gevaudan stiffened slightly; Helen winced. *Damn it, Alannah, did you have to say that?*

"– we started picking up a radio transmission. The listener who picked them up at first thought they were some kind of code, but that wasn't it either. They were *en clair* – just not in English."

"What language *were* they in?" But Gevaudan knew, Helen could tell.

Alannah handed him a signal flimsy. "See for yourself."

Gevaudan traced Stock's spidery capitals. They were large and clear; Helen could read them from where she sat.

ANGANA SOR VARALAKH KAI TORJA ANGANA SOR VARALAKH CHA VORAN MANTAKHA SA NIROLEPH CHIR KARAGH INSAPA VEIR BERELOTH INSAPA MAENGREPA GIR TREQUEFA GLA DETIRESH MEIRKA ANGANA SOR VARALAKH KAI TORJA ANGANA SOR VARALAKH CHA VORAN

"Tindalos," said Gevaudan. He pushed the paper away from him, then wiped his palms on his long coat. Had they shaken slightly? Helen told herself she'd just imagined it. "Well," he said at last, "it should hardly be a surprise. We knew they hadn't wholly abandoned Tindalos. That's how Kellett created the Catchmen."

"But it wasn't a Reaper transmission," said Alannah. "We triangulated the signal."

"And?"

"We've checked and rechecked the bearings," said Helen. "It's coming from Hobsdyke."

"I see," said Gevaudan. "And?"

"Can I be blunt?"

"Why break the habit of a lifetime?"

"We need to get you back in action. The Reapers are doing their best to spin what's happened to their advantage."

"Something of a challenge, I'd have thought."

"The one thing they've got is the idea that they broke you."

"So I need to do something visible. Let the rank and file see me."

"Basically, yes."

"So you want me to investigate."

"I want you to come there with me."

"Are you insane?"

Helen managed a smile. "That a trick question?"

"This isn't a joking matter, Helen."

"We need people there who know Hobsdyke. And what it does."

"Yes, and you know what it does far too well. You're susceptible to their influence – the last time you were there –"

"Yes," said Helen. "I know." She remembered the Sound, in her head, wandering blank-eyed through he caverns in a dream towards the Night Wolf and its endless hunger. "That's why I want you with me."

"Wholly against my advice, I might add," said Alannah. "It's too big a risk, and it could be a trap."

"And your objection's been noted," Helen told her. Too valuable to risk; stuck in the War Room like a specimen in a glass case, sending others out to die. Sending Gevaudan. "I'm not asking you to risk anything I'm not."

"You could be risking more." Gevaudan sighed. "When do you leave?"

"In half an hour."

"Short notice."

"You've been hard to find. It's just going to be a quick recon, Gevaudan. In and out, then decide on the next step."

Gevaudan breathed deep, then nodded. "Very well."

4.

Wakefield's Quarters, Ashwood Fort
18th July, Attack Plus Twenty-One Years
0510 hours

The morning sun lit the walls and floor. Wakefield lay on her back and watched it play across the ceiling. She'd been awake nearly an hour. Filly lay in the crook of her arm, warm and naked against her; she wasn't sleeping either.

Neither moved or spoke, save the fingers of Wakefield's right hand, which ran lightly up and down Filly's upper arm.

The light crept and filled the room, and they both moved, turning to face one another. Filly stroked Wakefield's cheek, then shushed her when she opened her mouth. "Save your breath," she said. "I'm coming with you."

Wakefield sighed. "You should rest up," she said. "Get better."

"I'll be fine," said Filly. "You're not keeping me away."

She cupped Filly's breasts, and Filly's hand slid between her thighs; no words after that, because there was nothing to be said. What would be, would be: in the meantime, there was this.

*

WALL ONE, ASHWOOD FORT
0800 HOURS

The gates opened; the landcruisers rolled out into the summer sun. Behind her, Helen heard Gevaudan draw a deep breath. "You okay?" she asked.

"I'll be all right."

Slumped in the flatbed, he looked shrunken again, smaller and tireder than before. Perhaps this had been a mistake, after all; perhaps he wasn't ready.

Well done, Helen; you're going to get him hurt, maybe killed.

Another stone on the cairn, as if she hadn't enough already – or, when it came to Gevaudan, enough guilt.

"Let's go," she said, and the convoy started down the hill.

*

WINTERBORN'S OFFICE, THE TOWER
0903 HOURS

"So you've cast your runes again?" said Winterborn.

Mordake responded with a silent stare. Winterborn knew he shouldn't mock – the good doctor and his apparent hocus-pocus had proven reliable enough so far, and was no less ridiculous, on the face of it, that Project Tindalos or the CATCH Programme – but such matters had never influenced his strategic planning, and Grimwood, among others, would have delightedly painted Winterborn as a madman if they'd known.

"The probabilities are very encouraging," Mordake said. "The current chain of events may well lead to Helen's death – or something even better."

"Better?" Winterborn reached into his drawer, stroked the music box. He had *no* feelings for Helen: only hatred and the desire for her death. Nothing more. "Is that possible?"

"Her fall from grace," said Mordake. "If she lives, we'll have struck a blow at the heart of the rebellion, when she..." He trailed off.

"When she what, Doctor?"

Mordake didn't answer. His eyes had glazed; he swayed in his chair.

*

Beneath the hood, the second face writhed in fury but dared not not rage aloud; Winterborn must see no hint of division in itself, must have no cause to doubt Mordake.

But division there was. *When she what?* When she returned, Mordake realised; *if* she returned. When she met what waited for her there. When she –

The second face asserted control. "When she returns from where she's going, assuming she does. Do you need me for anything else just now?"

"I don't think so. Feel free to amuse yourself in whatever way you prefer."

"Thank you, sir."

Of course Winterborn would rather Mordake wasn't there; now his plans were coming together, he'd much sooner feel as though he'd come up with it all himself. Mordake was more than happy to let him think so.

When Helen meets what lies beneath; when she sees what I've seen.

Mordake was vaguely aware of standing up and going to the door. The devil twin, in control. Winterborn's office door closed behind him. Mordake's body strode back along the Tower's corridors towards his quarters, while inside, silently, he began to scream.

*

THE WASTELANDS
0923 HOURS

The landcruiser's engine hissed and clanked. Carson huddled in one corner of the landcruiser's flatbed; a crowded space, but she had room. The others all sat clear of her: would neither speak to nor touch her.

Didn't matter. She looked out, to the hills and valleys on either side of the road. Another bright day, with clean sweet air, a warm sun on her face. As if the War had never been. *Blessed.* Each new day was a blessing, one she must earn. And she would. She was where she'd wanted, *needed* to be, now. She wouldn't let them down.

*

CORRIDOR, THE TOWER
0929 HOURS

Mordake leant against a wall, head burning; sweat trickled down his face. A spasm went through him; the twin trying to reassert control again. *Walk. Get back. Stop making a spectacle of us.*

Normally he simply accepted that the twin was in charge and allowed it to drive the machine that was their shared body. But the memory of what lay beneath, of what Helen was to encounter, was rising slowly towards the surface of his mind, its outline blurred but appalling, and it made him recoil from the twin's touch, like a convulsion. And so the more it tried to regain control, the more violently he reacted. It wasn't rational or conscious; it was a reflex.

The twin seemed to have recognised this on some level; for now, at least, it had stopped trying to take full control and focused its efforts on driving him back through the corridors back towards his quarters. Mordake didn't resist, as he wanted to go there as well: privacy, a place to hide. Thankfully no-one was about. Wouldn't do to see the Commander's Adjutant in this state.

Mordake flung the door wide, then slammed it behind him. Another convulsion hit him; he staggered sideways. A final effort from the twin sent him lurching back to the door to fumble with the lock. When it finally clicked, his knees gave way, and the floor rushed up to meet him.

*

Outskirts of Gaffer's Wood

1024 hours

The landcruisers came to a halt, fell silent. Gevaudan knelt up in the flatbed. The woods were green and lush in the summer sun, the air thick with their scent.

In the pines, in the pines, where the sun never shines…

"Bad place," muttered Wakefield; she cupped a small talisman in her hands, stroking it with her thumb.

"I know," said Gevaudan.

Wakefield slipped the talisman into a pouch around her neck, picked up her Thompson gun.

"Hack?" said Helen.

"Yo."

"You wait here with D Section. Guard the vehicles."

Hack scowled, plainly disappointed. "But –"

"Problem?"

Hack stiffened. "No, ma'am."

Gevaudan had glanced, out of curiosity, at Danny's report on his rescue; it had been strange, to see himself reduced on paper to a target, an objective. He knew what Hack had done to the Reapers attempting to surrender. Helen would have read that too. "You're sure this is the best way?"

"It's the least exposed," said Helen. "Our best chance of getting there undetected."

"I think we're expected," he said. "What other purpose would that broadcast serve?"

"We've still got to check it out. And it's strictly a recon mission – fact-finding, not fighting. Any sign of trouble, we pull back."

"Hopefully a trap's less of a trap if you know it's there."

"You're a real ray of sunshine, Gevaudan."

Gevaudan picked up his GPMG and climbed out. *I won't fail you. I won't.* "Shall we?"

*

GAFFER'S WOOD

1035 HOURS

As the woods closed around them, Carson heard whispers; tiny movements flickered in her peripheral vision. She jerked her rifle round towards them, but there was nothing there.

"Always like this." Carson turned: Wakefield, holding the little talisman-pouch around her neck between her free hand's fingers and thumb; the other rested on her Thompson gun. "Voices. Shadows. Don't look or answer. Bad if you do."

"Thanks," Carson mumbled.

Wakefield shrugged. "You start something, maybe we all die."

She wasn't even trying to hide her contempt for Carson. And it was only justice, Carson reminded herself: she deserved every insult, every bit of distrust and dislike. *Penance.*

They kept walking. The whispers kept up. Carson tried looking straight ahead, but the Raider directly ahead of her was Brant; he turned, feeling her gaze on the back of his head, and glared. "Fuck you looking at?" he whispered. After that, Carson looked down, kept her eyes on the ground. Pieces of bone showed yellowish-white against its carpet of rust-red needles: a rib, a pelvis, a femur. She looked away, looked up – and saw a skull grinning down at her from the fork of a tree.

Don't look or answer. Bad if you do.

"Bad place here," Wakefield said. "Bad things live here." She was murmuring one of the tribes' weird prayers or incantations. Barbaric shit, but Carson envied her.

The voices whispered; the half-seen shapes danced and capered, always just out of sight. *Devils. Demons.* Carson kept her eyes on the littered ground. Her head began to ache, and sweat trickled down her face.

"Down here," she heard Helen say.

The Grendelwolf was walking up ahead. As Carson watched, he crouched and jumped, then vanished. Helen climbed down after him, seemingly into the ground; the others followed. Carson saw a trench in the earth; the others were clambering into it too. Running water glistened at the bottom: a brook.

Carson climbed down, thick-fingered, near-blind with pain. She slipped, and almost fell, grabbing hold of a protruding tree-root just in time. She breathed out, climbed the rest of the way down, then followed the others, boots splashing in the shallow water. Brant turned at the noise and gave her a cold look, then headed up along the stream.

Christ, her head – she shouldn't blaspheme, she knew, but the pain was brutal, blurring her vision. She gripped her rifle tighter; whatever happened, she mustn't fuck up. *You have dues to pay, so pay them.*

Tall grass grew on either side of the bank, long, high and lush, with flurries of some tall pink-flowered plant. It blocked out the light; the brook became a cool green tunnel with a lush summer smell. It was pleasant, especially after the wood and its voices.

Carson touched her temple; the voices and flickering shadows were gone, but the ache remained. A hard finger poked her arm: Wakefield held something out to her. "Willowbark," she said. "Chew."

Wakefield moved on after the others. Carson popped the brittle bark into her mouth and began chewing, as instructed. She grimaced at the bitter taste, but swallowed, and soon the pain began to fade. By the time they started climbing back up out of the brook, it had gone completely. Carson slipped the bark's remains into a pouch. Old habit: you didn't leave anything behind to show you'd been there. Yes, the Jennywrens had taught her that: she might as well use the knowledge for good.

There was a small stone bridge up ahead. There'd been one like it on Ashwood Hill; it had survived the War and the Civil Emergency, only to be blown up during the battle. This one, though, was undamaged. There were creepers on it, sprouting flowers, but it wasn't that overgrown. Not as much as it should be, if it *had* been abandoned so long.

Carson crawled up the slope, pushing through the barrier of grass. Around her the others crouched or lay prone, weapons ready. She shouldered her rifle, knelt, and scanned her surroundings.

A cracked road surface. Stone cottages either side. An overgrown village green: the dark green glimmer of a pond. A war memorial, worn and duty but intact. A church, and beyond the village, a hill, on top of which Carson made out a watchtower and some low buildings.

"Hobsdyke," Wakefield said. The knuckles of her small hand were white where they gripped the talisman-pouch. The village would have been pretty, once; still was, in its quiet way. Untouched by the War, well-preserved, crumbling slowly and softly.

Carson loved places like this. She had only the haziest memories of the world before the War – blurred sense-impressions and little more – but the abandoned villages she'd passed through in her Jennywren days had brought her as close to them as she was ever likely to get.

And yet, she didn't like this place. Nothing she could have defined, but it was there. She hadn't lived this long without being able to sense a threat, and there was one here, even if she couldn't hear or see it.

"We're clear," said Helen. But of course, they weren't. Clear of the woods, yes. But whatever lived within them watched this place too.

*

As Gevaudan passed the church's main door, the brook chuckling soft and faint in the background, the ex-Reaper – Carson, that was her name – drew level with him and stopped, gazing at the lintel. "Isn't that –"

"It is," said Gevaudan. At first glance, it looked like an ordinary cross; the differences only became apparent when you looked closely. Unless, of course, you were used to carving that exact symbol onto your weapons; then you'd see it at once.

Carson looked up at it, swallowing. Gevaudan had seen her with a crucifix in the past, a real one, not one of these. She probably saw, and felt, the difference more than most. "We need to keep moving," he said.

She blinked at him. "Right. Yes."

Gevaudan strode away from the church, towards Helen, then past her. *Keep low; scout ahead.* The empty village, the houses: Jo would have loved to have lived in a place like this.

Gevaudan saw a group of people up ahead and raised the GPMG, then stopped. Those faces: he knew them.

He lowered the gun, and took a few steps forward.

His parents stood hand in hand; Michaela, Keith's arm around her waist, tousled Gloria's and David's hair. Beside them stood Jo. Only Gideon was missing: his brother, as lost in death as he had been in life. Gideon, and, of course, Gevaudan himself.

It wasn't true, wasn't real.

"It's real, sweetheart," Jo said. "It is."

Michaela tapped the children on their shoulders. "Go see Grandpa, babies." They giggled and ran forward; Gevaudan thought of clockwork toys newly set in motion, but the sight set off a wave of tenderness and yearning in him. He knelt, arms extended.

"Gevaudan!" Footsteps clattered on the road. He blinked; his family was gone. He leapt to his feet and turned, furious; Helen halted a few feet from him. "Gevaudan?"

He blinked, breathed out. "I'm sorry." He glanced at the empty space where they'd been. "I was ghostlighting."

She reached out, then drew back. "You okay?"

"Yes." He wasn't, of course. To be distracted by that. The Night Wolf had been killed, but something remained. He had to be on guard. "I'd forgotten," he said. "This place."

"We need to get up there next," Helen said, nodding to the hill. "I think whatever we're after is up there. Or under it."

Gevaudan grunted. "Joy."

"You okay going first?"

"It's what I was made for." She didn't answer. Once she'd have said something about how he was more than that. Perhaps she didn't want to patronise him; perhaps she couldn't be bothered. "I'll lead the way," he said.

*

Mordake's Quarters, The Tower
1117 hours

The twin spoke in a low insistent murmur, repeating the same phrase over and over. It seeped into Mordake's brain like fine oil: coating everything, covering it all. *Take back control. Take back control.*

"I'm not listening." Mordake heard his voice rising, almost a shout. "I won't."

The devil twin broke off and snarled at him. "Shut up, you loopy cunt. The neighbours will hear."

"Fuck the neighbours."

"Not my type. Now shut up, shut up, shut up."

"No. No, you shut up. I'm trying to think."

"Think about what?"

"None of your damned business."

"We know better, Doctor. Don't we?" It giggled. *Devil twin. Devil twin.*

"Shut up."

"Ah. You think you can remember something, don't you?"

"Shut up!"

"Shan't. Oh yes, yes. Now I see it. You think you remember something. From way way back, before the War."

"Yes!"

"You remember nothing. Nothing."

"I will if I damned well want."

It giggled again. "We know better. We know better."

"Shut up!"

It began murmuring again, a rising chant. Louder and louder, to drown Mordake out. To drown thought. To make him forget.

I want to remember. I will *remember.*

*

GRASPEN HILL

1134 HOURS

The grass on the hill grew waist-high in the lush summer heat and rustled in the breeze; it was perfect cover to close in on the base.

Gevaudan crawled up the slope, weapon shouldered. There was no sign of life: all above was silent and still. It would have been stupid to just walk up, open and exposed, but whoever had sent the signal must have known someone would come. The approach felt like a pointless ritual; nonetheless, he'd perform it properly. Keep low, watch, listen. Clear his mind of all other considerations, and do the job. Oddly, it helped.

Near the summit, the grass thinned out. Beyond it, the gates hung open; one creaked softly in the wind. A rust-pitted machine gun drooped from the watchtower. Gevaudan watched and waited, but nothing stirred.

Just waiting. The spider and the fly: come into my parlour.

"Take it easy," Helen said. "Eyes open, and ready to fall back if anything kicks off."

Gevaudan took a deep breath and stood, walking to the gates. Beyond them, he could make out the fire-blackened buildings that had survived the destruction of Project Tindalos, and the sagging, gaping hole in the centre of the compound.

"Gevaudan?" said Helen.

The gates creaked open at a push; Gevaudan stepped through. Behind him, he heard the others' soft footfalls on earth and grass, then their boots on the concrete as they followed.

*

REAP HOBSDYKE

Weeds sprouted across the compound, moored in cracked concrete and drifts of windblown dust. The burned-out prefab blocks, soot smudged around the empty holes of their doors and windows, were peeling and flaking, but already further gone in decay than anywhere down in the village.

Helen peered into the crater where the Adjustment Chamber had stood. The Sound had come from here, drawing those who'd heard it down into the depths. She'd almost died down there. Worse than died. Others hadn't been so lucky. Like Danny's friend, Thursday. Helen had been deep in the trance the Sound induced, barely aware of what had happened. Sometimes she thought she could remember something of it – vague hints, glimpses – but nothing definite. Danny had seen, though. He'd told her how Thursday had died. How Helen would have, and Alannah. Trex, too, Wakefield's friend from the Fox Tribe. Trex had died anyway, of course, killed at Ashwood Fort, but still a cleaner death than that.

"Helen," said Gevaudan. "Have you seen this?"

She turned with an effort and looked; Gevaudan was gesturing to a wooden shack, not far from the edge of the hole.

Helen frowned. "Was that here before?"

"I don't think so," Gevaudan said. "Keep back."

He moved towards it, the GPMG raised, then reached for the door.

"Gevaudan –" Helen began. But he had hold of the handle and pulled, stepping back, the gun aimed. Nothing happened; the shack's door creaked softly, rocking in the wind.

Helen approached and peered inside the shack. She saw a double bunk, a pot-bellied stove and a table with a rusted radio transmitter perched on it. There were bullet holes in the transmitter's casing.

"Hasn't been used in a while," Gevaudan said. "But this definitely wasn't here last time."

"Think you're right."

"He is," Wakefield said. "New. Built since. What for, though?"

"I don't know."

It didn't seem important, anyway; not as important as the faint noise Helen could hear now. It was coming from the hole in the ground. She turned towards it, took a step. What was that noise? It was a sort of humming sound, weak and blurred. It rose and fell, the pitch and tone changing. Simple, but oddly fascinating. Someone was down there. Singing?

A hand caught her arm. "Helen?" It was Gevaudan. "Helen, are you –" He frowned, clicked his fingers in front of her face. "Helen, can you hear me?"

"Of course I can hear you." She looked down and saw she was standing on the very edge of the hole; another step and she would have fallen. "Christ."

He drew her back. "What did you hear?"

"How did you know that –" And then she understood. Of course. "The Sound," she said. "It was the Sound."

"We need to pull back," said Gevaudan. "Rethink our approach while we still can."

"Right." Helen raised her voice. "Out!" She shouted. "Everybody, out of here now!"

*

Carson had no idea why, but she'd wanted to get clear of the compound the second she'd set foot in it; as with the village, but even more so, the place repelled her in a way she couldn't pinpoint or define. Discipline and faith had held her in place; now they were cleared to go, she couldn't head for the gates fast enough. But as she ran for them, they swung closed in her face. She pulled at them, but they didn't budge.

"Help her," Helen shouted. A moment later Wakefield was beside Carson, Filly too, then Brant: the four of them tried to open the gates, but it felt as if there were a dozen people on the other side, pulling against them.

"Shit," someone else shouted. Carson turned, and saw they were no longer alone in the compound.

A semicircle of figures in ash-grey robes stretched on either side of the gate, enclosing the rebels. And then they stepped forward, closing in.

*

Mordake's Quarters, The Tower
1200 hours

The devil twin chanted louder. "*Mantakha sa niroleph chir karagh. Insapa veir bereloth. Insapa.*"

"Shut up." Mordake pulled himself into a sitting position. "Shut up!"

It chanted on, gloating triumph in its voice; it knew it was winning, fracturing his concentration like glass. "*Maengrepa gir trequefa gla detiresh meirka.*"

Mordake's ability to fight back, move, think, all were failing. Another minute, and it would all be gone. He sank forward, took a deep breath.

"*Angana sor varalakh kai torja. Angana sor varalakh cha v –*"

Mordake snapped his head backwards, smashing the back of it into the wall. The incantation broke off in a muffled scream; there was an explosion of pain, but that other pain stopped and his head was clear.

"All right," snarled the second face. "If that's what you want. Remember, then!"

Another convulsion hit Mordake; something shifted in him, like a bubble of foul gas rising from the disturbed mud at the bottom of a deep pool. *I don't want to remember this. I don't –*

"Too late," the second face crooned, and laughed as the bubble burst. It had stopped fighting him to let him remember, and suddenly Mordake was terrified to – he mustn't remember, at any cost. But it was too late.

Mordake was aware of himself pitching sideways onto the bed, his limbs jerking, of foam spilling from his mouth.

And then of nothing else, except the waiting past.

5.

Mordake's Quarters, The Tower
18th July, Attack Plus Twenty-One Years
1200 hours

"Fuck sake, you lazy bastard, now look what you've done. Will you cunting well get up? We've work to do."

The voice raged on, muffled by the bedclothes, but Mordake heard nothing. He stretched out stiff on the bed, hands clenched, drool seeping from his mouth; he stared at the ceiling, seeing nothing.

"Move, you bastard!" the second face raged, but Mordake was beyond its reach.

*

BOWLAND BAR, UNIVERSITY OF LANCASTER
MARCH 7TH, THE YEAR OF THE WAR
ATTACK MINUS TWO MONTHS

"Dr Mordake?"

He half-rose from the chair, but was waved back. "No, no, park yourself. Need to take weight off the old fetlocks anyway. At my age."

A small sharp-featured woman with gold-rimmed spectacles and an untidy bird's-nest of salt-and-pepper hair lowered herself into the chair across the table from him and offered a hand. "Miriam Cohen."

"Pleasure to meet you, Professor."

"Likewise, I'm sure." Professor Cohen eyed the near-empty cup of coffee in front of Mordake. "See you're avoiding the food. Very wise. I can recommend any number of vastly superior eateries – but forgive me, you didn't come here for the good food guide."

"Well, I *do* need to take Mrs Mordake to dinner later, so any recommendations would be gratefully received."

Cohen chuckled. "Remind me later. But, to business. I understand you're something of an amateur archaeologist?"

"Afraid so."

"Nothing wrong with that. The passion's what counts – with the proper training, it can do a great deal."

"At some point, I'm hoping to take a degree, maybe a doctorate."

"Admirable. So, you're currently a doctor of..?"

"Psychology."

"Ah, yes. Archaeology is the study of how we got here, psychology of why we bothered."

Mordake laughed. "You could say."

"You were asking about a specific place, weren't you?"

"Yes. A DMV site in the Forest of Bowland area."

"Yes, yes. There are one or two. But this is the one I think you were after." Cohen opened her bulky raffia bag, pushed a buff folder across the table. "Gaffscote, about a mile or so from the present-day village of Hobsdyke. It was a few unusual features there you might be interested in."

"Yeah?"

"Mm." Cohen sighed. "Bloody smoking ban. I much prefer conversations like this when I can enjoy a cigarette. Helps me think. No matter, no matter. Where was I?"

"You mentioned some interesting features –"

"Ah, yes, yes. A lot of villages in this neck of the woods were destroyed in the Harrying of the North – you're familiar with the term?"

"Yes –" began Mordake.

"Norman Conquests. The Northern earls put up a stiff resistance to the Normans when they invaded. William the Bastard – as he was known then, the 'William the Conqueror' tag didn't come along till somewhat later – had to come up to York to put down each new revolt, and another one would flare up whenever he went back. So he devised a final solution – and I do not use that term by accident."

Mordake took a sip of his coffee. "Would you like one, by the way?"

"No, thank you. Far too susceptible to diuretics at my age. Actually, would you mind awfully if we stepped outside? It's a pleasant day and some fresh air would be good. Besides, I like to try and keep mobile. Have you seen Lake Carter? It's a short walk, but worth it."

"Yes, of course."

They found a bench overlooking the lake; below the green slopes, the water shone blue in the unseasonably warm sun. Cohen sat, sighed gratefully, and slipped a box of Sobranie Black Russians from her pocket. "Do you partake?"

"Er, no, thanks. Trying to quit."

Liz's doing; Mordake had tried quitting half a dozen times without success, but one day she'd just said *Eddie, you need to cut them out. They'll kill you. I'm not having kids just to tell them Daddy's gone while they're still at nursery.* He'd been cutting down ever since; he allowed himself two a day, no more. First thing in the morning, last thing at night. Next, he'd cut back further: just one cancer stick of an evening. And then, not even that. For Liz; for the family they'd raise. Although the world looked less and less like one to bring a child into every passing day.

"Wise man. Sadly, I'm too old to change my ways." Cohen lit one black and gold cigarette. "Now, where was I?"

"William the Bastard and the Harrying of the North."

"Ah, you're paying attention. Would my students were all so alert, instead of treating my lectures as an opportunity to sleep off last night's alcohol and drug abuse. William pursued a scorched-earth policy against the Northern earls. Cut off their support mechanism by sending raiding parties out to raze every village they found. They killed the inhabitants and animals, and burned houses, crops, food stores, weapons, tools. Some accounts even claim they salted the fields. It ended the rebellion, at least – caused mass starvation and cannibalism that left over a hundred thousand dead. This at a time when the English population was something like two million at most. Twenty years later, the Domesday Book described the region from the Humber to the Tees in two words: *Wasta Est.*"

"'All is waste'?" Latin had never been Mordake's best subject even then.

"Quite. Many villages were destroyed in this period. Since this was pre-Domesday, the full extent of the destruction may never be known – our information on Anglo-Saxon or Anglo-Danish settlements in the area is sketchy at best. A number of extant villages are believed to have been built on the sites of destroyed Saxon settlements that were, er, re-stocked. Gaffscote, however, is an interesting case."

"How so?"

"Reportedly razed and its inhabitants massacred, but actually some time *before* the Norman invasion. Apparently the Saxons destroyed it themselves and forbade building on the site – a new village was built a short distance away. Exactly what it was about the original site they disliked so much we're not clear on."

Mordake thought he knew, but said nothing. It was tempting to lay all he'd found in front of a professional, but what if Cohen dismissed the whole thing – or worse, set out to investigate for herself, with expertise and resources he didn't have? "Interesting," he said.

"Of course, the name 'Gaffscote' is Cumbric in origin – Celtic, that is – so an element of ethnic strife may have been involved. 'Cote' means wood – like the Welsh 'Coed', you see?"

"And the 'Gaffs' part?"

"Whatever's left of the village is in a nearby woodland called Gaffer's Wood – so the original meaning still lingers, it seems."

"Gaffer? Who'd have that been? Local noblity?"

"Not remotely, Doctor. 'Gaffer', I believe, also derives from the Cumbric. Something along the lines of the Welsh 'Gaufr'."

"Meaning?" Mordake's Latin was sketchy, but his Welsh was nonexistent.

"Goat."

"Goat's Wood?"

"Interesting, no? Information is very sketchy, but the implication was that the villagers practised a religion other than Christianity."

Yes! "Paganism of some sort?"

"Most likely. Of course, one has to taken it all with at least a pinch of salt. In the first place, what information there is derives from oral traditions recorded a couple of centuries after the Harrying. And secondly, the claims they make – devil-worship, human sacrifice, eating babies et cetera – that kind of demonisation is par for the course when you're trying to legitimise a bit of ethnic cleansing."

"Yes, of course." And given what he knew of the North Sea Culture, any survivals of *that* would be viewed even more negatively.

"For whatever reason, though, the whole area seems rife with some fairly gruesome superstitions," Cohen went on. "Which is reflected in the place names. The Saxon village – which seems to have survived the Harrying of the North, at least in name – is called Hobsdyke."

"Old English?"

"Yes. 'Hob' meant a demon or devil, especially in the North of England. 'Dyke' is a ditch, or a defensive wall. The hill overlooking the village is another one, or was."

"Was?"

"Well, today it's known as Graspen, which would translate as 'Grass hill.' So far, so innocuous, but that name's comparatively recent."

"'Comparatively' meaning..."

"Oh, some point in the Middle Ages, say the 1400s or thereabouts. A couple of older documents – post-Domesday, you understand – mention Hobsdyke, but refer to the hill as Blypen."

"Meaning?"

"Cumbric again, of course – 'pen' was the word for hill. The 'Bly' part most likely derives from something like the Welsh 'blaidd', meaning wolf. Wolves were – allegedly – part of whatever religion they were supposed to have practiced at Gaffscote."

"Goat's Wood and Wolf's Hill." Mordake tried not to cough as Cohen blew out a particularly pungent stream of smoke. "Sounds like a regular menagerie."

"Doesn't it just?" said Cohen. "Has all that been any help?"

"A lot," said Mordake.

"Good." Cohen wagged her cigarette. "Come to my office when I've finished this. See if we can pinpoint the site."

"You're very kind."

"These are dark days, Dr Mordake. Anything that brightens them is welcome. But if you find anything, let me know. That's all I ask."

*

TOLL HOUSE INN, LANCASTER
MARCH 7TH, THE YEAR OF THE WAR
ATTACK MINUS TWO MONTHS

Mordake ran his fingers over Liz's ribs to the soft firm curve of her hip. "Sure I can't persuade you?"

"Sweetheart." She kissed the tip of his nose. "I've already told you. I want you to dig into this, make a name for yourself and all the rest. But no, I *don't* want to go traipsing around a bloody wood while you poke around in the soil, okay?"

"You wouldn't have to. Hobsdyke's supposed to be quite nice. Tea-rooms and so on. And the hill should be worth a climb."

"Eddie, I know what you're like. You'll be nosing around in those woods for hours. A shopping expedition around Hobsdyke will take an hour if I'm lucky. And I'm not climbing the hill by myself. No, I'll stay here and amuse myself with your credit card."

"That's the bit I was worried about."

"You knew I was high-maintenance."

"Bullshit." He kissed her. "I'm the difficult one."

"Not to me you're not. Just take me somewhere nice for dinner when you get back. Speaking of which, didn't you book us a table for seven?"

"And?"

"It's half-six now."

"Shit!"

*

HOBSDYKE VILLAGE
MARCH 8TH, THE YEAR OF THE WAR
ATTACK MINUS TWO MONTHS

Mordake set off almost at first light, to the narrow, tall-hedged lanes that wound around Bowland and Pendle. The place names were subtly different from the ones he knew, almost foreign: Blacko, Sabden, Crawshawbooth. *A long way from home.*

And, at last, Hobsdyke. Stone cottages with well-kept gardens, a High Street with quiet little shops, a war memorial and a pub. What vehicles he could see were battered old Landrovers, spattered with old mud. Mordake parked up and got out of the car. With his two-year-old Volvo saloon and well-worn but pricey hiking gear, he probably couldn't have looked more like a tourist if he'd tried.

It was far too early for a pint, but a cup of tea and a potter around the village would be in order. The church in particular - with any luck, he'd find a few clues to follow. In the tea rooms, he picked at a piece of cake, aware of the eyes on him. It wasn't new, or unfamiliar. Look from a high place by night in this part of the world, and you understood why: the towns and villages were tiny clusters of lights dotted across hill and rugged moor, alone in a dark sea. Island communities, almost. Anyone from outside was recognised as such instantly. It wasn't even hostility, although it never felt far from it.

Mordake filled his teacup and studied Cohen's map. Gaffer's Wood extended unevenly over about two square miles, and Gaffscote's location within it was a matter of conjecture. Three crosses on the map marked the most likely sites. There was a lot of work ahead; if he could even identify the site of Gaffscote, and make some rough guesses as to how it had been planned, he'd have done well.

Mordake wandered along the High Street, eyeing the buildings. None were less than two hundred years old; the pub, the Gaffer's

Arms, looked older still, although the sign, which depicted a grey-bearded gentleman beaming in welcome, was more recent. Remembering what Cohen had told him, Mordake wondered what the original sign might have shown.

Mordake made for the church, wandering in through the graveyard. There were graves dating back to the 1700s, but he guessed the church to be far older. The squared tower in particular and the small adjoining chancel in particular; the rest would have been added later. Turriform construction: a distinctively Anglo-Saxon mode of construction.

"Nice little place, isn't it?"

A man with thinning sandy hair got to his feet beside a grave. He wore black, with a white dog-collar. "You're a student of architecture?"

"Archaeology," said Mordake. "Strictly amateur." He nodded towards the church. "Tenth century Saxon?"

"Ninth," said the vicar, unable to keep the pride out of his voice. "And still in use." He offered his hand. "Stephen Balchin."

"Edward Mordake."

"Good to meet you. So is that why you're here – your hobby?"

Mordake had already decided to be honest, at least up to a point. "Yeah."

"Hope you find plenty to interest you. How do you like our little village?"

"Nice place," said Mordake, diplomatically. "Quiet."

"True. So sadly not exactly a draw for tourists. A pot of tea and a nose around the local antique shop, and you've largely exhausted Hobsdyke's possibilitie." Balchin smiled. "Unless of course you like old churches."

"Or a bit of a climb," said Mordake, nodding towards the hill that rose above the village.

"Yes, we do get some. Graspen can be an interesting ascent – not as much as Pendle, and the view's less rewarding, but it's not bad. Used to climb it once a week when I was a lad." Balchin patted his small paunch and chuckled. "Kept me in shape, anyway." He motioned to Mordake and started walking; after a moment, Mordake followed.

"So you're a local man, then?"

"Mm," said Balchin. "Went away and then came back. And then of course, I got the call –" He touched the dog-collar "– and as luck would have it the incumbent vicar chose to retire shortly after. It suited all concerned to have me succeed him. So, how can I help you, Doctor? I assume you were looking for me. Vicars tend to be a first port of call for those poking around in the past, amateur or otherwise. After all, we know where the bodies are buried. Often quite literally."

"I'm trying to find a deserted mediaeval village site in the area."

"Ah, of course – Gaffscote."

"You know about it, then?"

"Any child in Hobsdyke could tell you about the village where they sacrificed unwary travellers to the Devil."

"That seems to be the legend."

"Legend?"

"You believe it?"

"That there was a village called Gaffscote? Certainly. And that it was destroyed by the people who went on to found Hobsdyke? Every bit as certain, I'm afraid. But that it was a place of devil-worship? Of course not. I'm a Christian, Dr Mordake, not a murderous fanatic."

"I didn't mean to imply you were."

Balchin chuckled. "I encounter my share of militant atheists – mostly online, where I spend far too much of my free time – according to whom I'm a Creationist homophobe who gloats at the thought of unbelievers suffering in Hell. Amazing how some people know what I believe better than I do. I'm humbled by such intellects... But, we were talking about Gaffscote. What happened there? It's possible that some form of pagan worship carried on there, perhaps in secret after the Northumbrians converted to Christianity in the seventh century. Or perhaps their killers just wanted their land and made up the devil-worship story to justify the massacre after the fact. Records are scant, unfortunately."

"I know," said Mordake. "Even the exact site —"

"Which is why you're here, of course. See if there's anything in the parish records." They'd completed a circuit of the church and now stood outside the main door. "If you'd like to come back to the Vicarage with me, I believe I can help."

"Thanks," said Mordake, then broke off, looking up at the lintel over the door. Balchin followed his gaze and smiled.

"Quite impressive, isn't it?"

"Certainly is." Mordake dug out his smartphone. "Do you mind if I —"

"Be my guest."

Mordake focused on the carving in the middle of the lintel and snapped three pictures, focusing in particular on the crucifix in the centre of it. His heart had quickened; the more closely he studied the symbol, the more certain he was that it *wasn't* a crucifix. It resembled one at first glance, most people would *expect* to see a Christian cross there and none of them would have seen the North Sea Culture glyph the carving actually showed. "Thanks," he said, and put the phone away.

"Not at all. We're quite proud of our little church. Now, this way, and we'll see what we can do about those parish records..."

*

THE VICARAGE, HOBSDYKE

"Here we go." Balchin set an iron box down on the table. "Property of my illustrious predecessor, the Reverend Doctor Frederick Downham. He had a bent for archaeology himself, although unfortunately he didn't get to do much about it. He was only here a couple of years. Consumption, poor man — tuberculosis to thee and me."

"Not surprised," said Mordake, sipping coffee. "This place must have been lethal in winter."

"Probably pretty benign, actually, compared to the cities back in those days," said Balchin. "And I think he was an advanced case, already beyond such help as there was in those days. Anyway, he was trying to locate the site of Gaffscote. And he laid hands on this."

Balchin opened a black, leather-bound journal. "Downham traced a letter to the local bishop from back in the thirteenth century. The local priest described the woods as haunted, possibly by demons of some kind, and suggested exorcism. Nothing seems to have come of it, but you can probably guess the suspected cause."

"Gaffscote?"

Balchin nodded. "*The unquiet dead, and that which they venerated in life*. Something like that. But as you can see, he enclosed a rough map of the area showing the location of the destroyed village. He wasn't much of a cartographer, I'm afraid."

"He might have been enough of one," said Mordake. "Could I have a copy of this?"

"Of course."

"Thank you. You've been a huge help."

"No problemo, Doctor Mordake. Happy to help."

It was only later that Mordake wondered how Balchin had known his title, and by then it was far too late.

*

GAFFER'S WOOD

He found his way into the woods just before midday, the cool shade closing so tight around him he shivered in its pine-scented embrace.

According to Balchin, local people, even the children, rarely went there even now. "There are still superstitions about the place?" Mordake had asked.

"Not exactly. Just something *unpleasant* about it. Hard to define more precisely, but people tend not to go unless they have to. Or stay any longer than they must."

Despite that, there were two or three tracks into the woods – desire-lines, trenched into the earth. They might, just possibly, be the remains of holloways, the troughs ground into the land surface by centuries of foot or wheeled traffic. Making his way along one of them, Mordake soon understood precisely what Balchin meant. The air was not only cold but damp, which seemed to insinuate itself through his clothes through to the skin; it was like being touched by chill, clammy fingers. The shade felt oppressive too, less a shelter from the sun's heat than a place that conspired to shut him off from its light. Even the fresh smell of pine sap had a cloying, even stifling quality about it.

The woods seemed to be on slightly lower ground than Hobsdyke, so perhaps the cold air settled here and grew stagnant. Something like that. It didn't matter, anyway; he wasn't here to enjoy the scenery or atmosphere.

A brook wound through the trees; Mordake sat on a rock beside it, sipped bottled water. He'd picked up a cold pasty from the local bakery; it had looked appealing enough at the time, but his appetite was gone. Well, he could eat later.

He took out the photocopy Balchin had made and laid it beside the map Cohen had given him. Separately of limited use, when put together they were his best lead yet. Downham's crude sketch put the site of Gaffscote near the woods' northern edge; of the possible locations on Cohen's map, one was in the centre of the woods, one near its eastern periphery – and one to the north. That location *was* relatively detailed, and wouldn't be hard to find.

The brook ran down from the north; Mordake followed it upstream. Assuming its course hadn't changed too greatly since the thirteenth century, following the stream was a good bet for locating the site: any mediaeval village would have needed a water supply. The sound of it had the additional benefit of muting the way the trees rustled in the breeze; they sounded almost like whispered voices, and the constant twitching of the branches was maddening, little shadows tugging constantly at the edges of his vision.

The gloom became a little less oppressive. Gleams of light and glimpses of the landscape beyond showed through the trees. They were thinning out; he was near the woods' edge. The next step, then, was finding evidence of habitation.

Mordake peered through the trees, looking for any signs of the other tracks; holloways – if these were the remains of holloways – tended to converge on villages. He saw one of the other trails closing in towards the one he trod; when he looked up the trail, he could make out a clearing up ahead. That was where they'd intersect. He walked faster.

In the clearing, he crouched down and looked about him. *Be patient, methodical.* Nearly twenty minutes passed, and by the end of them he was ready to move on, but that was when he saw it.

Mordake moved closer and looked again. Yes – now he knew it was there, it was so obvious: a raised earth bank with what appeared to be a squared-off corner. Nature rarely dealt in straight edges and regular shapes. Mordake felt his heart quicken, just a little.

The embankment was overgrown, trees sprouting, and of course he hadn't the equipment for a proper excavation, but he was able to get some idea of the first structure's outline. It was substantial – the village's main hall, he guessed, if Gaffscote had been planned out like most Anglo-Saxon villages of the time.

Which it almost certainly would have been; the North Sea Culture's diaspora had survived for centuries by migrating southward through Scotland and Northern England and adopting their host communities' outward practices. Likewise, the children would have been raised Christians until old enough to be taught the truth. Over time, they'd either lost their true culture and been wholly assimilated – or, like Gaffscote, been exterminated.

As the site was undisturbed, there was a good chance of finding artefacts, but evidence of the North Sea Culture would be another matter. They'd tended, for obvious reasons, to hide it well, so any such proof, assuming it had survived the village's destruction, would be doubly buried.

It would take a *lot* of work to even start unearthing what remained of Gaffscote. Still, Rome wasn't built in a day; for now, he'd try tracing the earthworks and foundations, get some idea of the village's layout. There were clues; nettles sprouted, even on the shaded floor, which was often an indicator: the scraps of food and bone ground into earthen floors enriched the soil, making it particularly conducive to nettle growth.

Mordake took out his pad and sketched the outline of the larger building. Pacing the clearing, he found another set of earthworks – a smaller, but equally rectangular, building – which he added to his own crude map before heading further out into the woods, seeking traces of the rest of the village.

The trees rustled and whispered; they sounded more like voices than ever now. They weren't, of course. Just the wind. Just as the dancing, just-out-of-sight shadows were only branches twitching in the breeze.

Even if he couldn't feel any wind.

Someone's behind me. He knew it suddenly. Maybe more than one someone. Mordake spun, but there was no-one there.

Get out of there, Eddie, Liz would have said. But this *mattered* to him; he wouldn't just buckle and run. And run from what, anyway? Shadows? Voices on the wind? People who weren't there? A weak laugh escaped him.

His skin prickled with sweat; he felt a moment's dizziness. He should sit down, take a break – but then he'd only have to stay here longer. Get the job finished, draw as good a map of Gaffscote as possible, then go.

He paced and sketched. The trees rustled. He picked his way across the brook and found further traces on the opposite side;

the village had straddled the watercourse. He should have been excited – he'd taken the first step towards excavating a proper North Sea Culture site, a whole village – but his predominant feeling was a blend of anger and fear.

Fear? No: unease at most. No more than that. He was by himself in a lonely part of the Lancashire countryside, in an isolated woodland full of shadows and tiny sounds; his brain was making patterns of them, sensing threats where there were none.

The anger was real, though: after years of searching, he'd found this place, and his traitorous imagination was doing all it could to sour his triumph. Even when he finished his sketches and made his way back, he kept his head down all the way. Stupid, he knew, but he couldn't shake the dread that if he looked up he'd see whoever he'd sensed behind him earlier – not just one person, but many. And worst of all, that he would see their faces.

6.

REAP HOBSDYKE

18TH JULY, ATTACK PLUS TWENTY-ONE YEARS
1201 HOUR

Carson backed up against the gate, rifle raised. The robed men were all armed, submachine guns aimed at her and at the others.

"Please stay calm," called one of the robed men. "We don't wish to harm you." Like the others, he was shaven-headed, and his skin had a dull metallic sheen. "We called. You came. That's all we wanted."

"Well, we're here," Carson heard Helen say.

"We've been waiting for you," said the robed man. "Or rather, our leaders have." Carson let her rifle track towards him. Brant glanced sideways at her, and she saw his gun was aimed at the man as well. He half-smiled, then stopped – remembering who she was – before focusing on the speaker again.

The robed man gestured towards the hole in the centre of the compound. "They want to meet you, below."

"Like Hell," Helen said.

"We must insist."

Wind blew across the hill; dust snaked in ghostly trails across the cracked concrete before subsiding. Carson gripped her rifle till her fingers hurt.

"If we meant you harm," the robed man said, "we could have killed you before you even knew we were there. Even now –"

"If you tried it now," said Helen, "you'd get hurt."

The robed man smiled. "But you would all die. See?"

He was pointing beyond them. *Not falling for that one*, Carson thought, but Filly glanced behind her and muttered "Shit," so Carson looked, after all. Outside the gates, more robed figures knelt or lay prone in the grass, rifles at their shoulders.

"One hostile move from you," said the robed man – Carson wanted to wipe that smile off his face, preferably with a well-placed 7.62mm round – "would result in instant death for all of you. Alternatively, you can come with me, meet our leaders and hear what they have to say."

"And what then?"

The robed man shrugged. "Then you'll be free to leave."

"You expect me to believe that?"

Another shrug. "No more than the truth. Your choice."

All eyes were on Helen now. The Grendelwolf moved a step closer to her. Helen looked around; her eyes met Carson's for a second. Then she nodded and lowered her Sterling.

The robed man bowed slightly. "You are wise. My name, by the way, is Faarrgrepa. Please follow me."

The robed men parted ranks to let the rebels follow Faarrgrepa back towards the hole in the ground. He raised a hand; Carson heard a grinding of rock and then a soft, faint whirring sound and something rose from below, to the level of the hole. As they reached the edge of the hole, Carson saw it was a flight of metal steps, which Faarrgrepa now descended.

"The Hell?" Helen said.

Faarrgrepa looked back at them and smiled. "Come on down."

Carson looked to Helen; so, she realised, had everyone else. Helen sighed. "Sod it," she said, and started down the steps. The Grendelwolf followed, then Wakefield and Filly. Brant looked over at Carson and raised his eyebrows. She shrugged. He nodded, then went after the others. *Right*, thought Carson; *show what you're made of.* She followed, boots clanking on the steps.

*

Helen took slow deep breaths, held them and then releasing. All slowly, not too fast. *Breathing control. Stay calm.* Easier said than done, with all the memories flooding back: the Styr, the Sound, the Night Wolf taking shape, ready to devour the Earth. Gevaudan moved to her side, the GPMG aimed, for now, at the ground.

Light flashed; Helen stepped back, raising the Sterling, and collided with someone. She jerked round, raising the gun: it was Wakefield. "Sorry," she breathed.

"No harm."

The light flickered, then flared into steady life. Wakefield stared up. Helen looked too: bright lights glowed around them, inside the cavern and along several of the half-dozen tunnels ahead.

"We installed a few mod cons in your absence," said Faarrgrepa, then motioned towards one of the tunnels.

Once she'd established the tunnel wasn't the one they'd followed that first time they'd come to Hobsdyke, Helen nodded. "Let's go."

"I'm with you," Gevaudan murmured.

The tunnel walls were dry, with no signs of cracks or damage. When the Night Wolf had been destroyed, it had seemed as though the entire cave system inside Graspen Hill was collapsing. But it couldn't have been, really: the hill, honeycombed with caverns and tunnels as it was, still stood, after all.

The tunnel ended abruptly, in a blind face of black stone. *Trap*, thought Helen, and reached for her gun, knowing as she did it was too late.

"A moment," said Faarrgrepa, and raised a hand. The floor shivered; a soft rumble sounded, and the rock ahead of them slid upward. From the space behind it, soft pale light spilled out.

"This way," said Faarrgrepa, and stepped through. Helen felt the others' gaze on her back: there was no choice.

She took a deep breath, and walked into the light.

*

It was another world.

The new tunnel had polished metal walls, and wound in a slow spiral further down beneath the hill. At last it came to an end, and they stepped onto a metal gantry that overlooked what lay below.

Before Helen, extending out from the rock wall against which the gantry stood, was a town – no, a *city*. There were streets and houses, all gleaming and clean and laid out with geometric precision; parks and green lawns. The ceiling above it was lost in a pale haze of artificial light – it had to be artificial, but it more closely resembled natural light than Helen would have thought possible. She heard water running.

"Good God," said Gevaudan. Helen almost laughed at the genuine astonishment on his face.

"Welcome to Bereloth," said Faarrgrepa: Helen heard the pride in his voice.

"Bereloth?" said Helen. She recognised the word from the Hobsdyke incantation.

Faarrgrepa smiled. "There is no exact translation into English, but it would approximately be rendered as 'The Place From Which We Call'."

"To the Night Wolves?"

"Yes, that was its original meaning. Long ago. Won't you come and see?"

Helen followed him down the gantry. "Who *are* you people?"

"The *Garalakh Tep Sharhr*," he said. "Roughly translated, 'the Dwellers beneath the Hill'. I think you'll have heard about our ancestors from Doctor Mordake."

"The North Sea Culture?" said Gevaudan.

"That was his name for it." Faarrgrepa stepped onto a moving walkway at the foot of the gantry and glided away from them. Gevaudan and Helen exchanged glances, then followed. A panicked yelp sounded behind them: Helen spun to see Wakefield, arms pinwheeling as she fought for balance. Filly steadied her; the tribeswoman blinked, stared at her feet, then up at Helen. "Devilwork."

"No," said Gevaudan. "Just technology." But he watched Faarrgrepa through narrowed eyes, just the same.

"Look around you," said the Dweller. "See the world we've built, and how your world could also be."

It was beautiful, Helen had to admit. The parks had stands of trees, little dells, streams winding through them, ponds. The houses were bright and clean, and every single one was identical to the next: square-shaped, whitewashed, flat-roofed, with a door in the exact centre of the frontage and a tiny oblong of lawn out front. Small, neat boxes. The larger buildings were simply larger boxes – equally whitewashed, equally flat-roofed, equally neat, equally devoid of any individuality. Each building had a brass plate above the door; the sole difference between one building and the next were the symbols etched on it. Helen didn't recognise them, although she suspected that if anyone who'd worked on Project Tindalos had still been alive, they would've.

The walkway reached a platform, from which other walkways branched out. Faarrgrepa led them onto one that sloped upwards before levelling out over Bereloth. The city obviously extended beyond Graspen Hill itself: it must lie beneath Hobsdyke too, Gaffer's Wood – perhaps even further.

Bright, clean – underground, too, which made the achievement even more impressive. It was meant to awe them, she knew, and it was working. And yet Helen didn't trust it. It was *too* bright, *too* clean; too regular and regimented. People were messy, untidy things; they refused to fit easily into plans and blueprints. That was one thing she liked about them. Bereloth's perfection was a sterile one: either its inhabitants lacked some vital human quality, or it was ruled by an authority that imposed absolute order and demanded absolute obedience. The kind of society Tereus Winterborn might build.

They passed over a small woodland; Helen could smell the trees. But even here, there was a sense of regulation and control, with the woods barbered into a neat oval.

Of course there is: it had to be planned out carefully, to build it underground like this. Give them a chance; see what they have to say.

"Here," said Faarrgrepa, pointing.

Up ahead rose a silver dome, with a white pillar at – Helen guessed – each compass point. A statue of some kind crouched atop each pillar. "Where's here?"

"The Temple of the Elders," said Faarrgrepa. "Where Bereloth is ruled from."

"A theocracy?" said Gevaudan.

"It was, in the beginning, but things have changed. The Elders will explain."

The walkway descended back to ground level; they stepped off it and approached the Temple. Helen looked up at the white pillars. She could see two of the idols on top of them in detail. One was a snarling wolf; the other, with its horned head, looked like a goat.

Helen saw Wakefield reach up to touch, again, the talisman that hung at her throat, before returning her free hand to her gun.

The main entrance was a pair of brass doors, each one twelve feet high and five wide. Two robed guards, armed, stood in front of them: at a sign from Faarrgrepa they stepped aside, and the doors swung open.

*

A pagan place: that was Carson's first thought, soon put aside. This wasn't the simple nature-worship of the tribes; a God was venerated here, but no God she knew. Perhaps not any God known outside this place.

Although the space was lit by the same bright, sourceless lighting as the rest of Bereloth, mounted bronze braziers burned inside the Temple, their flames' glow flickering on the idols they flanked. Carson saw the wolf and the goat, a rearing serpent and a cruel-faced hawk. *Graven images.*

And in the centre of the temple, on a raised semicircular dais, thirteen men and women in white robes sat on tall, narrow wooden thrones, waiting for them.

The Elders. The priests of their false gods. But then Carson hesitated, reconsidered. How much of that was her true faith, and how much was what the Reapers had taught her? The Reaper Creed had been woven into the SpiriCon Chaplain's sermons as deeply as it had been into everything else of REAP Command's Carson had touched, or that had touched her. The filth of it was grained into the pores of her soul; try as she might, she couldn't wash it all out.

A dislike for the unlike; a loathing of all that wasn't them: that was the Reaper way, and not the rebels'. The tribals might worship different gods, but Carson could no longer think of them as damned or soulless (her Chaplain had told her the ferals and tribesfolk were never ensouled to begin with, so there was even less sin in killing them than in slaughtering anyone else who stood in the Reapers' way.) The repulsion she felt now might be no more than that – some teaching of the Reapers that she hadn't quite shaken off.

Perhaps, but Carson doubted it. She wasn't just a Christian here; she was a soldier. The Jennywrens had trained her in that too, and whatever else they were, they knew that trade. There were her instincts as a Christian, her instincts as a soldier and her instincts as a Reaper, all so tangled together Carson struggled to separate them.

It was her soldier's instincts she had to find and listen to; they were well-honed, and she couldn't remember a time they'd been wrong. If they had been, chances were she'd be dead. If it was the soldier in her that warned of danger here, she'd better pay attention.

The Elders of the *Garalakh Tep Sharhr* waited, perfectly still, their hands on their knees. Like the others, they were all shaven-headed – or were they all naturally bald? – and their skin had a metallic sheen, as if brushed with powdered steel.

One throne, in the middle of the dais, stood higher than the rest. The woman in it inclined her head. "Welcome," she said. "Thank you for joining us."

"We didn't get the impression," said the Grendelwolf, "that we had much choice in the matter."

"We apologise for that," the woman said. "But it was necessary that we speak. I am Karalagh, the Heresiarch of Bereloth."

"I'm –" Helen began.

"We know your name, Helen Winter. We know all your names."

Winter? Carson saw Helen flinch at that; then the other woman drew herself up and pressed on. "So you're in charge here?"

"Inasmuch as any one of us is." Karalagh's light, gentle voice was like someone stroking your forehead while you lay back on a soft bed. A lover, perhaps. Her face was smooth; with that and her lack of hair, Carson couldn't tell if she was young or old.

"So why are we here?"

"Common interests."

"Such as?"

"Defeating Tereus Winterborn, and putting an end to Doctor Mordake and *his* endeavours."

"You're a little behind the times," said Gevaudan. "Mordake's dead."

Karalagh sighed. "Unfortunately, not so. You know, of course, that Winterborn has a new adjutant?"

"We've been trying bloody hard to find out who," said Helen. "Mordake?"

"Yes. And you saw what he became."

*

Helen had seen, all right; she doubted she'd ever forget. "Yes. And he said he was to have been a priest of the Night Wolves, like you."

"Not like us," said Karalagh.

Helen looked pointedly at the wolf idol.

"We no longer worship them," said Karalagh.

"And the transmissions we picked up? The incantation used to invoke the Night Wolves?"

"Without the other components of the ritual, as you well know, Helen, they're just words." That voice: soft, gentle, smooth. "But they're the one part of our culture you would recognise. We knew it would bring you here, and it has." Karalagh shrugged. "We don't choose the race we're born into, do we? As for the Night Wolves – why should we want to resurrect them, and be destroyed along with everyone else?"

Karalagh allowed a moment of silence to let the point sink in, then gestured to the wolf idol. "Bereloth is an old city – a thousand years, more. How much do you know of our kind?"

"Mordake called it the North Sea Culture," Helen heard Gevaudan say. "Destroyed thousands of years ago in a failed attempt to resurrect the Night Wolves. The survivors migrated south through Scotland and northern England."

"Some practised their beliefs openly," said Karalagh, "and were exterminated by their neighbours. Others practised secret worship, but the Christians rooted out and destroyed those who didn't abandon their faith. One such massacre happened above us." Her face was placid and calm: so calm, so reasonable. Too smooth; Helen didn't trust it.

"Hobsdyke?" said Helen.

Karalagh shook her head. "The Saxons built Hobsdyke after razing one of our ancestors' last surviving villages. Gaffscote. It stood in the woods nearby."

"Gaffer's Wood," said Wakefield. She fumbled at the talisman pouch around her neck. "Bad place."

Karalagh gave the little tribeswoman an amused glance. "Traces linger there, yes. But some of Gaffscote's inhabitants foresaw what was coming. They had one advantage; the skills of their ancestors. Magic, most would call it."

"And they used it to hide," said Gevaudan. "Literally went underground, and created this place. Is that it?"

Karalagh smiled and nodded: a schoolteacher praising a bright pupil. For a second Karalagh seemed to have Mum's face; then Helen blinked, and the moment passed. "To survive, they had to hide – not just their faith, but their existence. So they dug from beneath Gaffscote to under the hill; they found and expanded the caverns there, and built Bereloth. They kept watch on the world outside, of course, and copied the technology developed there to make our city a better place to live in. We grew comfortable, and, in that comfort, questioned our beliefs."

Karalagh gestured around her. "We've preserved the Temple, because it was at the heart of the city when it was founded. Tradition, nothing more. The Council of Elders was originally composed of our foremost priests; now they're chosen from the wisest among us. 'Heresiarch' is nominally a religious title, but now denotes only seniority."

"Then why stay hidden?" said Helen.

Karalagh sighed; something in her face reminded Helen of Mum, when Helen had been slow to grasp some important piece of information. "*Look* at us, Helen."

"She has a point," Gevaudan murmured.

Karalagh looked amusedly from him to Helen. *Like he's a new friend I've brought home.* "We hardly had faith in your tolerance and compassion. And we're content in our world. The War has barely touched us."

"Because you've been isolated from the outside world," said Helen. "Until now. Why?"

"Mordake almost restored the Night Wolves," Karalagh said, nodding ceilingwards, "and directly above our city. The creature he's become will try again. He's already responsible for those abominations, the Catchmen."

"I thought that was Kellett?" said Helen; beside her, Gevaudan flinched at the name, and she quickly touched his sleeve. Karalagh's gaze shifted to Helen's hand, and she pulled it back; those eyes saw too much.

"Mordake left information in the ruins of the Hobsdyke base," said Karalagh, "and ensured the Reapers found it. Winterborn, of course, made use of it – with Kellett's help. And then Mordake made his way to Manchester and offered his services."

"To do what?"

"To develop a new weapon system for Winterborn. He must be stopped, so we offer an alliance. The old knowledge, the *true* old knowledge – we offer it to you, to defeat Mordake and the Reapers."

7.

HOBSDYKE
MARCH 8TH, THE YEAR OF THE WAR
ATTACK MINUS TWO MONTHS

The few locals in the Gaffer's Arms looked Mordake over as he came in: not hostile, but clearly saying *not one of us*. Well, he'd expected that, and it didn't matter right now.

He sank into a well-padded armchair at a table by the fireplace, studied the menu, then went to the counter. The dark-haired barmaid gave a half-hearted smile. "What can I get you, love?"

"The game pie, please. And a pint. What can you recommend?"

"Blonde Witch is good."

Mordake wasn't sure he cared for the name, under the circumstances, but just now he was more interested in alcohol content. "Why not?"

She shrugged and pulled the pint. "I'll bring your food when it's ready."

"Thanks."

Back at his table, Mordake sat, then downed nearly a third of his pint in one gulp. *Easy.* He pressed his hands flat on the table. *You're driving, remember?*

Already, he felt foolish. What had happened in Gaffer's Wood, really? Rustling trees, flickering shadows? Wasn't he supposed to be a scientist? *Nothing* had happened – nothing that couldn't be dismissed as a natural phenomenon, coupled with ridiculous, near-hysterical overreaction on his part. Still, there was plenty of time left; he could still go back, explore further.

"Ah, Doctor Mordake!" Balchin stood over him, a double Scotch in hand. "Mind if I join you?"

"Please." Company would be welcome.

"Many thanks." Balchin fell into another armchair with a sigh. "Been writing my Sunday sermon. As the song said, some days it don't come easy."

Mordake, having written his share of essays, dissertations and theses, smiled. "I know that feeling."

"Mm." Balchin leant forward, lowering his voice and glancing sideways at the other drinkers. "So – any luck?"

Mordake smiled at his furtiveness, till he realised Balchin was serious. He leant forward too. "I think so, yes."

"Think it's the place?"

Mordake nodded. "Unless there's more than one DMV site in Gaffer's Wood."

"Good." Balchin sank back in his chair, beaming. "Delighted I could be of help."

The barmaid came up. "Your dinner, sir," she said, and nodded to Balchin. "Vicar."

"Hello, Eleanor." Balchin smiled at her; Eleanor primped her hair, then coughed. "Enjoy your meal, sir," she told Mordake, and headed back to the bar.

Balchin sighed. "Nice girl."

"You and her..?"

"No, no. Of course. Doubt she's interested."

"Looked it to me."

"Do you really think so?"

"I'd say."

"Good Lord." Balchin took another swallow of Scotch; Mordake wondered if he shouldn't have kept his mouth shut. Setting someone up with a drunk wouldn't exactly be a proud achievement. "Well, then, perhaps... But anyway." Balchin set the glass down, glancing around again; he couldn't have attracted more attention if he'd tried. "Something else you may be interested in."

"Oh?"

"Up on the hill, the summit, there's a flat rock; the Wolf Stone, they used to call it. Allegedly – *only* allegedly, mind – it was supposedly used by the Gaffscote folk back in the day."

The Wolf Stone; Wolf's Hill. "Used for what?" But Mordake thought he could guess.

"Allegedly – as I say – human sacrifice. Tradition has it there was a stone circle, too, but it was pulled down. I wouldn't know about that, but there are a few other stones nearby, might or might not have been part of a circle."

"I've never even heard of a stone circle around here..."

"Pretty obscure local legend. Not sure how many people here still remember it. I only know it from browsing the ever-reliable parish records. You won't get anyone from round here going up on Graspen Hill of a night, though."

"Nor most people, I'd have thought," said Mordake.

"You'd be surprised how the youth of today spend their evenings," said Balchin. "The Forest of Bowland isn't exactly a thriving social hub." He drained his glass.

"I appreciate it. I'll go and have a look later. A bit of hill-walking'll do me good." Mordake patted his belly. "Got to keep in shape somehow."

Balchin gave a reedy, but appreciative chuckle, toying with his glass. "Glad to be of help," he said. When he finally shot a rueful glance at the empty tumbler, Mordake gave in. "Another?" he said.

"Oh, that's very kind of you."

"Not at all." If nothing else, Balchin might forget about the barmaid.

*

GRASPEN HILL

Halfway up the slope, Mordake hunched over, hands braced on his knees, and huffed for breath. He'd only been joking about staying in shape, but he was more out of condition than he'd thought. That, or the hill-slope was a tougher ascent than it looked. Maybe both.

There was a rock up ahead, half-buried in the ground. It was flat, and dry to the touch, so he sat down gratefully. He considered turning back, but decided against it; he might run into Balchin, wanting to quiz him about the Wolf Stone.

Besides, it had to be admitted, the vicar's information had, so far, been good. It was worth taking a look at the Wolf Stone, at least. What harm could it do?

"A potential bloody heart attack, that's what," Mordake muttered, but even so he stood up to set off again.

He looked back, out over the landscape. It wasn't a bad view: Gaffer's Wood bristled from the earth to his left, with wider expanses of woodland and other hills further off, along with a couple of other villages. And below him was Hobsdyke, the little cottages, the old church –

Mordake froze. After a moment, he blinked, then studied the village more closely, but nothing seemed out of place. The only change was that the village looked busier than it had before, with men and women bustling up and down the High Street. He thought he could make out Balchin, and a woman beside him; it might have been Eleanor. God help him if he'd ended up inadvertently playing matchmaker there.

Mordake turned away again and continued with the climb. What had pulled him up short hadn't had anything to do with Balchin; he'd had the impression that he'd caught the tail end of some kind of movement. It was absurd, but he could almost believe he'd glimpsed all the villagers, as one, turning away from the hill. As if they'd been watching him climb.

*

He reached the summit after another twenty minutes, struggling for breath. *Hit the gym when you get back*, he thought; *get a decent bit of cardio done before you start the day*. But he was here at last.

He'd climbed Pendle Hill once – when he'd been younger and, he had to admit, fitter – and like it, Graspen Hill was flat-topped and surfaced with sphagnum moss. He turned and looked out – away from Hobsdyke, towards the hills over to the west. Having done the work, his reward was the view; it took him four or five minutes to remember why he was actually here.

Finding it was easy enough; apart from the stumpy white plinth of a trig point, only one cluster of grey stones interrupted the level dark green. He trudged over to it for a closer look.

His first feeling was disappointment; initially, he saw nothing to suggest this wasn't a natural formation. The smaller stones lay scattered randomly about, and the large one in the middle – the Wolf Stone itself, presumably – was neither flat nor regular in shape. But he crouched, wincing as his knees protested, and looked closer.

It was hard to be sure, of course; the stone was worn and weathered by hundreds of years of wind and rain. But eroded or not, the marks were there – dents, pits, holes – where chisels and sledgehammers had been at work.

They tried to smash it up; tried to hammer it into dust, break it into pieces and scatter them.

Balchin had been right; the legends were true. This had been an altar – almost certainly the North Sea Culture's – used in their rituals, to worship their gods –

The stone rumbled under his hand.

Mordake recoiled; as he did, the stone glowed with within, like an ember glowing through a crust of ash. The light, though, wasn't the reddish one of a fire, but a cold, pale light like none he'd seen before. The glints of light resolved themselves into shapes. Glyphs. Not runes, not ogham: no symbols anyone living would know, other than Mordake. Because he'd seen them before, carved on cylinders of greenish stone.

The North Sea Culture, the Beloved –

There was a moment of wild joy – here at last was the proof he'd sought– then terror and shock as the glyphs continued to glow. It was one thing to know what the North Sea Culture had believed: to see evidence that it had been real was something else again.

Get away from it – back to the village, then drive like hell for Lancaster.

Mordake turned to run, and everything went black.

*

THE OUTER DARK

The sun was gone. It was as though night had fallen in a single second, except it wasn't a night sky above him. The stars and moon weren't obscured by clouds; they just weren't there. And the hill was silent, too; the wind, the bleating of sheep, the distant bird-calls and the growl of far-off motors were gone. In their place was a thick blanketing hush: soft as velvet, deep and killing as the snow.

The one source of light, anywhere on the hill, came from the luminous glyphs on the Wolf Stone. It lit the sphagnum on the ground; Mordake knelt and touched the moss, found it damp and rough beneath his fingers.

The air grew colder.

The sky above him was empty no longer. It remained black and starless, but there other, deeper darknesses moved within it; huge silhouettes who loomed above him. Then eight dull stars appeared in the sky; they shone with the same pale light as the glyphs on the stone. They were huge, like winter suns seen through layers of cloud, and in pairs; one pair to each of the titan shapes above him. Mordake realised that they were eyes.

Four shapes: one for each point of the compass. Hunched shoulders, pointed ears, the suggestion of a long muzzle. Like a dog's – no, a wolf's. The Night Wolves. They were real. Not myths, not legends, not metaphors: the literal truth of things.

And the Night Wolves looked down upon him, and they saw.

Their glowing eyes expanded and swallowed the world. Mordake felt their gaze reach into him, felt that terrible revealing light seep through flesh and blood and bone. They saw through clothes and skin and flesh; they saw down to the DNA that shaped his body, to the thoughts and memories that shaped his mind, to the molecules and atoms and subatomic particles that made everything he was. He was seen and known and classified, a microbe on a glass slide.

I am nothing to them; they could annihilate me with a thought.

And yet they didn't. Their eyes brightened for a second, and something seared through Mordake, down to the very core of him; he felt himself about to unravel, and cried out. But then the glow faded, and as their eyes dimmed away to nothing, light bled back into the sky. With it came sounds again: faint and distant though they were, they crashed into that silence like angry waves.

The Night Wolves were gone; the Wolf Stone was a cold grey stone again. Hobsdyke was just a village, the people in it tiny dots – but again there was that impression that they'd all just turned away, en masse, from looking up at the hill.

Mordake was shaking. But it would pass: what he'd seen couldn't have been real. Already it felt impossible – an hallucination, a waking dream.

There was a pain in his right palm, like a brand. Mordake slowly turned the hand palm-up, and saw a ridged red weal. It was already fading, the swelling going down, but its shape was too familiar; one of the North Sea Culture's glyphs. What did it mean? What did it mean?.

Mordake stumbled towards the hill-path back towards the village. He'd found what he'd come for; it was time to go and he could always come back – but right then he would have happily vowed never to come near Hobsdyke again as long as he could leave it, and as long as he could believe that none of what he'd seen was real. Hallucinations, nothing more, both in the wood and up here.

And the mark on your hand? I suppose that's a hallucination as well?

The journey down was easy, the gradient working with him now; in a few minutes he'd reached the stone where he'd rested. He didn't stop now – the sooner he reached the bottom, the sooner he could be in the car, heading back towards Lancaster and Liz – but he did risk looking at his hand again.

Let it not be there, let it not be there, let me only have imagined it –

Mordake thought there might have been the faintest red patch on the palm of his hand, but even that was fading, soon it would be gone, and Mordake was already doing his best to convince himself it had never been there. A dream, like his vision on the hill.

*

HOBSDYKE VILLAGE

"Hello again, Doctor," called a voice as Mordake walked – did *not* run, despite the temptation – down the High Street. He looked up; it was Balchin. "How did you get on?"

Balchin's smile was cruel and smug, his eyes cold, unblinking. No sign of the nervous drunk Mordake had met before. Mordake went by without a word, making for the far end of the High Street and the Volvo. Balchin called after him. "What did you find up there, Doctor Mordake? What did you see?"

People stepped out of the shops and houses: farmers in heavy jackets and wellingtons, men and women in jeans and shirts – commuters with jobs in nearby towns – and children. Mordake saw Eleanor from The Gaffer's Arms, the waitress who'd served him in the tea rooms. All of them were blank-faced and empty-eyed, gazing straight ahead. They didn't even seem to see Mordake, but spread out across the road to block his way.

"Leaving us already, Doctor?" Balchin called. "There's so much more, still to be revealed."

Mordake turned back towards him. If he could get past Balchin, perhaps he could skirt round behind the houses to the car. Once he was in the Volvo with the engine running, he'd be away from here, for good.

Something drew Mordake's gaze upwards, towards the hilltop. There were people standing there. Only tiny stick figures at this distance, but there was something *wrong* about them, and they'd started to descend the hill.

Balchin was chuckling; Mordake backed away from him. When he turned around, he saw the villagers advancing down the road.

Insane. Impossible. He must be asleep and dreaming. Dozing by the fire in the Gaffer's Arms. But even as the hope took shape, he knew it was false. This was real.

Mordake ran up the street. He'd shoulder-charge the crowd, break through them. But he faltered; a revulsion he couldn't name rose in him at the thought of touching them. And even if he could bear it, he wouldn't get past them; they were waiting for him to try.

Can't go forward, can't go back –

Mordake broke across the High Street towards the stream that chuckled alongside. He cleared it with the kind of leap he hadn't even attempted since his schooldays, crashed to the ground on the far side. He landed on a stone; pain burst through his hip, and he cried out.

He stood, and saw the villagers had formed into a line, facing him; they moved towards the bridge over the river.

There was only one way left to go. Gritting his teeth against the pain in his side, Mordake stumbled along the path to Gaffer's Wood.

*

GAFFER'S WOOD

The trees swallowed him. Needles crunched underfoot. A thick scent of pine sap. The shade cast a creeping chill that even running couldn't drive out.

The thought of re-entering the woodland hadn't been appealing, but it was preferable to letting the villagers lay hands on him. Besides, the wood wasn't *that* deep, and there was another village beyond it. But although the village might not be far as the crow flew, when you were on foot, injured, out of condition and pursued – it was far enough.

No buses, no taxis to flag down; his best hope was to clear the woods, get to a road and flag down a passing car, while hoping that the driver didn't turn out to be part of this. Some kind of mass hypnosis, had to be – God knew how it had been done, but it had been. Did it only affect the Hobsdyke folk, or would it extend beyond the village?

There had to be be limits, surely, or Mordake himself would be under that influence already. Perhaps there was something in the air or water. Or perhaps whoever was behind this – Balchin? – was simply enjoying Mordake's panic.

Surely the woods should have come to an end by now. Gaffer's Wood was perhaps two miles across. Unfit or not, Mordake should be out of here by now. He was tired and starting to flag, and God knew where the villagers were. The most horrible thing had been the total silence in which they moved. In any case, they couldn't be far behind. He had to find a way out, he just had to keep going.

But still the woods didn't end. And he was sure he'd passed this spot at least once before. Mordake's legs shook; he leant against a tree. He mustn't stop, or he'd never be able to start again. But he hadn't the strength; his legs were weak, the muscles little more than jelly, the bones aching as if they'd crumble at any moment.

Weak. Soft, spoilt, city-bred man, no stamina for a real challenge. He thought of Liz, in their bed at the Toll Booth Inn, the hot smooth silk of her skin on his. Her laughter. Her smile. Their ghost children, not yet born: he needed to see them come into the world, but most of all, he needed her.

He pushed himself away from the tree and staggered on. The woods blurred in and out of focus. His steps were slow and stiff and stumbling, his momentum and rhythm gone.

Until now, he'd been able to hear nothing over his rasping breaths and the thump of blood in his ears; now other sounds crept in. Cracking twigs. Needles underfoot. And something else. Whispers: half-formed words. Flickers at the periphery of his vision: shadows. Like people moving just out of sight, vanishing when he looked.

Mordake could no longer see clearly; he held his hands out ahead of him to avoid blundering into the trees. And then he was groping at empty air; the woods had opened out into a clearing.

Recognition dawned after a few seconds, when Mordake registered the vestiges of the earthworks he'd sketched earlier. He should have got straight back into the car, driven back to Lancaster. Liz. Liz was waiting for him. He'd never come home, he realised, and she'd never know what had happened. He was sure of that. Whatever Hobsdyke's people were, they covered their traces well.

There was a shimmer in the air, like heat haze. Mordake's legs shook; he couldn't run any further, and any way there was no point. Even though the DMV site was near the woods' edge, he knew now that he'd never get out of the trees.

The shimmer intensified, till it resembled smoke or shadows in the air. Parts of it turned opaque, becoming blurred inchoate shapes. And then, as though a lens had been adjusted, they sprang into focus. There were low timber-framed cottages with thatched roofs, with people in cloaks and tunics standing outside. People of a kind.

Gaffscote.

Mordake cried out, and the lens shifted again; the buildings blurred to shadows, a shimmer, then nothing. The people, however, remained, and began walking towards him.

Mordake backed away and turned to run, but they'd already reached him. Hands caught his arms, in a grip as gentle as it was unbreakable. Then a hand touched his forehead, and he slumped.

They carried him back to the village, and one of them pointed to the ground. The soil sank inwards, then fell away. A dark hole gaped in the earth; then light filled it, revealing a flight of steps leading downwards.

Mordake's captors carried him down into a stone chamber. When the last of the villagers had descended, one of them pointed upwards. The earth piled on the stone floor stirred, then flew upwards in flurries and clods. The light above faded as the sky was blotted out. For a moment a roof of packed earth hung overhead; then the edges of the stone walls flowed inwards like grey water, before hardening once more into solid rock.

"Bring him," someone said. "Don't be afraid, Doctor Mordake. You're going to live."

Mordake's eyes closed, and he sank into the blessed dark as his captors carried him away.

8.

The Temple of the Elders, Bereloth
18th July, Attack Plus Twenty-One Years
1256 hours

Behind Helen, the others murmured. For or against? She could see the temptation of it, but when she turned and studied Karalagh, the Heresiarch and the other Elders regarded her with placid smiles. *Take or leave it, we don't care. But, of course, we both know you'll take it.*

The smug certainty on their faces made her prickle with anger. But there was something else, something more. Their appearance, their strangeness? No, it wasn't that, she was certain. She couldn't define it except as instinct, or the conditioned reflexes that had kept her alive this long.

She surveyed the Temple again. Firelight from the braziers gleamed on the idols' faces. All freshly polished and cleaned. She turned back to Karalagh. "I don't think so," she said.

She ignored the gasps from behind her, watching the Heresiarch. Karalagh's face was composed, but for a split-second, there was real, baulked fury in her eyes. Then it was gone, and Karalagh smiled. "Really?"

"Really," said Helen. "I've seen where your 'true knowledge' leads."

"You've seen its perversion."

"I've seen what it was always intended to do."

"That may have been its original intent, but not the use we make of it."

"So you say." Helen could still hear voices murmuring behind her; the Dwellers' aid was still a tempting offer, at least to some of her party. And the *Garalakh Tep Sharhr* had waited till they were in the heart of their city before making their offer. A blatant trap, and they'd walked straight into it. *She* had. If Helen could get to the Heresiarch, put a gun to her head, could she force a way out for them? "The answer's still no."

Karalagh shook her head. "Really? How many lives could be saved with our help? How many lost without it? We can end this conflict quickly, with a minimum of bloodshed. Are you so in love with war?"

So soft, so reasonable. So much like – *No. You are not my mother.* "It's nothing to do with that."

"No?" Karalagh raised an eyebrow. "When was the last time your actions didn't serve your ego? You're really going to reject an alliance that would save thousands of lives, all in the name of purity, risk the deaths of those you claim to care for in order to further your personal crusade?" She smiled, and a chill spread through Helen. "But it wouldn't be the first time. Would it, Helen Winter?"

*

MORDAKE'S QUARTERS, THE TOWER
1301 HOURS

Mordake's convulsions had ceased; now he just twitched occasionally, foam drying on his lips. His eyes were closed, moving under their lids in dream, and in remembering

Pressed into the pillow, the second face chuckled. Its anger had passed; now it just had to wait. The fit would end, and when it did, Mordake would be its once more.

*

BENEATH GRASPEN HILL
MARCH 8TH, THE YEAR OF THE WAR
ATTACK MINUS TWO MONTHS

He was being carried shoulder high, on his back. Above him the stone ceiling scrolled past. Light that came from everywhere and nowhere.

He lifted his head. There was a city: streets laid out neat as grids, manicured lawns, parks with trickling streams, all lit without a sun.

A domed steel temple. Idols mounted on columns. Tall brass braziers where fires burned. An altar. He was laid upon it.

Faces appeared above him, gazing down.

Darkness flooded in, and their eyes began to glow. Soon he could only see the eyes in the blackness: a circle of lights that now began to spin, blurring into a glowing ring.

In the wheeling lights, a darkness formed, and reached down.

They were above him again, the shapes he'd seen on Graspen Hill. They saw him, through space, and time. Their time was not yet now, but soon, a day they'd awaited for millennia. And this time there would be no vast, complex ritual; this time, they would proceed slowly, by increments and experiments.

The North Sea Culture was gone; only these few remnants were left, to be husbanded and conserved. So they would not be risked: instead there would be emissaries, carefully chosen, who when the time was right would find reasons to pursue a goal they thought was their own, while in truth serving the Night Wolves, and the *Garalakh Tep Sharhr*.

A single word, whispered in the dark: *Tindalos*.

It snaked down into the dark of his mind, wormed into some hidden crevice there and slept, waiting for its time.

The dark shrank back within the whirligig of lights; they slowed and separated into pairs. The glow within them dimmed, and the eyes were only eyes again. The light returned, and those faces, sheened a metallic grey, gazed down at him.

"Forget," said one of the faces. A hand reached down, brushed Mordake's forehead. "Forget."

The faces and the domed ceiling faded into shadow, as though sinking away into deep water.

*

The Temple of the Elders, Bereloth
18th July, Attack Plus Twenty-One Years
1302 hours

"What are you talking about?" said Gevaudan. Karalagh's smile widened. Helen's stomach dropped away with a sick lurch. Karalagh *knew*. Helen had no idea how she could, but she did: she knew, and she was going to tell.

Helen wanted to fall to her knees and beg. *Please, don't*. But that would just tell everyone Karalagh was right, and it wouldn't do any good anyway.

"Why do you think she does this?" said Karalagh. "Freedom? Justice? All of this came from one thing – the hope that killing Tereus Winterborn would make her nightmares end."

Karalagh looked away from Helen, at the other. "She dreamt – still dreams – of a Black Road. Of her family, killed by the Reapers, because Winterborn betrayed the Refuge to them – a young man who worshipped her. Helen seduced, then rejected him. She shattered him, turned him into the monster he is now. Her family's ghosts torment her constantly, demanding Winterborn's death. If not for those, she'd still be hiding in the Wastelands. Instead, she came back, and started a war in which hundreds – thousands – have died or will. Because she can't sleep at night, because of all she's done. And then there's you, Gevaudan Shoal."

No, thought Helen. *No, not that*. The Sterling hung at her side; the .38 weighed at her hip. She'd be killed, but better that than hear what Karalagh had to say.

"There's what she did to you," said Karalagh.

"What?" said Gevaudan.

Helen raised the Sterling. "Shut up."

Karalagh barely even glanced at her, just flicked her hand; the Sterling flew from Helen's grip, up into the air. Karalagh's fingers flicked again, and a blow smashed into Helen's upper arm. She cried out, stumbling sideways into Gevaudan.

And Gevaudan stepped away from her.

There were shouts from the others. Gunbolts clicked; weapons rose. Faarrgrepa and his men raised their guns too.

"Remain calm," Karalagh said, a hand still raised.

There were gasps from around Helen, and Brant pointed. She looked, and saw the Sterling suspended in the air. Karalagh's hand curled into a fist; veins rose at the Heresiarch's temples as she did so. There was a screech and crunch of crumpling metal, and the Sterling collapsed in on itself like wet clay. Karalagh opened her hand, and a ball of crushed steel clattered on the Temple floor.

"You abuse our hospitality," Karalagh said, "but I don't hold the rest of you responsible for Helen's actions. You have, however, seen for yourselves that she risked all of your deaths to silence me."

Karalagh turned back to Gevaudan. Helen didn't look at him, couldn't. She still had the .38, but her gun arm was numb. She felt her upper arm, gasping in pain. She didn't think the bone was broken, but the bruise was cripplingly deep. In any case she wasn't sure, in that moment, whether she'd have tried to use the gun on Karalagh or on herself.

"She sought you out," said Karalagh, "didn't she, Gevaudan Shoal, to fight for her and her precious cause? Did she tell you that you mattered? That you weren't just a pawn in a game to her, but a *person*?" Karalagh shrugged. "I *do* know she told you she had her own supply of the Goliath serum, and that it was yours if you fought for her."

That wasn't true – she'd told him it was his whatever he chose. Wouldn't Gevaudan remember that? But one half-lie wouldn't taint this truth. "Shut up," said Helen.

"She'd found a supply in the Wastelands before returning to Manchester. That's what she told you, wasn't it?" Karalagh shook her head. "A lie, Gevaudan Shoal. She searched long and hard, but when the time came to enter the city, she'd found nothing."

Karalagh's gaze shifted. "Wakefield of the Fox tribe knows what followed. The crazy ginger gave her a map, had her search a list of locations while she went to the city to find you. A last-ditch gamble that they'd find the serum you'd die without."

Gevaudan looked slowly from Helen to Wakefield; the little tribeswoman shrank back, eyes widening. She looked at Helen; there was hurt and betrayal in her face.

"Wakefield knew nothing of Helen's game," Karalagh went on. "The map also listed weapons caches and other useful supplies. The serum was just one more item; Wakefield had no way of knowing that she was your one hope of survival."

The yellow Grendelwolf eyes turned back towards Helen.

"The gamble paid off, of course," Karalagh said softly, "and here you are. But if it hadn't? You experienced yourself, only weeks ago, the fate she'd have risked for you. She'd have seen you dead, just like all of you here. And for what? A few bad dreams."

Helen couldn't look at Gevaudan, and Wakefield wouldn't meet her eyes. In the others' eyes, she saw shock, pity, disgust. And she saw anger.

The anger was fiercest on Carson's face; the ex-Reaper's hands tightened on her rifle. The zeal of the convert: Carson had unpicked herself and stitched herself back together again, abandoned all she'd known for Helen's war: her ex-comrades would kill her, and her new ones would never truly accept her. And all for this? Stood to reason, she'd be the angriest of all. After Gevaudan.

"You..." said Carson. The rifle rose, but Gevaudan moved, one long white hand grabbing the barrel and pushing it down. "No," he said, and turned towards Helen. "Is it true?" he said at last.

"Gevaudan," she said; her voice was faint and weak.

"*IS IT TRUE?*" He bellowed it. Everyone stepped back from him, Helen included. She'd only ever heard him raise his voice in battle: Gevaudan never lost control.

He took a deep breath. "Is it true?" he said again. Very quietly. In a way, that was worse than the shouting. "I shan't ask again."

All she could think of was the meal in the garden, his white face in the candlelight, the tenderness there. *Where there is love and tender care, God is present.* Where had she heard that? She couldn't get the phrase out of her head. There'd been tender care, at the very least, and now it was gone. Whatever had been there had been driven away. Desecrated, quite literally: but hadn't Karalagh only revealed the truth? What Helen had done, what she was? And that that moment in the garden, and all it might have been, was founded on a lie, worth no more than dust?

Gevaudan's eyes, always like a wolf's in colour, had never more closely resembled those of the beast Helen had seen in the zoo as a child. She had to answer, and couldn't look away. If she felt anything for him, she owed him that. "Yes," she said at last.

Gevaudan's body tensed, shook for a moment; then he breathed out. "No-one harm her," he said. "If anyone's going to kill her, it'll be me."

He let go of the rifle; Carson checked the barrel for dents.

He will destroy you.

"I'm sorry for your distress," Karalagh said. "But it was necessary that you knew." She exchanged glances with the other Elders. "There's a meditation chamber here; Faarrgrepa will show you to it. You may wish to deliberate our offer together." Her gaze rested on Helen. "And, perhaps, your choice of leader."

"This way," said Faarrgrepa.

The group drew away from Helen as they were ushered across the Temple. Even Wakefield wouldn't look at her.

A flight of steps led downwards, into a corridor beneath. There were several doorways; Faarrgrepa stopped in front of one. "This one's the most spacious," he said.

The chamber was plain, with stone walls and floor, but warm, dry and well-lit. The air was fresh, and there were chair and couches. A comfortable enough place to die in.

"There'll be a guard outside," said Faarrgrepa. "Necessary for now, I'm sure you understand. Should you need anything, let me know."

He stepped back through the door and closed it. Helen turned slowly, to face the others. Only Wakefield still refused to meet her eyes. The others looked at her, but she wished they didn't.

"Leave her," said Gevaudan. His eyes glistened. "We have things to discuss."

They moved away from Helen to the centre of the room and sat down to talk.

And once more, she stood alone.

*

MORDAKE'S QUARTERS, THE TOWER
1311 HOURS

He was on a narrow bed. Grey walls around him. He twisted onto his side; a bare room, Spartan.

Liz.

"Ah," said a voice. When the lips moved it tugged at his scalp, and the voice vibrated in his skull. He felt it move in his own throat, wanting him to speak it too. "You're back."

Mordake lay there, shaking, as the jumbled pieces fitted back together. Who he was now; who he had been then.

What had he remembered about that day before? That he'd found the site of Gaffscote, pottered around, scraped away a little earth – and found, almost in minutes, his Rosetta Stone, the information he'd needed to unlock the North Sea Culture's secrets.

In retrospect, it was ridiculous: to stumble across that so quickly, on what should have been just the beginning of his study of the site. He'd never questioned it; he'd only mentioned it in passing to Liz herself, a month or two later. At the time, he'd told her he'd found something, nothing more.

"Well, come on," said the voice. He felt it pull at his skin and muscles again. This time it wasn't just in his scalp; his arms and legs jerked and moved. When the second face tried to move him it was always awkward and painful, and it always won in the end, so it was easier to obey it.

"Up!"

"You..." It wasn't easy to speak when the second face was trying to. "You programmed me. Like a machine. You knew the War was coming."

"The important part," said the face; that *voice*, grating on the back of his skull, "was that you'd work to restore the Night Wolves. Liz's death was just a convenient motive. If she'd lived, you'd have found another reason."

"And I'd have kept with it?" Mordake said. "Even if it cost me her. Right?"

The second face only laughed. To anyone but him, Liz's death had been less than a footnote to the War, and to the Night Wolves' servants, not even that; her only relevance was as an aid to motivating him.

"Up!" said the second face. Mordake stood, but its laughter faded when he lurched towards his desk. "Where are you going?" it said. "What are you –?"

Mordake jerked the desk drawer open; inside was a small, flat, grey pistol.

"Leave that!"

It tugged the muscles of his arm like puppet's strings, but his hand closed around cold metal and he took out the gun.

"Mordake. Stop."

"Fuck you," he said, and struck himself across the back of his head with the gun. The second face yelped; Mordake hit it, again and again. Each blow sent white pain spearing behind his eyes and he fell to his knees, but the face's screams faded, and with it the tugging on his limbs.

Grunting, shaking, Mordake forced himself to his feet, leaning on the desk for balance. Blood covered his right hand, and the gun. He was shaking. But – for now - he was something like himself again.

There was time, still, to set things right.

He pulled back the pistol's slide to chamber a round, stuffed the weapon into his robe and pulled up his hood over the battered second face.

"Winterborn," he said thickly.

9.

MEDITATION CHAMBER, TEMPLE OF THE ELDERS, BERELOTH
18TH JULY, ATTACK PLUS TWENTY-ONE YEARS
1322 HOURS

Helen sat in a far corner of the room, cross-legged, staring down at her folded hands; from time to time Carson saw her hand stray to the .38 at her hip.

Should someone take the weapon from her? No, Carson decided; she knew enough of Helen to guess who she'd turn the gun on if she did use it. Of course, that might be making things easier on her than she deserved.

On the other hand, Carson was here, now – and glad of it – because of Helen. Glad of the person she'd become, the faith she now had. That had been worthwhile; the rebellion was worthwhile. Helen's character didn't matter.

Feet of clay. She'd read that in her Bible at Ashwood. They hadn't been given their own in the Reapers, just the excerpts from it that the Chaplain picked. It wasn't until after Ashwood that she'd read it for herself. *Feet of clay.* Everyone, ultimately, had them. But what Helen had built was what matter. That was true; truer than her.

Carson was here – and might see Heaven – because of Helen. In that case, let Helen have the means to end it all. If that was her choice, she'd earned that, at least. God moved in mysterious ways, His wonders to perform.

"Why shouldn't we?" Filly was saying. "I wanna live through this."

Her fingers brushed Wakefield's. The tribeswoman's cheeks turned red. "Don't trust them," she said. "Not right. None of this."

"I never thought I'd live through this," Brant said quietly. "Joined up because it was better than waiting for the Reapers to get us. Recked I'd at least get to pay 'em back before I went. But now, we might win. I wanna be alive for that. So this lot? Don't have to like or trust 'em. Watch 'em close – but use 'em to get the Reapers." He looked at Helen. "Always our sort, getting shot at for hers."

"Gevaudan?" said Wakefield, looking deeply unhappy. Carson got that: she liked things simple and certain. Helen was a friend; whatever came out of Hobsdyke was bad.

The Grendelwolf was about to speak, but then the door opened and a Dweller stepped through.

She – it took Carson a moment to realise it was a woman, with her robes and shaved head – was frowning, veins popping out on her temples. She put a finger to her lips, shut the door behind her, then breathed out. The veins on her head subsided.

"Can we help you?" Gevuadan said.

"I hope we can help one another," said the woman, and came to kneel beside them. Helen stirred in her corner, studying the new arrival. "I'm Mantaaresh," the woman said. "I've come to get you out of here. Karalagh and the others lied to you."

Gevaudan glanced at Helen.

"Not about that," said Mantaaresh. She looked at Helen too. "I'm sorry. Karalagh told you that they don't follow their old religion, didn't she? That they just make use of their powers, but only to build and maintain Bereloth? She lied. The Elders are the most powerful of us. And that's because they've given themselves the most fully over to the part of the Night Wolves that's in them. That's why they rule. It's a theocracy, the same as it always was, and with the same aim."

Carson slid a hand into her pocket, gripped the crude wooden cross. Across the room, she saw Wakefield clasp her talisman-pouch between both hands; she looked as if she was praying.

"They told the truth about Mordake, though. He's developing a weapons system for Winterborn – like Project Tindalos, its ultimate purpose is to resurrect the Night Wolves."

"If that's true, why offer to help us destroy it?"

"Karalagh and the others have looked ahead," said Mantaaresh. "Even with Mordake helping Winterborn, you might still win. Anything using the Night Wolves' technology can be used to help them return. The Catchmen, for instance – when the time is right, they can be converted into Styr, to build new hives for the Night Wolves. Anything Karalagh offers you will be no different."

"So," said Gevaudan. "Both sides will be fighting with weapons that will bring the Night Wolves back. Whoever wins, we all lose."

"Clever," said Wakefield. "What if we say no?"

"They'll kill you," said Mantaaresh. "Especially now you know the truth."

"If it *is* the truth," said Brant. "How do we know *you're* not the one lying?"

Mantaaresh nodded. "I can show you proof, but it will be difficult. If you come and see, you must be silent."

Brant looked around at the rest. "We agree?"

"Yes," said Wakefield. The others nodded.

"And then?" said Gevaudan.

"Then I'll guide you out of here. You can get back to your people and warn them."

Carson looked at the others. One by one, they nodded. Brant sighed. "Should have bloody known it wouldn't be easy."

They stood; Helen remained seated in her corner. "What about her?" asked Carson.

"Leave her," said Brant.

"No!" Wakefield snapped. Filly shushed her.

"We bring her," said Gevaudan. Helen looked up at him. "It would be too easy to leave her here to die. She wouldn't have to face the rest of us."

Helen's grey eyes brimmed; she looked away.

"Right, then," said Carson. "Let's see this."

*

Mantaaresh stood in silence before the door for a nearly a minute before opening it. Her breathing grew harsher; veins rose at her temples again. When she opened the door, Carson followed her out, the others trailing behind. They let her go first, she knew, in case it was a trap.

Faarrgrepa and his men stood motionless in the corridor, frozen in mid-movement. Faarrgrepa's mouth was half-open, twisting into what Carson guessed to be a smile.

"Hurry," said Mantaaresh. Her voice was tight with pain. "I can't hold them long. And shut the door, or they'll be suspicious."

Brant, the last one out into the corridor, obeyed.

"Good," Mantaaresh said. "Now, with me. And keep silent."

She led them away. She glanced back at them once or twice, and Carson saw the veins on her head subsiding once more.

Carson heard chanting, growing louder as they went. Mantaaresh stopped at a bend in the corridor, holding up a hand. She turned back to them, the veins on her head more thickly swollen than ever before and mouthed "Look."

Carson peered around the corner. The corridor opened into a circular chamber; in its centre was a metal dome with brass doors, a white pillar at – Carson guessed – each compass point. It was, she realised, a miniature replica of the Temple. It was perfect in detail, too: only the doors – tall and wide enough to admit two people to enter abreast – were out of proportion.

Those doors were now open; braziers flamed on either side. Robed, bare-headed figures knelt before them in a triangle formation, its point towards the doors. They were chanting.

"Angana sor varalakh kai torja. Angana sor varalakh cha voran."

The woman at the front of the group raised her head, arms spread wide; it was Karalagh.

Wakefield touched Carson's arm; she moved aside to let the tribeswoman look. One by one, the others followed.

The chant ended, and the group stood; Karalagh closed the brass doors and the Elders filed back down the corridor. Carson and the others pressed back against the walls, but the Elders never looked once at them. *They don't see us.*

Mantaaresh breathed out; her head-veins subsided once more. "All right," she said. "Come and see."

They followed her to the dome. Mantaaresh took a deep breath, opened the brass doors, then turned back to them, a finger to her lips.

Wakefield and Filly were first to look into the dome. Wakefield's face drained and whitened; Filly gripped her arm. Carson went to join them.

A pale glow lit the inside of the dome, shining out from the thing inside. Sitting on its haunches, it was about twenty feet high, with long thin forelegs, a narrow head, and what might have been either ears or horns.

The wolf, or the goat. There was a vague resemblance in terms of outline, but nothing beyond that. The thing's hide was made up of greenish, overlapping plates of moist, leathery material. The light shone from the gaps in the armour, pulsating rhythmically. Around its neck was a ruff of what looked like exposed roots

– smooth, grub-white and pale – that rippled and undulated like weeds underwater.

The thing's eyes – huge, even in proportion to that body – glowed too, through thick, membranous lids. Under the lids, they moved, up and down and side to side.

"It's asleep," said Mantaaresh. "And dreaming."

When they'd all seen, Mantaaresh closed the doors. "Wakefield, and Gevaudan Shoal, you were at Hobsdyke. You've seen this before."

Wakefield nodded.

"A Night Wolf," Gevaudan said. "Albeit considerably smaller than the one we encountered."

"The creature you saw at Hobsdyke was created from the essences of many victims, in their entirety," Mantaaresh said. "They were drained complete, of all they were. Here, full sacrifices have been few."

"Yes," said Gevaudan. He glanced at Helen. "It's always easier to sacrifice others."

Mantaaresh shook her head. "According to the Religion, once absorbed into the substance of a Night Wolf, you become as a god yourself, so it's as high an honour as you can have. But there are only a few thousand of us, and the last of the faith's followers. So we're a resource, to be carefully husbanded. So we watch and wait. And the right conditions to attempt to resurrect the Night Wolves only arose recently."

"But they made this, even so," said Gevaudan.

"A handful of chosen sacrifices. For the rest, devotees donate a little of themselves, here and there. Enough to keep a part of the Night Wolves alive here. A symbol of their commitment, if you like. For now, it sleeps, until the time comes for it to wake. Have you seen enough?"

"Fuck, yes," muttered Brant. "Should've known it was too good to be true."

Mantaaresh closed the brass doors. "Now," she said, "we need to get you out to warn the others. Come with me."

"Where to?" Helen asked. Everyone looked at her; it was the first she'd spoken since the revelation in the Temple. Carson could tell Helen didn't want to meet the others' eyes, but was forcing herself to. That must have cost her.

"There's a way out," Mantaaresh said. "A second Temple, beneath the village ruins in Gaffer's Wood. It's a memorial, hardly ever actually used."

"Memorial?"

"To our ancestors." Mantaaresh started walking. Carson and the others followed; Carson saw Helen lingering, biting her lip, then following.

"The Saxons destroyed Gaffscote village," Mantaaresh explained, "but by then, a division had occurred among its inhabitants. Some wanted to keep to the old ways, hiding in plain sight. Others foresaw that could not continue: sooner or later they'd be either exposed and destroyed, or become assimilated and forget their roots. Their solution was to hide completely, unseen by normal humans."

"And they became the *Garalakh Tep Sharhr?*" said Gevaudan.

"Basically, yes. But they knew they'd have to manage their bloodlines carefully to avoid inbreeding, and to maintain some connection to the outside world. They thought it poetic justice that Gaffscote's destroyers gave them an answer to both."

"Hobsdyke." Helen breathed out. "Changelings, right?"

A few people glared at her, but Mantaaresh nodded. "Just so," she said. "The *Garalakh Tep Sharhr* stole children from the Hobsdyke natives, substituting their own, while raising the stolen children as breeding stock. As time went by they had to alter their children's appearance to hide their true nature, but it continued, almost up to the War. Within a few centuries, although they never knew it, almost Hobsdyke's entire population were at least partly of the *Garalakh Tep Sharhr* by birth."

Helen snorted. "Best way to hide in plain sight," she said. "When you don't even know you're hiding."

She spoke, Carson realised, as though she and Mantaaresh were the only people there. Mantaaresh inclined her head. "As you say. A few moments' concentration on the Elders' part would put some or all of Hobsdyke's population into a trance state in which they'd carry out any command the Elders gave, and remember nothing afterward. It gave the *Garalakh Tep Sharhr* eyes, ears and hands in the world above, while allowing them to remain undetected."

Mantaaresh led them down an unlit corridor branched off the main one; she raised a hand and gestured, and the lights flickered on. "Bereloth began under the Gaffscote site, but they tunnelled towards what's now Hobsdyke and Blypen Hill. The hill's the centre of it all, you see."

"The centre of what?" said Gevaudan. He didn't look at Helen.

"All this area is... sacred to the *Garalakh Tep Sharhr*," Mantaaresh said. "Or perhaps sacred isn't the right word. You understand that certain conditions, which have no effect on humans, can be highly significant to the Night Wolves?"

"Yes," said Helen and Gevaudan together. She looked at him; he gazed resolutely ahead. "Mordake," said Helen, reddening. "He told us the Night Wolves died out because something changed – something we wouldn't even notice, but that made it impossible for them to survive."

"Correct. Similarly, certain conditions had to be right to effect the Night Wolves' return, and certain locations are more propitious to such attempts. Mordake has power, even far from here, but he isn't like us. He was touched by the Night Wolves themselves. Away from here, we have little or no power – Gaffer's Wood, and to a lesser extent Hobsdyke, greatly amplify our abilities. But Graspen Hill is the most powerful of all. So the Beloved abandoned the village under Gaffscote and came here."

The lights flickered out behind them as they walked, and flickered on ahead. "We need to move quickly," Mantaaresh said. "When they realise we've gone, they'll search. You need to get clear by then – I assume your transport is at the edge of Gaffer's Wood?"

"It is," Gevaudan said.

"Then our greatest difficulty will be getting through the wood itself. There are *things* there – even if they can't harm us directly, they can alert the Elders. And the Elders can do us a great deal of harm."

"What if Faarrgrepa realises we're gone?" Helen said. "I'm guessing he's not still standing around like a statue."

That drew a few hostile glances, but not as many; the priority for now was to escape. But afterwards… what Karalagh and the others had revealed, Carson knew, wasn't going to go away.

"No," Mantaaresh said, "but I planted a command in his mind that he wouldn't need to check on you for a while. Unless someone else orders him to, of course – I can't do anything about that."

Minutes passed in silence after that; the corridor gave way to open chambers holding empty, cell-like rooms. In a larger chamber beyond were half-dead, overgrown gardens, a stagnant pond, a smell of dead and rotten things. "We're almost there," Mantaaresh said.

In the largest chamber of all were small houses – cruder-looking than anything Carson had seen in Bereloth, but the same design – and a gleaming, brass-doored steely dome surrounded by four white columns around it. Another duplicate of the Temple, but this one had a spiral staircase leading upwards from the roof. The steps seemed to literally wind *into* the stone, as if the rock had congealed around them.

Mantaaresh broke into a stride. She pointed at the brass doors, and they swung open; light bloomed inside the dome as the braziers lit.

The temple's interior was much the same as that of the main one in Bereloth, only on a far smaller scale: the same idols dotted around, the same raised dais and semicircle of thrones. The sole difference, again, was the spiral staircase; it wound down to ground level in the middle of the dais, covered in cobwebs and rust.

"Quickly," Mantaaresh said. The staircase creaked and shivered, shedding thin whispers of dust, as she climbed. Carson eyed it dubiously. "Hurry," called Mantaaresh. Helen brushed past Carson to begin climbing; after a moment, Gevaudan followed.

Carson breathed out. "Fuck it," she muttered, and glanced at Wakefield. "Gotta die of something."

To her astonishment, Wakefield grinned – for a moment, anyway – then stepped past Carson to the stairs. Filly eyed Carson for a moment, then followed.

The braziers' glow flickered on the metal ceiling. As they climbed, Mantaaresh made another pass with her hand, and a tiny hole appeared in the ceiling and widened until the bared staircase wound upwards towards the stone above.

Above, Filly's bottom swayed, round and firm; Carson did her best to ignore the thoughts it roused in her. Her faith as she'd been taught it in the Reapers would have denounced them as unnatural and vile; the Jesus she'd come to know at Ashwood had never spoken against such feelings, and the rebels, as a whole, seemed to have no issues. But it was hard to shake off a lifetime's learning overnight. Besides, it might be right for them, but should it be, for her? Might it be a penance for her, a cross to bear? Something to deny herself, in order to atone?

One thing was for certain, and that was that it was probably safest not to be caught eyeing up Filly's arse. If Filly didn't kill Carson herself, Wakefield would.

Firelight danced on the stone ceiling locked around the staircase. Mantaaresh raised both hands above her head, palms facing outwards, then began moving her hands apart. The rock rippled and trembled like disturbed water, then ran like wax. Carson recoiled as the liquefied stone oozed downwards, but Mantaaresh turned her palms upward and the stone hung suspended in the air.

Mantaaresh moved her hands further apart; the liquid stone was pushed back upwards and spread out across the ceiling. More stone poured down from above and joined the pool widening overhead, exposing more and more of the staircase.

"Up," said Mantaaresh, "quickly. I'll need my strength above."

Helen, then Gevaudan, climbed on up. Wakefield and Filly followed, with Carson right behind them. Carson looked away quickly from Filly's arse as Wakefield glanced down, studying Mantaaresh instead. Veins bulged across the woman's temples and forehead; her face shone with sweat. "Go!" said Mantaaresh; Carson kept climbing. The stone shaft around her glistened, not with water but with liquid stone.

Light broke in from above. Sunlight; screened through a haze of tree branches, but sunlight nonetheless, and fresh, pine-scented air came with it. A thin light shower of earth and pine needles fell; Carson spat out crumbs of soil.

The staircase shuddered and moved. "Whoah!" said Wakefield, clutching the metal banister. Above her Carson saw the small metal platform at the top of the stair case, rising up into the light. Then it stopped; the staircase shivered once more, and was still again. Helen reached the top, looked around, then stepped off the platform and out of sight. Gevaudan, Wakefield and Filly followed, and then it was Carson's turn.

The platform wobbled slightly under her feet; it was level with the edges of the hole in the middle of a small clearing. Surrounding Carson were the thick pine woods; Gaffer's Wood. In the clearing, she saw Wakefield and Filly holding hands as they glanced nervously about them. Gevaudan was silent, gazing at the hole; Helen stood, alone and apart, arms folded, looking off into the distance at nothing.

Brant poked Carson in the side. "Get a move on."

"Sorry." For once Carson felt as though she meant one specific oversight rather than her whole life; she stepped off the platform, followed by Brant and then the others.

Mantaaresh came last. She was swaying slightly, and almost fell when she stepped off the platform; Carson caught her arm and steadied her. "Thank you," Mantaaresh said; her voice was a reedy gasp. The platform sank back out of sight and the hole closed, the earth flowing back into place over the bedrock.

The veins on Mantaaresh's head subsided; she wiped away sweat, breathing heavily. "We must keep moving," she said. "If the Elders don't know already, they soon will."

"Which way?" said Helen.

Mantaaresh pointed and started walking. Carson followed, the others bringing up the rear, and Helen fell into step beside her. "One question," Helen said to Mantaaresh's back.

"Ask," Mantaaresh said. "And quickly."

"Why are you helping us?"

"Karalagh lied to you about the Council's intention," Mantaaresh said, "but some of us truly *don't* want to raise the Night Wolves. We don't want to become part of them. We have our lives and want to live them. The Elders are the most powerful among us, so they're in charge, and they've set us on this course. But not all of us want to follow it, and a few of us are willing to do what we have to in order to prevent it."

"Which would mean overthrowing the Elders," Gevaudan said.

"Yes," said Mantaaresh. "There are a few of us, but on our own it's hard to act. What I'm doing today makes it harder for the others to remain hidden – until now, the Council hasn't known any of us planned to oppose them." She smiled grimly. "I hope not, anyway, otherwise our rebellion's finished before it's begun."

No-one spoke for a few seconds. "The village was here?" Helen said, looking around.

"Yes," said Mantaaresh. "But it's been a long time. Over a thousand years. There are signs, traces, if you know where to look. Mordake did. But we haven't time for that. Your vehicles are to the west, yes?"

"Yes."

"Then walk faster and speak less. Once we're clear of the woods, the Elders can't harm us. Until then, we're still in grave danger."

Something moved over to Carson's left. She spun towards it, rifle raised, but there was nothing there – only movement out of the corner of her eye, to the left again. She pivoted towards it, and her rifle came to bear on Brant. He slapped the barrel aside. "Don't point that fucking thing at me!"

"Easy, Brant," said Helen.

"Shut up," he snapped. "I don't take orders from you now."

"Yes, you do," said Carson. "She's still your CO. We get out of here first, then deal with the rest."

Brant glared, then breathed out, grinning tightly. "All right. Any chance can you point that fucking cannon somewhere else, though?"

Carson smiled back. "Sorry."

"You'll see things," said Mantaaresh. "You'll hear them, too. Ignore them. They'll lure you away to be destroyed. Stay close to me. Things will get worse soon. I'll try to protect you from the worst of it, but I can only do that if you're near."

As they walked on, there were whispers and flickers of motion among the trees around them. The ground became softer underfoot, then wetter, stickier. Carson took a step forward, and her foot sank deep into what felt less like mud than glue. She tried to pull it free, but that meant putting her weight on her back foot, and that began sinking too. Cold wet mud rose over her ankles, then her shins. "Shit!"

Brant grabbed her arm and pulled, but he was sinking too. They all were. "No," said Mantaaresh. The veins on her head were swollen hard as rock. "It isn't real."

The mud shrank back; Carson staggered back into Brant as her feet came free. He supported her for a moment, then grunted, stepping away. "Best keep going," he muttered. "Come on."

They trudged after Mantaaresh. Carson saw Wakefield touch her talisman-pouch to her lips, mouthing a silent prayer. Whispers and twitters from the trees. Moving shadows. Bones among the pine needles. A skull swivelled on the ground and grinned at Carson.

The earth rippled. White domes rose through it, like mushrooms sprouting: more skulls emerged grinning from the earth, and kept rising, pulling fully-formed skeletons after them. The teeth were long and sharp; the fingerbones ended in sharp hooked claws. The hands flexed; the jaws opened and closed. The skeletons moved out to encircle the group. One slashed at Carson with its talons; she jerked her gun up.

"No!" shouted Mantaaresh, and raised a hand. The skeletons fell apart, clattering to the ground in pieces. Carson realised she was standing in front of Filly, rifle aimed at the girl's face; Filly's SMG was levelled at Carson's gut. They stepped back from each other, blinking.

Mantaaresh swayed and nearly fell; Wakefield caught her arm. "It's all right," Mantaaresh said. Bruises dotted her forehead; one eye was bright scarlet, and a tear of blood trickled down her cheek. "We're almost clear."

They kept going. Light gleamed through the tree-trunks up ahead. Nearly out. Nearly clear. Carson wasn't sure, but thought she could make out their landcruisers through the trees. She hoped she could, anyway; it helped her carry on, and she needed help to do so. There was a blinding pain behind her eyes, and she felt sick, ready to vomit at any moment. Her bowels churned, and cold sweat prickled her skin.

And there was a smell of burning earth. A haze in the air. Smoke. It was trickling up from the ground, from spots dotted all about the woodland floor around them. A tongue of flame darted out, licked at the air.

"Run!" shouted Mantaaresh. The rebels bolted for the woods' edge. Smoke caught at the back of Carson's throat. She coughed, choking; tears blurred her vision.

Flames shot up out of the ground in a gout, spraying charred earth; a rebel fell screaming, on fire. Three more blasting jets of flame roared upwards. The burning rebel twitched and was still, charred black. This wasn't an illusion, wasn't a trick: Carson knew that with absolute certainty.

Smoke billowed; the daylight winking through the trees faded and dimmed. More flames exploded upwards. There were screams. Brant was on his knees; he was bleeding from his ears and eyes. Gevaudan stumbled to him, picked him up. The Grendelwolf's ears were bleeding too.

Pain lanced through Carson's ears; wetness trickled down her neck and her hearing dulled. She was bleeding too. Pressure built behind her eyes; her legs buckled and she fell to her knees, vomiting. *Can't get up. Have to get up.* If she could get clear of the woods, this would stop – if not, she'd die here. She tried to stand, but fell back down. *No. No. Get up. Up –*

Hands caught her, pulled her to her feet. An arm around her waist. Carson managed to get her arm about her rescuer's shoulders. Stumbling, weaving, towards the treeline. The air full of screams. The earth on fire. Mantaaresh, her arms outspread, mouth moving in words Carson couldn't hear and wouldn't have understood if she had, blood gushing from her ears and eyes. Carson wasn't sure if Mantaaresh even *had* eyes any more.

Then through the trees and into the light. Air, clean air, the scent of pine gone. Carson had once liked that smell; now she didn't think she ever wanted to smell it again. She could see their landcruisers, the shocked looks on the faces of the sentries they'd left.

"Get in there," Carson heard her rescuer shouting. "We've got people still in there. Get them out."

Gevaudan laid Brant on the grass, then stumbled back towards the woods.

"No," said Carson's rescuer, "not you – Gevaudan, you're –"

But the Grendelwolf went past as if he hadn't heard. Carson's legs buckled again; her rescuer stumbled, gripping her tighter round the waist. "Whoa. Easy. Take it easy. Okay." Carson was lowered to the ground, propped against the side of a landcruiser.

"Thanks," she mumbled, as her rescuer's face swam into focus. "Thank you."

Helen smiled wryly back. "You're welcome."

The pain in Carson's ears had faded; the bleeding had stopped. She took deep breaths. Flames crackled in the woods. The last of the party emerged from the trees, unaided or otherwise.

Gevaudan came out last, swaying. Mantaaresh hung limp in his arms like a soiled grey flag; blood stained her robes and streaked her face. Gevaudan knelt and propped her up beside Carson. "Mantaaresh?"

The Dweller's eyes opened slowly. One eye, anyway; the other had ruptured, bleeding down her face. "I am here."

"Medic!" Helen shouted.

Mantaaresh caught Helen's wrist. "Much too late. This was inevitable."

"Inevitable?"

"Some must be sacrificed for all to live." Mantaaresh forced a smile. "We drew lots. I knew this would be the price." She reached under her robes and withdrew something. "Take."

Gevaudan took it before Helen could: some sort of brass capsule, made from two halves fitted together. "What is it?"

"Should have given earlier." Mantaaresh coughed blood. "Tells you how to contact others like me. You help us, we help you."

"How?" said Gevaudan.

"Karalagh, the Elders. Destroy them. Free us, and we'll fight with you against the Reapers. Haven't got their power, but can fight. Please."

Her head fell back, the breath rattled in her throat, and she was gone.

"Let's go!" Wakefield shouted from one of the landcruisers. Its engine was already clanking into life; the 'cruiser pulled out.

Gevaudan lifted Mantaaresh aboard another 'cruiser, brushing past Helen as he went. Carson got to her feet, wove towards a 'cruiser and climbed aboard.

Helen approached one of the 'cruisers, but one of the occupants said something to her and she stepped back. She came towards Carson's 'cruiser.

"Don't let her on," said someone.

"Yeah," said another. "We don't want you."

Carson looked around. No-one said a word for Helen. Even Gevaudan, in the neighbouring 'cruiser, gazed stonily ahead. Wakefield might have spoken for her, but she was in the lead 'cruiser, already some way distant and accelerating fast. Hack looked from face to face – she didn't know what had happened, but knew something had, and a smirk was shaping on her lips.

"Let her on," Carson heard herself say. "She's earned that much."

That got her a few angry glares, but a couple of the other fighters nodded, and moved up to let Helen sit with them. They purposefully drew back from her, though, and none spoke to or acknowledged her – even Brant, still bleeding and shivering, inched further up the flatbed so they didn't touch.

The landcruiser began to roll. Carson sank back against the side of the flatbed, and closed her eyes.

*

CORRIDOR NEAR WINTERBORN'S OFFICE, THE TOWER
1500 HOURS

Mordake leant against the wall and took the pistol from his pocket, pushing the magazine release and easing the grey metal box from the butt. His hands shook.

Seven bullets in the magazine, one in the chamber. The magazine held nine rounds, and he'd only ever fired one: he'd shot Dowson, Winterborn's old adjutant, in the temple. Never used a weapon before that day. But it had been easy; he'd done it without thinking.

"No." Inside the hood, the second face had woken again. It had kept waking, kept trying to reassert control. The pain he'd inflicted on himself in order to disable it had left him close to collapse. "You think you did that on your own? The Night Wolves, Eddie. You acted on their call, to eliminate a threat. This will be different. It'll be just you doing the killing, and you won't be able to. You'll falter and he'll kill you, or his guards will."

The voice was wheedling. "Let's be sensible about this, Eddie. Hm? No sense getting yourself killed, is there? Let's go back and talk. You're upset, of course you are. I shouldn't have shown you all that, not the way I did. Yes, yes, yes, you deserved to know, but I should have broken it to you more gently. Let you understand. I got angry. I shouldn't have."

The voice had grown silky and caressing. It had never sounded more feminine, more seductive. Mordake shook his head, thrust the magazine back into the pistol and shoved gun and hand back into his pocket. He focused on the bend in the corridor ahead; he lurched to the corner, peering round.

Winterborn's guards stood outside his office. In theory, every visitor was covered on sight and searched at gunpoint, but that didn't happen to Mordake any more. None of them wanted to touch him, and he was a familiar enough sight by now that he was generally waved through. As long as they did that now, when he was armed and in charge of himself, it would be easy. Walk up to Winterborn's desk, and then a single shot to the head, same as Dowson. Maybe another, to make sure. There'd be no way out for him, but what did that matter? There could be no life for him, not now, not any more. He was what he was now, bound together with his devil twin. He could just put the gun in his mouth, pull the trigger, and that would be all. Done.

"No," the second face whispered, tender and soft. "Come on, Eddie. You don't want to do that."

Want? It wasn't a question of wanting, but of necessity. For now, at least, he was still himself, and could choose to end this. End Tindalos and Sycorax; end Winterborn. Put things as right as he could.

Mordake drew himself up: one last performance, enough to get past the guards. And then: Winterborn.

"No," said the face, and the tenderness was gone; the old familiar gloat was back in its voice. Mordake's scalp pulled taut, and other muscles suddenly contracted too. He staggered, legs in sudden spasm, but his left arm shot out in another convulsion and braced itself against the wall. *No*, he tried to shout – but another spasm locked his jaw. He lurched upright; the hand thrust into his pocket clawed open and came free. *No, no, no.*

But he couldn't speak, couldn't move; he could only feel his muscles worked and manipulated by something that wasn't him. *Oh God, no.* He'd forgotten how vile this felt. He wanted to beg, but couldn't. Couldn't speak or move; only scream, silent, feeling himself dwindle away inside his own body as the second face turned it around and marched it back towards its quarters, back in command once more.

10.

HOBSDYKE VILLAGE
MARCH 8TH, THE YEAR OF THE WAR
ATTACK MINUS TWO MONTHS

"So, how was your day?" Mordake asked.

"Well, I enjoyed it, darling. Not sure about your credit card, though. What about you?"

"Yeah, not bad."

"Found anything interesting?"

"You could say."

In the bar at the Gaffer's Arms, Mordake sat beside the fire and nursed a pint of Blonde Witch. Good beer, and the food earlier had been excellent, too. Pity you couldn't smoke in pubs any more. Perhaps he should bring Liz here: a pub lunch, after a walk on Graspen Hill to get their appetite up.

After a few seconds he dismissed the idea; beyond the pub grub there wouldn't be much to interest her. When all was said and done, Hobsdyke just wasn't Liz's kind of place. Part of a happy marriage was knowing which interests were shared, and which were yours alone.

"So when are you gonna be back here?"

Mordake glanced at his watch; nearly four o'clock. "I'm going to make a move in a minute. Get to the hotel with time to kill before dinner. Freshen up, spend some time together." He lowered his voice to what he hoped was a suave purr. "And who knows what else?"

"In your dreams, pal. But get your arse back here anyway, and I might let you give me a back-rub."

"That's a date."

Mordake finished his pint and pottered up the street to the Volvo. The vicar, Balchin, waved from across the street; Mordake waved back but didn't speak. Had to be getting along.

A good day, anyway. Things had gone far better than expected: he'd found Gaffscote, mapped it out pretty thoroughly. And he'd found something else, too; it was in his knapsack now, bouncing against his back.

Mordake remembered the moment clearly: the ground had been split open - subsidence, perhaps – and inside it, caked with old earth, was a small ironbound chest. Very old – Lord knew how it had stayed preserved so long. And inside it were greenish, cylindrical stones, carved with those glyphs he knew so well. And with them, parchments inscribed with faded Latin – the lingua franca of the learned back then, be they Cumbric or Saxon – interspersed with the glyphs.

A Rosetta Stone; he was almost certain of it. A dictionary of the glyphs – a teaching aid for the village children, most likely, for when they grew old enough to trust with their true faith's secrets. No, it hadn't been a wasted trip at all.

But now it was time to go home to Liz. A shame there hadn't been time to climb Graspen Hill – the stones Balchin mentioned had sounded interesting – but he'd be back again, he was sure.

On reaching the car, he turned to study the hill. Yes, he decided; definitely worth a climb at some future point.

Mordake blinked, frowned, then chuckled. For a moment, he'd had the oddest impression that the villagers – and the High Street did seem oddly busy for the time of day – had all turned away from him. As if they'd all been watching him go.

Pure imagination, of course. Some of the villagers were talking – and why not idle around outside for a while, on a pleasant day like this? – while others vanished into shops, the pub or the tea-rooms, or back into their own homes. One man got into his Landrover; he drove past Mordake without sparing him a glance as he passed. And why should he?

Mordake put his knapsack in the car boot, then got behind the wheel. The engine growled into life, and he drove away.

*

The Devil's Highway

18th July, Attack Plus Twenty-One Years
1640 hours

The moors unrolled on either side. Stands of trees; old farmhouses dotted on the distant hills. Easy to bale out, Helen thought; jump over the 'cruiser's side and run. Who'd follow her? They'd be glad to see her gone.

Or perhaps they *would* follow, to ensure she came back to face the music. There'd be no direct punishment – she'd committed no actionable offence – but the damage was done. Who'd serve with her now? Sooner or later, she'd be relieved of command, shunted off to the sidelines. Simple necessity: who'd trust the judgement of a madwoman driven by nightmares of the dead, of a liar and manipulator who deceived those closest to her in order to get what she wanted?

She glanced around the flatbed; none of the others would even look at her. Except Carson; but then, she knew something about being a pariah, too.

Helen had repeatedly glanced towards Gevaudan's 'cruiser on the journey, unable to resist the pathetic hope he'd look her way; that there'd be a smile, some small gesture, something to tell her there might be a way back. There'd been nothing. He'd just gazed straight ahead, never once looking her way.

But others had looked – sidelong glances as they muttered to one another – and their looks had said it all. Her fate, her ending, was being written for her for when they returned to the Fort.

After the Pyramid, Gevaudan had seemed so fragile, despite his size and strength, but there'd been the hope his strength would return and he'd become again what he'd been before. But the damage this time was far less tangible, and what would that do to someone who'd taken so long to reconnect himself to the outside world, and who'd done so through her?

Helen looked out over the moor again; her gaze lingered on a nearby farmhouse. *Jump over, roll and rise, run low across the moor till you're there. Then make it yours; live out your days alone and in peace.*

The thought was as absurd as it was tempting. But whatever else she was, she wasn't that type of coward. She'd face what she'd brought on herself, and she'd take the reckoning and punishment due.

*

DEADSBURY

1700 HOURS

Darrow walked slowly, stiffly, up Wilmslow Road – away from the church, to the overgrown gardens nearby, then in through the gates and down the path through the thick vegetation.

Flaps waited till he was almost out of sight before following, easing her Browning from its holster. Some folk preferred revolvers, like she'd used to have, but the Browning hadn't let her down yet, and it was thirteen shots, 'stead of six. Her free hand drew a knife. Stealth'd be better: a silent kill, if it came to that. But old or not, Darrow was still fast, and good instincts had kept him alive this long.

Darrow disappeared around a corner; Flaps cat-footed to the tall thicket of bushes there and peered down the path, but it was empty. *The fuck?* She started forward, gun raised. He couldn't have gone that fast, could he?

Cold metal touched her neck; a hammer clicked back. "Please don't do anything foolish," said Darrow, emerging from the thicket to take Flaps' pistol. "The knife too, please."

She had other weapons hidden; just needed the chance to get to them. Not that she expected she'd get one; this was Darrow, after all. He *would* drop her though, if she didn't toss the knife. She let it clatter to the ground.

"So," she said. "Why?"

Darrow raised his eyebrows. "I was about to ask you that."

"Why do you think?"

He sighed. "I'm guessing this isn't the first time you've followed me."

"I saw you," she said.

"Saw me where?"

"Baguley."

"I see."

"So, why?"

"Why *what*, Flaps?"

"Think I'm thick?" Angry tears prickled her eyes. "You're selling us to the Reapers."

"*What?*" The gun muzzle left her neck for a moment, then pressed against it before she could turn. "How the hell did you get *that* idea?"

"You went to that place and left them a message," she said. "I went in after you, saw what you'd scratched there."

"What *I'd* scratched? For God's sake, Flaps, didn't you notice how old those marks were?"

Of course. "So they left *you* a message."

Darrow sighed. "I honestly thought you were brighter than this, Flaps. Or at least that you knew me better. Yes, there was a message, but not from the Reapers."

"Who, then? Who was it you weren't telling us about?"

"You really don't remember them?"

"Who?"

"The nursery crew."

"The –" A memory had surfaced. A quiet room, laughter, warmth. A round face, blonde hair. Other sprogs, too. An old memory, long-buried. How old had she been?

"How old were you when we found you?" Darrow said. "Nine? Ten? Near-feral, I expect. You went to Mary's crew quickly enough, but you were in the nursery crew first, along with all the ones too young to fight. We've had new recruits join over the years – did you never wonder where they came from?"

"Nursery crew." It was clearer in her head now.

"Do I have to keep pointing this thing at you?" said Darrow. "I'd really rather not, you know."

Flaps looked sideways at him, met his tired blue gaze. "Kay," she said.

Darrow lowered the Browning. "It was Kate's idea," he said.

"Kate?"

"Can we sit down?" He motioned to a bench. "Age do make bones to creak."

"You talk weird sometimes."

"So I've been told." Darrow holstered the Browning and sat down.

Flaps retrieved her weapons and sat at the far end of the bench. "Who's Kate?"

"A counsellor, before the War. After that... well, her speciality was helping children, so during the Civil Emergency she ended up on the side that tried to avoid killing any. At the Refuge, she was in charge of the nursery. We rescued a lot of children from the Reapers – ferals and so forth, did our best to give them a new life and a family. Sometimes we succeeded, sometimes we didn't."

"Like with Winterborn?"

"He was one. Kate tried to help him, but..."

"But he was a cunt."

"Flaps." Darrow frowned at the language.

"Soz."

"Hm." He sighed, went on. "Kate survived the Refuge Massacre, along with a few children – far too few of them, in fact. She was grieving badly. When we reached the cities, we started recruiting from all the orphaned and abandoned children – she didn't like the idea much, but she also knew a lot of them would have a better chance at some sort of life this way. A lot of the children were very young – not much more than babies, as I said – too young to train to fight, even had we wanted to. So Kate formed her own crew. They didn't fight, didn't have any contact with the others except through me; she just raised the little ones till they were old enough to join one of the main crews. We ended copying that set-up in most of the cities."

"What happened to her then?"

"That's what I've been trying to find out." Darrow sank forward; fucking hell, he looked so fucking *old*. "I tried to get them out during the December Rising, but couldn't make contact with them, and I had to get what was left of the other crews out. I just had to hope Kate would stay safe. That's why I had to come back. I had to know if they'd made it, or if I'd got them all killed."

"And?"

"They moved around, like any other crew. I went to the last place they'd been in, and there was nobody. It was burned out, in fact, but I couldn't tell whether they'd got out or not. But there were safe houses and bolt-holes all over the city. The idea was, if we found ourselves on the run and used one, we'd leave messages behind, to help the other crews find us. Who was there, how many, where they'd gone next."

"So that message at Baguley, that was from..."

Darrow nodded. His eyes were bright. Fucking hell, he looked like he was about to start skriking. "Yes," he said at last. "Finally."

"Shit." Flaps' face burned. "I'm sorry," she mumbled.

Darrow glanced at her, smiled. "It's all right. You have to watch out for traitors. But I'm not one."

"Good," she said. "Wouldn't have wanted to drop you."

Darrow raised an eyebrow. "Mutual, I can assure you."

*

Winterborn's Office
1720 hours

Winterborn leant back, studying Lewis as he entered. Scrubbed, clean, spick and span. He knew the signs: he'd just finished an interrogation. And his eyes were bright, there was a bounce in his step; that meant it had gone well.

If it hadn't, of course, he'd have hardly wanted to see Winterborn, and the plain manila folder under his arm was something of a giveaway. But it was amusing to watch for the little tells.

"Sir." Lewis saluted.

"At ease, Major. So, what do you have for me?"

"A person of interest, Commander." Lewis held out the file.

Winterborn took it, opened it. Inside, pictures: he leafed through them one by one. A tall grey-haired man. In most, the face was half-seen or blurred, but finally, there was one where it was clear and seen full-on. "Darrow," he said at last. "Where?"

"South Manchester, sir. He's good – we only managed a picture good enough for a positive ID today."

"He always had a knack for that. You picked him up?"

"Not yet, sir. We want his crew as well."

"Of course. No leads yet?"

"The approximate area, but we keep losing his trail."

"Another skill of his."

"He's looking for something, or someone. Personal, I think. And that's good. Means he'll slip up."

"Good." Winterborn handed the file back to Lewis. "Keep me posted. And I'll expect a result soon."

*

INNER COURTYARD, ASHWOOD FORT
1740 HOURS

The gates swung shut behind the landcruisers, but the crowd outside the Fort didn't move towards them as they halted; silence spread across the courtyard.

Helen sat in the flatbed as the others climbed out, one by one. She didn't want to follow them. The word was already spreading, inside the Fort and through the village and up to the inner and outer walls; someone must have radioed ahead.

If she went in now, she might manage a last normal conversation with someone, before everybody knew. But what would be the point? Anyone she spoke to would want to know what was going on, and what could she tell them? No, better to stay here; moving would take her into a future she wanted no part of.

There was no avoiding that future, though. Well, perhaps one. She touched her revolver; it, at least, had never let her down. Worst problem was the odd misfire, and if that happened, you just pulled the trigger again. It would be easy enough. What she'd started would carry on without her – perhaps better than if she was still alive.

A shadow fell on her. She looked up; Gevaudan. The Grendelwolf looked down on her. He was silent at first, breathing deep. Would he speak, or act?

If anyone's going to kill her, it'll be me. Had he really meant that? Helen hadn't feared him like this since the day they'd met. Her fingers brushed the .38 again, then fell away. If he was going to do it, let him.

"I'd have been naive," he said, "not to have considered the possibility. But I told myself that the past was the past. I wouldn't ask. But now it's been said. You would have risked not only my death, but *that* death."

Helen opened her mouth to speak, but Gevaudan had already turned away.

"I thought I had a family again," he said, his back to her, "but it seems I was wrong."

No, Helen wanted to whisper, but nothing else would come. And now Gevaudan was striding off towards his cottage, head down.

What could she have said, anyway?

Everyone had gone inside already; only Mackie still stood there, blinking at her. Then he turned away and walked quickly past her and through the inner gate, heading down towards the village, head down. His hand flapped at his ear as he want, as if to ward something off. An insect, maybe.

Helen got out of the landcruiser, and walked alone to the Fort.

*

Mordake's Quarters, The Tower
2000 hours

On Mordake's desk, the wolf idol's clay jaws opened and closed.

"Mordake."

"Masters."

"We have met with partial success. The rebels will not accept our aid, but they are divided now. We will deepen that division."

"Yes, Masters."

"You will see it, and soon. It begins this very night, and you will have a part to play, with Winterborn. A blow must be struck, to weaken and delay the rebels. But *not* to destroy them utterly."

"Masters?"

"End the rebellion, and Winterborn has no need of Project Sycorax. And without Sycorax, the Annihilation Sequence cannot begin."

*

LISTENING POST 2, THE WASTELANDS
2100 HOURS

Colby sat by the base of the pylon in the dusk, hugging her aching knees.

She still wore only her bindings, but now she shivered in them. She was in the pylon's shadow, and the heat was going out of the day. Her teeth had begun to chatter, but that wasn't important now. Nothing was.

"Colb?"

It was Swan. "Get back below," she muttered.

"Not till you do too. Make yourself sick."

"I'm already sick, Swan. I'm fucking dying, remember?"

She didn't turn around and look at Swan's face. There was a long pause before he answered. "Please?" he said.

"All right. All right." She pushed her stick into the ground and stood.

Swan looked back at her, red-eyed. "'S bad, in't it?"

"Yes." She shook her head. "It shouldn't matter. Should be something that can wait. But it won't, will it?"

Swan didn't answer. He knew her better than most, understood her too. "Come on."

"Coming." *Just wanted to see the Reapers fall; thought I might get that much.* But soon now she'd be gone, and the Reapers would still be there. For nothing, all of it. Colby let Swan take her arm and lead her below.

*

ALANNAH'S QUARTERS, ASHWOOD FORT
2250 HOURS

Danny spooned against Alannah's soft warm nakedness, touched his lips to the silver hair, but it was too fucking hot to snuggle, or even sleep.

Anyway, having woken, he wasn't tired; he slid out of bed and dressed in the dark, tiptoed into the corridor and put on his boots.

At the end of the corridor he squinnied out the window across the hilltop. There was Gevaudan's cottage; a light glowed in the window.

Danny'd heard, of course; it was all over the Fort, what'd happened at Hobsdyke, what Helen'd done. He glanced back towards Alannah's quarters. She'd sleep till dawn now; once she nodded off, she was like a corpse. So if old Creeping Death was up and about, it'd be a good time to go see him. Alannah'd never liked Gevaudan much, so it was awkward around him these days.

Danny went downstairs, then out through the Fort's main entrance. He glanced up and around; a sentry on the roof raised a hand in greeting. Danny waved back, then went towards the cottage. Bats flittered across the moon; the air was warm and thick and hard to breathe.

"Yo," called Danny at the cottage's front door. "You up?"

No answer. He tried the door; locked. He knocked; no answer. He wandered round the back, found the door there ajar.

"Gevaudan?"

Danny crossed the garden, went inside. Still no answer. Ice touched Danny's innards; that wasn't like the Grendelwolf. He went room to room, upstairs, downstairs: nothing. The cottage was empty.

Danny went to the inner wall, then climbed up to the parapet and looked out. Moonlight silvered the woods and hills; a fox darted from shadow to shadow on the hillside below. But that was all. Of the Grendelwolf, there was no sign.

*

Wakefield's Quarters, Ashwood Fort
2305 hours

Wakefield lay curled on her side, Filly spooned warm and naked against her from behind. Again, the room was silent; neither had spoken since making love.

She's used everyone, Filly had said. *My whole crew died for her.*

It's war, Wakefield had answered. *Do what you have to. Fight Reapers however you can, or die.*

Things had been said; Filly had been angry. In the end, they'd stopped talking and gone to bed. But still it hung between them: an open wound, slow poison. Helen and what she'd done.

*

Helen's Quarters, Ashwood Fort
2400 hours

Helen put her back against the door and slid down.

Unable to sleep – her rooms had felt like a prison, ridiculously small – she'd ventured out for a change of scene. But she hadn't left it late enough; not everyone had been asleep.

No-one had confronted her; that would have been easier to take. Instead, there'd been cold looks to her face and whispers at her back, silence falling when she'd entered a room. Her future; it would always be with her now.

She unfastened the pouch on her thigh and took out the Smith and Wesson. The milled hammer spur dug into her thumb as she pulled it back; a crisp triple click, and the gun was cocked.

Put the barrel in your mouth, pointing upwards. Or under the chin, that's surer still. Goes out through the top of your head that way, does the job properly. Lights out. All over.

Frank and Belinda were gone; no-one was screaming for Winterborn's blood. There'd been something more for her, briefly; the hope of something bright in her life again. Not just Gevaudan, but others, too. Belonging. But now, all that was gone, burned, the ashes scattered. And she didn't think she could bear what remained.

The gun would be easy, but it would be a coward's way out. Whatever she was about to receive, she'd earned, and there was still a war to fight. She'd play whatever part in that she was still allowed to. Friendless and alone, if need be.

Carefully, Helen squeezed the trigger with her thumb pressed to the hammer, and lowered it again.

*

ROOF OF THE TOWER

19TH JULY, ATTACK PLUS TWENTY-ONE YEARS
2230 HOURS

The crosswinds blew as Winterborn emerged onto the rooftop. The coolness was pleasant; the summer heat had made the Tower's interior close and sweltering. Discipline was strained, especially after the Pyramid business; it looked as though the rebels were going from strength to strength. The alliances with the other Commanders might help calm matters, but he couldn't announce those yet.

Scattered points of fire and candlelight gleamed around the Tower. There weren't many; the night was warm and clear, belts of stars scattered around the bright half-moon that lit the streets, and the Pennines were sharply delineated against the deep blue of the sky.

It had actually grown hotter since nightfall. Or perhaps only more humid. In either case, the air felt thick and close, muggy. At least the city was quiet; humidity or heat, either way it sapped all will and strength. Tonight at least might be peaceful, whatever the new day bought.

"Commander," called Mordake's weird, doubled voice. He stood near the edge of the roof, his back to Winterborn and his hood down; the second face blinked at him. Winterborn grimaced and strolled over; he was the Commander here, not some dog to come running on command. "Yes, Doctor?"

"Good news of several kinds."

"Oh?"

"The rebels are in turmoil. Helen's position has been greatly weakened by certain... revelations."

"Oh?"

"You'll hear more very soon from your agents, Commander. But Operation Long Knife will be able to proceed within the fortnight – perhaps sooner." Mordake chuckled; the second face, as smooth and flawless as ever, contorted in silent laughter. "Meanwhile, we must leave the Tower for a moment."

"What?"

"There's something you should see." Mordake turned and smiled; he looked exhausted, but triumphant. "Trust me, Commander. I guarantee you will not be disappointed."

Winterborn hesitated; to leave the Tower, at short notice? But Mordake's excitement was plain to see. "Very well," he said. "Let's go."

*

CITY GATE, CHEETHAM HILL ROAD, CITY OF MANCHESTER
2250 HOURS

The four landcruisers shot along the road, sirens wailing. There was no-one on the streets at that hour, but the landcruisers' .50

cals swept back and forth while Winterborn's guards kept their rifles and submachine guns locked and loaded.

The Reapers at the gate sprang to attention. Climbing down from his vehicle, Winterborn saw them gawp – half-astonished, half-terrified – at the sight of him. He returned the salute, lazily, smiling; the fear was sweet, the knowing he'd be obeyed. "Open the gates."

"Sir!"

The gates swung wide; Winterborn glimpse the tall figure standing outside them, and then Mordake clicked his fingers. The gate guards froze, then straightened up, gazing blankly ahead. A light breeze rose; Winterborn assured himself that was the only reason he felt cold.

"They'll remember none of this," said Mordake. He nodded to Winterborn's escort. "I'm assuming these ladies and gentlemen can keep a confidence?"

"I sincerely hope so." The words came out of Winterborn's mouth mechanically, as if by rote; what he saw standing in the moonlight outside the gates was impossible, but it was there.

Heavy boots gritted in the dust. A long black coat flapped; long, fine black hair blew back from a pale, high-cheekboned face, and moonlight gleamed in pale, yellow eyes.

"Winterborn." Its voice was deep, sepulchral.

Winterborn tried to speak its name, but the words wouldn't come.

"Commander Winterborn," Mordake said. "Allow me to present your newest military asset. Gevaudan Shoal."

Part Three:
Tindalos Rising

1.

Armoury, Ashwood Fort
July 24th, Attack Plus Twenty-One Years
1830 hours

Helen took aim and squeezed the trigger. The Sten gun's T-stock slammed back into her shoulder, but not too hard; recoil was light, and the three-round burst punched a trio of holes at the edge of the target's inner ring. She sighted and fired, sighted and fired, again and again until half the clip was used up. Then she allowed herself a tight smile and pulled the trigger again, emptying the rest of the magazine in a burst that blasted the target to shreds.

As the gun's echoes and the thin whining in her ears faded, Helen heard a slow handclap from behind her. A small, trim-built Asian woman, dressed in black, with a round, pretty face and black hair with a silver streak. "Bravo," said Zaq. "Feeling better for blowing the shit out of my firing range?"

"Isn't that what it's there for?"

"Actually, I was trying to grow magic mushrooms. No place else for it round here." Probably sarcasm, but as the armourer's face was set in its usual permanent scowl Helen couldn't tell for sure. You rarely could with Zaq. "Back to the fucking drawing board."

Helen walked back to the tables where Zaq's weapons lay, tapping the Sten's hot barrel. "Good gun," she said.

"Well, duh. Course it is. I made the fucking thing."

"I know."

"I suppose you want it? If so, don't expect any further instructions from me. I'm going to assume you know how to strip and load it."

"I'll manage."

"Your look-out if you don't. I'd keep it under your bed if I were you. Might need it."

"Might at that."

Zaq banged down four magazines and a box of ammunition onto the table. "You can load them yourself," she said. She didn't look at Helen.

"You hate me, Zaq?" said Helen. Why had she asked that?

"I hate everyone." Zaq still didn't look up.

"Even Gevaudan?"

Now Zaq *did* look up. "You hurt him."

"I know."

"So what are you going to do about it?"

Helen shook her head. "I don't know."

"Well, if I were you, I'd think of something. But don't take too long."

*

THE TOWER, CITY OF MANCHESTER
1858 HOURS

Sweat stung the corner of Wearing's eye as she strode down the corridor. *Look confident. You've every right to be here. Don't let anyone see your nerves. Worry about the Reapers, not Alannah Vale. Or Sycorax.*

Not that Sycorax wasn't worrying; Soper had come along and spooked Wearing before she'd had a chance to do more than glance through the file, but what she'd seen had been bad enough. Bad enough that there was no doubt, no conflict in her about giving this to Alannah. The item in her current report was urgent, but everything she knew about Sycorax would go in her next one, and she'd get that done today, despite the risk. Someone needed to know; someone needed to put a stop to it, before –

I'm being followed.

She'd turned two corners now, and someone was still behind her. The same person? She wasn't sure. But that didn't mean anything: one person dropped out, another dropped in. She didn't need proof: she knew. Instinct. Desk job or not, she hadn't lost that.

Shadowing someone wasn't easy in the Tower; plainclothes Reapers were more used to working in the city, pretending to be scavengers dressed in stinking rags. She deliberately hesitated at a junction of two corridors; from the corner of her eye, she saw the young Reaper behind her desperately study the clipboard he held, trying to look occupied.

"Problem, soldier?" she said.

He snapped to attention, red-faced. "No, ma'am."

"New here, aren't you?"

"Yes, ma'am."

"Where are you looking for?"

"Um – er – MediaSec, ma'am."

"MediaSec are on seven. You shouldn't be up here if you're not on business. Off you go. Chop-chop."

"Yes'm."

Wearing started walking again, quicker now, but not too fast. *You knew this day would come. Thanks a fucking bunch, Vale.*

If she got out of here, Wearing vowed to find Alannah Vale and shove a rifle so far up her arse the business end came out through her nose for blackmailing her back into this game. But she already knew she wouldn't get out. She was blown; she'd never leave the Tower alive.

The message capsule dug into her sweat-damp palm. It was the only thing that could betray her: there was nothing else on her, or in her quarters. She could swallow it, maybe. But if they picked her up, they'd watch for it to pass out the other end. Root through the shit bucket. That or just cut her open for it. No – safest way was to ditch the capsule, and the safest way to do *that* was to get the capsule where it was meant to go. Then the next link in the chain could pick it up, whoever they were. The fewer names you knew, the fewer you could betray.

If she was lucky, she was only under suspicion. If she disposed of the capsule and brazened out the interrogation she might, just might, stand a chance.

No-one in sight as she rounded the next corner, but they'd come soon – either another shadow, or they'd lift her there and then. She had to get rid of the capsule before then.

One more corner. Wearing heard footsteps; were they behind her, or ahead? If behind, she still might have a chance. Might.

She rounded the corner; the corridor ahead was empty, but the footsteps were louder. They weren't hiding; they were running.

Quickly, then. Wearing tugged at a section of wood-panelled wainscot that ran along the wall. It pulled partly free; on the inward side a small, neat hollow had been carved in the message capsule's exact shape. She tucked the capsule into it and pushed the panel back into place.

Now move. Wearing broke into a fast stride – she had to put distance between the capsule and her. Then let them lift her and hope for the best.

"Wearing!"

She turned. A young officer, flanked by four Reapers, came down the corridor towards her. All wore the white shoulder-flashes of the Jennywrens. When the officer saw her, he smiled.

They don't suspect, she realised; *they* know. *They wouldn't have sent the Jennywrens otherwise.*

"Take the bitch," the officer said.

Wearing saw her future in that second. No brazening it out: only a world of pain without hope, and then a bullet. If she was lucky

The Jennywrens came towards her, and Wearing ran.

"Get her!"

Around the next corner was the door to the staircase; she slammed it wide, unfastening her uniform jacket as she went. Staff officers didn't go armed in the Tower, which was why she carried the pistol in the secret holster. It was only a .32, a mouse gun, but better than nothing.

She pulled it from its holster as the first Jennywren rounded the corner, and fired four shots; he fell, screaming and thrashing. Wearing ducked through the door onto the stairs. As the door swung shut behind her bullets smashed into it, splintering the wood and shattering the glass.

She was at the bottom of the first flight when a second Jennywren burst through the riddled door. Wearing shot him in the throat and he fell, choking, the submachine gun clattering down the stairs to land at her feet. She grabbed it and ran on.

Stairwell, The Tower
1910 hours

Thorpe leant on the stair-rail, wheezing. He was dripping sweat and his face was burning. Bloody stupid idea, taking the stairs from the canteen to the Ops Room. All right, no-one liked anyone who looked too well-fed, not these days – and if you were a staff officer, you were never going to win any popularity contests anyway. But Christ Almighty, this wasn't fitness, it was attempted suicide.

That was when he heard the gunfire – single shots, then the stutter of a submachine gun. Thorpe froze: which way should he run? Back down the stairs, or up to the next flight, where there was a door?

Boots thundered on the staircase. A Reaper officer burst around the corner, clutching a Sterling. Thorpe yelped, fumbling for his pistol; the SMG swept towards him. "Don't!" the woman snapped.

Thorpe blinked: it was Wearing. "Lee?"

"Richard," she said, then raised the Sterling again. "To me," she said. "Now."

Thorpe moved up the steps, the pistol on his hip forgotten. He hadn't fired a shot in months, even at the range, and in all truth he'd never so much as pointed his gun at another human being. Besides, Lee was probably the closest thing he had to a friend; surely she wouldn't harm him? But the Sterling's barrel was levelled at his face, wavering in her scared grip.

When Thorpe reached her she pulled him back against her, an arm across his throat and pushed the Sterling to his temple. "Come on," she said, "move." She backed up towards the door at the top of the flight, pushing it open with her backside. "Take your pistol out. Carefully, between your forefinger and thumb, then drop it."

As he obeyed, two Jennywrens came down the stairs above, SMGs raised. "Don't move!"

"Drop 'em," shouted Wearing, pushing the gun harder into Thorpe's temple. "I'll kill him."

They didn't drop their weapons, but remained still as Wearing backed out into the corridor. She dragged Thorpe around the corner, then shoved open the door of a meeting-room and pushed him inside, herding him into the far corner. "Down on the floor," she said, then lay on top of him, aiming over him at the door. The Reapers' running footsteps approached, then faded as they ran past. Wearing breathed out.

"They'll come back," Thorpe whispered.

"Shut up."

"They will, though," he said. "You try and fight, they'll kill you."

"They will anyway," she hissed back. "It's what the fuckers'll do to me first."

"Why would they –?"

"What else do they do to a rebel agent?"

"They think you're a –" Thorpe felt her breathe wearily out, and realised. "Oh no. Lee, no. They'll bloody kill you."

She snorted. "Yes, I *know*."

She slid off Thorpe and sat back against the wall, studying him. Glancing at the door, Thorpe sat up too. Wearing held the Sterling across her knees; it wasn't quite pointing away from him, but it was no longer aimed directly at him either. She looked tired and pale, almost grey.

"Bloody hell, Lee, why?" he said.

"No choice," she said. "Not this time around."

"This time?" He stared. "How long have you been –"

"Since the Civil Emergency."

And he'd never known. Then again, nor had anyone else, it seemed. "Why?" said Thorpe. "Why would you –"

"Five minutes' worth of stupid idealism," said Wearing. "Alannah Vale ran me. Once she got back in business, the bitch wasn't taking no for an answer."

"The rotten —"

Wearing sighed. "Shouldn't have been so daft." She trained the Sterling on the door. "Anyway, we might need 'em."

"The rebels?"

"Winterborn's lost the plot, Rick. You've seen the Catchmen."

He grimaced. "Yes."

"They're just the start. Remember Project Tindalos?"

Could he hear movement nearby? Best to keep her talking. "Just the name, really."

Wearing shook her head. "Fucked-up stuff. Wouldn't believe it myself if I hadn't read the file. But it worked. That's what destroyed the Hobsdyke base."

"Thought the rebels —"

"They destroyed what was left, and good job too. Tindalos was out of control. Kellett made the Catchmen using some of Mordake's notes. They're bad enough, but Tindalos would have been a million times worse."

That name. "Mordake?"

"Yeah. He created Tindalos."

"He's the new Adjutant."

Wearing frowned. "Mordake's dead."

"Someone forgot to tell him, then." Although having seen Mordake, Thorpe wondered.

Wearing shook her head; too much to absorb, Thorpe guessed, and no time to try. "There's a new project," she said. "Sycorax. Based on Tindalos, maybe worse. Only got a few details — I was trying to find out more." She eyed the door again. "Probably how they got onto me."

Voices outside; footsteps. "Oh shit," said Wearing.

"Lee —" Thorpe reached for her. She raised a hand to ward him off, but then reached out too, fingers briefly clasping his. "Over in the far corner," she said, letting go his hand to put down the Sterling and take a .32 automatic from her pocket. "Let's not get you killed too."

Thorpe wriggled backwards, realising he was crying. "Lee," he said again.

"Yeah." There were tears in her eyes too, but they might just be for herself. You could never be sure what was going on in someone else's head. "I know." She glanced at him once more. "Sycorax, Rick. You've got to –"

A boot kicked the door wide, and the Jennywrens came through. "Fuck," said Wearing, and as they ran towards her she stuck the .32 in her mouth and fired.

*

CORRIDOR, THE TOWER

1730 HOURS

One last gunshot, and then silence. Reaper Axon dried his sweaty palms; summer or not, he was shivering. You didn't get shooting in the Tower; did that mean they'd found the agent?

Might do, but Axon had a job to do anyway. He felt a moment's temptation to forget it, to leave it just this once. But he wouldn't. He wasn't a coward.

Axon glanced around as he reached the spot. No-one there. He eased the wooden panel out from the wall, took out the message capsule and slipped it into a pouch on his belt. Then he replaced the panel, and walked.

*

INTELLIGENCE CENTRE

1900 HOURS

"Killed resisting arrest," Kingfisher said. "That's what they're saying anyway. Least they didn't get to interrogate her."

"Shit." Alannah rubbed her eyes. "One asset we really didn't need to lose."

"I know, Osprey. I'm sorry."

"Not your fault, Kingfisher. Anything else?"

"Far as we can tell, the rest of the Tower network hasn't been compromised. No other arrests."

"They must have guessed we had someone," said Alannah. "Fed different suspects different intel, then waited to see whose we responded to. It's what I'd have done."

"You think the rest of the network there's safe, then?"

"Nowhere's safe, but if we're lucky, they don't have a line on anyone else. All the same, watch yourselves."

"Will do. She managed to make a final drop before they lifted her. Could be a plant, of course, but –"

"Sure." Alannah took a sip of dandelion-root coffee and grimaced; stone-cold. But it would keep her awake, so she took another. "What have we got?"

"No specifics, so potentially suss. But she claims there's a traitor at the Fort."

"Ashwood?"

"That's what it says."

"Clever," said Alannah. "If it *is* a plant, I mean. We can't ignore it, but it's just vague enough to send us chasing our tails."

"That, or it's on the level."

"Yeah. Okay, Kingfisher. Watch your backs and keep listening in."

*

WINTERBORN'S OFFICE, THE TOWER
2000 HOURS

Thorpe stood before Winterborn's desk, fighting back the tremors in his legs.

Winterborn barely looked at him; just sat there, turning a small flat shiny metal box this way, then that. *Does he know? About me and Lee?* If he did, he'd never believe Thorpe hadn't known about her. Guilt by association. Thorpe hated Lee for a moment, but only for a moment; *I loved her*, he realised. Too late to do any good.

After a moment, the Commander reached for the intercom and pressed a button. "This is Winterborn. Contact Agent Shoal; instruct him to proceed."

"Yes, sir."

"Good. Out." Winterborn stroked the lid of the metal box, then became still. He looked up slowly at Thorpe, never blinking, a half-smile on his lips. Then he stood. "Something, Colonel?"

"Sir?"

Winterborn moved around the desk, towards Thorpe. "Perhaps you have a question you'd like to ask," he said. "Such as whether I can arrange a transfer to a front-line combat role? I'm sure GenRen would benefit immeasurably with an officer of your experience and ability to lead them against the rebels. Well, Colonel? Do you have any questions?"

"No, sir," Thorpe managed at last. "No questions."

"That's what I thought." Winterborn smirked. "Dismiss."

Because what was Thorpe going to do about it? About anything? Desk-jockey. Wimp. That's all he was to Winterborn.

I'll show you what I'll do, you bastard. Shaking, Thorpe straightened up, turned and left the room.

*

St Martin de Porres Church, Ashwood
2030 hours

Carson had thought she was alone in the church, so she jumped, starting out of her reverie, when footsteps sounded on the stone floor. Halfway down the aisle, she saw Helen halt and stare at her; Carson guessed the other woman had thought she'd been alone too.

"Ma'am." She stood, starting to salute. For now, at least, Helen still held command.

"Siddown." Helen waved her back into her pew. "Don't mind me."

Carson sat. The two of them studied one another. The silence stretched out, till Carson broke it. "Didn't know you were religious," she said.

"I'm not," said Helen. "It's quiet here, though. Peaceful."

"Yeah," said Carson. "That's good. You're safe here, kind of. Even if people don't like you, they leave you alone. Mostly."

"Yeah. Hard to find that around here."

"Why are you still here?" said Carson. She broke off, winced; that hadn't sounded right. "I mean, weren't you supposed to've gone back to wherever?"

"It's on an island," said Helen after a moment. "Tiny little island. And I'd have to face everyone there. Go through this all over again, but with nowhere to hide. I'd go crazy." She shrugged. "Here's not so bad." She started for the door. "At least for now."

*

WINTERBORN'S OFFICE, THE TOWER
2100 HOURS

"So," said Treloar. "Where are we now?"

She was dark-haired, dark-eyed and olive-skinned – but both hair and eyes were dull and lustreless, and there was an underlying sickly pastiness to her complexion. Rumour was she was an alcoholic, but managed to function well nonetheless. A far-right activist of some kind before the War, if Winterborn recalled, constantly vowing to pay back 'traitors' with 'good old British justice' in the form of a length of rope. After the War, she'd had plentiful opportunities to do so.

She was stupid, small-minded, petty and cruel; and she admired Winterborn for his ability to get things done. Treloar always been a natural ally, albeit one he wanted as little contact with as possible.

"So far," he said, "Wales and the North are with me, along with the Midlands, Northern Ireland and Mann."

Treloar whistled. "You got Drozek on-side? That must have taken some work."

Winterborn smiled. "In addition," he said, "all of Scotland will be consolidating into a single bloc – with the possible exception of Commander Scrimgeour – and a treaty of cooperation is already being finalised."

Treloar lit a Monarch, chuckling. "Poor old Scrimgeour, eh? Stupid cow."

"Things are taking shape," said Winterborn. "We're approaching a state of de facto unification – except for a few Commands."

"Well, I'm on board," Treloar said. "You know me."

Winterborn smiled. "I certainly do."

"Wexford, too," said Treloar. "Already made sure of that. So you might wanna copy him in too."

"Will do." Winterborn already had, of course. *Wexford of East Anglia is largely indifferent to Unification, as long as his Command remains untroubled,* Mordake had told him: *Ending all unrest quickly and decisively means he can go back to his quiet life.* "Thank you."

"No worries, Tez."

Winterborn felt his face stiffen. "Please don't call me that."

Treloar blinked. "No offence."

Winterborn forced himself to smile. "None taken."

*

WALL ONE, ASHWOOD FORT

2230 HOURS

Bats squeaked; night-birds called. The sun set, westward, in gold and purple; the air was cool and fresh. Blob looked east again, to where the hills were melting away into the dusk.

She stole a glance back inside the Fort complex. The Grendelwolf's cottage stood alone and lightless. She hadn't seen him make for the hills, but she guessed he was there; where else would he go?

Shadows moved below her; Blob aimed her Sten gun downward. Something long and fluid and black flowed across the ground below. A white face looked up at her, and then the black shape was sliding up the wall.

Blob had her finger on the trigger, then she realised who it was and lowered the gun, stepping back as the dark shape leapt over the parapet and landed in a crouch. She grinned. "Lo, Gev. You okay?"

He didn't answer as he straightened. Moonlight gleamed in his yellow eyes. And when he smiled, Blob took a step back. There was something different about it, something wrong; it was hard, cruel.

The smile widened, and he stepped towards her. Claws slid from the fingertips.

Blob remembered the Sten, started to raise it. But he was already moving impossibly fast, and was on her before she could fire.

2.

THE WAR ROOM, ASHWOOD FORT
25TH JULY, ATTACK PLUS TWENTY-ONE YEARS
0800 HOURS

"Take a seat," Alannah said, flashing Danny a quick smile – only quick, cos they were working; they weren't lovers, not in here. "This won't take long," she said. "We've only one matter to discuss."

Danny looked at Helen; she was paler than ever, hands to her mouth.

"A lookout was killed last night," Alannah said. "Name of Blob."

"Blob?" said Danny. *Ah fuck, no.*

"You knew her?"

Everyone was looking at him now. Danny coughed. "A bit," he said. "Applied for Raider training, couple months back. Didn't quite hack it, but she was close. Told her to try again." A scrawny kid; reminded Danny of Scopes. Still surprised him how much he missed Scopes.

"Sorry," said Alannah. "This bit isn't pleasant, I'm afraid."

"S'all right."

"She was hanging over the battlements," said Alannah. "The killer picked her up and slammed her down across the parapet, smashed her spine. But Nestor says she was already dead then. The killer tore her throat out."

"Fuck," said Danny.

"What was it?" asked Thorn. "Catchman?"

Alannah shook her head. "Catchmen have big thick talons – they're designed to grip, crush and tear. These claws – they were sharper, thinner. Made for *slicing*. Nestor said he'd only seen injuries like this once before. During the Civil Emergency." She wouldn't look straight at Helen. "After a Grendelwolf attack."

"No way," Danny said at last. "No. This is *Gevaudan* you're talking about."

"I don't like saying it." Helen shook her head. "I *don't*," Alannah insisted. "But we can't deny what's in front of us. No-one even knows where he is right now."

"It could be some kind of Reaper trick," Helen said at last, looking down at her clasped hands.

Jazz snorted.

"It could be," Helen insisted. "Discredit him. He's one of our biggest assets."

"Used to be," said Jazz. "Till he found out what you did."

"Jazz –"

"People don't like it when you play games with their lives, Helen. We're funny like that."

Danny could see the hurt on Helen's face, but Jazz wasn't wrong about *used to be*. First the Pyramid, then Hobsdyke, had taken something out of the Grendelwolf. He'd played his guitar in the canteen once since he'd been rescued; it'd been dull, dead-sounding, empty. And when he wasn't locked away in his cottage, no-one knew where he went.

"Let's not do this now, shall we?" said Thorn. She reached out and touched Jazz's hand. "God knows you've every right to be angry, Jazz. It's fairly safe to say my people wouldn't have become part of this if we'd known then what we know now. But we are where we are. There'll be no mercy from the Reapers, no forgiveness. We're in it now, for good or bad."

Malik cleared his throat. "On the subject of forgiveness –"

"Jav," said Thorn, "with the greatest possible respect, we're not going there today."

"Let's stick to the matter in hand," Alannah said, still not looking at Helen. "Helen's right – it *is* possible, just about, that this is some sort of disinfo campaign by the Reapers." But she didn't sound like she believed it. She couldn't think that about old Creeping Death, could she? Not really? "Either way," she went on, "we need to talk to him. He's not in his cottage, so – any thoughts on where he could be?"

"The caves, maybe," Loncraine pointed at the floor. "Down there."

"Fuck that," said Stewart. "Go looking down there, we'll never come out again. Specially if he *has* gone bad."

"He hasn't," said Helen. No-one answered; no-one even looked at her, 'cept Malik. Stewart looked at his fingernails – there was nowt Helen'd done he wouldn't have, Danny knew, but he wasn't gonna say owt. Far as Stewart was concerned, Helen was fucked and he wasn't going near her. None of them wanted to know her any more, by the look.

Even Alannah'd said to Danny – quiet, in bed one night – she didn't think Helen should still be on the Council, not after everything. Or here at Ashwood. She should've gone back to Piel weeks ago, but here she was. Maybe it was cos Gevaudan was here and she was hoping to make it right. Or she was just scared of having to face the crowd at Piel after what'd happened. Helen too scared to do something? Danny would've pissed himself laughing at that normally, but this wasn't something you could fight with a gun, or anything else. What'd happened at Hobsdyke, it was touching everything, poisoning it, fucking it all up.

"I want guards on all entrances to the cave system," said Alannah. "Heavily armed. If he has gone bad –" Helen shook her head "– *if* he has, he'll take a lot of stopping."

"You really think he'd stick us?" said Danny. "Gevaudan? I know you're not keen on him, but..."

Alannah looked at him, stung; she hadn't expected that off him, Danny realised, and felt a pang of guilt. "Maybe not before," she said. "But he's been through a lot." Danny saw Helen put a hand to her mouth. "And we know now there's a Reaper agent here. So – let's find him."

*

St Martin de Porres Church, Ashwood
1340 hours

"Right, then," Danny said, and nodded.

"Ten*sion*!" said Wakefield. Wasn't sure what it meant, but she knew what it did. The Raider recruits outside the church slammed their heels together and stood up straight.

Danny looked at her, winked. "Not too bad," he said. "But you've all got a long way to go."

He paced up and down in front of them. Wakefield bit the inside of her mouth so she didn't laugh. She'd seen him do this a few times now. She needed something to make her smile: she'd had to help Danny search for Gevaudan most of this morning. No luck, but the idea that someone might think that of the Grendelwolf shook her. Cracks. Weaknesses in the alliance.

Thinking like that made the smile fade. *Stop thinking: watch Danny, listen to him.* Wakefield was glad they'd decided normal life had to go on, the induction for the new recruits. It took her away from the thought of the Grendelwolf being a traitor. She didn't, couldn't, wouldn't believe there was truth in it.

"You've been picked for Raider training," Danny said. "But it's just starting. Next few weeks are gonna be tough. And I'm not gonna lie to you, not everyone can hack it. Usually, 'bout half of you'll quit before it's done. But a lot of folk don't get this far. Don't forget that. And," he folded his arms, "if you can't hack it as a Raider, you're better off finding out now than –"

A flash, and the ground jolted underfoot; three windows on the Fort's third storey burst outwards, spraying smoke and dust and glass. Wakefield dived, hands over her head.

Shouts. Screams. Wakefield's ears hummed. She got up. Blood trickled down her neck; she plucked a sliver of glass from her cheek. A black cloud hung over the Fort; smoke and dust billowed through the courtyard. She coughed and spat.

Danny stood, staring up. The recruits got to their feet. A young boy knelt near the church, screaming, hands to his face. A woman knelt by him and pulled his hands away; she screamed too when she saw the dozen glass daggers buried in his face, his eyes.

*

The War Room, Ashwood Fort
1516 hours

"He targeted the sick bay as a diversion," Alannah said, keeping her voice as level as she could. "Luckily there weren't many people in there. Nestor's okay, thank God, but four of his staff are dead, a dozen more injured."

"Sick fuck," said Stewart, and lit another cigarette. The air in the War Room was hot, and thick with smoke.

"And that was just a diversion," said Alannah. "While we were worried about the sick bay, the bastard was planting another device in the armoury."

"Jesus Christ." Thorn coughed. "Sorry," she muttered to Malik.

Malik smiled wanly. "Understandable in the circumstances."

"The timer was defective," said Alannah. "Good job too, or we'd have lost half the Fort, the amount of ordnance we had in there."

"Why wasn't the armoury under guard?" Helen said.

"It was," snapped Alannah. "They stayed in place even when the sick bay blew. Stop trying to change the subject, Helen."

"I'm not –"

"Everyone can see it, Helen," Jazz snapped. "Everyone but you, it looks like." Beside her, Thorn nodded.

"He wouldn't do this," said Loncraine. "He wouldn't."

Alannah's fists clenched on the table. Loncraine was pretty much the one ally Helen had left at this table; everything was black and white to him. Them versus the Reapers, and anything went when it came to beating them. Same with Wakefield, with nearly all the tribals. Couldn't understand the damage that'd been done, and they all practically worshipped the Grendelwolf – the perfect warrior, after all, and he played music, too.

But no, not her; she wasn't fooled. Alannah had never really trusted the yellow-eyed bastard, and she'd been right. She blocked out the hurt on Helen's face; friend or not, that didn't matter now. Helen couldn't, wouldn't see it, wouldn't accept it or understand. So she, Alannah, must. She had to do whatever she had to to stop the threat. "They were killed," she said. "All six of them. Three with their throats ripped out, like Blob's. The rest were blunt force trauma. Blows and kicks way beyond normal human strength. Smashed bones, crushed internal organs." Alannah held Helen's gaze until she looked away. "Every bloody one of them was a Grendelwolf kill."

*

Winterborn's Office, The Tower
1631 hours

"Well," Winterborn said, as Cadigan and her team worked. "This one should be... interesting."

Mordake chuckled. "Do I detect a certain trepidation, Commander?"

"It's easy to tell that you've never tried having a conversation with Commander Fowler."

"Only glimpsed her at the video conference."

"This will be an experience, I can assure you. I'm not sure how I'm expected to persuade her, frankly. She's barely connected to reality to begin with."

"So I'm told," said Mordake. "But if you'll let me step in, this may be the easiest one yet."

"Not even sure why we're bothering, frankly," sighed Winterborn. "Greater London's no use to anyone."

"Symbolic value," said Mordake, "as the former capitol. Besides, you want *complete* Unification, surely?"

"Even so, Fowler's more trouble than she's worth."

"As I said, Commander, I can deal with her."

"You're more than welcome to try."

"Ready, sir," said Cadigan.

"Give us the room," said Winterborn.

Cadigan and her techs cleared out with their usual grateful speed; Mordake resumed his seat in the corner. "Call on me whenever you need me, Commander."

Winterborn nodded, watching Elizabeth Fowler's face appear out of the murk on the screen. The image flickered, then stabilised. "Commander Fowler."

Fowler smiled, showing stained teeth. "Tiberius."

"Tereus."

"That's what I said, isn't it? Yes, of course it is. So – the rebel problem."

"We're in the process of attempting to unify the Commands –"

"About time. Disgraceful, cowardly opposition to the proposal at the last video conference." Fowler shook her head. "I never thought I would see fellow Reapers defend anarchists and traitors. But they did. Whatever form it took... they did."

"Well, quite."

"There's only one solution to these people. Unity, action."

"I agree."

"Naturally, I will assume Supreme Command."

"Eh?"

"I'm the obvious choice. As the former capitol, RCZ1 is the most important Command. It's also the most peaceful, which shows my ability as a leader and organiser."

"It's peaceful because there's nobody there," muttered Winterborn.

Greater London and its surrounding areas had suffered the heaviest bombing of the War. Most of the former UK had been peppered with low-yield weapons, designed to throw the country into chaos without rendering it uninhabitable or beyond exploitation; London, though, had been devastated.

The Reaper forces there, skeletal though they were, quite possibly outnumbered the civilian population, which, lacking the Reapers' access to clean water and food, were thought to be numbered in the low thousands, or possibly the hundreds.

The scale of the damage and the tiny labour pool made reclamation work an impossibility, and it was hard to imagine anyone stupid or demented enough to attack it. The Reaper force, made up of those without the resources or influence to obtain reassignment, was largely symbolic. RCZ1 was a Command in name only, a joke.

Which made it the perfect home for Elizabeth Fowler. A one-time local authority Housing Officer, she'd worked her way up through the old Regional Commission through flattery and manipulation, then made the jump to the REAP Command system that had replaced it.

The other senior Reaper officers, having realised how hopelessly devastated and contaminated the area was, had begged, stolen or otherwise wangled transfer to somewhere less hopelessly ruined. However, RCZ1 *was* at least nominally a Command, so there had to be a Commander; Fowler had got the post simply because nobody else wanted it, while announcing it as proof that everyone recognised her brilliance.

Her one real achievement – other than the unintentional amusement she gave her colleagues – was the tiny reclaimed area surrounding the bunker in which she spent her entire life. When she looked outside, she saw a restored world; no-one told her that it was less than a mile square, or that her ever-more grandiose plans for reclaiming the rest of RCZ1 would never – could never – be implemented. RCZ1 existed inside her head, like her genius as a Commander, her peers' respect for her and her status as the most powerful and influential Commander of them all.

"The rebels," she said, gazing up at the ceiling and steepling her fingers, "must be dealt with once and for all."

"I agree."

"So I shall deploy our remaining nuclear weapons to eliminate them."

"*What?*"

"It's rather poetic," she said, "when you think about it. These vermin were created by a nuclear attack, so let them perish in one."

"You want to drop nuclear bombs on our own territory?" The next time anyone accused him of making far-fetched or insane plans, he'd tell them about this. Or perhaps not; *not as demented as Commander Fowler* was hardly an accolade.

"I appreciate the rebels are most active in your Command," she went on, "but your people are efficient, aren't they, Thrombosis?"

"Tereus."

"That's what I said. They'll soon decontaminate the area again. The land will recover, but the rebels won't, and you'll have shown yourself to be a leader who won't be defied, and who gets the job done."

"I was rather hoping to continue reclaiming RCZ7," said Winterborn, "not start again from scratch."

"You're either committed to destroying the rebels by whatever means necessary, or you're supporting them," said Fowler. "Like Scrimgeour. An appeaser. She'll be dealt with, naturally, when I assume power."

"Commander Fowler, I was hoping we might discuss –"

Mordake coughed gently from his corner, raising his eyebrows. After a moment, Winterborn nodded. "Bear with me for a moment, Commander," he said.

"The first priority will be a series of reconnaissance flights..."

Mordake came over and motioned politely to Winterborn's chair. Winterborn stood and stepped aside, clenching and unclenching his hands. The chair was *his*. So, of course, were the office, the Tower and RCZ7 itself, but the chair most of all. After eliminating him, Winterborn had had his predecessor's chair burned, and this one built from scratch. No-one, *no-one*, had ever sat in it but him.

"Commander Fowler?" said Mordake.

"...and follow up the nukes with a final round of air strikes, using gas to finish off any... who are you?" Fowler blinked, sitting up straight in her chair.

"I'm Doctor Mordake, Commander." He leant forward. "Very pleased to meet you. I've wanted to for some time."

Fowler preened. "Well, naturally."

"I've heard so much about your wisdom," said Mordake, "about your wonderful plans to make Britain great again. Everyone agrees you're the only choice for Supreme Commander, apart from the rebels and the traitors who collaborate with them."

"Exactly!"

"So please," said Mordake. "Tell us more. Commander Winterborn and I are among your most loyal supporters. You can trust us."

Fowler didn't need any encouragement. "Once the rebels are eliminated, I'll requisition resources to complete the reclamation of Greater London. Then my neighbouring Commands – I'll show them the way – and then we'll progress east and west. Devon and Cornwall, Wales, East Anglia. Winterborn, naturally, will be responsible for maintaining order in the North until that phase of the work is complete." Fowler's voice had lost some of its animation, winding steadily down.

"Well, naturally," said Mordake.

"Meanwhile, our Naval units will blockade the Orkneys and Shetlands to isolate the traitor Scrimgeour. When the mainland is under control, the various islands will be next," Fowler's voice was by now a murmuring drone. "The Hebrides, the Isle of Man. Finally..."

Fowler's voice trailed off and she began to rock back and forth in her chair, staring blankly out.

"Commander Fowler," said Mordake softly. "It seems to me that what a leader of your vision needs above all is time. Wouldn't you agree?"

"Time?"

"Well, of course. Time to spend in quiet contemplation, in order to answer all those pressing questions about Britain's future."

"Time," Fowler repeated.

"The last thing such a person needs, surely, is to be burdened with the cares of day to day Command. They're a distraction from the main task. Wouldn't you agree?"

"Yes," Fowler murmured, "I suppose I would."

"Exactly. That sort of thing's beneath you, Elizabeth."

"Yes. Yes. Of course, you're right. But someone has to assume the responsibility."

"Of course they must. Someone like Commander Winterborn, for example. Your most steadfast ally."

Fowler blinked. "Is he?"

"But of course he is. Surely you remember?"

"Ah, yes, of course. Dear old Tantalus."

"Ter –" Winterborn broke off.

"Commander Winterborn is the man you can trust with those cares," said Mordake. "That's why you want him to be appointed Supreme Commander of a unified Britain."

Fowler blinked again. "Do I really?"

"But of course, Commander. A stroke of genius, I thought."

"Well, naturally."

"You'll be our Oracle," Mordake said. "You'll devise the blueprint, the *vision,* for a Greater Britain, and Winterborn will make it a reality. He knows you alone can show us the way."

"Well, of course he does. Clever boy, young Tumulus."

Winterborn gritted his teeth.

"And so," said Mordake, "where do you stand on Unification, Commander?"

"Naturally, I support it."

"And the Supreme Commander?"

"Trichinosis Winterborn, of course. My right-hand man."

"Thank you." Mordake stood and motioned to the chair.

Winterborn sat, surreptitiously brushing the seat. "Commander Fowler?"

"So, Tuberculosis, I assume there's a treaty to sign."

"Yes."

"Then send it to me at once. We mustn't delay. It's the first step to bringing Britain back together under my rule."

"Of course."

"Good. Good. Good! I'll look forward to it. Anything else?"

"I can't think of anything."

"Then I'll say goodbye for now. I've a future to plan! Thank you, Testiculos."

Thankfully, the screen went blank at that point. "Very impressive," Winterborn said at last.

"I thought you might enjoy it," smiled Mordake.

"We should have done that with all the other Commanders," said Winterborn. "Save a great deal of time and effort."

"Sadly, my abilities here only work on the weak-minded and deranged. For stronger intellects, more subtle methods are required."

Winterborn felt a stir of unease; was he, too, being played? But then he shook his head; this was his destiny, and thanks to Mordake it was now almost in his his grasp.

*

RECORDS DEPARTMENT, THE TOWER
1710 HOURS

Thorpe took a deep breath and glanced around him one more time to ensure there was no-one to see – *get on with it, for God's sake, you couldn't look more suss if you tried* – and stepped through the door onto Records.

A smell of old paper; dim light from where the stacks and shelves blocked out the light. Lee's domain. She'd been well-liked; he could hear more than one set of muffled sniffles coming from among the crowded shelves. How many of the tears were for Lee herself, though, and how many for the betrayal? No way of knowing. But there was only one set of tears that mattered here.

Thorpe squeezed down one of the aisles – not easily, since they were very narrow and he wasn't – and found his way to the little cubby-hole, tucked away in one corner of the floor, that he was after. He listened at the door: he could hear muffled sobbing.

You sure about this, Richard?

No. But fuck it. That last brief clasp of Lee's fingers in his; what he'd seen when she'd pulled the trigger, before he could look away; the smirk on Winterborn's face. He was sick of cringing, of squirming in front of that vicious lunatic. Thorpe took a deep breath and tapped on the cubby-hole door.

"One minute," mumbled a wavery voice, then a few seconds later: "Yes?"

Thorpe opened the door. "Hello, Soper."

Soper wiped his eyes. He was fair-haired and blue-eyed – somewhat red-eyed now, too – with a pale, open face. "Colonel." He started to stand.

"Sit down." Thorpe shut the door behind him. "We need to talk," he said. "About Lee."

Soper's face quivered. "You're going to kill me, aren't you?"

"What?"

"I don't blame you." Soper's voice was crushed and empty. "I got her killed. I deserve it."

"Whoah. Run that by me again."

"I didn't know. I mean, I didn't mean to."

Thorpe's fingers dug into his thighs, wanting to become fists. "Mean what?"

"I saw she was reading the Sycorax file," said Soper. "So I logged it. I didn't know she was – I mean, I thought she was doing it on orders. Had authorisation. I didn't know, Colonel, I swear to G –"

"Okay." Thorpe held a hand up. "It's okay, mate, I believe you." *Mate*: how long had it been since he'd called someone that? But it came naturally now. There was a bond here: *we both loved her*. He wanted to tell Soper it wasn't on him, but didn't. There was guilt here, as well as grief, and he could make use of that. "You want to make up for it?" he said.

Soper looked up, blinking.

"Well?"

"All right." Soper nodded. "How."

"I want to know what Lee died for," said Thorpe. "I want to read the Sycorax file. And I don't want anyone else to know. Least of all Winterborn. Can you make that happen?"

"Yes," whispered Soper.

"Then do it. Now."

*

Gevaudan's Cottage, Ashwood Fort
1802 hours

The grass in Gevaudan's garden was up to Helen's shins. It grew thick and lush in the summer heat; normally Gevaudan's garden was neatly kept, but in the last few weeks it had grown wild, twining up the legs of the chairs and table in the middle of the garden. The one part of it kept neat was the corner holding the two cairns, Gevaudan's and Flaps'.

Her foot caught something. She looked down; a candle lantern glinted in the grass. From that meal with Gevaudan – had it really only been a month ago?

A footfall, behind her; she turned. "Gevaudan?"

"Soz," Danny said. "Only me."

They stood in silence for nearly a minute, before Danny spoke again. "Just wish he was here."

"You and me both."

"Can't believe it, what Alannah's saying. No way would he do that, not to us. Not after everything."

Helen sank into a chair. "After what he found out..."

"Dun't matter," said Danny. "Even if he's fucked off at you, he wouldn't shaft us all like that. I mean, he's a *mate*."

Helen could have laughed, or cried; Danny had grown up fast, but he was still a boy. "I hope you're right," she said. "But the Pyramid – I think they broke something in him. And then after Hobsdyke, I just don't –"

"You were fighting a war," said Danny. "And he wasn't a mate then. But you wouldn't trick him like that now, right?"

Wouldn't she? Was there, ultimately, anything she wouldn't do to get what she wanted? "No," Helen said at last.

"Right, then. And he knows that. Or he will. Just give him time."

Helen wanted to believe it, of course she did; what was the alternative? That she'd wounded Gevaudan to the point of betrayal? That Blob's death, the butchered sentries, the sick-bay explosion, were all on her?

You didn't force him to become a Reaper, Gevaudan had said of Winterborn: Percy, Tereus, had made his choice, Helen shouldn't hold herself responsible. Would he say the same now? First Winterborn, now Gevaudan; it was a pattern. She used and wounded those who cared for her, betrayed them and was betrayed in turn. She couldn't clear herself of responsibility in that.

Danny opened his mouth to say something else, but before he could utter it, they heard the screams. "Fuck," said Danny, and ran back through the cottage.

Helen followed him; they ran back towards the Fort, but the screams weren't coming from there. They came from beyond the inner wall. Helen unfastened the pouch on her thigh which held the .38, closing her hand around the Smith and Wesson's grip.

The gates were already being pulled open and Helen sprinted through, Danny behind her. Outside St Martin's Church, a crowd had already gathered. Helen pushed through it.

Inside the church, a young boy, maybe eleven or twelve, was still screaming. An older man cradled him, trying to soothe him, but the cries didn't stop. Helen couldn't blame him. She knew the boy; he came from a religious community deep in the Wastelands, one left largely untouched since the War: they'd been lucky enough never to have encountered the Reapers, or even brigands, so violent death was still new to them.

And what was above the altar would have troubled even a battle-hardened warrior's sleep. From the big crucifix, a man hung upside down. He'd been eviscerated, his eyes put out; his throat was slashed open in three or four places. *A Grendelwolf kill*; that was what Alannah would say, and would she be right?

"Oh fucking hell," Danny said as they approached the altar. Helen wasn't sure if he meant the savage mutilations the corpse had sustained, or if he'd seen what she had; the grey hair, the weathered body criss-crossed with white scars, and the fox-skin headdress – crumpled, sodden with blood – laid out like an offering on the altar.

*

Gevaudan sat with his back against the stone, gazing sightlessly ahead. Water dripped.

Jo stood before him. His parents stood to his left, Michaela and Keith to his right. David and Gloria stood by Jo, holding her hands.

None of them spoke. There was nothing left to say.

*

CANTEEN, ASHWOOD FORT
1930 HOURS

The moment she entered the canteen, Helen felt the anger in the air, like the heat from an opened oven door. And as eyes turned her way, the temperature rose.

"Wondered when you'd show your face," someone called. "Or if you'd have the guts."

A fortnight ago, no-one would have spoken to her like that: not because of her rank, but because of who she was. Now even her rank was meaningless. She could see Brant in the crowd – had it been him who'd shouted? – glaring at her with the kind of venom he'd previously reserved for Carson.

Wakefield was leaning on Filly; the little tribeswoman was crying openly. "Wakefield," said Helen. "I'm so sorry –"

Wakefield turned away. Filly held her close; her eyes met Helen's over Wakefield's tangled bird's-nest hair, and she shook her head.

Alannah climbed up on a table, banging on it with an earthenware mug. "Right," she said, standing. "Everybody listen up."

The filthy, broken woman Helen had met when she returned to Manchester seven months before was gone: this was the Alannah of old. Tough, organised, capable. A fighter, and a leader. "Chief Loncraine is dead," she said. "And not just dead. The bastard defiled his corpse, like a fucking Jennywren. There's a traitor here."

Voices muttered agreement. Helen saw Mackie – big, daft, gentle Mackie – nodding along.

"And not just any traitor. A vicious one. Cruel. Savage."

More sounds of agreement.

"And inhuman. Quite literally. The Grendelwolf."

"Yes!" Mackie shouted.

"He's got to be found," said Alannah. "And immediately. We can't wait any longer."

"Found and killed," someone shouted – Hack, Helen realised. "Bastard's a mad dog. Put him down like one."

Someone had to speak for Gevaudan, but who? As things were, Helen's support might only make things worse. Surely someone else would, after all they'd undergone? But no-one did. Where was Danny? Helen saw him in the crowd; he met her eyes miserably, then looked at Alannah and the others. He hadn't expected this division – who had? However hard things had been, up till now they'd all been on the same side. But now?

A few faces showed uncertainty, but Helen could tell that none of them were going to speak up. It would be her, she realised, or nobody. "Wait," she shouted.

Heads turned; there was a silence, but it was a sullen, hostile one. Alannah put her hands on her hips. Hack looked at Helen, and spat on the floor.

"We don't know for sure it's Gevaudan," she said, but a chorus of jeers drowned her out. "Wait," she yelled again, climbing up on a table. *Two can play that game, Alannah.* "Think about this. The Reapers tried to turn Gevaudan once. He's one of our most valued allies. He's fought beside us time and again. Half of us here owe him their lives –"

"I don't owe that freak fuck-all," Mackie shouted.

"How many Reapers did he kill here when they attacked? How many Catchmen?"

"That was then, Helen," said Alannah. "Things have changed. Maybe they did break him at the Pyramid. Or maybe it was Hobsdyke that turned him." Alannah's mouth didn't say it, but her eyes did: *in which case, you can thank yourself.*

Dozens of voices shouted agreement with Alannah as Helen tried to speak.

"*Wait*," she yelled again. The noise diminished, but only a little. They weren't listening. She had to say her piece while she still could. "We have to at least try and take him alive – this could still be the Reapers trying to fit him up. If they turn us against each other –" She had to shout now, over the rising jeers. "He's the right to a hearing at least."

"No he doesn't," said Hack. "Traitors don't get rights."

"Take him alive?" said Mackie. "Just killing him'll be tough enough. How many of ours you want dead?"

"Fuck him," Hack shouted. "He's a fucking freak who can't be trusted. We don't need him. Kill him now and be safe."

Helen opened her mouth again, but this time the yells and jeers were too loud, and didn't stop. Not until Alannah signalled for silence; even then, she cut Helen off before she could speak.

"Enough," she said. "Helen, stop now. While you still have some friends."

The air went out of Helen at that.

"You just don't want to face the truth," Alannah said; Christ, there was actual *pity* in her eyes. "I'm sorry. All the evidence points one way. So now we have to act for the best. We find Gevaudan and yes, if we can, we take him alive. But the priority's got to be to put him out of action before anyone else dies."

"Alannah," said Helen, but the other woman had turned away. "Danny? Wakefield?"

But no-one would face her; the whole crowd turned its back and clustered around Alannah's table. Brant gave her one last look then turned away, shaking his head.

Alannah crouched to speak to them. Helen stood for nearly a minute, waiting for someone, anyone, to look her way. At last she climbed down, and walked slowly from the canteen.

3.

EASTERN HILLS, NEAR ASHWOOD FORT, RCZ7
26TH JULY, ATTACK PLUS TWENTY-ONE YEARS
2240 HOURS

Dusk was settling, softening the landscape's contours as the sun died in splendour to the west. A wind blew across the hill, cooling and welcome in the close summer heat. Gevaudan emerged from the cave, took a deep breath of air that didn't smell of damp stone.

He was still; only his long black coat and long black hair, flapping about him in the wind, moved. His long, sombre face remained impassive, the yellow wolf's eyes hooded; what went on behind them, no-one else, even if there'd been another present, could have told.

The wind blew, and the night came on.

And Gevaudan Shoal descended the hillside and walked into the deepening night, where Helen Damnation, and Ashwood Fort, awaited him.

*

WALL ONE (EAST), ASHWOOD FORT
2350 HOURS

The Fort's lights burned in the dark; like a moth in the night, Gevaudan circled towards them, low and silent, flitting from shadow to shadow.

Stealth and speed; the Grendelwolf's hallmark. That and the destruction they'd been shaped to wreak, by Kellett.

Shaped to die by him, too, without their serum. Helen had saved him from that. *Helen*; to think of her brought pain, and the pain in turn brought fury.

He pushed the anger aside, or tried to.

The sentry above didn't even see Gevaudan as he reached the wall and began to climb.

*

ROOF OF THE TOWER
27TH JULY, ATTACK PLUS TWENTY-ONE YEARS
0002 HOURS

The wind sheared hard across the roof, blowing Winterborn's hair back from his face. It was pleasant, cooling; he stood awhile in silence, savouring it, before turning to Mordake. "Well?"

"Things are coming to fruition among the rebels, I think. Wait for word from our agent at Ashwood. It'll come soon. Is everything else ready?"

"Operation Long Knife can be launched at a moment's notice. We're all just waiting on you, Doctor."

"Soon, Commander. And then the tide will begin to turn again, this time in your favour."

"*Our* favour, Doctor Mordake, surely?"

"Of course." Mordake smiled. "But yours most of all, Commander. I am but a humble servant."

"Humble in roughly the same way as a dog is a herbivore," said Winterborn, "but no matter."

"Indeed," said Mordake. "Does't not go well?"

"It does, yes. Now we've only Scrimgeour, Grimwood and Holland to contend with."

Mordake nodded. "Scrimgeour is an efficient administrator of her little domain, but has no aptitude for politics and only a tiny Reaper force to back her up. Without the others' support, she becomes irrelevant. As for Holland, he's old school – genuinely believes the REAP Command exists to serve the greater good and that the time isn't right for unification. But if the new reality is presented to them as a *fait accompli*, he'll accept it." Mordake smiled. "He won't like it, but he have no choice. Leaving us only with Grimwood."

"Grimwood," said Winterborn. "Yes."

"The one you fear most."

"I don't *fear* any of them, Mordake."

"My apologies, Commander. A poor choice of words. But Grimwood, nonetheless..."

"He's the only one who hates me more than he does the rebels. If I supported breathing he'd oppose it on general principles. He'll never join, at any price, might even work actively to break up the alliances I've built..."

"Yes, the danger he poses is quite clear. Did you obtain what I require? Hair, nail clippings?"

"I did, yes. We all have agents in one another's camps, as you know."

"Oh yes." Mordake smiled; then it faded. "Bring those items to me as soon as you can, Commander, and Grimwood will cease to be a problem."

"We can't assassinate..."

"There'll be no assassination, Commander. Rest assured of that. No suggestion of foul play, and certainly nothing that points towards you."

*

Gevaudan's Cottage
0014 hours

Gevaudan dropped unseen from the inner wall into a silent crouch, and ghosted to his cottage.

He allowed himself a smile as he let himself inside. No-one had seen him come. "The hand hath not lost its ancient cunning," he muttered.

The smile faded, and he wandered through the dark to the kitchen. No need to light a candle; he could see all he needed to. He drew back a chair and sat at the table, silent, for a little while. Then he went out.

*

Roof of the Tower
0030 hours

"What about the rebels in the city?" said Mordake. "You've made progress there?"

"We have a lead," said Winterborn. "Roger Darrow – he's been sighted in South Manchester, so we're fairly certain he's based there. We're watching for him now; he only needs to break cover once more, and then..."

"You track him to his lair."

"We can spare a little manpower from Operation Long Knife," said Winterborn, "to extract that particular thorn from our side."

"I'd think your CorSec personnel would be admirably suited to the task."

"Quite." Winterborn sighed. "I'll almost miss the old goat."

"All things must pass away."

"Try not to wax philosophical, Mordake. It's not what I pay you for."

*

WALL TWO, ASHWOOD FORT
0100 HOURS

Danny climbed the steps to the top of Wall Two, wincing as his knees twinged. Fuck sake. No way was he getting old, not already. Few more years left, weren't there? *A man's as young as the woman he feels* – Alannah'd said that once, laughing. Fucking hell, if that was true he was up shit creek. Though he'd better not say that around her.

Candles flickered in the battlements' shrine. Inside were little effigies of clay and twig. Danny always tried to make one before anything big kicked off; he hadn't when the Reapers attacked the Fort back, and that psycho bitch Jarrett had shot the shit out of him. Then again, some folk had made effigies and not lived through that day. Scopes, f'r instance. After the battle, he'd found one of hers; twigs and hair stuck together around a rifle bullet. She'd been weird as fuck, but he'd liked her. Missed her too. Wasn't the same without her around.

Danny climbed down from the wall, went out through the gate towards the church. Some twat'd parked a cart full of hay outside. Have a word with someone about that. He stood outside the church for a sec, then went in.

They'd cleaned up inside. Candles burnt round the altar – special ones, tribal – and they'd left offerings where Loncraine had been. Bunches of flowers, jugs of wine and ale, food. A fresh-flayed fox skin, too, flies buzzing all over it. *Ugh*. Wakefield'd said that's what they did when a chief died.

Danny stood at the altar for a bit; felt like he should say or do something, but he didn't know what. He didn't know the Fox Tribe's ways, or the old church's. Hadn't really known Loncraine either, but he knew Wakefield and how bad it would've hurt.

She'd liked the Grendelwolf too, though. Old Creeping D – no, Danny couldn't call him that, not now. Maybe never again. He wished he'd said something in the canteen, but what? That he didn't believe it, or that he didn't want to? No-one *wanted* to, not even Alannah, and she'd never been mad keen on the fucker.

Gevaudan'd saved his life enough times. They might even have called themselves friends. Danny still had the jacket Gevaudan had given him. Back in his quarters right now, cos it was way too fucking hot – he'd nearly boiled alive in those Reaper leathers back at the Pyramid.

Danny turned from the altar, found the door to the church tower. Bullet-holes in the walls, where Trex had dragged himself up the stairs, bleeding and dying. Danny climbed to the top, reached out and touched the door handle. Hesitated. He'd only been up here once, before the battle. After it was over, he'd been in the sick bay – and after *that*, he'd had better things to do. But tonight seemed a good time to look back; he didn't fancy looking forward.

Danny stepped out into the roof, lit the candle lantern hanging by the door, watched the glow spread out through the gloom. The stains where the blood'd soaked in deep showed on the reddish sandstone. They'd never been managed to scrub it all out. Bullets had smashed and hammered the parapet and the walls around the door ragged.

They'd fought hard here, Trex and Scopes; held the church against the Reapers while Danny'd been pinned down behind Wall Two, unable to do a thing. He tried not to think of how it'd ended, of their stripped bodies hanging from the church tower, but couldn't: out of everything he remembered from that day, *that* was the worst. He'd never been up here, couldn't face seeing it. Not till now.

Gevaudan had seen it happen; he'd tried to stop Danny looking, hadn't wanted him to see. He'd saved Danny's arse how many times, that day alone? And now they wanted him dead – *Alannah* wanted him dead.

He didn't know which way to go. But if Alannah pulled hard enough one way, Danny thought he might end up going with her. Even if she was wrong.

Miserably, Danny scuffed the rooftop with his boot.

And something moved in the dark.

Shadows flickered in the candle-lantern's glow. He spun, looking round; a low chuckle sounded. One he knew.

No. Oh fucking no.

Something squatted on the parapet; its eyes gleamed yellow. *No. No.* It jumped, landed in a crouch at the light's edge, then flowed to its feet and stepped fully into view.

"Hello, Danny," said Gevaudan, claws sliding from his fingertips.

No. Danny fumbled for his .38, knowing he'd never be fast enough and that even if he was the pistol wouldn't stop him. The Grendelwolf leapt, closing the distance between in a split second. The claws flashed; there was a white sheet of pain. Then the parapet hit Danny in the back. He tipped over it; then he was falling, and there was only the dark.

*

ROOF OF THE TOWER
0106 HOURS

Mordake had moved to the roof's edge, leaning out into the wind. Winterborn grimaced; even the sight made him queasy.

Mordake stared out into the distance – was it towards Ashwood? A long, eager sigh escaped him. "Soon now," Mordake said; the second face grinned, black eyes fixed on Winterborn. "We're very close."

Mordake turned to face Winterborn; it was a relief to see that human face, however harrowed, whatever terrible things those eyes had seen. "We're almost there," he said. "Shoal has almost served his turn. And then..."

Winterborn smiled back. Mordake turned away again to gaze out once more, seeing who knew what. In a moment or two he seemed to have forgotten Winterborn entirely, and Winterborn found he didn't mind that at all. He'd been up here for more than an hour, and the wind seemed particularly cold here, of a sudden; he went, as quietly as he could, back down inside the Tower.

*

TEMPORARY SICK BAY, ROOF OF ASHWOOD FORT
0214 HOURS

Nestor's patients – some of them his staff until earlier today – lay under canvas awnings. Candle-lanterns lit the roof. *Bloody firetrap*, Helen thought: *let one lantern break and Christ help them.*

She wove between beds and pallets, still rubbing the sleep from her eyes. A nurse wove past; Helen reached out and touched his arm. "Where's Nestor?"

The nurse eyed her with plain dislike. "That way."

Nestor sat on the cowling of an air-vent, smock bloodied, and looking more drained and tired than ever. There were cuts on his face, a plaster on his cheek. He'd been lucky; the explosion had only left him with minor injuries. Was that down to Gevaudan, too?

Alannah sat beside Nestor, crying. *Oh Christ, Danny.* Helen sprinted over. "I just heard. Is he –?"

"Still be touch and go for a while," said Nestor. "But I think he'll pull through."

"Thank fuck. Alannah —"

"Don't," Alannah said. "Just don't." She turned back to Nestor. "Can I see him?"

Nestor hesitated, then nodded.

"Can I —" began Helen. Alannah opened her mouth to speak, but Nestor said "Anything for a quiet life. Just take it easy on him. Both of you."

Alannah gave Helen a last glare, then stalked after Nestor.

Helen followed. It didn't matter if she wasn't welcome. She kept seeing Danny at their first meeting — a spiky-haired boy, puppy-dog eyes and a wild grin, all eager for the fight and with no bloody clue of how to go about it. And now, this. The fighting had put grey in his hair, taken light from his eyes. The boy was a man now, but with how much of himself left behind? *Just let him live*, she begged whoever or whatever might listen: his death would be too much to bear just now.

She had to ask him; she knew she'd come here for that cold, selfish purpose as much as any other, and despised herself for it. But she had to, nonetheless. She might be every kind of manipulative, selfish thing, but that had kept her alive this long, had helped her win.

Danny lay on a bed salvaged from the sick-bay after the bombing, the covers pulled up to his throat; Alannah stood over him, fingers to her mouth, then reached down and took his hand. Helen moved to the other side of the bed. Alannah glared at her, then nodded; a truce, however brief, had been declared.

"He was lucky," Nestor said. "Landed in the haycart when he fell. Otherwise..." he shrugged.

Alannah drew the covers back. Dents of shiny white scar tissue, from when Jarrett had shot him, dotted his once-smooth torso; bandages swathed his chest, dotted red.

"What did this?" Alannah's voice was thick and shaking.

Nestor pulled the sheets back up. "I don't know exactly," he said. "Some kind of sharp implement. Implements."

"Claws?" said Alannah.

"Alannah," began Helen.

"I don't want to hear it, Helen." Alannah brought Danny's hand to her lips and kissed it. "I don't."

"Can I leave you two unattended?" said Nestor. "Believe it or not, I've got other patients."

Helen nodded.

"Right," Alannah said. Her eyes filled; more than anything Helen wanted to go to her, but she could feel the anger that battened on the grief too, like the heat from a fire.

Danny murmured faintly, stirred. Helen stroked the hand she held. She didn't want to keep still, she wanted to go and *do* something – but this was the closest she'd known since Bereloth to anything like peace, any sort of companionship. It rested on a paper-thin veneer of civility, but it was something.

"Uh." It was less a word than a loud breath; Danny blinked up at them, gummy-eyed. He looked blearily from Helen to Alannah. "Fucking hell," he muttered at last.

Alannah let out something between a laugh, a gasp and a sob, and kissed his hand again.

"Welcome back," said Helen.

Danny tried to smile and winced. "Fucking hell," he said again.

"Can you say anything else?" Helen asked. "Or did you knacker your speech centres back there?"

Danny grinned again, with a little more strength. "How about – ow, that fucking hurts?"

"Sweetheart?" Alannah cut in; glaring at Helen before switching her attention back to Danny. "Sweetheart, what happened?"

Danny's smile faded. "I was up on the church tower, and..."

"And what, honey?" Alannah kissed his hand again.

Danny's breathing hitched. "Alannah, take it easy," said Helen.

Alannah held her free hand up; the other kept a tight hold of Danny's. "Who did this?" she said. "Who hurt you?"

Danny's eyes filled. He shook his head.

Oh no, thought Helen. *No*. She could see the pain there.

"Was it him?" said Alannah. "Was it him, Danny?"

"Alannah –" Helen began.

"Shut up, Helen. Was it, love? You can tell me. You don't have to say the name if you can't. Just a yes or a no. Was it the Grendelwolf? Was it Gevaudan?"

Danny looked miserably from her to Helen, then back again. After the longest of moments, he nodded. "Yes," he whispered, and closed his eyes.

"Danny?" Helen said.

"Leave him," said Alannah. "He's sleeping."

Helen looked at her. "Don't," Alannah said. "Not a word."

"Alannah, come on. At the least, he deserves a fair trial."

"Fair trial?" Alannah snorted. "Anyone else, Helen, anyone other than that *thing*, you'd have had them hung, drawn and quartered by now. What more proof do you need? What else does he have to do?"

She kissed Danny's fingers, then laid his hand on his chest, resting both hands on it for a moment. Then she stepped away. "Wherever he was," she said, "he's back at the Fort. We're going to find him, and we're going to deal with him. Permanently. And if you don't like that, Helen, then I suggest you stay out of my way."

Alannah wheeled and strode off. Helen stayed there, holding Danny's hand. He was sleeping again, his eyes moving to and fro under their lids.

The sensible thing would be to stay here. Let Alannah do what she had to. Accept the evidence; forget Gevaudan Shoal and cauterise whatever part of her felt anything for him.

But she remembered the candlelight, shining in his eyes that evening. What he'd said after the battle for Ashwood: *I don't fight for a cause. I fight for you.* To have come so far, shared so much – was all that gone, now? Had she destroyed him as she'd destroyed Percy? Percy had become Tereus Winterborn; what had she made of Gevaudan?

But if she didn't let him go, what then? Fight Alannah and the rest? What friends would she have left, assuming she had any at all? And all for what? The regard of someone who despised her, who'd like as not kill her on sight?

The easy thing versus the right thing; it had rarely been any contest for Helen, even when her idea of the right thing matched almost no-one else's.

Tonight, she wasn't even certain what the right thing *was*. She needed to decide though, and soon. Before the chance to do so was taken out of her hands.

She stood stroking Danny's hand in the flickering light that held the darkness back, trying to choose.

4.

GEVAUDAN'S COTTAGE
27TH JULY, ATTACK PLUS TWENTY-ONE YEARS
0300 HOURS

In the garden, lit only by the moon and stars, Gevaudan sat cross-legged on the grass; it felt pleasantly cool. The shrine was close; he reached out and touched it lightly.

"Jo?" he whispered. "Talk to me. Please. I need to hear your voice."

No answer; if she was there, she stayed voiceless and unseen.

"The choices I've made," he said. "The things I've chosen to believe. I can't tell any longer, you see. Whether I've been right or wrong. Or just a fool."

The night was his only answer: the crickets chirruping, the bats' shrill distant peeping. Crickets chirped. Nothing more. Alone with the silent dead.

*

Canteen, Ashwood Fort
0340 hours

A dull silence had settled in the canteen; the rebel fighters sat scattered round their tables.

In one corner, Lish nursed a mug of dandelion-root coffee long gone cold. She'd kept quiet while the others had argued and raged, not knowing what to think; the thought of Danny wounded and near-death blotted out everything else. Shock, grief, fury. Yes, fury; yes, grief. Danny might be with Alannah and she herself with Harp, but Lish couldn't help how she felt for him. Anyway, he'd switched partners before, hadn't he? Poor Flaps.

In which case, of course, Lish shouldn't want him at all. If he'd cheat once, he'd cheat again. But logic never came into matters like this.

And now they were saying Gevaudan had done this. He'd saved Lish during the battle – saved Danny too, she'd seen it. And Harp. He'd saved them all, one time or another. How could he be a traitor? But already those memories seemed faint and faded.

And things had changed since then; no point clinging to how it had been. Everyone knew what had happened at Hobsdyke, and Lish'd seen what the Reapers did to him at the Pyramid herself; either of those things would have shaken not just her loyalty, but her sense of who she was. What would both together have done?

But even so – *we came for you at Stockport, you bastard. We got you out.* Part of her might try to understand such a betrayal, but the part that had *been* betrayed spoke up louder and stronger. The bomb in the sick-bay; Loncraine hung up and gutted, his eyes put out; and now Danny. No. No excuses for that.

If he'd killed Helen, she knew, people might have understood, even have forgiven him for it. But he was killing everyone *but* her.

Lish wanted to believe Helen was right: it was all some horrible mistake, or a fit-up by the Reapers. She wanted that to be true, because then they wouldn't have been betrayed, not like that. They could put things back together, to something like what they'd been before. But that was clutching at straws; every scrap of proof pointed one way. What would Harp have thought or done? He was out in the Wastelands, on manoeuvres out of one of the field-bases; Lish could have done with him here now. But no, that wouldn't have been any good. She had to think for herself.

The canteen door banged; Lish jumped, almost spilling her drink. Alannah strode in, fists balled at her sides. Snatched an empty mug off a table and banged it for silence. On the third try, it smashed; she swept the pieces to the floor and climbed on the table-top.

"Still alive," she said, hands on hips, "but no thanks to that *thing*. It was Gevaudan, all right. So now we find him, we deal with him. No more talk."

"How do you know it was him?" Lish heard herself say. That last defiant sliver of her, that didn't want to believe.

Others in the canteen glared at Lish; Hack walked towards Lish, moving in close. Brant tried to catch her arm, but Hack shook him off and took another step towards Lish. Alannah just looked at her.

"Danny told us," she said. "And the bastard half-killed him, so I think he should know. Don't you?"

Hack smiled, then put a finger to her lips, mouthing *Shh*.

Lish's face burned, and she looked down.

"This is bollocks." Zaq strode forward. "You all know the big fucker. He's saved our arses, all of us."

"Shut up," said Hack.

"Fuck off," said Zaq, turning from her to the crowd, hands on hips. Thank God; they'd listen to Zaq, she'd find the right words. "This is a fucking set up –"

Lish saw the glint of brass in Hack's hand and opened her mouth to shout a warning. Too slow: Hack kidney-punched Zaq with the knuckleduster and Zaq fell to her knees with a cry. Hack punched down, and Zaq fell forward groaning.

"Cunt!" Wakefield ran forward. Hack stepped back, arms spread, smirking. "Problem?" she said.

"Wakefield!" It was Filly, on the edge of the crowd. She caught Wakefield's eye, shaking her head. Wakefield clenched her fists. Hack blew her a kiss, beckoned her. "Anyone else soft on traitors?" she said.

"That's enough," said Brant. Hack rounded on him but he looked calmly back at her. "We've got other stuff to do."

Filly moved to Wakefield's side and touched her arm. They knelt by Zaq and sat her up.

"Right then," said Hack. She nodded to Alannah.

For a sec, Alannah looked uncomfortable; maybe she could stop this, even now. *You're better than this*, Lish thought. But then Alannah nodded. "The armoury," she told Hack. "We need to go hunting."

*

Timperley Golf Course and Driving Range, South Manchester
0400 hours

Flaps followed Darrow along the cinder path, Sterling braced against her hip. On either side, green land spread out, grown wild, ending at a wall with a road beyond it. There were clumps of trees and hummocks of ground that were grass on one side and sand on the other. Each road had a row of big, ornate houses.

"The fuck is this place?"

"Golf course," Darrow said absently, looking ahead.

"What's one of them?"

"Golf was a game," said Darrow. "You played it on an open green like this. Never saw the appeal myself, but it tended to be popular among those who could afford it."

Flaps eyed the tents and shelters dotting the green. Beyond a copse of gnarled trees, ragged figures crouched in the pre-dawn twilight, dangling fishing lines into a pond. "They were rich around here, then?"

"For the most part." Darrow glanced around. "It was considered a nice place to live, once upon a time."

They emerged from another thicket; something big and grimily white showed through the branches. Darrow stopped and took a deep breath.

"What's up?" said Flaps.

He pointed. "That's the place."

It was a big house – or was *house* the right word? Flaps wasn't sure; it was the right shape for a house, but bigger than any she'd seen.

"The Old Hall," said Darrow. "Used to belong to some wealthy family. It was a restaurant, back when I knew it. A steakhouse."

"And she's there?"

"We'll see, won't we?"

They crossed to the building itself and stood before the main entrance. Soot blackened the windows and doorframe.

"Looks a bit fucked," said Flaps.

"That's the idea," said Darrow. "Look closer."

He pointed; when Flaps got close enough, she saw what he meant. The soot-smudges weren't the random patterns left by a fire. They'd been applied deliberately. In places, she could almost make out the fingerprints. Little hands, too. Children's.

"Clever," she said.

"Exactly," said Darrow. "Plenty of other empty buildings in better condition around here. So this place gets left alone." He took another deep breath; nervous. "Okay," he said, "let's have a look."

They went inside, down a hallway and into a wide open room filled with dark wooden tables and chairs with padded seats. "This was the restaurant," said Darrow.

It reminded Flaps a bit of the canteen at Ashwood. "So what now?"

"Kate?" Darrow called. "Kate, it's Roger."

"I know," said a voice. Flaps spun round. A round-faced, blonde-haired woman stood in the doorway. Behind her were a bunch of sprogs, most no older than ten. One girl who might've been eleven, maybe twelve held a Sten; so did another lad, about Flaps' age, with a mop of curly hair. The guns were pointed at the floor in front of Darrow and her – not aimed at them, but ready to go if owt kicked off.

"Kate," said Darrow.

"Roger." Kate smiled at Flaps. There was something *warm* about her; only word Flaps had for it. "And this is..."

"Flaps."

"Dene," said Darrow, nodding to the curly-haired boy. "I thought you were dead."

"Me too, for a bit," Dene said. "Ashton sent me looking for this lot."

"Ashton?"

Dene nodded. "Right before we hit Station Five. He knew it was gonna kick off. Said to find Kate and help get her out."

"Good old Mike," Darrow sighed. "You managed the first part."

"Reaper shot me," Dene said. "Was half-dead when I found 'em. Kate looked after me, but the bastards had the whole city locked down by then. Best thing was to lay low. After that... well, someone's gotta look after 'em."

Darrow smiled. "You've done a good job." He nodded at the girl with the gun. "Is this your second in command?"

"Yup. Meet Spike."

Spike nodded. She had frizzy hair, buck teeth, and very sharp, bright hazel eyes.

"I've been looking for you," Darrow told Kate.

"I know." She stepped forward, holding out her arms; Darrow went to meet her, and they hugged tightly for nearly a minute. Flaps heard Darrow make a noise; sounded almost like a sob. She didn't know where to look; when she looked at the sprogs they looked terrified.

"So." Kate stepped back. "What's the plan now?"

"We get you back to Deadsbury, first of all," Darrow said. "After that, we smuggle you out of the city to the Wastelands." He smiled. "We control quite a lot of them now. You'll be safe."

"Safe," said Kate. She smiled, too. "Not felt that way for a while." She took a deep breath. "Get your things, kids. Just what you can carry. We're going home."

*

Canteen, Ashwood Fort

0430 hours

The canteen rang with the sound of metal on metal: bullets were slotted into magazines, magazines slotted into guns, bolts pulled back and safeties applied.

Lish watched, her Thompson gun held across her knees. The canteen's main door flew open: four fighters came in, each one pushing a crate-laden goods cart. Alannah went to meet them.

The door flew open again; a young fighter ran in. "He's been spotted!"

Alannah went still. "Where?"

"You're not gonna believe it. His cottage."

Alannah snorted. "He must be losing it."

She opened one of the crates and took out an M20 rocket launcher. "Now we're ready," she said. "Who's coming?"

Chairs scraped back; everyone else in the room stood. After a moment, so did Lish. She saw Filly and Wakefield exchange glances, then stand. Lish met Wakefield's eyes, and they nodded to one another.

*

Timperley Golf Course and Driving Range
0432 hours

In the sand of an old bunker, Reaper Ellen Harris lay squinting through her binoculars at the little procession making its way from the Old Hall and down the overgrown driveway that led to the main road. She adjusted the focusing wheel; Darrow's grey hair and lined face spring into focus.

Harris touched the rifle beside her. She could kill him now; could probably slot the whole lot of them inside a minute. But what'd be the point? Their time'd come, soon enough.

Harris' hand shifted from her rifle to her communicator, raising it to her lips. "Trap One," she said. "He's on the move. Travelling towards Stockport Road."

"Trap Two here," came the reply. "Will pick up."

When the group was out of sight, Harris tucked the communicator into her poncho and picked up her rifle. She'd need to move into an intercept position to take over the job of following them again, further down their route. Between them, they'd track Darrow every step of his way.

"Wee wee wee, little pig," she muttered. "All the way home."

*

Gevaudan's Cottage
0442 hours

He had no idea how long he'd sat there, wanting Jo and the others to come to him, wanting them to speak, but there'd been nothing, no sign. He'd never needed them so badly, so, of course, they were nowhere to be found. Wasn't that always the way?

Sounds in the distance; angry voices, running footsteps. Didn't matter; another move in this endless, grubby conflict. He was no longer sure if he cared; just now he had no interest in running to their aid.

Away from the cave, he'd hoped to find them again. But there was nothing. Was that approval, disapproval, a sign of some other kind? Or only a delusion that – for now, at least – had stopped?

He was still trying to decide when the voices and the footsteps became louder. They were approaching – coming his way. Then he heard the cottage doors crash open, booted footsteps storming through his home. He spun, rising.

Alannah strode into the garden, aiming her Sten at him. Other faces he recognised, too – Lish, Brant. Some held rifles and submachine guns; two or three even pointed rocket launchers clumsily at him.

"Don't move," Alannah said.

Gevaudan spread his hands; gun-bolts clicked back. "Keep the claws sheathed," Alannah said. "Where've you been, Gevaudan?"

"Away," he said.

"With your Reaper friends?"

"What?"

"Don't *what* me."

"I was in the hills," he said. "For the past few hours, I've been here." He nodded at the cairn. "With my family."

"Your Reaper family?" called the bony girl with the pitted face – what was she called? Hack, that was it.

"What are you talking about?" Gevaudan motioned to the cairn once more. "My memorial to my family. Surely you –"

"Memorial?" Alannah strode past him, circling round towards the cairn.

*

Lish gripped the Thompson tight, watching the Grendelwolf for some final proof of innocence or guilt. But that long white face gave nothing away; no knowing what lay behind it.

Alannah reached the cairn. "This where you hide your transmitter?" she said. "So you can talk to your *friends*?"

On the last word, she kicked out, catching at the cairn with her boot; the heaped stones spilled and clattered to the ground.

The Grendelwolf's yellow eyes flared; red lips drew back from sharp white teeth; claws slid from his fingertips, and he stepped towards Alannah.

Alannah fell back, the Sten aimed. "Take him!" she shouted. "Take him out now!"

And Lish, without even meaning to, raised her gun to fire.

5.

GEVAUDAN'S COTTAGE
27TH JULY, ATTACK PLUS TWENTY-ONE YEARS
0444 HOURS

Running in through the open front door, Helen reached the kitchen in time to see it through the window. Alannah kicking out at the cairn: stones tumbling, and rage flashing across Gevaudan's face.

What did you expect, you idiots? All that's left of his loved ones is there, and you defile it? But it didn't matter now; the guns were rising, and she heard Alannah shouting the order to fire.

A chance to escape; she owed him that. She burst out through the back door. "Gevaudan, run!" As heads turned, she raised the Sten and pulled the trigger.

She aimed high, over their heads; as they ducked she saw Gevaudan bolt, across the garden to vault the low wall. But then the crowd was wheeling, guns aiming towards her.

When fired on, return fire. She dived back in through the back door, tucking and rolling. *Shit, I taught the fuckers too well.*

The cottage windows burst inwards. Helen covered her face to avoid the spraying glass. "No," she heard Alannah shout. "Not at this range, you'll blow us all up."

Had someone been pointing a rocket launcher at the cottage? If so, what had Alannah thought would happen if they'd blasted Gevaudan with them at point-blank range? More gunfire hit the cottage; someone ran towards the door. Helen aimed high once more and fired again, wriggling back along the floor till she reached the front room – and then she was up and running, head down.

*

BETWEEN WALLS ONE AND TWO, ASHWOOD FORT
0447 HOURS

Gevaudan scrambled across the battlement to the parapet and jumped, legs pumping at the air. He hit the ground in a crouch, rolled and stood.

He summoned the Fury and ran; to the east of his cottage, the gap between Walls One and Two was narrower that at any other point – during the attack in the spring, a Reaper unit had scaled the outer walls, almost got into the inner compound. Wakefield had caught them in time.

Wakefield; had she been with the mob? Gevaudan hadn't seen her face among them. But he'd seen enough faces he knew there. More than enough.

Bullets cracked and buzzed past him. Gevaudan zig-zagged – the temptation to run in a straight line was strong, but potentially fatal – and leapt for the outer wall.

*

WALL TWO, ASHWOOD FORT
0451 HOURS

Helen ran to the parapet; Gevaudan was scaling Wall One, bullets punching the stonework around him.

"Get into position," she heard Alannah shout. Helen looked to her right; about fifty yards away, a pair of two-man teams were aiming Carl Gustaf launchers at Wall One. Blasting their own defences from the inside: didn't that just sum all this up? Hilarious, if it hadn't been pitiful.

Gevaudan reached the battlements. A sentry came at him; the Grendelwolf picked him up and flung him aside like a toy.

"Fire," Alannah shouted.

*

WALL ONE, ASHWOOD FORT
0452 HOURS

A loud *whoosh* sounded, then another. Gevaudan looked around, two white vapour trails, tipped with fire, streaked towards him.

He leapt for the parapet –

*

WALL TWO, ASHWOOD FORT

Smoke and fire erupted where Gevaudan had been. Helen ducked; a hail of stone-chips smashed into the battlements above her like gunfire.

When she looked again, smoke and dust hung over a jagged gap in Wall One's battlements. Of Gevaudan, there was no sign.

"We get him?" Alannah shouted. "Did we get him?"

Rifle shots sounded: a sentry on Wall One, firing down at something. Hope rose in Helen: you didn't shoot a corpse.

Unless you hate it, or want to make sure it's dead.

But the sentry kept firing, and she was aiming further and further out from the wall. A moving target.

"He's getting away," Alannah yelled. "Get after him."

Helen had to get after him too; had to try and stop this, if she could. She turned to head for the steps, and someone punched her hard in the stomach.

Air whistled out of her; *knuckleduster*. She fell to her knees. The Sten was pulled from her weakened grip; she pawed for the Smith & Wesson but another blow to the stomach – a kick this time – doubled her up. Her gun arm was grabbed; she felt the pouch on her thigh pulled open, the revolver yanked out. Other hands grabbed her free arm, pulling her to her feet.

Her vision was blurred – her eyes, tearing up from the pain. She blinked, trying to clear her vision. Nausea rolled through her – serve the bastards right if she puked on them. She heard pops and spatters of gunfire, the whoosh and crump of another rocket. "Lost him," someone shouted. Despite everything, Helen smiled, and someone slapped her face. Her teeth clicked together; blood in her mouth. She spat at where she thought the slap had come from.

"Bitch," someone grunted. She'd hit her target; that, or she'd spat on the wrong person and someone else now wanted to punch her. *What, Helen, making new enemies wherever you go? Surely not.* She blinked the last of her tears away. In front of her, Hack was wiping the spit from her face. She glared at Helen, balling her fist for a punch.

"That's enough," called Alannah. Hack lowered her fist. Good job, too: Helen saw she was still wearing the knuckleduster. Her stomach throbbed: *I'll remember you, love.*

"Break it up," Alannah said, striding up. Her eyes met Helen's; for the first time they seemed uncertain. *Didn't plan for this, did you? Now it's all slipping out of control.*

"She helped him get away," said Hack. "Fucking traitor." She pointed Helen's revolver at her. "Should do her now."

"Give me that." Alannah took the .38 from her. "Wakefield?"

"Alannah?" The little tribeswoman appeared, Filly at her side. Both looked deeply unhappy.

Alannah handed Wakefield the Smith & Wesson. "Take her to the detention block. Lock her up for the duration. We'll decide what to do with her afterward."

Wakefield nodded, looking more miserable than ever. "Filly?" she said.

They took an arm each, and led Helen away.

*

GEVAUDAN'S COTTAGE
0503 HOURS

The cairns had been kicked apart. Stones were scattered on the grass, but that was all they'd found. Lish looked back towards the cottage: from inside, she heard things broken and smashed.

She went in; as she did, Hack swept past her, stomping through into the kitchen. In the kitchen, a carpet of broken glass and china crunched underfoot. In the living room, three boys with knives hacked at the sofa and armchair with knives, tearing out the stuffing. Lish saw Hack look about her, fists clenching and unclenching, them storm upstairs.

Lish went upstairs too. Shouts and sounds of destruction came from the rooms. Hack came out of one of them, Gevaudan's guitar in her hands. *Oh no; no.* How often had Lish seen Gevaudan play it in the canteen? It brought back memories, good ones. Hack looked at her and smirked; knew Lish knew what was going to happen, knew she didn't want it, knew she wouldn't dare try and stop it happening.

Hack smashed the guitar down twice on the banister rail. Wood splintered: Hack flung it to the floor and stamped on it, grinning at Lish. Did she think he'd hidden a radio in there? Or was just it an excuse to smash something? Probably the second one. *Is this all we are? Another fucking mob?*

More ripping and tearing sounds from the bedroom. Down and stuffing billowed through the air. Laughter sounded; whoops of joy.

Lish walked back downstairs, feeling sick.

*

DETENTION BLOCK, ASHWOOD FORT
0516 HOURS

Neither Wakefield nor Filly had marched Helen from the wall in silence, but as they neared the barred gate the Wastelander spoke. "Don't believe it."

Helen looked at her.

"Gevaudan," said Wakefield. "Don't believe it's him."

"Wakefield..." said Filly.

"I know," said Wakefield. "Don't understand." She tapped her temple, then her chest. "This says yes. That says no."

"I know." Filly squeezed Helen's arm. "We saw them going, thought we'd try and stop it going too far." She laughed bitterly. "That went well."

They'd reached the gate leading to the detention block; Wakefield clanged the butt of Helen's revolver against the bars. "Yo!"

"Coming." Someone jogged towards them along the corridor. It was Carson, Helen realised; the other woman froze when she recognised Helen. "What?"

"Long story," said Filly. "We'll fill you in, but..." She looked at Helen, then away. "Need to lock her up first."

Carson stared at them and swallowed. "Okay," she nodded, and unlocked the gate.

This part of the building had been office space – two long, wide rooms on either side of a corridor. Zaq, with her usual grumpy efficiency, had knocked up sets of bars and gates to partition each one into separate cells. Carson had been here for a spell herself, Helen recalled, after she'd recovered from her wounds. While they'd decided what to do with her.

And now they'll decide what to do with you. I wouldn't hold my breath for a quiet and honourable retirement, somehow.

Carson unlocked a cell door. "This okay?"

Helen looked inside: a pallet bed, a shit-bucket in the corner. "Any chance of a room with a view?"

"Don't, Helen," Filly said. "Please."

After a moment, Helen walked into the cell. The door clanged shut behind her, the key sounded in the lock.

She looked back at the others; if anything, they looked even more miserable than she felt. Wakefield and Filly bringing Helen here, Helen stepping into the cell, Carson turning the key: *we all hate it, but we're doing it anyway. Maybe there's a lesson there.*

Filly touched Wakefield's arm. "Best go," she said.

Wakefield nodded, handing Helen's revolver to Carson. She gave Helen a last forlorn glance – *goodbye, crazy ginger* – and the two of them left.

Carson eyed Helen through the bars. "Need anything?"

"Nothing you can give me," Helen said. She sat down on the pallet bed, her back against the bars. She rubbed her throbbing belly, and blinked back tears.

OUTSIDE WALL ONE
0530 HOURS

"Nowt here."

"No, looks like they were right. Must've gone that-a-way."

"Making for the Devil's Highway?"

"Get him back to Manchester, won't it? To his *mate* Winterborn."

"Fuck. Come on."

When he was sure they'd gone, Gevaudan emerged from the grass-covered hollow he'd lain in. They'd been half-right: he'd feinted towards the Devil's Highway before doubling back towards the Fort. Risky, but worthwhile.

Besides, the day he couldn't lose a bunch of pursuers in the dark would be a cold one in Hell. He was a Grendelwolf, after all. He had so much to hate Kellett's ghost for, but so much, too, that he'd have been long dead without.

Blood dripped into the grass. Gevaudan muttered a curse, dug a scrap of cloth from his pocket. The wound should have healed by now, but for some reason it was doing so slowly. Perhaps he'd actually get a scar.

Gevaudan pressed the cloth over the jagged wound in his cheek, and headed towards the Eastern Hills.

6.

Former Ashwood Village
27th July, Attack Plus Twenty-One Years
0600 hours

The Fort was hushed as Mackie slipped down the High Street; the half-dozen people he passed on his way home blinked at him, stunned and dazed.

"They can't believe it, can they, *mate*?" said a voice to his right. Mackie didn't look. "Never easy to get your head round, is it," Cov said, "when a *mate* stabs you in the back?"

Mackie walked on, shaking.

"Or shoots you in the face," Cov called after him. For a moment Mackie thought he was being left alone, for now at least, but Cov's boots clicked on the road till he was beside Mackie. "Now *that* really takes some getting your head round.

The betrayal, I mean. Not the bullet. Your head's around *that* before you know what's happened."

"Will you fuck off?" Mackie said through his teeth.

"Will I fuck," said Cov as they reached Mackie's door. "What you gonna do? Shoot me?"

Mackie fumbled the door open, slammed it in Cov's face before he could step through. It was hot inside; the one-room structure was solidly built, the stones mortared thickly to leave no crack for the wind to get through. He'd built it himself. He was good with his hands; it had been something to occupy himself with after the fighting at Bowkitt.

"After you killed me, you mean?"

Cov was sitting on the floor. Mackie stared at him; Cov shrugged. "I'm dead, remember? Didn't really reckon you'd keep me out with a shut door, did you?"

Mackie would be glad when winter came; it was boiling in here, the air thick and hot. He clenched his fists. "Fuck off," he said. "Leave me alone."

"Or what?" Cov laughed. "Got 'em all fooled, haven't you? Poor thick Mackie. And this," he gestured round, "well, this is fucking brilliant, isn't it? Hiring yourself out to work on people's homes –"

"I don't hire. I do it free."

"Yeah. And all the while you're trying to help the Reapers kill the people who live in 'em. What do you reck, Mackie?" Cov pretended to balance weight on his upturned palms. "That supposed to balance it out?"

Mackie swung a punch at him. Cov laughed; Mackie overbalanced and fell to his knees. When he opened his eyes, he was alone. Mackie knelt there, shaking. Then took a deep breath and crawled into a corner.

He swept the straw and rushes from the stone-flagged floor. They were thickest over one particular flag, to hide the lack of mortar. Mackie prised the loose flag up and lifted out the transmitter. His hands shook. This close to the Fort and the Intelligence Centre – every time he used it he was scared. But the cellar at the Reaper station had scared him more; the calm, quiet IntelSec Major with the dead, empty eyes and level voice, and the broken, tortured things, once people, that he'd wheeled out to show Mackie what would happen.

There aren't any heroes here, Mackie, Lewis had said. *Everyone breaks in the end. Oh, now and again you get the odd one who really doesn't tell you anything, but you're not one of them. You can try, of course, but you won't hack it. And then where are you? All the suffering and none of the reward. Or...* he'd smiled and spread his hands. *Or you can spare yourself the pain and walk away now. In exchange for one small favour.*

Mackie fished the hidden wire from the stonework above the fireplace and connected it to the transmitter. How would things have gone if it'd been Cov the Reapers had lifted instead of him? Would Cov have held out, or given in? Would Cov have blown his cover on the Devil's Highway, shot Mackie in the face to keep him quiet?

The air in the room stirred, as if Cov's ghost were drawing breath to speak. Mackie forced himself to think of other things. He wound up the transmitter to charge it, took out his codebook, pad and grease pencil, and started tapping out his signal.

*

Detention Block, Ashwood Fort
0613 hours

"Here." Carson held a bowl and spoon through the bars. "Not much cop, I'm afraid. I'm not much of a cook."

Helen prodded the bowl's contents. "Is it supposed to be a soup or a stew?"

Carson gave a weak smile. "Didn't wanna make up its mind."

Helen tried a spoonful. "Not bad," she said. Bit bland, but she'd eaten worse. Much worse.

"Yeah?" Carson brightened a little.

Helen sat down and began to eat. She'd need her strength, especially if she wanted to help Gevaudan. Assuming he wanted her help. Or deserved it.

"Ask you something?" said Carson.

"What?"

"Why'd you do it?"

"Do what?"

"Help him. He was seen. There's witnesses. I know you and him go back, but..."

Helen chewed and swallowed.

"He's fought for us in the past," she said. "Saved my life. Other people's, too. Half the ones trying to kill him now'd be dead if it wasn't for him."

Carson looked down. "People change."

"True."

"But not him?"

Helen shook her head. "No," she said. If she said it firmly enough, she might flush away that shred of doubt. "I can't believe it. I won't, not till I hear it from him."

"Why, though?"

Helen could have given any number of answers, but looking at Carson, she saw the one she'd need to give. Not the honest answer, but one that might turn Carson like a key.

"Sometimes you have a feeling about someone," she said. "Just – instinct. That you can trust them. Like I had about you."

*

WINTERBORN'S OFFICE, THE TOWER

0640 HOURS

The desk intercom buzzed; Winterborn pushed the music box to one side and pressed the button. "Yes?"

"Thorpe in the Ops Room, sir."

"Yes, Colonel Thorpe?"

"Two signals, sir. Both priority."

"Well?"

"One's from Major Lewis at IntelSec. Darrow and his friends just entered Deadsbury."

Winterborn breathed out, chuckling. "Of course."

"Sir."

"I disregarded Deadsbury as it was supposedly too contaminated for anyone but Shoal. I should have known better to believe the Grendelwolf. So Darrow's been under our noses all along?"

"Appears so, sir."

Winterborn nodded. "Have the IntelSec agents continue surveillance, but they're to avoid detection at all costs. I want a precise location on where Darrow's people are based. Secondly, seal every potential exit from Deadsbury. Nothing else gets in or out. Understood?"

"Yes, sir."

"Good. And the second message?"

"From Ashwood."

Winterborn gripped the arms of his chair. "Read it."

"Phoenix arrested. Cormorant on the run. Manhunt under way."

Winterborn breathed out. "Confusion to our enemies, indeed," he said. "I think the time's unlikely to grow any riper. Instruct Colonel Majid to initiate Operation Long Knife, Thorpe. Immediately." He saw Thorpe hesitate. "Is there a problem, Colonel?"

"Our CorSec units, sir. Most of them are detailed to support the Jennywrens for Long Knife."

"Reassign one company to go into Deadsbury. Assign CiviSec units to make up the numbers and to maintain the perimeter. Anything else, Colonel Thorpe? Perhaps you'd like me to send the Catchmen in instead? No? Then get on with it."

*

DETENTION BLOCK, ASHWOOD FORT
0658 HOURS

Footsteps approaching; Helen looked up.

Carson was studying her from the other side of the bars. Helen put down her food bowl. "Something on your mind?"

Carson bit her lip, then took the keys from her belt, unlocked the door and pulled it open.

"What's this?" said Helen.

Carson took Helen's revolver from her waistband and held it out to her. After a moment, Helen took it.

"Now punch me," said Carson, "and make it look good."

Helen hesitated. "Why?"

"You're not the only one with instincts. Okay? Now get it over with."

Helen punched Carson square in the face. Carson's head snapped back from the impact and her knees buckled; Helen caught her jacket and pulled the keys from her belt, then kicked Carson's legs out from under her. When she fell to her knees, Helen pulled her jacket off, looped it through the cell bars and knotted the sleeves around Carson's wrist. *Gag her, too.* Helen cut a strip from the jacket with Carson's boot-knife, pushed it in Carson's mouth and knotted it tight behind her head. "Convincing enough?" she asked.

Carson nodded, bleary-eyed.

Helen nodded back, tucking her revolver back into its pouch. "Thanks," she said, and ran.

*

REAP Station 14
Wythenshawe, Manchester
0730 hours

"Stretch a leg, boys and girls. Double time now, move it."

Twemlow helped Ahmad down from the landcruiser and they quick-marched with the rest of their platoon to the parade ground. "Fuck's this?" he muttered.

"Oh *shit*," muttered Ahmad.

"What?"

"There."

Twemlow looked where the older man was nodding. There was already a company's worth of Reapers standing to attention. Automatic rifles, Sterlings, pistols on their hips. There'd be knives in their boots too. Most of the shoulder-flashes were pure white: GenRen. The others were red: CorSec.

The sergeant ordered them into their formations. Three officers formed up to address them: a Major, two Captains.

"At ease," the Major said. "All right, listen up. We're about to move out into the Wastelands for a surprise attack on rebel positions."

"Fuck," muttered Ahmad, not moving his lips. Twemlow couldn't find anything to add to that.

"CorSec units will be supporting us for the operation. However," said the Major, "another issue has arisen closer to home. There's a rebel group operating in the city – we've known that for some time, but haven't had their location. Now, though, we're onto them. They need dealing with immediately, before they twig we're onto them. That's where you come in." He nodded towards the CiviSec Reapers; for a moment his eyes actually met Twemlow's. "You'll be supporting Captain Hawkins and her platoon here in going in to clear them out."

Ahmad nodded to a Reaper in the Jennywren ranks – another Asian bloke, with the nametag PATEL on his uniform. Patel nodded back, then turned his eyes front again.

Hawkins stepped forward. She was stocky, with cropped, curly hair and a scrubbed, heart-shaped, emotionless face. "Right, you lot. We move out in five."

"The rest of you, with Lieutenant Lezard," said the Major. "Good hunting."

"Marching there and back like bloody toy soldiers," Ahmad muttered as they climbed back aboard the landcruiser.

"Beats the Wastelands, though," Twemlow said.

"There's always that."

Neither said anything else as the 'cruiser pulled out. Twemlow's hands were shaking; he gripped his Sten tighter till they stopped.

*

WALL ONE, ASHWOOD FORT
0740 HOURS

The sentries had been doubled on the outer wall, but they avoided the ragged section the rockets had blown out of the battlements. In any case, they were watching for something trying to get back into the Fort, not someone else trying to get out.

Helen let the scaling rope fall groundward, then peered up and down the battlements. In the early morning light, it would take all she had to avoid detection. But she was an old hand at this, with years of practice; with luck, her skills would still be sharp enough. As would her judgement.

Helen shinned down the rope and dropped, landing in a crouch at the foot of the wall. Then she began crawling, keeping low, towards the Eastern Hills.

*

RECORDS DEPARTMENT, THE TOWER
0802 HOURS

The file pressed against Thorpe's skin under his jacket; he could feel it sticking to him. Sweat. He tapped on the cubby-hole door. "Yes?" said Soper.

"Me."

Soper opened the door, glancing left and right. *Nearly as scared as me.* "Have you got it?" he whispered.

Thorpe nodded. Soper motioned him in, shut the door behind him. Thorpe took out the Sycorax file and handed it to him. "There."

"I need to get it back where it belongs," said Soper. "Scuse m —"

"Not yet. Wait."

Soper blinked at him.

"Sit down," said Thorpe. Soper obeyed. Thorpe sat in the other chair.

"We both loved her," he said. "Didn't we?"

"Yes," said Soper. His eyes filled; he dragged his sleeve across them.

"I don't want her to have died for nothing. Do you?"

"No."

"Have you read the file?"

"No. Of course not. I don't have the —"

"Read it," said Thorpe. "We're in the hands of a madman."

He watched what he'd said sink in. Soper looked around again, even though they were alone in the cubby-hole. Not surprising; Winterborn had that effect on people. "You mean the Commander?" he said.

"I mean the Commander," Thorpe said. He watched and waited some more; this was the moment of danger. But he couldn't achieve this alone; he would need help, and that would begin with trust. He had to hope he'd judged Soper correctly.

Fear cramped his belly. *I'm not the stuff heroes are made of,* he thought. *If you could see me now, Lee, what would you say?* "Soper, can you find me some Reapers I can trust? Who'll do as they're ordered – exactly as they're ordered – and say nothing?"

"Yes." Soper nodded. "Yes, I think so."

"Okay, then. Find them. Right now."

*

Perimeter of Reaper-controlled Territory, Sector 18
0846 hours

Saeed Patel clenched and unclenched his hands on his rifle, keeping his finger clear of the trigger. It wasn't cocked – not yet – but better safe than sorry.

A knife in his boot, a pistol on his hip, a Sterling SMG slung across his back. Fully kitted out, trained to take whatever came, but even so he was nearly hyperventilating as the landcruisers reached the high wire fences and the watchtowers – those, and the big gates that were even now being pulled open.

Off we go again, out into the Wastelands. The whole point of being a Jennywren, after all. Clear the Wastelands, to destroy whatever didn't belong to the Reapers' vision. But he hadn't been out there in months, not since Ashwood. And now Ashwood was all he could remember. The slaughter on the hillside, at the walls, in the ruined village: Pete Walters, ripped open by machine gun fire, bleeding out in his arms.

He was sweating. Patel wiped his hands on his uniform and took hold of his rifle once more.

The landcruisers rolled through the gate, out into the Wastelands.

*

ST JAMES' CHURCH, DEADSBURY
0858 HOURS

Flaps sprinted to the church door, knocked it wide as she charged through.

Guns swung towards her, then lowered. Darrow was by the altar with Kate, the kids gathered round her. He was laughing – didn't see that often – but it vanished when he saw her. "Flaps?"

"Reapers," she said. "They're setting up all around Deadsbury, fully armed. We're surrounded."

They always had been, obvs – they were in the middle of Reaperland – but the Reapers hadn't known that. Till now, anyway.

Darrow was pale. "They followed us."

A couple of the littl'uns started skriking – too young to really understand, just picking up on the fear. Kate knelt to shush and hug them; when they'd quieted, she looked up at Darrow.

"They're gonna come in, aren't they?" Flaps said. "Probably go street by street. Pin us down, then –"

"Yes, Flaps, I know." Darrow took a deep breath. "All right. Contact our perimeter look-outs. I want them looking for the slightest hint of a weak point in that cordon." He picked up his Thompson gun. "We need to find a way out."

*

NORTHENDEN, MANCHESTER
0904 HOURS

Landcruisers, sirens wailing, rolled through the middle of Northenden.

Huddled in the back, Reaper Twemlow saw the ruined town go past; the ragged scavengers who clawed their living from the wreckage stared, watching.

A few older ones caught his eye; old enough to be his parents. Might even have been them. Twemlow couldn't remember what they looked like; they'd offered him up to the Reapers when he was three, knowing they wouldn't see him again. When you became a Reaper, your family ceased to exist.

Ahmad poked Twemlow's booted foot with his own. "You all right, kidda?"

Twemlow nodded.

"You'll be okay. Just stick with me and –"

"Don't," said Twemlow. "Last time you said that, rebels blew fuck out of us."

"Good point." Ahmad grinned; it faded as he peered down the road. "Aw, shit."

"What?" But then Twemlow saw where they were heading. "You're fucking shitting me now."

Ahmad stood, peering over the landcruiser cabin. "I bloody wish."

Twemlow stood and looked too. Further up, a bigger crowd of scavengers had gathered either side of the road as a team of Reapers, the yellow shoulder-flashes of CivEng Division on their shoulders, worked on the rubble barricade blocking the bridge across the Mersey. The Reapers heaped the rubble into carts and dumped it at the roadside beside the sawhorses and razor-wire, where the scavengers fell on it, carrying the choicer pieces off. Building materials were always in demand.

The landcruiser column halted; Captain Hawkins jumped out and approached the CivEng team, who snapped at once to attention. "Carry on," Hawkins said. "Who's in charge here?"

"Me, ma'am." A young officer saluted. "Lieutenant Spode, ma'am."

Hawkins nodded at the barricade. "How long, Spode?"

"'Bout twenty minutes, ma'am."

"You've got ten." Hawkins motioned to one of her sergeants. "Smoke break. Pass it along."

"Ma'am." The sergeant strode along the landcruiser column. "Light 'em if you got 'em, lads," he barked as he went. "Light 'em if you got 'em."

Ahmad offered Twemlow a packet of Monarchs. Twemlow took one; they lit up and smoked in silence, waiting.

*

EASTERN HILLS
0910 HOURS

Helen looked back; in the distance, the Fort looked tiny. Far behind and left behind; she was beyond that now. On her own again.

The hillside stirred in the wind: grasses waving, bright with flowers. Her way was clear; she began to climb.

She'd find the cave and Gevaudan would be there. Where else would he go?

Manchester, if he was a traitor. He might be on the Devil's Highway already.

No, she refused to accept that. If he was hiding up there, it would prove she'd been right about him. That he was loyal.

Unless, of course, he hadn't finished whatever task they'd set him. Unless he had further attacks to carry out.

Helen hesitated, but carried on. She'd find him and she'd face him; whatever happened next, she'd deal with. She was responsible: if he'd gone to the dark, it was her fault.

And if she was wrong, then at least she'd be dead and all pain, she hoped, would be at an end.

7.

THE WAR ROOM, ASHWOOD FORT
27TH JULY, ATTACK PLUS TWENTY-ONE YEARS
0914 HOURS

"Still nothing?" Alannah rubbed gritty eyes, swallowed a speed pill dry. Just needed to keep going a few more hours. "Okay. Recall all search units. He's probably a long way from here by now, but I want perimeter and wall patrols doubled till further notice."

Hei nodded. "Anything else?"

"Instructions to the field-bases. they're to watch out for him. Shoot on sight, to kill. We try to take him prisoner, we'll lose more people."

Hei hesitated. "Problem?" said Alannah.

"No," said Hei after a moment, and made a note on his pad. He was disappointed in her, Alannah realised. Expected some level of fair play, a fair hearing. Hadn't got his head round the level of betrayal, the level of threat the Grendelwolf now posed. "Anything else?" he said.

This wasn't the time to have it out with him. Give some orders, restore control, reassure people: that was the priority now. "Call a meeting."

"The War Room?"

"No. Canteen."

"Canteen?"

"As many people as we can get. Whoever's not got orders to carry out. I need to talk to them. Get things calmed down."

Hei nodded again. "Will do."

*

GEVAUDAN'S CAVE, EASTERN HILLS
0923 HOURS

Helen took one last look back towards the Fort. Would there ever be any going back to them, and did she even care? She had no answers, or at least none she wanted to hear.

The light was behind her; ahead, there was only the dark.

All roads lead here, Helen.

She reached the cave's threshold. The entrance was a deeper shadow against the wider blackness of the hill. She swayed: she was tired to her bones, and not only physically. Helen reached into a pouch on her coveralls, for the small jar of amphetamine pills. She'd taken a couple earlier, for the journey, but they already seemed to have worn off. She squeezed the jar briefly, then let it go. She wouldn't need them for this. One way or the other, she'd know if she'd succeeded or not soon enough.

He will destroy you.

With a last deep breath, Helen stepped into cold damp shadows.

"Gevaudan?" She eased the Smith and Wesson from its pouch. "You there?"

The cave was silent; the dark waited and watched.

"I'm sorry," she said. "I tricked you. I used you." She felt her voice growing ragged; she fought to steady it. "You've every right to hate me. But I don't believe you're a traitor. I've been wrong about a lot, but not that. And if I am…"

She held up the revolver, then threw it aside to clatter on the cave floor and held up empty hands.

"Here I am. No lies, Gevaudan. No tricks. You want revenge? Take it. I'm the one who deserves it."

The darkness stirred, and moved towards her.

He will destroy you.

Helen closed her eyes, and held her breath.

*

Roof of the Tower

0930 hours

Mordake knelt, clenched fists pushed into the rooftop. Below him lay a pile of twigs and hair; on it, two crossed sticks pinned down a crumpled photograph. A man in Reaper uniform – skeletally lean, unsmiling, thinning grey hair cropped short.

The crosswinds blew cold across the roof, but Mordake barely felt them. "So, Commander Grimwood," he murmured. "Let's see what we can do with you."

He struck a match and lit the kindling. When the flames lapped at the corners of the photograph they turned green; the picture blackened and shrivelled. Mordake inhaled the hot smoke that poured up into his face and then held his breath, while his second face began to first murmur, then chant out loud.

SENLAC HILL, BATTLE, NEAR HASTINGS, RCZ13 (FORMERLY SUSSEX)
1000 HOURS

Grimwood stood on the hill looking out towards the sea; he almost thought he could hear the English Channel hiss on the shingle and sand.

They'd landed just a few miles away at Hastings, William the Bastard and his Norman, Angevin and Breton mercenaries. And here on Senlac Hill had been Harold Godwinson – King Harold II of England – and his army, fresh from defeating Harald Hardraada and his Norwegians at Stamford Bridge in Yorkshire. Battle-weary and exhausted from the long march south, they'd nonetheless held their ground against the Normans, till a single tactical error had undone them. The Normans had feigned a retreat; the Saxons had broken ranks to give chase, and then the Normans had turned and attacked.

Senlac: supposedly from the French *Sanguelac*, meaning *Lake of Blood*. The Normans had paid dearly for their victory – but the victory had been theirs nonetheless. Tradition had it that Harold had been killed with an arrow to the eye, but Grimwood knew it hadn't been so: England's last Anglo-Saxon King had been surrounded by four Norman knights and hacked to pieces. A vicious, ugly, cowardly way to kill a man; Grimwood knew there was no honour in war, that if you wanted to win you used whatever means achieved that, but Harold Godwinson had been a brave man; he'd deserved a better ending.

Before the War, Grimwood's father – something of an amateur genealogist – had claimed that an ancestor of theirs had been one of the thegns who'd stood by Harold on Senlac Hill. Grimwood had never been able to quell a small thrill of pride at the thought. Ironic, really: though he'd never wanted anything but to serve as a soldier, sworn to defend the social order that had been, at least in part, created that day, he'd always fantasised about being one of Harold's guard, fighting off the Normans – perhaps even helping Godwinson turn the battle and alter the course of history.

Grimwood had started in the ranks; by the time the War came he'd been a Captain in a Guards Regiment. And when the Reapers had been formed, he'd been among the first to join, rising to become Percival Holland's adjutant in RCZ12. Nothing would have made him leave the side of the man he admired above all others, the man he lov – no, nothing would have made him leave Holland's side, except that Holland had asked him to go.

Back in the Civil Emergency the rebels had assassinated RCZ13's Commander and his staff and were wreaking havoc against its surviving, scattered Reaper divisions. The RCZ had seemed certain to fall entirely to the rebels, the first Command the Reapers utterly lost. Holland had sent a dozen of his best officers, under Grimwood's command, to reorganise the Command and put down the rebellion. Grimwood had succeeded; in fact, he'd succeeded too well.

The posting had only ever been intended as a temporary measure to restore order. Grimwood had come in from outside the Command and started ordering its men around: surely, he'd reasoned, they'd be as glad to see the back of him as he'd be to return to RCZ12, and to Holland's side.

But instead, they'd grown to love him. He'd won their loyalty and their devotion; by the time the Civil Emergency was over they remembered no other Commander, nor wanted one.

That was an achievement, at least, he thought, watching the Sussex landscape in the morning sun. He clung to that now; it was all that made the parting bearable.

Duty. Honour. Sacrifice: that was what it was to be a soldier. *Service.* To serve a land, a king, a Commander. To do what had to be done, no matter the cost to himself or others, to ensure something great survived and prospered.

And none of those things even registered in Tereus Winterborn's world-view. Command wasn't a sacred trust to him, but a springboard from which to leap to ever-higher status.

Command, Unification – all of it was just a means to crown himself king of the ruined land.

Unification would come – Grimwood wanted nothing more. He loved his land, the Britain that had been before the bombs fell. It was less a memory now than an idol and ideal: to restore that, as far as might be possible, was his deepest desire, beyond even what he felt for Percival Holland. But better the country be sundered into RCZs for a hundred, a thousand years, than it be unified in Winterborn's image.

It was getting late; he should go. Grimwood started down the hill, but as he did, a horn sounded low and mournful on the wind.

Grimwood froze, reaching for his pistol; the horn blew again, above him on the summit, and a voice shouted.

"To me, Gesith! To me, fyrd-men of England! To me!"

Horse-hooves thundered in the distance, and other voices drifted on the wind: Danish, French and Breton, in three massed groups, cavalry and infantry. They charged, brandishing sword and spear and axe. Arrows whistled through the air; a Norman knight fell choking, an arrow in his throat.

Grimwood ran up the slope: he was a fit man, exercising regularly and running each day, and soon opened a gap between him and his pursuers. Even though, he realised, he too was weighed down with chainmail, a battle-helm and a longsword.

He stumbled, fell; hands clapped his shoulder, hauled him to his feet. "Well done, lad," shouted the tall man who'd helped him up. "Stay beside me and guard my back."

The man was bare-headed and fair-haired, blue-eyed, with a long flaxen moustache. It was Harold Godwinson, of course – that face was the essence of a hundred mediaeval portraits and drawings in children's history books – but it was somehow Percival Holland's too.

Bowstrings twanged; arrows whipped and whistled in flight, darkening the sky. The arrows hailed down. Screams; Saxons falling. Bellowed battlecries from below; the Normans charged up the hill.

Sword and shield; Grimwood held them ready. He and Harold, he and Holland, still stood. The Normans closed in, hacking down the last few soldiers around Harold. Two of them rushed Grimwood; he blocked a sword thrust with his shield, split one man's skull with a sword-blow and stabbed the other in the throat. More of them came at him: he hacked, slashed, stabbed, used his shield to deflect blows and to bludgeon his attackers.

Harold/Holland cried out; Grimwood spun and saw him falling, a spear in his side. He cut down the spear-man, laid about him with the sword, but four Normans charged him with lowered shields; they crashed into him and Grimwood flew back, winded. He tried to rise, but the Normans had already surrounded Harold, and their swords and axes rose and fell. Harold cried out; so did Grimwood as he got up and attacked, knowing already that it was too late.

The Normans laughed as they retreated, and laughed louder when Grimwood fell weeping by his beloved King's butchered carcass and gathered it in his arms, kissing the ruined face.

The Normans rushed in into finish him, swords and spears lowered. Grimwood didn't care; it would be over in a moment. He held Holland's, Harold's, remains to his chest and waited –

But the end didn't come. Instead, silence fell; footsteps squelched in the sodden earth. Grimwood looked up; a hooded man in a soft grey robe stood above him. He looked tired, but a strange, bitter fire lit his eyes.

"Do you want to save him?" the man said. His voice sounded like two voices together, one deep and male, the other female and higher-pitched.

Grimwood's grip was all that stopped the cloven fragments he was cradling from falling apart; they slid against one another in their own blood, threatening to escape his embrace. "Fuck off," he said, trying not to weep.

The robed man cocked his head. "No way to talk to someone who can help you, surely?"

"Help me?" said Grimwood. They were alone on the hill, he realised; there were scattered weapons, blood on the earth, but no other people. "How can you help me? He's dead."

"He doesn't have to be," the robed man said. "I can give you another chance to save him. I can give you as many as you need. I can put you back in the moment before he fell, and you can prevent it. Would you want that?"

Grimwood didn't even need to think about it. "Yes."

"Then ready your sword and shield."

And Kevin Grimwood did as he was told, lowering Harold/Holland's remains to the ground and standing again.

The battle sounds crashed in and he saw, as if a clear light had fallen on the Norman, the spear-man charging, the weapon aimed at the King's side. Grimwood sprang forward, and the sword swept down; it cut through the spear's haft, then rose to impale the spear-man as his momentum carried him forward.

Grimwood whooped. He'd done it – but a swordsman ran at Holland/Harold's back. Grimwood blocked the sword with his shield, stabbed the attacker in the groin, but an axe-man buried his weapon in the King's neck –

The King fell, and the weapons hewed down and cut him apart –

The hill was silent again, deserted except for Grimwood and the sundered body of Harold Godwinson, of Percival Holland –

And then he was back in the moment before the axe-man struck, charging to stop the axe with his shield, hacking at the man's neck with his sword. And he fought on until a sword killed Harold/Holland –

And then an arrow killed Holland/Harold –

And then it was another spear –

And then another axe –

And on and on and on; there was always another chance. Hope rose, to be dashed again; or was dashed, to rise once more. Heaven or Hell, depending on how you looked at it.

The cares, the responsibilities of Grimwood's Command, of the year of Attack Plus Twenty-One, fell away. Only this fight mattered now. And he dimly knew that it would never end, and he made his peace with that.

And that was how Grimwood's men found him; fighting ghostly enemies with a ghostly sword to save a long-dead King, now and forevermore.

*

Field-Base Nineteen, The Wastelands
1048 hours

Explosions and gunfire sounded up ahead as the landcruiser pulled in. Smoke billowed into the air; around the big farmhouse on the steep hillside above, machine-guns chattered and flashed.

Bullets tore up the earth; one clipped Patel's helmet and he ducked down into the landcruiser's flatbed. The rebels had chosen their field-base well: high ground, surrounded by flat open land. Reaper landcruisers raked the farmhouse and gun emplacements with their .50 cals, giving covering fire to the teams setting up mortars on the ground.

"De-bus!" a grey-haired sergeant shouted.

Fuck fuck fuck, thought Patel, baling out of the landcruiser. The first mortars whistled down and exploded on the hillside. A fusillade of machine-gun fire swept down in response. A landcruiser's windows shattered, and there were screams; two mortar teams collapsed beside their weapons and lay still.

"Take positions," Lezard shouted, pointing up the slope. "Advance on my command."

Patel stared up the hillside, then at the lieutenant. "Are you *high*?" he demanded, then quickly added. "Sir."

Lezard flushed red, glared. He opened his mouth to speak, but a line of bullets ripped along the ground and found him. He dropped, coughing blood; Patel dived into the grass and did his best to burrow under it.

The turf in front of him erupted. Dirt and grit sprayed into Patel's eyes. He yelled, clawing at them. His vision cleared; his eyes streamed, and he spat out earth. Mortars whistled, then a series of dull, thudding explosions.

"Go! Go! Go!" Someone kicked him in the side; Patel twisted round, grabbing for his rifle. The grey-haired sergeant jabbed a finger at him. "Even *think* of pointing that my way and it goes up your arse sideways," he shouted. "Now *get up that fucking hill.*"

If only for a moment, the sergeant was more frightening than the rebel machine-guns. Whole point of his job really, Patel supposed, as he ran towards the hill.

Bullets whipped and cracked overhead, but Patel realised they weren't hitting the Jennywrens any more; the bullets flying overhead were going the other way, from the Reaper positions. Dust and stone chips flew from the farmhouse walls; black smoke plumes poured from its windows. More smoke still hung over ragged craters in the hillside. There were bodies scattered round them.

"Fuck it," Patel muttered, and charged.

*

Harp dived to the floor as a fresh hail of bullets spewed through the shattered window frame, smashing into the far wall. "Return fire, for fuck sake!" Jazz shouted.

A rebel fighter aimed her Bren gun through the window and triggered a burst; a second later her head and upper body exploded as a .50 cal below fired back.

"Can't even get a shot off at 'em, boss," shouted one of her fighters. "No way we can hold."

He was right, Harp knew; he looked at Jazz, who gritted her teeth but finally nodded. "Newt, get on to Osprey. Tell 'em we're abandoning the base." She turned to Harp. "Get everyone out, now. While we can."

"Osprey, this is Yellowhammer," Newt shouted into the mic. "Yellowhammer calling Osprey. Osprey? Osprey?" He stared at Jazz. "They're not responding."

Jazz shook her head. "The hell's going on?"

*

CANTEEN, ASHWOOD FORT

1100 HOURS

Wakefield huddled close to Filly, clasping her hand beneath the table. The canteen was crowded; some rebels were there with their families, belongings packed, ready to flee. Others from the Council were present: Malik, Stewart, and Thorn. Jazz was in the Wastelands, inspecting field-bases, and Wakefield knew too well where Helen was. She saw Lish, too, and Brant; even Nestor was there.

Most of the guns had been put away for now. Two or three people in the crowd still carried their weapons, and a couple of Danny's Raiders flanked the door – Hack, and a man Wakefield didn't recognise. She wasn't sure why they were there. It didn't feel right.

Alannah came in, climbed up onto a table. "The Grendelwolf's gone," she said at last. "Heading for the Devil's Highway, we think. We're going after him, but he's good at what he does." Her voice had turned bitter; so she cleared her throat.

"The priority now's to get reorganised, so that by the time the Reapers find out about this it'll already be too late to catch us on the wrong foot. And that's exactly what we're gonna do. I want everyone here to know that, and to make sure everyone else does. It's been a bad time, but it's over. We've found our traitor, and everything's back under control."

*

INTELLIGENCE CENTRE, ASHWOOD FORT

1102 HOURS

"Yellowhammer calling Osprey. Osprey, please respond. Osprey!"

The shadow in the doorway lay across the blood and bodies, the torn and scattered flimsies and splintered desks, that strewed the Intelligence Centre's floor. One last look at what it had wrought. Then it fell away, and was gone.

"Yellowhammer calling Osprey – Field-Base Nineteen has fallen, repeat fallen. We're falling back. Please acknowledge."

Hei coughed blood, fumbling for the edge of a desk, and pulled himself to his feet. Swaying to and fro, he stumbled towards the still-functioning radio set, weaving drunk with pain.

"Osprey, please acknowledge. Osprey!"

Hei's knees buckled and he fell. He tried once more to rise, then fell back and lay still.

*

CANTEEN, ASHWOOD FORT

1105 HOURS

It felt as though everyone in the canteen had breathed out in relief as one: a warm, slightly sour-smelling gust that washed over Alannah and blew away her own tension. It really *was* done. Now the harder work began, of pulling things back together, fixing the damage. "Now the harder work begins," she said. "We have to repair the damage, regain our purpose."

We have to decide what to do with Helen. Should she raise that point now, or was it better to give it time, allow feelings to cool?

Alannah was still trying to make up her mind when the canteen doors burst inward.

Hack and the other guard spun to meet the intruder, but they fought a blur. The man smashed into the far wall and slid down, leaving a trail of blood; clawed hands seized Hack's head and twisted it till her spine snapped, then snatched her Sten gun as she fell.

There were only three other armed personnel in the room, apart from Alannah; the blur fired three quick bursts as it moved, and each of them fell. Alannah fumbled for her revolver on her hip, but the Sten was already aimed at her.

The Grendelwolf smiled at her, finger tight upon the trigger. Then, with a grunt, he bent the Sten in half, tossing it aside to clatter on the floor.

In the silence, he advanced, still smiling, yellow wolf-eyes mad and bright.

Gevaudan looked back and forth across the crowd. "Women and children," he said, and spread his bloody hands; the claws slid from the fingertips. "First."

8.

Canteen, Ashwood Fort
27th July, Attack Plus Twenty-One Years
1106 hours

It was true, then, Lish realised. Here he was in his long black coat, the long white fingers that had teased tunes from a guitar in this same room now dappled with rebels' blood. The smile on his face, the cold light in his eyes – there was nothing there. Nothing to be reached or mended, only fled from or destroyed.

Except that there was no means to destroy the Grendelwolf here; as for flight, there was an emergency exit at the back of the canteen, but against Gevaudan's strength and speed, what chance was there of reaching it alive?

"Gideon!" called a voice, and the Grendelwolf stopped.

He slowly turned, and another Gevaudan stepped through the canteen door. The same long black hair and coat, the same long pale face and hands, the same red mouth and yellow wolf-eyes. The only difference was that the new Gevaudan had a faint, crooked, blue-black mark on his left cheek.

The first Grendelwolf studied the second and released a long, almost weary sigh. "I see things haven't changed," he said. "Whenever I start to gain some pleasure in life, you come along and fuck it up."

The second Grendelwolf shook his head. "Gideon," he said; Lish heard actual sorrow in his voice. "What have you done?"

The first Grendelwolf – Gideon? – sighed again. "I'd have thought it was self-evident, brother of mine."

"You are fucking shitting me," Alannah said.

"Quiet, love," said Gideon lightly, "or I'll rip your cunt out."

"You joined with the Reapers," Gevaudan said. Helen slipped through the door behind him and moved to his side.

"Of course I did. Some of us are loyal. Some of us understand sacrifice."

"Gideon..."

"Stop whining, Gevaudan."

Gideon turned and look over the crowd. When his gaze swept across Lish she shrank back, feeling as though cold hands wet with slime and blood had trailed across her bare skin. But she wasn't the object of his attention. "Alannah Vale," said Gideon. "You've been useful. But now..."

He crouched; there were cries, and the crowd scattered from Alannah, but in the confined space there wasn't really anywhere to go. Someone cannoned into Lish, and she went sprawling; looking up from the floor, she saw Gideon grin, then leap – but something blurred through the air and crashed into him, something black with flickers of white and two gleaming specks of yellow fire for eyes. The two of them crashed into a table, crushing it to splinters as they clawed at one another.

One of the Grendelwolves pinned the other to the floor. "Helen," the one doing the pinning shouted as the other raged and thrashed. "Get everyone out."

Alannah caught Lish and pulled her to her feet; her face was paler than ever, like snow or bleached bone. Helen was already holding the main doors open. "Come on," said Alannah. "Help me."

Everyone was screaming, trying to get away; half a dozen people crashed to the ground, knocked over in the rush. Lish helped one of them to his feet; Alannah pulled a young girl out of harm's way before she could be trampled. Brant shouted, waving the crowd around the others who'd fallen so they could get up. As the canteen emptied, one Grendelwolf – Gevaudan, she guessed – dragged the other towards the far end of the canteen, away from the exodus. Gideon broke free and tried to rush the crowd; Gevaudan leapt on him and flung him bodily down the canteen.

Gideon bolted for the fire door, kicking the emergency exit open. Alarms shrilled; he ran outside, Gevaudan in pursuit.

"Intelligence centre," Lish heard Helen shouting. "Alannah, come on."

*

St James' Church, Deadsbury
1112 hours

Another explosion sounded outside, and dust streamed down from the ceiling. Flaps squinnied through a shattered stained-glass window, saw a landcruiser's .50 cal track towards her again, firing. "Down," she shouted. One fighter, too slow, was blasted from his position, landing like a bundle of sodden rags on the floor.

Flaps fired back through the window, then ducked down as another fusillade hit the church. Might as well be cobbing stones at them, all the good it was doing. From the bell tower above, the rebels' GPMGs chattered in response. At least they were doing some good – for now, anyway. She jumped back down, ran up the aisle. "Darrow!"

He knelt by the altar over charts and maps, looking tireder than Flaps had ever seen him. From time to time he looked over at Kate and the children, huddled in a terrified little group.

Flaps knelt beside him. "We're fucked," she said. "We gotta get out of here."

"Don't you think I know that?" He glared. "There's nowhere to – wait."

He gripped her shoulder. "There might be a way out. We just have to get there. Not sure if we can make it –"

The walls shuddered; more dust showered on them. "Well we fucking won't make it here."

Darrow gave a tired smile. "I suppose not. Get everyone ready. We're moving out. And bring the explosives. We'll need them."

*

WILMSLOW ROAD, DEADSBURY
1115 HOURS

"There," someone shouted; Twemlow jerked round, the Sten tucked into his shoulder. A tall, grey-haired man came out through the church's side-door, a Thompson gun in his hands. Bullets chipped the stonework behind him, and Twemlow aimed to fire too, but then something whooshed through one of the shattered windows, a fireball pulling a stream of smoke after it, flying towards his position.

Twemlow hit the ground, rolling. *Call me Water all you like, Stone, but you're the fucking dead one.* Impact. Bright flash. The ground bounced under him, flung him upwards. Steel and stone flew past him, plucked at his uniform. An explosion, like a door slamming on his head. The ground knocked the wind out of him; he rolled, heaving for breath.

Gunfire. Another *whoosh*; another explosion, but further off. Shouts. More gunfire. Twemlow looked up, fumbled in the dust for his gun. A bunch of ragged figures poured out of the church and away from it, a few hanging back as a rearguard to lay down covering fire at the Reapers. No more fucking rockets, at least.

Twemlow raised the Sten and fired, more because everyone else was than any other reason. One, then another, of the rearguard fell. The others broke and ran. One of the fallen rebels rolled over and started crawling towards the church; the other lay still. A CorSec Reaper ran up and fired a burst from her Sterling into the crawling rebel. "After them," she shouted; as she turned to follow, the top of her helmet shattered and she fell to her knees before pitching forward.

"Move," yelled Hawkins. Her helmet was gone and blood streamed from a cut on her forehead. She jabbed her Browning towards Twemlow. "Get after them!"

Twemlow stumbled towards the church, reaching the bodies by the side-entrance. The rebel who hadn't been crawling lay on her back staring up: there were bullet holes in her chest and neck. Frizzy hair, buck teeth, hazel eyes; she couldn't have been twelve.

A hand grabbed his arm. Twemlow looked up, blinking: it was Ahmad. "Let's go, mate. Got to keep moving."

Twemlow glanced back and saw Hawkins marching towards them, pistol in one hand, rifle in the other. He ran.

*

CORRIDOR, ASHWOOD FORT
1116 HOURS

Gevaudan brought Gideon down with a flying tackle; Gideon howled, thrashing and laying about him with his claws.

Gevaudan hooked his arms and legs around his brother's, trying to immobilise him.

Gideon writhed and heaved. "Stop trying to fuck me," he shouted.

"In your dreams," said Gevaudan. An automatic response – they'd bantered like this when they'd play-fought as boys. Old habits died hard.

What was he supposed to do? He'd never stopped trying to save Gideon, not since it had all started going wrong. That was family; that was love. Didn't matter if they hated you: they were family, they were blood. That had been Dad's philosophy, and Gevaudan had never relinquished it.

"Stop this," he said. "I'll speak for you. I'll get them to spare your life. You can –"

Gideon's head snapped backwards to smash into Gevaudan's face. He felt his nose break; pain speared through his head and his vision blurred. Gideon thrashed harder in his grip. "You pathetic twat," Gideon said. "Still trying to save me? I don't want saving, you stupid cunt. Won't you ever get that?"

Gevaudan's grip broke, and he rolled clear as Gideon sprang to his feet. They circled, claws extended. Then Gideon grinned at him, turned and ran again.

Gevaudan ran after him, feeling the helplessness of it even as he did. He could chase Gideon, even catch him – but what then? He couldn't kill his brother.

Although Gideon, he knew, might well be able to kill him.

*

Intelligence Centre, Ashwood Fort
1117 hours

Both Helen and Alannah ran every day, and were pretty much a match when it came to strength and fitness; Alannah's longer legs gave her the edge, though, so she was the first to reach the Intelligence Centre.

She froze at the door, and cried out. Seconds later Helen reached the door too, and saw what Alannah had.

Radio sets were smashed, filing cabinets tipped to the floor, bodies scattered everywhere. A couple of radios the attacker – Gideon Shoal, of course – had somehow missed crackled weakly.

"Oh Christ," said Alannah. "Christ." Her voice was thick with tears. "Hei," Helen heard her shout; she ran to a body on the floor. Hei's eyes stared blankly up at the ceiling. "Fucking bastard evil tw –"

Helen held up a hand. "Listen."

Now they both heard it – a human voice, weak and faint. "Help," it said. "Please."

"There." Alannah pointed, wiping her eyes with her free hand. The filing cabinet she indicated had tipped over, but wasn't flat on the floor; something, some*one,* was under it.

They levered up the cabinet and shoved it aside. A small figure with dirty blonde hair lay underneath. "Stock," Alannah said.

"I've got her," Helen knelt beside the girl. "Get on the blower, Alannah. Tell them about Gevaudan. And Gideon."

Alannah nodded. "Helen," she began.

"Later," Helen said. "We've got to sort this out."

Alannah nodded and ran off in search of one of the surviving sets.

Helen propped Stock up against the wall. "How you feeling there?"

"Squashed," said Stock.

Helen grinned. "Bit less now, though, right?"

"I'll let you know when I've gone back to my normal shape." Stock flexed her fingers, then her booted feet.

"No bones broken?" said Helen.

"Don't think so." Stock winced, prodding her stomach. "It's here I'm worried about."

Helen remembered her now. "We'll get you to Nestor."

Stock shook her head. "You're gonna need all the help you can get. It was coming through just before that fucking traitor hit us."

"Gevaudan isn't –" Helen broke off; she'd explain later. "What was it?"

"Reapers," said Stock. "They're pushing into the Wastelands." She motioned round the room. "Kept listening, while I was pinned down. Get information. We've lost two field-bases already, maybe three."

"Repeat," Alannah was saying, "disregard previous instructions regarding Gevaudan Shoal. Reaper disinfo campaign. Attacks committed by individual impersonating the Grendelwolf."

Helen got up and went to her, stomach cold and clenched. "It's an all-out invasion."

"They're trying that shit again?"

"And it looks like they're succeeding this time."

"Stock," said Alannah. "how are you feeling? Can you work?"

Stock got to her feet; she grimaced, but nodded.

"I'll send anyone I can find to help," Alannah said. "Get onto the field-bases first, see who's still active, who's under attack, who's not. Find out where the Reapers are and how far they've got. Then the listening posts – see what they're picking up."

"Check."

Alannah stopped halfway to the door. "Join me in the War Room, Helen?"

Helen smiled. "Happy to."

*

St Martin de Porres Church, Ashwood Fort
1121 hours

Zaq stood on top of the church tower, leaning on the broken parapet.

The bruises Hack had given her throbbed. She'd find a way to pay the bitch back, in time, but for now she only wanted some time to nurse the pain. Not just the physical kind, either. Up here it was quiet, and she could be away from people without having to leave the Fort.

All evidence said it was Gevaudan; every instinct she had denied it. He pissed her off, but there was something about him. The dryness, the humour – she liked that. And if she was honest, there was the solidity and size of him. He was handsome. And tireless. Hard not to muse on what it would be like, or how it would feel.

Feeling and thought, instinct and calculation; it was all a hopeless tangle within her. She didn't believe it. More accurately, she didn't *want* to. But what difference did that make?

"Grendelwolf!" someone shouted. Zaq swung around. Danny had been attacked here, after all; was Gevaudan about to spring onto the roof and show her how wrong she'd been to doubt his treachery? But there was no sign of him.

"The gates," the same voice shouted. Zaq ran to the parapet, and saw the Wall Two gates starting to close. Then they flew open, and a familiar figure in a long black coat burst through.

Followed, a second later, by another figure, identical – as far as Zaq could see – in every way.

"Hold your fire," someone shouted from the battlements. "He's on our side."

"Which one?" another voice answered.

"The fuck should I know?"

The black-clad pair barrelled across the courtyard, then down through the old village towards Wall One. Shouts and screams echoed from the village as pursuer and pursued tore through it, bounding and zig-zagging through the makeshift dwellings. Then they were clear of the village and one of them was scrambling up the face of Wall One like a lizard, followed by the second. They reached the battlements; the first one leapt onto the parapet. Zaq heard him laughing; there was something ugly and wrong about the sound. Then he spread his arms and leapt out into space. After a moment, the second Grendelwolf jumped after him.

*

Approach to Ashwood Fort
1128 hours

Gevaudan hit the ground and rolled to his feet. Gideon, running ahead, had leapt over the stream; Gevaudan followed, closing the gap. "Gideon," he shouted.

Gideon whirled, snarling; a beast at bay. "Come on, then. Kill me if you can, brother of mine."

"I don't want to kill you, Gideon."

"Fine by me, Gevaudan. Makes my job very easy."

Gideon leapt, claws aimed at his brother's eyes. Gevaudan blocked the blows and kicked Gideon under the knee with bonecracking force; Gideon yelped, his leg buckling.

The combat training that had followed his Grendelwolf conversion had conditioned Gevaudan to react to any assault with lethal force; he'd been fighting those instincts with Gideon, but now his control slipped. As Gideon fell, Gevaudan grabbed his hair and bent him backwards across his knee, throat bared.

A slash or chop would end things, here and now. But his hand wouldn't descend, refused to deliver the killing blow.

Gideon laughed, and punched Gevaudan in the throat. Something crunched and cracked; Gevaudan toppled, choking. Gideon leapt astride him, hands closing on his windpipe. Gevaudan tried to speak, but nothing emerged.

Shouts and running footsteps sounded from inside the Fort, but they were faint and far-off. This would be over before they arrived. Gideon squeezed. His eyes seemed to glow as Gevaudan's vision dimmed; so did his white teeth. *Cheshire Cat*, Gevaudan thought.

Was this how it ended, how he allowed himself to die? The world was fading; the only person left in it who shared his blood was sending him from it. Easy to give up, and allow events to take their course. But he could see Helen's face: coming to him as she had in Deadsbury and in the cave, to call him back into the light.

Fresh pain bloomed in the flesh of Gevaudan's throat; Gideon's claws were extending. *Two can play*, thought Gevaudan, and extended his own.

One blow, that was all he'd manage. Gideon's eyes gleamed above him. *Brother. I don't want to do this.* But he acted now, or was dead.

Gevaudan struck with his right hand, aiming for Gideon's left eye. Blind him and he'd be weakened; his grip would break. Gideon turned aside from the blow, but wasn't quite fast enough; Gevaudan felt the strike connect, and heard a howl of pain. The grip on his throat slackened and he twisted free of it, bucking and heaving to throw Gideon clear.

Gideon hit the ground and rolled. Gevaudan glimpsed a bloodied, feral face. Then the Fort's outer gates crashed open, and Gideon whirled away, plunging down the slope.

"Gideon," Gevaudan shouted after his brother, but Gideon never looked back.

A voice shouted an order. Guns chattered and crashed; Gideon spun and fell, rolling down the hillside till he was lost to sight in the summer grass. A cry tore out of Gevaudan; bereavement, loss. To have found his family, only to lose it again.

"Get the body," shouted the voice. "And watch. Grendelwolf." Footsteps approached, swishing through the tall grass. "Gevaudan?" Wakefield knelt beside him, a hand on his arm. "Gevaudan? You okay?"

"You'll have to define your terms a little more clearly," he said at last.

Wakefield frowned. "You hurt?"

No more clever retorts. "Nothing that won't heal. How did you know?"

"Know?"

"Which of us to shoot."

"Back of your coat."

"Eh?" Gevaudan removed the coat; there was an X on the back, drawn in yellow chalk.

"Helen," said Wakefield.

"Of course." Where had she got the chalk from? It must have been in one of the endless pouches on her coveralls; Helen had a magpie's eye for any item that might prove useful in the future. Surprising she'd managed to do it without him noticing, but then he'd been somewhat distracted. A clever move, anyway. Gevaudan put the coat back on.

Wakefield squeezed his hand; he glanced down at the small thin fingers gripping his own, surprised. The tribeswoman looked up at him. "I'm glad," she said.

"Glad?"

"That it wasn't you. Didn't believe it. Ever."

With someone else, Gevaudan might have suspected a lie, for his comfort or to salve the other's conscience, but Wakefield had no guile; it was one reason he liked her. "Thank you," he said.

"He's gone," a voice called up the hill. Gevaudan closed his eyes: *Gideon, dead again.*

"Gone?" called Wakefield.

"Not here," came the reply. "He's cleared off."

That should have been bad news; in many ways, it was. But it was a relief, too. There might be no reaching Gideon now. Even if there was, what he'd done here wouldn't be forgotten; if he were honest, Gevaudan knew there was likely no way back from what Gideon had become. But he couldn't afford that honesty today. There were things he hadn't the strength to face.

"Come on," said Wakefield. "Get you inside."

She was still holding his hand; Gevaudan felt the warmth of the little tribeswoman's touch and was glad of it. He let her lead him back to the Fort.

9.

Deadsbury
27th July, Attack Plus Twenty-One Years
1136 hours

Darrow was badly out of breath; most of his crew were ahead of him. He halted, panting, gripping the Thompson gun. "Peepo."

"Yo?"

"Set up a perimeter, keep watch. Hold them back as long as you can."

"Darrow?"

He turned, saw Jukk, looking grim. "We *did* bring the explosives?" he said.

"Yeah," said Jukk. "But we lost some getting here. One crate of gear, at least."

"See what we still have and use it to mine the houses. I want to take as much of the street out as we can when the time comes."

Jukk ran off. "What's the plan then?" said Flaps.

Darrow pointed to a manhole cover in the middle of the street. "There's a way out. Danny used it, when he and Helen first found the Grendelwolf."

Flaps' face tightened at the mention of Danny, but she nodded, then ran to the others shouting orders.

Gunfire; the distant crump of explosions. Only waiting now remained, and the hope that Peepo could buy Jukk sufficient time. Darrow went to Kate and the little ones. "You're all right?"

"You really know how to show a girl a good time, Rog." Kate forced a smile; she was pale and shaken, but composed for the sake of the children around her. But it was an effort – her smile trembled and her eyes glistened. Spike, Darrow remembered; she hadn't made it. Dene was still alive, though currently slumped against a wall nursing a shattered hand.

Darrow thought of Niamh. All the *what ifs* and *might have beens*. He pointed to the manhole cover that several fighters, under Flaps' supervision, were now dragging clear. "There's a tunnel. Comes up in Northenden."

"Still in the lion's den."

"But outside the cordon. From there, we can find a way out of the city."

Kate nodded at the houses. "And blowing them up covers our trail?"

"With any luck, they'll think it's mass suicide, or an accident. Either way, it'll buy us time."

Kate smiled, her hands stroking the hair of the children gathered round her. "Doesn't exactly feel like our lucky day."

Darrow felt the warmth of her, the gentleness; even now, she had an open heart that drew others to it like a fire in the cold night. He was in awe of her for that, always had been. Had things been different, perhaps, there could have been something between. But he'd thought that, once or twice, of Alannah too. And others; it had never come to anything. He'd never known that completeness, that warmth. He would have liked to. Just once. "Perhaps our luck's about to change," he said.

"Darrow!" Jukk ran up. "Problem."

"Excuse me," Darrow told Kate, and went to him. "Don't tell me we've lost the explosives."

"Nah. Whole street's ready to blow. It's the detonators we've lost."

"You mean we've no way of –"

"No. We got this." Jukk held up a short metal cylinder with a lever sticking out from it. "And some detonators that go with it. But there's a problem."

*

Ashwood Fort

1142 hours

The landcruisers rolled through the village, heading for the open gates. From the passenger seat Wakefield saw Gevaudan sitting by the road, head bowed. She'd got him this far before, and no further. Something reserve of strength had gone out of the Grendelwolf; Wakefield had wanted to help him find it, but all the Raiders were heading for the Wastelands now.

A jar of speed pills was being passed round. Wakefield swallowed two, grimacing: she hated them, but she'd need them today. In the back, Lish was thumbing bullets into magazines; Brant sat silent, his gun across his knees. Wakefield waved to Gevaudan; his eyes met hers, and at last he raised a pale hand in response. She nodded back. And then they were past. She forced herself to keep looking ahead; she had a battle to fight.

*

Gevaudan watched the landcruisers go, and the Wall One gates swing closed.

Those left behind were watching him. They knew, of course, by now, that he wasn't a traitor – some would even have seen Gideon themselves – but even so, he was an object of fear again.

Thank you, brother. You took even this from me.

He had to get up, go back to his cottage, hide from this. But not just yet; at that moment, he felt weary beyond words.

*

DEADSBURY

1145 HOURS

A young fighter – smoke-stained face and reddened eyes, blood running from a cut on her forehead – ran up. "Peepo says we can't hold them."

"Jukk?" said Darrow. The crewboy looked at him. "All set?"

Jukk nodded.

"All right." Darrow raised his voice. "Everybody into the tunnel."

Kate looked at him, close to tears, holding them back only so she didn't distress the children. A kind of love swelled in Darrow at the sight. If he'd made the time, if he'd only tried – but it was too late now. He touched her face with his free hand; she kissed it, hugged him for a moment, then shepherded her charges towards the tunnel. Jukk followed, helping Dene down after them.

"Darrow!" Flaps tugged at his sleeve. "Come on."

"I'm afraid not."

"What?"

Darrow showed her his left hand; in it was the cylinder Jukk had shown him. "It's a dead man's switch," he said, fingers resting on the lever. "When I close the circuit, it arms the detonator. When released, it sets it off."

"Which fucking idiot came up with that?"

"They have their uses, but for this situation, I'll admit, it's not ideal. Not least because underground, we'll lose the signal. And if we're directly under the street when it blows, the tunnel will come down on us. Unfortunately, it's all we have."

"So what do we do?"

"*We* don't do anything," said Darrow. "You continue with the plan."

"But someone's gotta stay up here and —"

"Yes."

Darrow saw the realisation on Flaps' face. "No," she said. "No fucking way."

"I can't ask anyone else, Flaps. Now go on."

"Like fuck," she said. "I'll do it."

Darrow closed his fist. The lever resisted stiffly for a moment, then clicked against the side of the cylinder. There was a beep, and a red light came on. "No."

There were tears in Flaps' eyes. "You fucking —"

"Language." Darrow smiled as best he could. "Now, don't distract me — you might break my grip. Just get in the tunnel, get them clear, and get them out."

At last, Flaps nodded. She opened her mouth to speak, but there were shouts and yells, and Peepo's unit came running down the street.

"No more time," Darrow said gently. "Go on, Flaps."

She backed away, shaking her head, then turned and ran for the manhole.

Peepo's squad dashed past Darrow; Peepo jumped feet-first into the tunnel. There was yelp of pain, and Flaps shouted "Watch what you're fucking doing, you bell-end." A weak ripple of laughter; even Darrow smiled. The last of Peepo's squad climbed down; with a metallic scrape, the manhole cover was pulled back into place.

Darrow walked towards the top of the street. His left hand held the dead man's switch shut; his right closed around the pistol grip of his Thompson.

So much done, so much undone. The lives sacrificed; the lives saved. Did it balance out, or come down on this or that side? Would it even matter, once he was dead? He'd never believed in anything afterward, but he wanted to, now. Perhaps he'd have that meal with Niamh again; do right whatever he'd done wrong. Or perhaps it would be Alannah, or Kate. Or someone else, someone he might have met and loved, if not for the Reapers, if not for the War.

Darrow heard running footsteps, the hiss and clank of engines.

Reapers charged around the corner, rifles raised. Some dropped prone when they saw him; others knelt. Others ran on down the street, keeping clear of their comrades' fire-lines, weapons trained on Darrow as they took up their own positions.

Landcruisers rounded the corner. Their .50 cals swivelled back and forth, searching for targets. Two came to bear on him.

"Quite sure you're pointing enough guns at me?" Darrow murmured.

The landcruisers halted; the street grew still. A distant crackle of flames; somewhere, a bird began to sing.

"Drop your weapon," shouted a voice.

The Reapers inched closer. How long now, since Flaps had climbed into the tunnel? A minute? Less? More? How long would they need, to get out of range?

Darrow stood his ground and held the Thompson at his side. There were tremors in his arms and his right leg. His teeth, despite the warm day, were chattering; he clenched them tight.

"Drop your weapon," the voice shouted. "This is your final warning."

No more time. He'd bought Flaps and the others every second he could; he'd just have to hope it was enough.

Roger Darrow raised the Thompson submachine gun, braced his forearm across the barrel to steady it, and smiled.

*

TUNNEL UNDER DEADSBURY

Flaps heard a distant, muffled crash of gunfire. There was a moment's silence, then a barrage of heavy, ground-shaking thuds that shook the tunnel. Dust showered from the roof. There was a crash; the littl'uns with Kate screamed as a section of tunnel roof collapsed behind them, as if stomped down by a huge foot.

Dust filled the tunnel, making Flaps cough and choke. Her eyes streamed; she told herself it was only the dust. She spat to get its taste out of her mouth. In the distance she heard screaming, shouts for help.

The littl'uns wailed; Kate shushed them, hugging them close. "Let's go," said Flaps. "Get out while we can."

They carried on down the tunnel. Flaps gripped the Sterling as she went; it was something small and concrete, something she could control.

*

DEADSBURY

Someone was shaking him. Twemlow grunted and tried to shrug the hand from his shoulder; he wanted to sleep, it wasn't time to get up yet. But they wouldn't stop, and they were shouting his name.

"All right," said Twemlow, and opened his eyes. Ahmad was kneeling over him. The air was full of smoke and dust; it caught at Twemlow's throat and he coughed.

"Thank fuck for that." Ahmad wiped his eyes. "Thought you were dead."

Twemlow sat up. The houses on either side of the street were gone – burning, gutted shells with most of the frontages blown out. Bricks and concrete littered the road. Those, and bodies. Blood and cement dust, thickening into a paste.

With Ahmad's help, he stood, looked around. There were maybe a dozen men and women left standing, plus half a dozen more injured. Hawkins lay in the middle of the road, or at least her lower half did. Her upper half lay on the rubble-covered pavement to Twemlow's left, still clutching her pistol. Twemlow wasn't sure, but he thought he saw her lips moving. Some blood was still pumping out of her, anyway. Other things were sliding out from what'd been her stomach: he looked away.

"What a fucking mess," said Ahmad.

The man they'd found when they came down the street was nowhere in sight, but there was a heap of masonry stretched across the road. Blood pumped out of it, like a bright red spring, but the flow was slowing even as Twemlow looked. And finally, it stopped.

*

The War Room, Ashwood Fort
1240 hours

"Unit 3A," said Helen, "take up positions at the Bowkitt Library and hold there." She looked up at Alannah. "That completes the defensive line."

Alannah nodded.

"Sparrowhawk?" Helen ground her teeth; she could taste the blood where she'd chewed the inside of her mouth. She'd taken more speed pills – her and Alannah both, to stave off the exhaustion threatening to overwhelm them. "Talk to me."

"Here." Wakefield's voice came from the radio. "Holding. Just."

"Stand by. Starling? What's your status?"

"Retreat underway." Jazz's voice was bitter.

"Fall back towards Bowkitt."

"They'll come after us."

"Let them, Starling. We're ready for them now."

"Wilco, Phoenix."

Helen heard the anger, the sorrow, the broken pride. She'd talk to Jazz later, reassure her she'd done well. Later; when the battle was done.

Defeat: a bitter pill to swallow, but you couldn't fight without tasting it at least once. Part of your education, in a way. Victory, today, wouldn't be driving the Reapers before them, or throwing back a larger force, but in falling back and holding a line, preventing a retreat from becoming an utter rout.

"Just get your people out of there, Starling," she said. "They've done enough for today. Sparrowhawk?"

"Hoy, crazy ginger." Wakefield coughed. "Mean – Sparrowhawk here, Phoenix."

Helen tried not to laugh. "You're the rearguard. Cover the rest of the frontline units as they fall back."

"Will do."

Helen leant on the chart table, breathing out. "They gonna hold okay?" Alannah asked finally.

"Should do," said Helen. "They caught us off-guard. We're not off-guard any more."

Alannah shook her head. "Helen, I'm so sorry –"

"It's okay." It wasn't, not really, but that was for later. Despite everything, Alannah was a friend, one of the few Helen still had. Gideon had played her, and countless others; it had almost worked, almost led to irrevocable things, but it hadn't. Helen, at least, would get past that. Whether Gevaudan would, she didn't know.

"For now," she said, "we hold. Let Winterborn have his victory. When we're secure again, we'll start working on taking the territory back." They'd have to, of course; by winning battles, they'd shown that the Reapers could be beaten. Let the Reapers un-teach those lessons, and their support would fall away. "We fall back, and hold the line."

*

NORTHENDEN
1249 HOURS

Jukk pushed the manhole cover back; weak light spilled down into the tunnel. Flaps squinted, dazzled after more than an hour in the dark.

"Clear," Jukk whispered.

"Then let's go."

Jukk clambered out; one by one, the rest of them followed. Kate and her children went last, followed by Flaps herself. She glanced back down the darkened tunnel, then climbed up to join the others. "Help," she said, tugging at the manhole cover.

No-one moved or answered. Flaps looked up, glaring. "I said," she began, then stopped.

A side-street, full of half-collapsed, burnt-out houses – but they'd clearly been intact enough to serve as hiding places, because now the street was full of Reapers, guns levelled at Flaps' group.

"Hold your fire," called a voice. Flaps squinnied, trying to see who'd spoken; she thought it was coming from one of the buildings. "Who's in command?"

No-one answered. "I could kill you all now," the voice said, "take you back to the Pyramid for interrogation, or I could let you go. But for that to happen, I need to talk to whoever's in charge."

Half the fuckwits in the group were looking at Flaps already. If the Reapers didn't already know, they'd guess pretty quick. She took a deep breath, raised a hand. "Me."

"Over here," said the voice.

Two Reapers came forward; one reached for her, but Flaps pulled back. "Touch me and you'll fucking lose it," she said. "Just lead on."

One of them motioned to the ruined house. Flaps moved through the crowd, the Reapers flanking her.

A candle-lantern flickered in the shadows; a tubby, balding Reaper officer sat beside us. "Leave us," he said. The two Reapers backed out. "I want to make a deal with you."

"I'm listening," she said. He was plump and sleek, like a rat who fed on the dead.

"Do you know who Alannah Vale is?"

"Oh yeah."

"She needs eyes and ears inside the Tower," he said. "She doesn't have them any more. But she can again." He tossed something to Flaps; she caught it. "Get that to her. Have her get in touch."

"And we can go?"

"Yes," he said, and smiled. "Just don't get caught."

She weighed up the message capsule. "You'd be right up shit street if we did, wouldn't you?"

The tubby man let out a nervous laugh. "Suppose I would." He stood up. "Best get back to the Tower before I'm missed. Safe journey."

Flaps pocketed the capsule and went back outside in time to see the Reapers jogging away up the street. She looked behind her, but the officer had vanished; the candle-lantern burned alone.

"Let's move," she told the others. They were nowhere near safe yet – whatever safe meant now. They still had to reach Worsley, stow away on an outbound supply barge. But they were out of Deadsbury – any luck, the Reapers still thought they'd all topped themselves rather than get taken.

They'd make it. She'd make sure of that. She owed it to Darrow.

Flaps sucked in a hard breath; the memory of him was too sharp, too fresh. She breathed out, focussing only on what lay ahead. The rest could come and get her in its own time. And she knew it would.

*

ST MARTIN DE PORRES CHURCH, ASHWOOD FORT
1600 HOURS

There were no cheering crowds whooping in victory in the Fort – after all, this hadn't been a victory but a tactical retreat, a Dunkirk rather than an El Alamein – and that more than suited Gevaudan's mood as he sat, exhausted, beside the church. Had sat there ever since. But the glances he was getting – half-suspicious, half-guilty – had begun to irritate him.

Gevaudan and stood and crossed the courtyard behind Wall Two. Smiles faded as he approached; people stepped out of his way. Which was the best idea most of them had had in a long time.

He knew some had believed in him as Helen had, but too many others had joined the lynch-mob or done nothing to stop it. He was a living reminder of that, and some people would never forgive him for it.

He was in no hurry to return to the cottage, either. Gevaudan was under no illusions what he'd find, and he'd rather have avoided facing it if possible. But while the cave on the hill was a tempting option, it hadn't the energy for the trek – and besides, if he was too far away, the ground might shift again in his absence.

Helen was here; that was the closest thing he had to a fixed point right now. Whatever else she'd done, she'd been willing to gamble her life on his innocence.

There was a persistent twinge of pain coming from Gevaudan's cheek. he reached up and touched it, found something hard under the skin. A splinter or rock-chip, embedded in the wound he'd sustained earlier: he remembered that it had been taking a long time to heal. Carefully, Gevaudan extended a claw and slit the skin of his cheek. Blood made his thumb and finger slippery, but he managed to pull the object free. Yes, a rock chip. He let the blood trickle down his face, washing any other, smaller fragments out of the wound. Soon the flow diminished as the wound healed: by the time he'd reached his cottage the bleeding had stopped, and when he touched his cheek the skin was unbroken.

The cottage's windows were broken, and the grass outside was littered with torn pages and smashed china, splintered wood and buckled brass.

Stupid, really. The church in Deadsbury, the cottage, the cave – in all of them he'd sought a sanctuary from this world, in a futile attempt to preserve what had been. Nonetheless, it was his, or had been.

Gevaudan went through into the living room. Slashed, broken furniture and wads of stuffing, books torn into scraps. His guitar was matchwood on the floor. He was tempted to walk away, but where else had he to go? In the kitchen, broken crockery crunched underfoot; outside the window, in the garden, the grass was gouged up and churned, the lanterns, chairs and table smashed, the cairns scattered –

Someone was in the garden, rooting through the grass. A growl escaped Gevaudan; he threw the back door wide, strode into the garden. "Whatever you plan on taking, I suggest that if you enjoy having lungs, you put it back –" He stopped. "You."

Alannah stared back at him, a pebble in each hand. "Gevaudan."

"Put them down," he said.

"I just wanted to –"

"I'm not going to ask again."

Alannah let the stones fall. "I just wanted to put it right."

"You can't," said Gevaudan. "And you know it."

Alannah's eyes filled. She opened and closed her mouth; she even took half a step towards Gevaudan.

"Leave my house," he said. A candle flame wouldn't have stirred at his lips. "While you can."

She circled around him towards the back door; he heard her run through the house. Then he knelt in the grass, feeling in it for the fallen stones.

10.

Approach to Ashwood Fort
29th July, Attack Plus Twenty-One Years
1000 hours

The landcruiser bounced over cracked tarmac, bulbous with tree roots. The trees on either side gave way to open grassland. There were hills in the distance and another one closer to, the Fort rising from it behind its defensive walls.

Flaps wiped her eyes with her sleeve. Her first sight of the Fort had been like this, that snowy winter's day as Darrow had brought them in, those last few survivors of the crews he'd raised in the city. He'd blindfolded them all for the journey to the Fort, only letting them see when they were almost there.

Of course, back then the Fort's location had been secret; that didn't matter now. Flaps wasn't sure if anything still did.

She hadn't been crying that day; she'd been empty, a wrung-out rag. She'd done all her crying before, after she'd got away from the house where Mary and the others had died, when Darrow had found her hidden in Steel City. She hadn't wanted to, she'd wanted to be strong as Mary had trained her to be, but she'd skriked away like a littl'un in Darrow's arms. Only time she'd given way like that. After that she'd stayed strong.

Someone was crying. Flaps looked across the landcruiser's flatbed: it was Kate. For all the older woman's seeming softness, there was a strength to her, but at last it was giving way.

The landcruiser's radio crackled; Flaps heard the driver speaking. She closed her eyes; the landcruiser's bouncing diminished as they laboured up the hill. When she looked again, the outer gates were opening.

They drove on and stopped, at last, outside the Fort. Flaps saw the crowd gathering outside. Helen was there, Alannah too. Her hostility to them both twitched once inside Flaps, sluggish and weak, then subsided. She hadn't the strength today.

Flaps climbed out of her landcruiser. Helen and Alannah were scanning the weaving, soot-stained figures climbing out of the landcruisers. Looking for one face in particular, and slowly realising it wasn't there.

Flaps had let them know as little as possible after the escape from Deadsbury. Just that they were out, and heading home. Nothing more; nothing about who'd made it and who hadn't. Easy for Helen to give the orders; twice now the city crews had died for her. Flaps wanted to see her face when she heard, see if there was any fucking feeling left in her.

Nestor and a couple of nurses came forward to meet them; Dene and a couple of other wounded were ushered away. Kate was shepherding the littl'uns off the landcruisers, a mother hen with her chicks. Nestor went to her, saying something. She said something back, and he smiled. Let them; Flaps cared more about the ones on Helen's and Alannah's faces.

A weak smile still fluttered on Alannah's lips as Flaps approached, but Helen had already stopped. When their faces were as empty as hers felt, Flaps nodded a greeting to them. Helen was silent, ashen: she knew.

So did Alannah, really, but she had to be sure. "Darrow?" It was practically a whisper.

Flaps shook her head. She hoped there was nothing in her face; she wanted to be blank, empty, for it to be as easy as it was for Helen to give the orders.

Alannah made a noise Flaps didn't have a name for and put a hand to her mouth. The dark eyes filled, and overflowed. Flaps felt guilty; it was Helen's reaction she'd wanted. Flaps turned back to study her. Helen swayed, white-faced, and closed her eyes. "God," she said at last.

At least she felt something. Flaps nodded, then turned back to Alannah. "I'm sorry."

Alannah nodded, and the grief Flaps had locked down welled up in her; she choked on it, felt her face crumple like dead leaves. *No, for fuck sake, not in front of everyone.* But she couldn't help it. And Alannah moved forward, and took Flaps in her arms.

*

The War Room, Ashwood Fort
1140 hours

Helen had splashed the coldest water she could find on her face, again and again, till it and her hands were numb. Now feeling was slowly returning to them both.

The War Room was empty, for now; standing idle, waiting to be of use again. Much like Helen herself. People were still awkward with her, could find little to say beyond the obvious and necessary.

She'd been alone before, in the Wastelands after the Refuge fell, but she'd been *on* her own then; being alone in a crowd was something else. her isolation then had been self-imposed; this time, though, it was different. It would heal, she hoped, in time. If only because that wholeness would help them win at last.

The door opened. "You wanted me?"

"Flaps." Helen motioned to a chair.

Flaps sat down. "I'm sorry about Darrow," Helen said at last.

Flaps looked at her without speaking for some seconds, then nodded. "Reck you are," she said.

"You've been in command, Flaps. You know the decisions you have to make. They're not easy, but they have to be made."

"Especially when it's us in the city crews, right?"

Helen clenched her hands under the table. Who was Flaps to judge her? Then again, everyone else had been doing it. "I need someone to go back into the city," she said. "Finish what Roger started. Build the crews back to what they were."

Flaps stared at her. "Are you fucking high?"

Helen held up a hand. "Strictly intelligence-gathering and recruitment only. We'll sneak the Raiders in to carry out any ops. They'll only liaise with you if there's absolutely no alternative. From now on, the city crews stay out of the fight until they're good and ready. I'll make that promise to you now, Flaps. Next time I call on you, it'll be for the final battle."

"You want my answer now?"

"No. Think about it. Sleep on it. I want you to be sure. I know what I'm asking. If you're not up for it, I'll look elsewhere." Helen damned herself mentally; even now, she sounded manipulative. And that wasn't what Helen wanted, not today. "I mean it, Flaps. Your choice, no-one else's. If you don't want to do it, don't. You've more than done your part."

"I'll think on it."

"Okay. Thanks."

"That everything?"

"Yeah."

"See you, then."

*

Winterborn's Office, The Tower
1400 hours

"The new frontline's stabilised, anyway," said Winterborn. "We attempted further advances, but they dug in and re-established their defences. Trying to push any further, for now, would cost more than it gained us."

"Quite," said Mordake. "We achieved what we set out to do."

"Yes. A shame we couldn't eliminate at least some of the rebel command while we were at it, but it's an imperfect world."

"You got Darrow."

Winterborn chuckled. "That was an unexpected bonus, I'll admit. Surprised there was enough left of him to identify. If we could only have arranged the same for Helen."

"Her time will come," Mordake assured him. "Operation Long Knife was never about a final victory. Only *a* victory. It's ended the myth of rebel superiority, of our inevitable defeat. Fewer new recruits will come forward; those who would have aided them will, at the very least, hedge their bets. There'll never be a better time to call a Unification Conference."

"Supreme Commander." Winterborn breathed it, tasting the words. "As long as the final piece of the puzzle is in place, of course. What news on Project Sycorax?"

"These things can't be rushed, Commander. It will take time for it to be ready. But once certain processes are set in motion, we need only wait until they're completed. I'll be able to give you a date within the next week. Then all you need do is schedule the Conference. A small demonstration will be more than enough to convince the others."

"Then don't let me detain you," said Winterborn. "You may return to your work, Doctor."

Mordake bowed.

*

GEVAUDAN'S COTTAGE, ASHWOOD FORT
1600 HOURS

The warm thick air wrapped close round Danny like damp, hot rags; the sky overhead was nearly black. A thin white thread of lightning flashed between it and a hilltop to the west. Danny counted two before the thunder reached the Fort.

Fat drops of rain hit him as he limped towards the cottage with his sack. By the time he'd reached the front door it had begun falling heavily.

Garlands of flowers and stacks of books were heaped around the front door. The flowers twitched in the warm, heavy rain, and it spotted the books' covers.

Danny tapped on the door; no answer. When he tried the handle it was locked. He breathed out and went round the back and climbed the low garden wall. The kitchen door was also locked, so he knocked on it, too. The rain quickened to a drumming rhythm that hissed in the grass and clattered on the roof. "Bollocks," Danny muttered. He knocked again, harder. "Oi, Creeping D – I mean, Gevaudan! You in there or what?"

He squinnied through the cracked glass panes in the door, then went to the window. They'd replaced the smashed glass with scraped hide, but all you could see through it were shadows –

The door lock clicked, and it swung open. "Hello, Danny."

Danny swallowed. "Yo."

In the shadows, Gevaudan smiled. "Good to see you," he said quietly. "I'm glad... you're well."

"Always keep bouncing back," Danny said.

"So I heard. Literally, when you hit that damned haycart. Would you like to come in?"

"Please. Fucking drowning out here."

Gevaudan motioned him inside, shutting the door behind them. Danny tried not to look at the ruined kitchen, bullet spattered walls, or the hacked kitchen counter. The shattered crockery had been swept, at least; a few new dishes stood by the Belfast sink, which had somehow escaped the damage.

Rain drummed on the roof, pattered on the windowsill. Danny held out the sack. "Here."

"What's this?"

"Present. Thought you might want a new one."

Gevaudan opened the sack and drew out the guitar, turning it over in his hands. "I doubt I'll be in any mood to play in the canteen any time soon."

"Doesn't matter."

"It's good guitar," said Gevaudan. "A Martin."

Danny shrugged. "Told the Raiders to keep their eyes out for one. Lish found it. Music shop in some old village."

Gevaudan stroked the strings, listened, adjusted the tension. "Extraordinary condition," he said at last. "Please thank Lish for me."

"Will do. Oh, and – this is from Zaq."

Give him this, would you? Zaq had said gruffly, not looking at Danny. She'd actually asked instead of ordering. Gevaudan took the battered harmonica from him, played a few experimental notes. "Thank her for me."

"Will do."

"Don't forget to throw some raw meat in ahead of you, though."

Danny laughed, then stopped. It didn't feel right, not in here. The air inside the house was stale and hot; the windows hadn't been opened in a while. In the living room were two wooden chairs, a small table with a spirit stove. "They're a little Spartan," said Gevaudan, "but they'll serve." He was silent for a moment, then added: "I'm sorry about Darrow."

Danny sucked in a deep breath, as if someone had just poked an open cut. Felt a bit that way, too. "Thanks."

"How are you..." Gevaudan trailed off.

Danny shrugged. "Nowt I can do, is there?"

"No. Death's final like that. Well, unless you're Helen. There's no chance he could have survived?"

"Nah. Nowt like that happening this time, mate. Alannah –" He broke off when he saw the look on Gevaudan's face "– they got Kingfisher to check and re-check, just in case. But..." He shook his head, feeling his eyes prickle and fill. Fuck. He was a man now. No more skriking. "No," he said. "He's gone."

"I'm sorry," Gevaudan said again. "He and I, we weren't exactly friends, but... I had great respect for him. He was a good man."

"Yeah. Yeah, he was."

Neither of them spoke for a few seconds after that. Gevaudan cleared his throat. "Would you like coffee?"

"Thanks. Not had any in a while."

"I didn't ask about your love-life." Gevaudan smiled, then stopped – he'd have just remembered who Danny's love-life was with.

Danny coughed. "You got some more stuff out front."

Gevaudan put a pan of water on to boil. "Have I indeed?"

"Books and stuff. They'll be fucked if you don't get 'em in. Pissing down out there."

The Grendelwolf went to the front door; Danny looked around the room. It was barer than it had been. The surviving books were piled in corners, and the house seemed darker than it had. The new windows weren't as clear as the glass ones, obvs, but it was more than that. Something had gone out of the place, and out of Gevaudan.

The stuff they'd lost cos of those Reaper fuckers. Danny was doing his best not to think of Darrow. Funny, but it wasn't that hard – the idea of Darrow being gone, just *not there* any more, was too big for Danny's head to fit around. Easier just not to think of it, then everything else carried on as normal. For now.

Gevaudan came back in with an armful of books and dumped them on the floor. Danny stared: the Grendelwolf always treated books like something precious. Gevaudan looked up at him. "I'll sort them out later," he said. "I just... can't be bothered right now."

He sat and watched the stove. *He's not all right*, Danny realised. *He's nowhere near back to what he was. Might never be.* That was a hard, painful thought. There was more than one way to lose someone. He saw there were small, half-healed wounds in Gevaudan's throat, scabbed over.

The Grendelwolf saw him looking. "Grendelwolf claws," he said.

"Eh?"

Gevaudan touched the wounds. "Gideon did this. Grendelwolf claws exude a sort of toxin. It's harmless to normal humans, but it affects the accelerated healing process in other Grendelwolves. Basically, any wound they cause on a Grendelwolf are as damaging – heal as slowly – as they'd be to someone like you. If one ever went rogue, his brothers would finish him quickly. Anyway." Gevaudan held out a mug of coffee. "Here."

"Thanks."

"So, how are you?"

"Still a bit stiff. But I'm all right."

"Really?"

"I'm sorry, if that's what you mean."

"Sorry? For what?"

"I told 'em, didn't I? That it was you."

Gevaudan shook his head. "Gideon half-killed you," he said. "And he was the image of me. You were fooled, briefly. But that was the whole point. And that's all you did. You didn't go further than that."

Danny's eyes and throat hurt. "Like Alannah?"

"This place," said Gevaudan. "It wasn't much, but it was something. And now..." He gestured round.

"She was tricked too," said Danny. "Everyone was."

"Not everyone," said Gevaudan. "Some doubted. And some refused to believe."

"Yeah, but Helen fancies you."

Gevaudan raised an eyebrow. Danny shrugged, felt his face get hot. "Looks like it to me, anyway."

"Thank you for the observation, Casanova."

"Eh?"

"Never mind."

"She thought I was gonna cark it, too," Danny said. How much of a grudge did Gevaudan bear, and what was he gonna do about it?

"It isn't an easy thing to forget, Danny," said Gevaudan, almost gently. "Seeing the people you thought were friends turn on you like that."

"Spose not." Danny sipped his coffee, barely tasting it.

"She thought she was facing the hard facts," Gevaudan said. "That's her job, after all. The evidence pointed my way, and then Gideon went after you. So I do understand, Danny, and one day I'll probably forgive her." The Grendelwolf sipped his own coffee. "Just not today."

*

Danny's Quarters, Ashwood Fort
1800 hours

The door closed; Alannah sat up in bed. "Sweetheart?"

"Yo." Danny sat on the edge of the bed, and kissed her; his hands were warm on her bare skin, but she felt them shaking. When he pulled away, there were tears in his eyes.

Alannah held her arms out. He nodded. "One sec."

When he was naked, she drew back the covers; he climbed in alongside her.

"Can't believe it," she heard him whisper.

"What?"

"That he's gone."

"Gevaudan?" An unpleasant flicker of hope in her – that might make things a little easier, on her at least.

"Darrow."

Alannah's breath caught; she held him tighter. "Me neither."

How many years had it been? Darrow had been nearly the last of her old friends: Mary, Ashton, Noakes, and others too, more than she could count – all gone. She remained, and Helen: that was all. Winterborn didn't count: the boy he'd been had died long ago. The time before the War was fast fading into mist, and she found it hard to recall a time after it when Darrow hadn't been there. For Danny, of course, there'd never been such a time for him, and Darrow had been the closest thing to a father he'd known.

Alannah held him in the dark, stroking his hair. "He did all right, though," she heard him say. "Last thing he did was make sure they got away. Did all right." His voice choked and hitched; Alannah hugged him tighter. He shook and began to sob, then to bawl; something like a scream escaped him. Alannah kissed the top of his head and held him close, crying her own silent tears.

*

Gevaudan's Cottage, Ashwood Fort
2000 hours

"Gevaudan."

"Helen." A smile touched the tired, pale face. It wasn't as bright as it would once have been – before the Pyramid, before Bereloth, before Gideon – but it was something, at least; an echo of what once was. And what might be again? Perhaps. With luck. "Come in," Gevaudan said.

Following him through the cottage, Helen studied him from the back. His shoulders seemed rounded, bowed, but the strength of him was still there, the easy, fluid motion. It was muted, had been battered and shaken, but it hadn't broken. She wanted to lean on it, to let it hold her – but that couldn't be. Not tonight, at least.

The cottage still bore the scars, but outside, in the garden, candle-lanterns glowed; a pot hung over a fire. Helen sniffed the air, and smiled. "Stew again?"

"I'll attempt something more adventurous next time."

She reached out to touch his arm, then let her hand fall. There was a time it would have come easily, but that had been before Bereloth. Some things couldn't be put right quickly, if at all. "Stew's fine."

"No shortage of ale or wine to accompany it, either," said Gevaudan. "Gifts pile up outside my door. Guilt can be a wonderful provider."

"They know they were fooled," said Helen. "They're trying to make things right."

"I know. It's just... hard."

"You gonna actually serve dinner any time this evening?"

"As you wish." He ladled stew into bowls. "Still, they weren't all fooled."

"Wakefield wasn't, or Filly." Would Darrow have seen past the deception, with his cold clock of a mind? Except that he hadn't been cold, not in the end. *The end.* Helen almost swayed for a moment. The fact of Darrow's death was still like a stone in her gut, swallowed whole and stuck fast: it would neither be digested nor pass through her. *Enough.* "And then there was Carson," she said, forcing herself back to the present. "Got to say, she surprised me."

"People do change," said Gevaudan. "All too often, for the worse. But... not always."

"You're such a ray of sunshine, Gevaudan."

"I merely speak the truth."

"Yeah, yeah." Helen ate a mouthful of stew. "Mm. Good."

"Beer or wine?"

"Wine, please."

Gevaudan filled their cups. "Thank you, by the way," he said.

"What for?"

"You know what for."

"Yeah." Helen resisted the impulse for a moment, but then gave way to it and reached across the table; her fingers brushed against his. "And you're welcome."

"When do you go back?"

"Tomorrow," she said. A part of her ached for Piel, and a part of her dreaded it. There would be people there she wouldn't enjoy facing, but too much had happened at Ashwood. Her one reason for staying here had been Gevaudan, but even that wasn't enough to keep her here any longer.

"I shall miss you," he sighed.

"Same."

His eyes didn't leave hers. One of those moments where something, anything, could happen.

Then he smiled, and picked up his cup. "Safe journey."

"Thanks. And I hope you're safe here."

"So do I."

*

REAPER CAMP, THE WASTELANDS
2100 HOURS

Saeed Patel sat on a chunk of rubble, smoking a Monarch cigarette and drinking Monarch gin. Raw grain spirit flavoured with berries. It would do.

Nearby was the perimeter; CivEng troops were already at work, building fences and a watchtower.

There was laughter from a bunch of younger recruits a few yards away. Half-pissed already. Some of them recked this was it, the turning of the tide. After this, they'd keep shoving the rebels back, till they were gone. And that was bollocks. They always came back again, twice as strong.

Patel only just remembered his Dad. Old fucker'd given him to the Reapers when he was seven or eight. Give your kids a better chance – and give yourself one less mouth to feed, plus food, booze and cigs in exchange. Still, Patel'd been fed, trained up, looked after. It was a life. He'd never had any reason to doubt being with the Reapers.

Not till now.

Patel heard shouts, screams; people were running. *Fuck.* He grabbed his rifle, got to his feet. *Fucking counter-attack, already?*

He ran towards the perimeter, then stopped. A figure strode towards him. Six and a half feet tall if it was an inch; a long black coat flapped round it, and long black hair blew back from its long white face. Something was wrong with that face.

It was bandaged, Patel realised; one side of it, including the eye, was covered over. The other eye, cold and yellow, fixed on him; he backed away.

The red lips smiled.

"I take it you have a commanding officer?" the Grendelwolf said. "Take me to them, please. I'm Gideon Shoal."

Epilogue

Sick Bay, Ashwood Fort

6th August, Attack Plus Twenty-One Years

Nestor Shelley rubbed his eyes, reached for his mug. The coffee was cold, but he drank it anyway.

"Okay," he called. "Next."

A chair, a table and a couch, screened off from the rest of the sick bay. The curtain rustled back. "Yo."

"Hi, Danny." Nestor managed a smile. "Take a seat."

The boy sat – but he wasn't a boy any more, was he? Before the War, he wouldn't have been old enough to drink or smoke or drive a car, but now he was a man, and there were the grey flecks in his hair to prove it. Under his shirt, the scars: from Jarrett's gun, from Gideon's claws. The last were still red, but fading.

"You're healing up," said Nestor. "Take it easy for a couple more weeks."

"Do me best." Danny refastened his shirt. "You okay?"

Nestor smiled. "As long as I keep working."

"You never do anything else."

Nestor watched him go, then stood and stretched before stepping outside the cubicle. The sick bay was more or less fully restored; here and there were scars left by the shrapnel, but he'd had plenty of volunteers to replace the people he'd lost. *Healing.*

You never do anything else. Nestor smiled again; that wasn't true any more.

A warm hand touched his. "You all right, love?" said Kath.

He took her hand and squeezed it. "I'm good."

"Need some counselling?"

"Not when I'm working." He grinned at her. "Maybe later."

She smiled too, and squeezed his hand back. "Look forward to it."

She went to her cubicle, and Nestor to his.

Healing.

*

St Martin de Porres Church, Ashwood Fort

The church was cool after the heat outside; Carson paused to savour it, breathing deep, before walking down the aisle to the altar.

She knelt, the stone floor hard against her knees, and bowed her head in what had become her familiar prayer: *make me worthy of forgiveness, Lord, if only Yours*. She didn't hear the footsteps behind her, was only aware she had company when someone knelt beside her at the altar.

She glanced up, saw who it was, and made to rise, but Brant shook his head. "It's okay," he said. "Don't mind." He bowed his head, then glanced up at her and scowled. "Carry on," he said.

Carson knelt again, clasped her hands. And in silence, they both prayed.

*

Intelligence Centre, Ashwood Fort

Weird being sat behind Alannah's desk, weirder still being in charge while she was gone. Felt like a fraud, a con – waiting for someone to say so, to twig she was making it up as she went, hoping to fuck she was getting it right.

Still – Stock looked around – so far, so good. She turned as someone came in. "You the new boy?"

He nodded. Thin and curly-eyed, big dark eyes. *Pretty*, Stock thought. "Dene," he said.

"And I'm Stock." She nodded, stood up. "With me," she said, and led him over to a corner of the room. "Your desk."

"Thanks."

"And your radio set." Awkwardly, Dene took the headphones from her, then the pad and grease pencil. "Don't dick around with the controls – it's already covering a specific frequency and area. Write down anything you hear, best you can. Got it?"

"Got it."

Stock nodded, went back to her desk. Dene put on the headphones, picked up his pencil.

*

Wall Two, Ashwood Fort

A bright, clear day: blue sky, hot sun.

The battlements were quiet. Filly hissed as she lowered herself into a crouch; the chest wound still pained her at times.

Wakefield ran a hand down her back, then crouched beside her, drew her close.

Filly took a shuddering breath; her eyes glistened. Then she unwrapped the two tallow candles and handed one to Wakefield. A couple were already burning in the shrine; Filly lit her candle from one of them. "Darrow," she said softly.

After a moment, Wakefield lit her own, and whispered: "Loncraine." *Fox's Spirit, run with us...*

Filly took Wakefield's hand and they leant close together, silent, before the shrine.

*

CANTEEN, ASHWOOD FORT

"Bet you're happy," Cov said.

Mackie heard him, but didn't look up, didn't answer. He shoved the rag-mop back in the bucket, squeezed it almost dry, worked it back and forth across the patch of floor.

"Got away with it, didn't you, mate? Least for now."

Mackie heard him, but didn't look up or answer. Just shoved the rag-mop back in the bucket, squeezed it almost dry, worked it back and forth across the patch of floor. The canteen was nearly empty; Harp and Lish sat at a nearby table, her hands held tight in his. Probably too wrapped up in each other to notice if he ripped his clothes off and danced bollock-naked on a table, but even so, best not to answer Cov with any fucker else around.

"Gonna remember sooner or later, though, aren't they?" Cov went on. He climbed up on a table and sat there; Mackie made him briefly out from the corner of his eye – hands clasped, leaning forward, a cold smile on his dead ghost's face – before returning his attention to the canteen floor again. "That if it wasn't the Grendelwolf, there's still a traitor here. And then they'll starting looking again. Won't they?"

Mackie didn't look up or answer. Shoved the rag-mop back in the bucket, squeezed it almost dry, worked it back and forth across the patch of floor. He could see his face in it.

*

GEVAUDAN'S COTTAGE, ASHWOOD FORT

The garden was bright with flowers; the two cairns stood again at the end.

Flaps picked up the pebble she'd taken from Gevaudan's cairn at Deadsbury, leaving speckles of white paint on the grass. It was dry now, so she took the brush from the water jar and dipped it in the pot of black paint.

She wrote slowly, carefully: it had never been easy for her. But she always made the effort for something like this – for this one, most of all.

She drew each letter with care, then blew gently on them before setting the pebble back down in the grass to dry. *Darrow*, it read. She stretched her legs and pressed her bare feet to the ground, clenching and unclenching her toes. Funny thing to do – kind of thing she'd done when she was a littl'un – but it felt nice.

Kate's idea. Flaps had talked to her a bit. Felt weird, talking about stuff like that, how she felt – but it was helping. She'd been worried she couldn't do what she had to if she wasn't angry any more, but so far it seemed to be okay. A simple thing that felt good. She lay back, looked up at the sky.

It was a day of warm peace, and her grief had lessened; in fact, for now at least, she felt something close to happiness. Flaps closed her eyes and smiled. There were only moments, Kate had told her; good and bad. You coped with the bad as best you could, relished the good while they lasted. So Flaps lay in the sun, barefoot in the grass, and smiled.

*

LISTENING POST 2, THE WASTELANDS

Colby leant back against the base of the pylon in the warm sun.

They'd fallen back, but the line had held. Cracks had formed in their unity, but had closed again. They'd turned on one another, then stopped.

Hope? She didn't dare use that term, not even to herself. But she could see the possibility again, at least, that she might see the Reapers fall before she died. And that was something.

Colby coughed, spat blood into the grass. Although, if the possibility existed, it would have to happen soon.

"Colb?" It was Swan, his head sticking up through the trapdoor; he blinked and squinted in the light. "Come on. Gotta get below."

"I know," she said. There was work to be done.

Grunting and wincing, Colby climbed to her feet.

*

WINTERBORN'S OFFICE, THE TOWER

"I have sad news," Winterborn said, "regarding Commander Grimwood. We've had our differences over the years, he and I, but I've never doubted his commitment to our cause. I'm sorry to announce that his breakdown appears to be irreversible."

He didn't look directly at Holland, who looked weary and ashen; there was no pleasure to be had in wounding the one Commander he respected. Instead he smiled at Scrimgeour, who glared back at him.

"A bilateral treaty has been agreed in principle with Acting Commander Denyer," he continued. "Final ratification will take place shortly."

"Bloody outrageous," said Scrimgeour.

"As you yourself pointed out, Naomi, my Command is the flashpoint. But anti-Reaper movements throughout the British Isles have taken succour and inspiration from the rebels here. So yes, I've sought to forge closer working relationships with other Commands to resolve the situation. And we've made significant progress, as you see."

"The rebels haven't been destroyed," said Holland.

"No," agreed Winterborn. "But it *is* their first significant defeat since the December Rising. The impact on morale has been huge – on both sides. Productivity has increased in all Reaper divisions, while support for the rebels has fallen – recruitment's stopped almost entirely, and there've even been desertions."

"Reversals," said Drozek, "can prove temporary."

"I agree." Winterborn smiled. "So we must be ready. We've allowed petty divisions to keep us separate for too long. Remember the symbol of the REAP Command? A sheaf, a bundle of stalks – fragile alone, but strong together. That's how we will defeat the rebels, once and for all. And how we'll reunify our country. Make it Britain again, not just scattered kingdoms. We'll do it – with co-ordinated effort, military alliances, and..." Winterborn glanced at Mordake, over in his corner; Mordake smiled and inclined his head. "...some new weapons."

"New weapons?" Treloar raised her eyebrows.

"Destroy them with tactical nuclear strikes," said Fowler, "then reclaim the land afterwards. Only way."

"We have a weapons system in development," Winterborn said. "Unlike anything else you've seen. I can't say any more at this stage, but I should be able to provide a demonstration no later than the autumn."

"The autumn?" said Probert.

"Yes. I would like to propose that we set a date for the next Unification Conference: Manchester, in October. We can review our progress against the rebellion, discuss the timetable for unification, and all being well, witness the new weapons system in action." He smiled. "I guarantee you will not be disappointed."

"Fine by me," said Probert.

"Me too," said McMahon.

"Count me in," said Johnstone.

One by one, the other Commanders nodded assent, till only Scrimgeour, Holland and Denyer remained.

"Commander Denyer?" said Winterborn.

Denyer swallowed and nodded.

Holland breathed out. "Bit of a *fait accompli*, it seems," he said at last. "All right, Winterborn. But you'd better know what you're doing."

"I do," said Winterborn. "Naomi?"

Scrimgeour glared. Winterborn smiled and waited; she had no choice, he knew. "All right," she said.

"Excellent," said Winterborn. "Then, if there's nothing else, it only remains to settle the date."

*

When they were alone in the room, Winterborn turned to Mordake. "Leave me now," he said. "I want some time to myself."

"Of course, Commander." Mordake bowed and went out.

Winterborn turned in his chair, looking out across the city. He laid the music box on the table beside him, stroking the lid. He wasn't afraid any longer; he could feel the pieces being drawn into place. His destiny.

Winterborn lifted the lid and let the music play. It wasn't to soothe his fears any more, but to celebrate what was to come.

I dreamt I dwelt in marble halls, with vassals and serfs at my side...

*

Eastern Stairwell, Fourteenth Floor, The Tower

Thorpe plodded down the stairs, dabbing sweat from his face, till he reached the half-landing between the fourteenth and thirteenth floors. No-one in sight.

Quickly. Thorpe pried the newel post's plastic cap loose, tugged the message capsule from his pocket and dropped it inside.

Thorpe replaced the cap, wiped his forehead once more and carried on down the stairs. As he went, he passed a young Reaper, coming up. Thorpe had seen him around: Axon, that was his name. The boy saluted him. Thorpe returned it.

*

Roof of the Tower, City of Manchester

Mordake walked widdershins around the cowlings on the roof, murmuring to himself as he went. Then he stood to the centre, arms outspread, and looked skyward.

He smiled, breathed out, closed his eyes. "Almost," he whispered.

He inspected the cowlings one by one, then knelt and lifted one of them.

The face beneath it was bloodless and faded from being so long in the dark; the eyelids were stitched together over the empty sockets. But still the lips moved; still the face, sealed in its trance, spoke.

"Angana sor varalakh kai torja. Angana sor varalakh cha voran."

Mordake replaced the cowling and went to the roof's edge, leaning out into the wind.

"Almost," he said, again.

*

Piel Island, Barrow-in-Furness

The bright summer day turned the Piel Channel's waters blue, and wildflowers speckled the grass' vivid green.

Helen sat on the wooden jetty, her boots beside her, dangling her feet in the water. They were pale and dappled with sunlight, the water pleasantly cool between her toes. The day was quiet; all she could hear was the sea lapping softly at the shore.

"Helen."

Helen turned. "Alannah?"

Standing at the landward end of the jetty, the older woman nodded. "Having fun?"

Helen smiled. "It's quite nice. Something Kate said. Supposed to help you relax, feel connected, something like that."

"Is it working?"

"I'll let you know. Doesn't feel bad, anyway."

"Join you?"

Free country, Helen almost said – Mum had often said it when Helen had been little – but of course it wasn't. The possibility now existed, though. "Be my guest."

Alannah pulled off her boots and socks, lowered her feet into the water. "Yeah," she said. "Not bad at all."

"Told you."

Alannah nodded. "Kate might be onto something. Maybe I should spend some time with her." She squinted out over the water towards Barrow. "Might do me some good."

"So," said Helen, "to what do I owe the honour?"

"News of several sorts."

"There's a thing called radio."

"Gave me an excuse to leave the Fort."

"Since when do you get the urge to travel?"

"Thought a change of scene would do me good."

"As long as the scene didn't have Gevaudan in it?"

"I'm not exactly his favourite person right now." Alannah shook her head. "Those fuckers played me."

"Played a lot of people."

"Not you, though."

"I didn't want to believe it." Or she quite literally couldn't have; accepting it would have destroyed the last of her. "You know me. Stubborn."

"No shit?"

Helen smiled.

"Looks like the alliance is holding, anyway. The new Fox Chief's on the Council – Rotherham, he calls himself."

"Any relation to Wakefield?"

"I didn't ask. Anyway, we're safe with them. As far as they're concerned, you walk on water."

Helen studied the patterns of sunlight dancing on the water. "What about the rest?"

"You know Javeed. It's all forgiveness and oneness with him. And Stewart thinks you're great now, of course."

"Why the hell does he think that?"

Alannah shrugged. "You won."

"Won? Doesn't feel like I won anything."

"You were right about the Grendelwolf, and got him back onside. And saved half our arses from Gideon. Safe to say you scored a lot of brownie points with that one. So you're popular again."

"Right." Helen closed her eyes, let the sun warm her face. She'd have to go in soon, of course – red-headed as she was, she burned in the heat – but for now she'd enjoy it. "So now he's my best mate and he always believed in me."

"Pretty much."

"What about Thorn? And Jazz?"

"Do you really want to know?"

"Probably not."

"They're on board. They know there's no choice – hang together or hang separately and all that. Best you can hope for, sometimes."

They sat, waving their feet under the water.

"I'm sorry, Helen," Alannah said at last.

"Why?"

"You know why."

"Not like I'm in any position to judge, is it?" Helen shrugged. "You fucked up. Join the club."

"Yeah. Suppose we're both members."

"Members?" said Helen. "I bloody founded it."

Alannah snorted, then began to laugh. Helen did too. Alannah wiped her eyes; Helen held out a hand. Alannah squeezed it for a moment, then let go. "You know how long it's been since I saw the sea?"

"Long time, I bet," said Helen.

"Years." Alannah looked down at the patterns of light on the water. "We got word from Kingfisher," she said. "The new source, inside the Tower. They're active."

"Good?"

"This asset's a real peach, believe me. Just given us the date of the Unification Conference."

"What?"

"Manchester. This October. They're all coming. All the Commanders. And the word is that this time it's actually going to happen. Unification, I mean. And the Supreme Commander..."

"Tereus Winterborn."

"Yeah," said Alannah. "He's been busy."

"All the Commanders," said Helen. "Every single one of them, in one place, at one time. You thinking the same as me?"

"Security would be almost impossible to get through."

"But could it be done?"

"I did say *almost*." Alannah breathed out. "Yes," she said. "It bloody could."

"October," said Helen. "One way or another, it's nearly done."

Winterborn's Office, The Tower

"Your quarters are satisfactory?" said Winterborn.

"Adequate."

"And is the uniform comfortable? I had to have it specially made."

Black leather creaked. "Perfectly."

"I understand that in the dim and distant past there were… issues with your conduct. Not your discipline or loyalty – they've never been in question – but in terms of how far you were prepared to go to get the job done."

A shrug. "You can't fight a war by the Marquess of Queensberry rules."

"No, you can't. To be fair, even your former paymasters knew that. They just had to pay lip service to the notion, and find a scapegoat should circumstances dictate. Be assured you that you won't find any such hypocrisy in my Command."

"That's why I joined."

"Good. Serve me well, and you'll be rewarded handsomely."

A low chuckle. "I have a feeling that the job itself will be reward enough, sir. But I'll happily accept any additional benefits."

Winterborn smiled. "I think you and I will get along very well. All right, dismiss. I'll let you know when I have work for you. It won't be long."

"Yes, sir."

Gideon Shoal saluted and turned away to leave.

Reaching up, almost unconsciously, to touch the jagged, Y-shaped scar that disfigured his left cheek.

THE END

# THE BLACK ROAD CONCLUDES IN ROAD'S END

ACKNOWLEDGEMENTS

Thanks, as ever, are due to Emma Barnes at Snowbooks, and to Anna Torborg and Tik Dalton, without all of whom the story of the Black Road would not have been told.

The music of Dark Sanctuary, Helen Marnie, Jan Garbarek, Nick Cave, PJ Harvey and Claudio Monteverdi provided the soundtrack to *Wolf's Hill*.

My thanks to all the reviewers and bloggers who've sung the praises of *Hell's Ditch* and *Devil's Highway*, or otherwise spread the good word. Special hugs to Lisa DuMond, Matt Fryer, Black Static's Peter Tennant (enjoy your retirement, Pete, and we'll miss you!) and all at Ginger Nuts of Horror and This Is Horror.

Richard Muir's *The Lost Villages Of Britain* was a fascinating and instructive guide to Britain's lost and abandoned communities and the reasons for their desertion, not to mention how to spot a DMV site.

Big thanks and additional hugs go to Laura Mauro, for a) reading an early draft of this novel, b) sending me furious allcaps emails saying "I CAN'T BELIEVE YOU KILLED [NAME REDACTED] YOU UTTER BASTARD" and c) proclaiming me the official King of the Bastards. It's much appreciated!

Hugs and thanks also go to Priya Sharma and Mark Greenwood just on general principles, for being such awesome friends.

Finally and far from least, my thanks – and love – go to my wonderful wife, Cate Gardner, for her unfailing support, for making life generally worth living, and for believing in me even when I struggle to. *Diolch yn fawr, cariad.*

Lightning Source UK Ltd.
Milton Keynes UK
UKHW02f1044230718
326137UK00003B/26/P